"What I feel when I kiss a woman is desire," Jeffrey said. "I think the feelings you are describing are part of being in love."

"But I felt nothing," she said in a small voice. "Nothing at all. Shouldn't I have felt *something* when William kissed me?"

"You're not in love with him, Yvette."

"Perhaps there's something wrong with me," she murmured.

"There's absolutely nothing wrong with you." Gently, he placed a hand under her chin, tilting her face to his. "Absolutely nothing."

At his touch, Yvette's pulse began to quicken. Her heart fluttered for a moment as she looked into his eyes. Her fingers itched to run along the length of his jaw, to feel the slight stubble on his cheek. What would it be like to kiss his lips? What would it feel like to be kissed by Jeffrey Eddington?

He stood so close Yvette could smell the now-familiar scent of him. Masculine. Clean. Sandalwood. A sudden crackle of excitement filled the air around them.

"Jeffrey, would you kiss me?"

Her whispered plea seemed to unlock something in him, for in the next instant he lowered his head and she closed her eyes, the sense of expectancy almost too great to bear. When his lips finally met hers, Yvette thought she would perish from the sheer pleasure of it . . .

Books by Kaitlin O'Riley

SECRETS OF A DUCHESS

ONE SINFUL NIGHT

WHEN HIS KISS IS WICKED

DESIRE IN HIS EYES

IT HAPPENED ONE CHRISTMAS

TO TEMPT AN IRISH ROGUE

HIS BY CHRISTMAS

YOURS FOR ETERNITY
(with Hannah Howell and Alexandra Ivy)

AN INVITATION TO SIN
(with Jo Beverley, Sally MacKenzie, and Vanessa Kelly)

Published by Kensington Publishing Corporation

His
By
Christmas

KAITLIN O'RILEY

ZEBRA BOOKS
KENSINGTON PUBLISHING CORP.
http://www.kensingtonbooks.com

ZEBRA BOOKS are published by

Kensington Publishing Corp.
119 West 40th Street
New York, NY 10018

All Kensington titles, imprints, and distributed lines are available at special quantity discounts for bulk purchases for sales
promotion, premiums, fund-raising, educational, or institu-
tional use.

Special book excerpts or customized printings can also be
created to fit specific needs. For details, write or phone the
office of the Kensington Special Sales Manager: Attn. Special
Sales Department. Kensington Publishing Corp., 119 West
40th Street, New York, NY 10018. Phone: 1-800-221-2647.

Zebra and the Z logo Reg. U.S. Pat. & TM Off.

ISBN-13: 978-1-4201-1241-2
ISBN-10: 1-4201-1241-4
First Printing: October 2013

eISBN-13: 978-1-4201-3267-0
eISBN-10: 1-4201-3267-9
First Electronic Edition: October 2013

10 9 8 7 6 5 4 3 2 1

Printed in the United States of America

To my little sister Jennifer

My playmate, my confidante, my best friend.

*For Daisy and Rosie
and twelve o'donkey and a million others.*

*I cannot begin to imagine my childhood,
my life, without you.*

Thank you for everything.

Acknowledgments

This is the last of the Hamilton series and the central theme in all of the books has been about the bonds of family and especially those between sisters. The universe has blessed me with the most incredible family in the world and the most amazing sisters, all four of them. To Jane, Maureen, Janet, and Jennifer . . . thank you for long lunches by the fire, spa days, big family dinners, Christmas shopping, endless phone calls and texts, hysterical card games, laughing until we can't breathe, crying together, sharing clothes, calling the front seat of the car, making fun of each other, eating things we shouldn't, trying to get me to exercise, and for being my best friends as well as my sisters. I love you so much.

I thank my many friends and family on both the east and west coasts for their continued support of my writing career and for reasons far too numerous to list: Jane Milmore, Shelley Jensen, Maureen Milmore, Janet and Scott Wheeler, Jennifer and Greg Malins, Adrienne Barbeau, Billy Van Zandt, Jeff Babey, Kim McCafferty, Michele Wiener, and Yvonne Deane. To my incredible friends at CH: Cela Lim, Gretchen Kempf, Lynn Abbott, Jill Shapiro, Jensie Kainz, and Melanie Carlisle, thank you for everything.

Thanks go to my lovely cousin, Laurence Cogger, who patiently translated into French all of Genevieve Hamilton's comments for five books. *Merci!*

I also thank the talented Rebecca Harris Zaccagnino for my beautiful website.

And as always, I give thanks to my wonderful agent,

Jane Dystel, and my extraordinary editor, John Scognamiglio, for guiding my publishing journey so skillfully.

*

A very special thank you also goes to all the people who have read my books about the Hamilton sisters and loved them almost as much as I do.

*

Once again I must thank the inspiration behind the character of Jeffrey Eddington, for without him the character would have never been created. Thank you, JME, for French fries, sloe gin fizzes, and all the laughter we've shared together over the years, my friend.

Note to Riley
Thank you for being the best son.
I love you more than you will ever know.

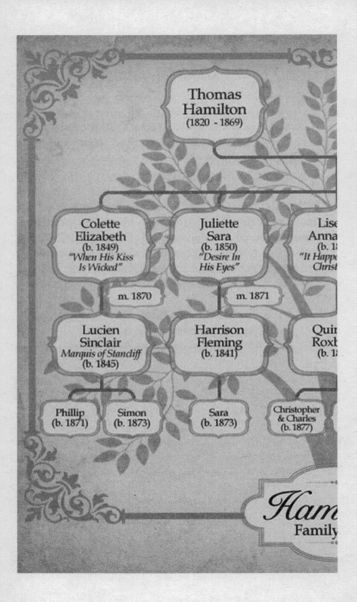

Thomas
Hamilton
(1820 - 1869)

Colette
Elizabeth
(b. 1849)
*"When His Kiss
Is Wicked"*

Juliette
Sara
(b. 1850)
*"Desire In
His Eyes"*

Lise
Anna
(b. 1)
*"It Happe
Christ*

m. 1870

m. 1871

Lucien
Sinclair
Marquis of Stancliff
(b. 1845)

Harrison
Fleming
(b. 1841)

Quir
Roxb
(b. 1)

Phillip
(b. 1871)

Simon
(b. 1873)

Sara
(b. 1873)

Christopher
& Charles
(b. 1877)

Ham
Family

Genevieve
La Brecque
(b. 1830)

m. 1849

[ette
belle
853)
ned One
mas"]

Paulette
Victoria
(b. 1856)
"To Tempt An
Irish Rogue"

Yvette
Katherine
(b. 1858)
"His By
Christmas"

m. 1874

m. 1876

[nton
oury
846)]

Declan
Reeves
Earl of Cashelmore
(b. 1851)

Elizabeth
(b. 1878)

Mara
(b. 1872)

Thomas
(b. 1877)

ilton
Tree

1

Signs of the Season

London
September 1878

"Will you do me a favor, Jeffrey?" asked Lucien Sinclair, the Marquis of Stancliff.

"That depends entirely on what it is." Lord Jeffrey Eddington smiled lazily at his oldest and closest friend. He settled into the large leather armchair, stretching out his tall form and placing his feet upon an upholstered footstool, quite at home in Lucien's grand study. "It's good to be back!"

"It's good to see you here again," Lucien said. "Everyone has missed you."

"Of course they have." Jeffrey had spent the better part of the last year in France on business and had just returned to London. "So," he prompted Lucien, "this favor of yours . . . what is it?"

"It's rather important. . . ." Lucien hesitated, looking

slightly uncomfortable. "Something only you can do for me. And I need your utmost discretion."

"Sounds serious." Jeffrey's blue eyes narrowed and his lazy smile disappeared.

Lucien began reluctantly, "It is. . . . And I'm not quite sure how you'll feel about it."

"Go on then." Jeffrey inclined his head.

"I need you to keep an eye on Yvette while we're in America," Lucien asked.

Jeffrey blinked. "You're jesting."

"I wish I were." Lucien's mouth formed a grim line.

"I don't understand." Jeffrey sat up, suddenly not as comfortable as he had been. "Isn't she going to New York with you and Colette?"

Frowning, Lucien shook his head. "I would much rather she come with Colette and me, but Yvette is quite determined to stay in London without us."

"That's ridiculous!" Jeffrey wondered at the wisdom of allowing Yvette Hamilton, the youngest of the five sisters, to remain at Devon House without her family. It was unthinkable. "You should insist that she go with you."

"Believe me, I have tried, but you know Yvette as well as I do." Lucien sighed in heavy resignation. "She can be headstrong, like all the Hamilton women. Being the youngest, she's used to getting her own way. And she has made up her mind to stay in London and my wife has given her permission to stay. Naturally, I can't fight them both. Yvette's not foolish, but I don't like leaving her behind."

"But who will be here with her? Who will look after her?" Jeffrey asked, incredulous at this turn of events. They couldn't simply leave the girl alone!

"Well, Paulette and Declan are in Ireland until Christmas as usual, so Mrs. Hamilton has agreed to come up from Brighton to stay with her daughter here at Devon House.

That way Yvette will not be unchaperoned at home. As much as I don't care a great deal for them personally, the girls' aunt Cecilia and uncle Randall Hamilton have agreed to escort her to any social events. They are actually looking forward to it, with the hope of arranging a successful match for her. And of course, Lisette and Quinton are in town as well, but with Lisette just having had the baby, they won't be much help on that score." Lucien paused, giving his friend a pointed look. "You understand what I'm saying, Jeffrey. I need someone here who will know what is truly going on." He flashed a knowing glance in Jeffrey's direction. "Keep an eye on her."

Yes, Jeffrey knew exactly what his friend meant. It had been the same with all the Hamilton girls, this quintet of lovely women who had become like his very own sisters. In one way or another Jeffrey had been there to protect each of them over the years and they had grown to trust him. Oh, the stories he could tell Lucien! But since he was a gentleman, and he loved each one of the girls dearly, Jeffrey would never betray their trust by telling anyone what he knew about them.

Now Yvette was the last unmarried Hamilton sister and she would more than likely need the most looking after. With her soft blond hair and sparkling blue eyes, pretty little Yvette had always been a charming, flirtatious, and social creature seeking out grand, romanticized ideals and splendid dreams. She wanted to live her life as a princess. Yet after a Season or two she still remained inexplicably unattached. Jeffrey wondered at the reasons for that. Why hadn't his little Yvette married already? Why hadn't some eligible nobleman snatched her up and made her his wife? She would be an asset to any man, for Yvette was very beautiful, well educated, and utterly charming.

Although he hadn't seen her for the last few months, he

had known Yvette since she was a young girl and had always thought her the most striking of all the Hamilton sisters.

Having just returned to London that morning, after spending the better part of the last year working in France, the very thought of reuniting with everyone at Devon House tonight had kept his spirits up while he was away. This wonderful family, *his* family, meant more to him than any of them realized. And Yvette . . . well, little Yvette Hamilton had a special place in his heart.

"Do you know why she's so insistent on staying in London?" Jeffrey asked.

"No." Lucien gave him another knowing look. "But I'm sure you'll find out what her reason is before long. Or who."

"So you do think there is someone in the picture then?"

"That would be my guess." Lucien shrugged helplessly. "But she hasn't mentioned a word to me about him. Or Colette for that matter."

Now that was surprising news. Yvette had always been quite keen on romance and most vocal about her romantic pursuits. Why was she keeping it such a secret now? What had happened? And who could have captured her attention enough for her to pass up a transatlantic trip to visit her sister in New York? It was quite unlike Yvette. Was there a valid reason for her secrecy? Could she have fallen under the spell of a gentleman unworthy of her? Perhaps someone with an unsavory background or a man with questionable honor?

Someone had definitely caught Yvette's interest and in his mind the need for concealment did not bode well. A twinge of worry coursed through Jeffrey, though he was reluctant to mention it to Lucien. There was no need to make the man more anxious than he already was about leaving his youngest sister-in-law behind.

"You'll do it, then?" Lucien asked.

"Yes, of course, I'll look after Yvette," Jeffrey promised. He could not refuse his childhood friend. He and Lucien had looked out for each other since they were young boys at Eton, bonding over the unhappiness that was rife in both of their families. They were as close as any brothers could be. He would do anything for Lucien.

Besides, Jeffrey could never ignore one of the Hamilton sisters, least of all sweet, little Yvette. He would readily and gladly give his life for any of them. In all honesty he would have watched over her even without Lucien asking him.

"Thank you," Lucien said with relief in his voice as he handed Jeffrey a glass of bourbon. "Here," he added with a rueful laugh. "You'll probably need this."

"You're the one going to visit Juliette. You'll need it more than I," Jeffrey retorted with a wicked grin. "Hell, take the whole bottle."

Jeffrey and Lucien laughed together, for Juliette Hamilton had given them both cause to lose sleep at one point or another. However, the second Hamilton sister had calmed considerably since marrying Captain Harrison Fleming and happily settling down in America.

"No, my friend." Lucien's face turned serious. "I'll leave this for you. I'm not sure what she's up to, but if anyone can drive a man to drink, it might just be Yvette."

Jeffrey was inclined to agree in spite of himself. "You're more than likely right about that." The girl was too pretty and too romantic to be trusted to act rationally.

"Whatever you do," Lucien added with a note of solemnity, "don't let Yvette know I asked you to do this. Be subtle in your watching over her. Anything heavy-handed and she's likely to rebel out of sheer stubbornness."

"I'm not an idiot, Lucien. She is the fifth Hamilton sister, and not my first go-around. Didn't I manage to help get the others safely married? I know how to handle this situation." At least Jeffrey thought he did. He was like Yvette's older brother, for Christ's sake. He could handle a little girl like her. "You and Colette should enjoy yourselves in America. Don't give another thought to what's going on here. I'll make sure Yvette stays out of harm's way and doesn't do anything too foolish." Jeffrey raised his brows in mock alarm. "Although if she takes after her older sisters, I can only hope whatever she does isn't as drastic as any of their adventures were."

Lucien smiled at Jeffrey. "Just try to keep her from doing anything reckless. Quinton will do the best he can also, but he's preoccupied with Lisette and the baby. Colette and I will be home in time for Christmas. Just keep her safe until then."

"That's three months," Jeffrey said.

"I have complete faith you can handle things until then."

Jeffrey paused in thought. "So do you have any idea who he is?"

Lucien sighed in weariness. "Look at her. It could be any one of a dozen young men. I've had offers of marriage for her from some of the best families and she has turned down each one, most graciously. Flowers and cards arrive for her on a daily basis. She is flooded with social invitations. I can't keep them all straight. Colette and I have escorted her to more parties, balls, and soirees than I can count, where she is sought after by all the young gentlemen, and yet she favors no one in particular that we can see. Here I thought all along she would be the easiest of the sisters to marry off, with her always dreaming about romance and princes and such things. Now her second Season has come and gone. She's almost twenty-one. What is she waiting for? Someone has caught her fancy, I'll warrant, but I can't figure out who he is. Honest to God, I won't rest easy until this girl is safely married."

"How we've managed with the other three sisters is a miracle in itself."

Lucien raised his glass. "You said it."

Jeffrey asked, "Is Colette worried?"

"Not in the least. But then she's not a man and doesn't see the world the way we do." Lucien shrugged in disbelief. "Please don't mention to her that I've asked you to do this, by the way. This is just between us. And Quinton."

Jeffrey nodded. It was good to know he'd have a ready ally in Lisette's husband if he needed one.

"Thank God I have only sons," Lucien groaned. "I don't know how I'd go through this again if I had daughters of my own."

Laughing, Jeffrey agreed with him. "Daughters would no doubt kill you, my friend."

"Don't I know it?" Lucien took a swig of his bourbon. "Send word of any important developments, would you?"

"Of course."

The door to Lucien's study opened and Colette Sinclair, Lucien's wife, entered the room. The oldest of the Hamilton sisters, and the reason why Jeffrey was considered a part of this family, Colette was a strikingly beautiful woman. With her coffee-colored hair and deep blue eyes, she carried herself with a regal bearing. She was the epitome of the wife of a marquis. One would never know that she had grown up working in a bookshop.

"Hello, darling—oh, Jeffrey! You're here!" she declared with delight as Jeffrey hugged her tightly. "You're home! When did you get back?"

"Yes, I'm home!" Jeffrey echoed happily. "I just arrived."

"And we're leaving," Colette said with a sudden frown.

"It's too disappointing! We haven't seen you in months and months and now we're going away. I don't like that at all. But look at you! You grow more handsome as you age, Jeffrey Eddington. It's entirely unfair!"

"You look more beautiful every time I see you, Colette!" He flashed her a smile.

"And you still know how to turn a girl's head." Colette laughed and placed a kiss on his cheek. "You're joining us for supper, aren't you? We need to catch up on all the news. And you must see Phillip and Simon. You won't believe how much our boys have grown since you've been gone! Oh, and my mother's here and will be thrilled to see that you're here too! You know how much she loves to see you!"

"I'm very happy to be here with you all again." Jeffrey found he couldn't stop grinning. He had been away far too long and he had missed this family. His family. The family that had embraced him as one of its own.

And, yes, now he was home again.

2

Christmas Wishes

Yvette Hamilton glanced around the glittering ballroom in annoyance. Where had that man gone now? She'd lost track of him when she had been cornered into discussing the merits of gardening with the overbearing Mrs. Ashby, who also talked endlessly about her only son. Yvette had no interest in Mrs. Ashby's prominent-toothed boy. No, she had set her sights on someone much higher than that. But somehow she had managed to lose him!

And the last thing she intended to do was to lose him.

With hurried steps, she moved through the crowded and festively decorated ballroom, carefully making her way toward the exit, while she nodded and smiled in greeting to everyone she knew.

"Kate, did you happen to see where Lord Shelley went to?" she whispered to her dearest friend and the only other person who knew of her secret dream.

Lady Katherine Spencer glanced around with her big brown eyes. "I'm not entirely positive, but I think he went that way a few moments ago." She gestured to the arched doorway leading to the hall. "But you mustn't chase after him, Yvette!"

"I'm not chasing after him," she protested heatedly. Yvette never chased after any man. Or at least it never looked that way. Lord Shelley must have gone to the card room. Perhaps she should linger in the hallway for a little while and just happen to be there when he returned. "I simply wondered where he had gone is all."

Kate gave her a skeptical glance, her freckled face looking a bit amused. "Don't worry though. Your competition, Jane Fairmont, is over there dancing with Lord Calvert."

Yvette spied her rival and then relaxed knowing that the girl was not with Lord Shelley either. Yvette had worked too hard to gain favor with the most eligible bachelor in all of London to lose him to the likes of Jane Fairmont.

"I wasn't worried really," Yvette murmured to her friend. "Simply curious."

"I don't know why you're throwing yourself at Lord Shelley when there are dozens of handsome men who would die to marry you." Kate gave her an exasperated look.

"I am not throwing myself at him. Honestly, Kate! You know me better than that. And I have explained all of this to you before. It's quite simple. Lord Shelley will be the Duke of Lansdowne when his father passes away."

In Yvette's eyes, there was no need to say more. She had longed for an opportunity like this her whole life. Nothing could be more romantic than marrying a duke and becoming a duchess! To be considered important and grand. To be a stylish and elegant lady, admired by all. Lord Shelley was able to give her the title that would allow everyone to call her Your Grace. No one could deny her significance then.

At almost twenty-one years of age, Yvette would be entering her third Season next spring. She should be married by now for heaven's sake!

It wasn't from a lack of offers. That was most definitely not the case. Yvette had been the toast of her first Season and again in her second. She had been practically drowning in proposals from fine young gentlemen from good families with excellent prospects, and even a few from those of questionable standing in society. She could have been satisfied with any of them as her husband.

But she was not.

She wanted something more. Something romantic and dramatic. Something quite special and exceptionally wonderful. Something her older sisters didn't already have. As the youngest of five sisters, Yvette had watched each of her siblings marry in thrilling and dramatic ways, being swept off their feet by romance, head-over-heels in love with dashing husbands who adored them.

Yet, after two Seasons and a few stolen kisses, she had not encountered anyone who made her feel the way she believed she ought to feel. Not one single man had captivated her with his charm or enchanted her with his being. Her heart had not been stolen by a good-looking rogue, nor had she been swept off her feet by a handsome, dark-eyed stranger. Yvette was beginning to fear romance and adventure would never happen for her. Weary of waiting for something dreamy and magical to happen, she had decided to pursue her own romantic dreams instead. Yvette had her sights set on making the most brilliant match she could.

And what was more brilliant and romantic than a handsome duke?

She wasn't bold or brazen enough to think she could snare a prince, even though two of Queen Victoria's sons were still unmarried. But as luck would have it, earlier that summer she had met William Weatherly, Marquis of Shelley, Earl of Cheshire, and best of all, the future Duke of Lansdowne. Handsome and distinguished, Lord Shelley had been traveling abroad for several years, and having just returned home, he was now in the market for a wife, his future duchess.

The competition for his attentions had been quite fierce all summer long, for a prize such as Lord Shelley was rare indeed. But as summer turned to fall, Yvette had emerged as one of his favorites, and she had become determined to win him over. Her hope was to be his by Christmas, which gave her only three more months to win over and become affianced to the handsome Lord Shelley.

"Oh, here comes your future duke now," Kate whispered with a conspiratorial giggle. "I shall leave the two of you alone. Good luck!"

Her loyal friend fled the scene just as Lord Shelley arrived at Yvette's side.

"As usual, you are looking quite lovely this evening, Miss Hamilton," he said. A warm smile lit his face.

"So you tell me every time I see you, my lord." She cast a flirtatious eye around the ballroom, as if she had already tired of him, and fluttered her new lace fan, which matched her elegant, rosebud-pink silk gown with lace edging. Acting a bit unattainable had been her strategy with him from the start. Lord Shelley was an attractive and powerful gentleman accustomed to having women fall at his feet. Yvette refused to be one of them.

Lord Shelley whispered close to her ear, "That is because I can think of nothing else but your beauty when I look at you."

A thrill of delight raced through her and Yvette tallied his compliment to the growing list she kept in her head to mark her progress with him. Although Lord Shelley as yet had not shown her any more attention than he had to the other girls, Yvette sensed a subtle change in his behavior. One by one, the young ladies vying for his attentions all summer had fallen out of favor with him, leaving only Yvette and her greatest rival, Jane Fairmont, left to battle it out.

Yvette was quite determined that she would win her romantic ideal in the end. It was the reason she had refused to accompany Colette and Lucien to America. She simply could not leave London now, not when she was so close to taking serious steps forward with Lord Shelley. Through single-minded perseverance and much cajoling on her part, she had somehow managed to convince them to let her stay. So she remained in town, while her sister, brother-in-law, and nephews had set sail across the Atlantic the day before. Yvette was free to pursue her dream of becoming the next Duchess of Lansdowne.

Now Yvette turned and gazed into Lord Shelley's thoughtful hazel eyes, which had been giving her quite intent stares of late, she had been pleased to note. With fair hair, almost silver in color, William Weatherly was a very good-looking man, despite his maturity. She guessed he was close to forty years old but wasn't certain of his exact age. Always clean-shaven, he had straight teeth, a well-proportioned nose, and a strong jaw. He was muscular and taller than average height, but his title and position added to the powerful air about him. His good-natured charm and dashing manner appealed to her. He looked the epitome of a duke and all the girls were mad for him.

"You are very kind, my lord." She cast her eyes down at his second compliment.

"I confess that I am very happy to see you here tonight."

"I wasn't sure if I could manage to attend at all. My aunt and uncle were escorting me this evening and my aunt was not feeling well," Yvette said.

"I would have been very disappointed had you not been here, Miss Hamilton."

She glanced up at him with an indulgent smile. "I am happy to save you from such disappointment then, my lord."

"As am I." His eyes twinkled at her. "It's rather warm in here. Are you thirsty, Miss Hamilton? May I get you something to drink?" he asked.

"Oh, that would be quite nice. Thank you very much."

"I shall return to you shortly." Lord Shelley walked off toward the refreshment area and Yvette watched him make his way through the crowd.

How positively wonderful! He would have been disappointed not to see her! She could barely contain her excitement at his confession.

Kate hurried back to Yvette's side as Lord Shelley disappeared into the dining room. Her friend asked, "So, how is it progressing this evening?"

Yvette grinned, pleased with her evening's endeavors. "I believe quite well, Kate. Quite well. He's coming back with punch."

Kate's freckled face wrinkled in amusement. "Really, Yvette, I don't understand why you're in such a rush to marry him."

Yvette remained silent for she could not quite put into words why she felt such a need to hurry or why she had chosen Christmas as a goal for herself. But she just knew that if she became a duchess her life would instantly change for the better. She would lead society and host the most fashionable parties and events. She would wear the most stylish clothes. Everyone would love and admire her. Being married to a duke would be the most romantic thing that could happen to her.

"If I were you, I'd try for Lord Eddington," Kate continued in a voice full of utter longing. "He's the most dashing gentleman I've ever met. He's the one you ought to marry, Yvette."

Yvette laughed at the absurdity of such a prospect. "Lord Eddington? I could never marry him!"

"Why ever not? He is so devastatingly handsome and charming. He's terribly rich too. And he's known to have made all the ladies swoon. You know what they say about him . . ." Kate gave a little sigh and fluttered her fan.

"Putting aside the fact that he's been like a brother to me, he's . . . he's . . ." Yvette struggled to find the proper words.

Yes, Jeffrey Eddington *was* indeed all of the things Kate had said. He was also funny, sweet, and unfailingly loyal. In fact, he was quite dear to her. Yvette had to admit that he held a special place in her heart. He had been a part of her life since she was a young girl and she could hardly recall a time when she had not known him. But as for marriage? To Jeffrey Eddington? It was completely ridiculous!

"I know you used to be sweet on him, Yvette."

She paused. Perhaps she had nursed a childish infatuation for Jeffrey years ago, but as a mature woman of almost twenty-one she had quite outgrown such juvenile illusions. "Well, I was a silly little girl then. Besides Jeffrey is not what one would call marriage material."

"Is it . . . is it because he's a . . . he's a . . . he was born on the wrong side of the blanket?" Kate asked in a furtive whisper.

It was common knowledge in society that Lord Eddington was the illegitimate son of the Duke of Rathmore and a ballet dancer. Although the duke had long ago claimed Jeffrey as his son, no one ever forgot he was illegitimate.

"Well, yes . . ." Yvette responded, wondering why they were discussing this at all. "Besides I can't very well marry Lord Eddington if I wish to become a duchess, now can I?"

"How are you enjoying the ball, Yvette?"

At the sound of a very deep familiar voice, Yvette's heart raced as she turned in his direction. There stood the very subject of their conversation, Lord Jeffrey Eddington, and from the look on his face, Yvette was fairly certain he had heard everything she had just said.

"Oh, Lord Eddington!" Kate's freckled face turned a deep shade of scarlet. "Good evening!"

"Jeffrey!" Yvette cried out in surprise. Fluttering her fan as if she hadn't a care in the world, she murmured, "I didn't know you were in attendance this evening."

"I only just arrived. And here I find the two prettiest girls in London standing alone among the potted plants. How is such a thing possible?" He gave them his signature heart-melting grin, completely ignoring the fact that he had just overheard them gossiping about him.

It was so utterly Jeffrey to save them from embarrassment that Yvette wanted to hug him, in spite of her own feelings of discomfiture. Looking up at him, she could not deny that Jeffrey Eddington was an exceptionally handsome man. Tall with broad shoulders and hair the color of ebony and clear, deep blue eyes, he was muscular and strong, wearing his evening clothes with careless elegance. His classically sculpted, clean-shaven face had a devil-may-care allure that caused women to swoon when he looked their way. But now he was looking at Yvette with an intense gleam in those eyes and she felt unexpectedly warm.

"We're very happy that you're here now to keep us company, Lord Eddington," Kate said with a tone in her voice that Yvette had never heard before. "I fear we have been quite bored so far this evening."

Why, Kate was flirting with Jeffrey! Yvette struggled to contain her giggles. Levelheaded Kate, who was already engaged to her childhood sweetheart, looked about ready to swoon at Jeffrey's feet.

"It would be my great pleasure to keep you amused,

Lady Katherine," Jeffrey said mischievously. And in rare form, he bowed over her hand in a gallant gesture.

Yvette tried not to roll her eyes at his flirtations. It was so typical of him. He had behaved the same way with her mother the night before last at Devon House when they had all gathered to say good-bye to Colette and Lucien.

At that moment, Lord Shelley returned with a cup of punch for Yvette.

"I'm afraid that took longer than I anticipated, Miss Hamilton," Lord Shelley apologized, while handing her the crystal glass filled with a fruity concoction. He glanced to the others, his hazel eyes questioning Jeffrey's presence. "Good evening."

Yvette thanked him for the punch and introduced him to Lord Eddington. She added, "Lord Shelley, both you and Lord Eddington have been on extended trips abroad this year. Lord Eddington has just returned from France this week."

Interested, Lord Shelley asked, "Is that so? I was in Paris a good part of last year. Were you there for business or recreation, Lord Eddington?"

Jeffrey favored the ladies with another mischievous look. "A little of both."

Kate giggled and fluttered her fan. Yvette could not help but smile.

"I'm surprised we've not met before," Lord Shelley stated, his eyes moving to Yvette. "How are you acquainted with Miss Hamilton?"

"Lord Eddington is a very close friend to my brother-in-law, Lord Stancliff," Yvette explained with a calmness that belied her excitement. Thrilled with Lord Shelley's obvious jealousy, she smiled at him. "Consequently Jeffrey has been a part of our family since Lord Stancliff married my sister, Colette."

"I see." Lord Shelley looked intrigued by this. "You must tell me more for I am most interested in everything about Yvette, Lord Eddington."

"Yes, it's true," Jeffrey began in a light-hearted manner. "I've known Miss Hamilton since she was a bit of a thing, climbing ladders in her family's bookshop. Although she always tried to act like a lady, she was a little mischievous. One Christmas I even caught her hiding behind a sofa, so she could get a peek at her presents."

"Jeffrey!" Yvette cried. She had almost forgotten that Jeffrey had caught her doing that. She had been only thirteen or fourteen at the time, but she recalled that he had let her see one gift and had never told her mother or sisters what she had done. He had always been good to her that way.

He continued, "But as pretty as Yvette is, I knew she would be a heartbreaker even then. Although I'm afraid I used to tease her quite terribly."

"Is that so?" Lord Shelley asked, looking carefully between the two of them.

"I must confess that I more than likely deserved his teasing," Yvette explained with a laughing smile and a knowing glance at Jeffrey. Who winked at her.

"I doubt that could possibly be the case," Lord Shelley said in her defense, noticing the interplay between her and Jeffrey. "Miss Hamilton could never warrant teasing."

"On the contrary," Yvette protested. "I was quite the nuisance to my sisters in my younger years."

"I could never imagine you being a nuisance to anyone, Miss Hamilton." Lord Shelley made his statement firmly, as if that settled the matter in his eyes. "It was a pleasure speaking with you again, Lady Katherine. And you too, Lord Eddington. I'm sure we shall meet again. However, Miss Hamilton has promised me the next dance and the orchestra is about to begin a waltz."

"Oh, yes, my lord, please forgive me." Yvette grinned in happy triumph. "I had quite forgotten about our dance." She had not promised Lord Shelley any such thing, but she played along. Handing her cup of punch to a passing footman, she allowed Lord Shelley to take her arm.

"Please excuse us," Lord Shelley said to the others. He then led her to the main ballroom.

Yvette glanced back to see Jeffrey Eddington staring after her, an odd expression on his face. Dismissing the unease within her, she focused her attention on the handsome man in front of her instead as they began to move in time to the strains of a familiar waltz.

"So, Miss Hamilton." William Weatherly smiled at her, his hazel eyes twinkling. "I am more intrigued by you by the minute. Please tell me more about your life at your family's bookshop."

3

A Gentleman's Wager

Jeffrey Eddington spent the rest of the evening covertly watching Yvette Hamilton. After all, he had promised Lucien that he would. Not that keeping his eyes on Yvette was a hardship. She looked like an angel in that shimmering pale pink gown that accentuated her small waist and sweet feminine curves. With her blond hair arranged like a golden halo around her beautiful face, she moved with elegant grace on the arm of Lord Shelley as he walked her about the perimeter of the room.

Jeffrey hadn't expected to discover her secret so soon. It was only his first night on duty.

Clearly, Yvette had set her cap for William Weatherly, Lord Shelley.

What on earth did Yvette see in him? He was too old for her, first of all! He was twice her age if he was a day. The man's hair was almost completely silver, for Christ's sake! Although Jeffrey hated to admit it, Lord Shelley was good looking in spite of his age. But he wasn't worthy of a woman like Yvette. Well, yes, Lord Shelley would inherit his father's dukedom. The Duke of Lansdowne was almost as powerful as Jeffrey's own father, the Duke of Rathmore. But titles meant nothing to Jeffrey. He had learned the hard way that their true value was meaningless.

However, it was quite apparent they mattered to Yvette.

After overhearing her conversation earlier that evening with her friend, he now understood her refusal to leave London. She had set her sights quite high. Yvette was angling to become the next Duchess of Lansdowne. An unexpected feeling of distaste washed over him.

"She's quite gorgeous, isn't she?"

Jeffrey turned to see his cousin, James Granger Eddington, who had just walked over to stand beside him. His cousin's dark eyes were locked on Yvette Hamilton.

"Yes," Jeffrey agreed without hesitation. "She is beautiful."

"I don't know why I haven't noticed her before," James mused aloud.

"Haven't you?"

James Granger Eddington turned to face Jeffrey. "When did you get back from France?"

"Just this week." Jeffrey shrugged indifferently. He was not interested in talking to his cousin. Glancing back at Yvette, he saw Lord Shelley lower his head to whisper something for her ears only. He could almost hear Yvette's sweet laughter. A cold tightness knotted in Jeffrey's stomach.

Seeing Yvette Hamilton again had quite surprised him. She had changed while he'd been away. He had always thought of her as a pretty little girl even as she had grown into a lovely young lady and made her debut. But now . . . now there was something noticeably different about her. She had developed into a woman and he couldn't reconcile the two images in his head.

"I'd heard that you returned." James continued his line of questioning, "Have you seen your father yet?"

"Yes. I saw him last night." Jeffrey glanced at his cousin again.

James Granger Eddington was the legal heir to Jeffrey's father's title, estate, and money. He did not begrudge James this ducal inheritance, for nothing could be done to change the order of things. The already married duke had had an affair with Jeffrey's mother and therefore he could not legally claim Jeffrey as his heir, although he acknowledged him publicly. Being illegitimate excluded Jeffrey from inheriting his father's dukedom and he had accepted that fact many years ago.

However, Jeffrey noted that James's gaze was fixed on Yvette once again. He could not help but ask, "What's your interest in Miss Hamilton?"

"She is truly stunning." James sighed heavily and added with regret, "I wish I could have offered for her."

Jeffrey started at his cousin's unexpected comment. James had had a suitable marriage arranged for him years ago. Being the acknowledged heir to the Duke of Rathmore, he had no lack of options. His grand wedding to Lady Amelia Wells was set for next summer. But the idea of James with Yvette? It was beyond ridiculous.

"I know Yvette Hamilton quite well and you are not her type, James."

"A high-ranking title is her type." He stared pointedly at Jeffrey. "In which case I suit her perfectly."

Jeffrey remained silent. His cousin was correct. The thought rankled as they both watched Yvette. Her blue eyes wide, she gazed with rapt attention as Lord Shelley spoke to her.

James Granger Eddington scoffed, "I could get her away

from that old man if I wanted. I've got just as much to offer as he does, and I'm younger. A lot younger."

Jeffrey's mouth set in a grim line. He wasn't sure which notion suddenly upset him most, the thought of Yvette marrying James or the thought of her with Lord Shelley. Both ideas were completely preposterous. Neither man was half good enough for her, in his opinion. Lord Shelley was entirely too old for Yvette. And James, well . . .

Aside from the fact that he was already engaged to be married, James Granger Eddington was utterly wrong for a girl as beautiful as Yvette. James had excellent prospects and was considered a catch by most standards, but unfortunately he was not an attractive man. Proof again that he was a distant branch on the Eddington family tree. Wide of girth, shorter than Jeffrey by a full head, with a bulbous nose and receding, thin brown hair, he was not at all Yvette's romantic hero type. Not even close!

Jeffrey glanced down at him in amusement. "I seriously doubt you could capture Yvette Hamilton's heart."

"And you think you would be able to?" James challenged, his dark brow raised in a mocking question.

Jeffrey barely paused. "Certainly."

"You're a good-looking and charming gentleman and all the women love you, to be sure, and I am quite the opposite." James shook his balding head with conviction. "But I have something to offer her that you do not."

Jeffrey did not meet his cousin's eyes for he spoke only the truth. Jeffrey had nothing to offer Yvette Hamilton, or any other woman for that matter. That fact had saved him on more than one occasion, as he used it to escape the marriage noose of certain persistent females who were determined to marry him for his looks, even if he was a bastard. Being an illegitimate son had its advantages at times.

Jeffrey remained silent, focused on the object of their

discussion. Lord Shelley was now escorting Yvette from the ballroom, his hand holding her arm possessively, his tall form hovering over her petite body.

As he watched her, Jeffrey thought of the little girl he knew. A sweeter, lovelier, brighter girl he had never met. Even at that young of an age Yvette carried herself with an elegance and grace unmatched by any female he knew. They had always enjoyed an uncomplicated relationship, even if he had teased her too much, and he'd regarded her as a little sister. But looking at her at this moment . . . Yvette had certainly matured over the years.

How had he not noticed until tonight the beautiful and desirable woman she had become?

She was no longer a little girl and she was definitely *not* his little sister.

"I don't think you could do it, old chap."

"You don't think I could do what?" Jeffrey turned back to his cousin, startled out of his errant thoughts. He'd almost forgotten about him.

James wrinkled his wide nose in derision. "I don't think you could get Yvette Hamilton to marry the likes of you."

Keeping his eyes on Yvette, Jeffrey watched her walk out to the terrace on Lord Shelley's arm and his gut tightened in reflex. "You don't know what you're talking about."

"Yes, I do and I bet you couldn't do it."

"Is that a challenge?" Jeffrey asked, staring at James. Their conversation had taken a surprising turn.

"Yes. A challenge." James crossed his arms in defiance. "Let's wager on it."

"Wager on what?" Jeffrey questioned incredulously.

His eyes glinting, James made a proposition. "Let's bet to see if you could win Miss Hamilton over the future Duke of Lansdowne or not."

"You've lost your damned mind, James." Jeffrey shook his dark head with determination. "I would never bet on Yvette Hamilton that way."

Once again, James arched a knowing brow, his expression quite superior. "It's because you know you would lose to Lord Shelley's title, isn't it?"

He laughed at his cousin. "No. I could easily make Yvette mine, if I wanted to. And I don't have to place a wager with you to prove it."

"Coward."

Jeffrey bristled at that. "What did you call me?"

"You heard me, Cousin." James snickered with delight. "You know I'm right and you would lose out to the heir to a dukedom. The title of duke always trumps good looks."

"You've no idea what you're talking about, James." Jeffrey itched to deck the shorter man. He gritted his teeth in annoyance. "You barely know Yvette Hamilton."

"I don't need to know her. She's like all women and they all want the same thing. But I do know you're afraid of losing."

"Is that truly what you believe?"

"Yes, it is. That girl wants nothing more than to be a duchess and not even your charm and good looks are worth more than that. You know it as well as I do. It's as plain as the ugly nose on my face." James smiled in satisfaction.

Jeffrey considered Yvette's motives. Surely that wasn't all that inspired her pursuit of Lord Shelley? Could she be so mercenary and cold? No, not his sweet little Yvette. He refused to think of her that way. His cousin was wrong, certainly. And Jeffrey would prove him so.

There had never been a woman Jeffrey couldn't get if he wanted her. No woman had ever turned him down. Yvette, a sweet little romantic, would be no match for his skills of seduction.

He paused in thought. There could be some merit to a wager with James after all.

If Jeffrey made an effort to win Yvette's affections, he would be able to accomplish two goals. For if Yvette truly loved Lord Shelley then she wouldn't be swayed by Jeffrey's charm, and then he could give her his blessing to marry the man and they would have his best wishes for every happiness together. But if Yvette was only seeking the title of duchess, Jeffrey would be stopping her from a loveless marriage. And doing so would also provide him with a way to keep his eye on her while Lucien and Colette were away.

It was not a bad plan, at that.

There was one risk though. A mighty risk. At the end of it all, Yvette could wind up hating him for what he'd done. But that was a risk Jeffrey was willing to take to save her from making the most irrevocable mistake any woman could make in her lifetime. Marrying the wrong man.

It was his duty to protect her. He had promised Lucien to keep her away from certain types of men and to prevent her from making foolish choices. And if wooing her away from the wrong man, Lord Shelley, would be the best way to do that, then by God he would do it.

Jeffrey looked his short cousin in the eye. "I accept your wager."

"You . . . you do?" James sputtered in disbelief. He had clearly not expected his challenge to be accepted.

"Yes, I do."

"What are the terms?" James asked hurriedly, his round face now lit with gleeful excitement.

"Whatever you like," Jeffrey responded with a shrug. He couldn't care less about the terms of the wager. Proving his cousin wrong and winning money meant less than nothing to him. His only concern was keeping Yvette Hamilton from possibly marrying the wrong man and ruining her life.

"Since we're gentlemen of means," James Granger Eddington continued, "let's make it interesting, shall we? How about a thousand pounds?"

"Whatever amount you wish. It's your loss."

"Fine. A gentleman's wager." James grinned with undisguised glee. "I'll bet you a thousand pounds that you can't win Miss Yvette Hamilton away from the future Duke of Lansdowne by . . . by when?"

"By Christmas, if not sooner." Jeffrey could pass the care of Yvette back to Lucien and Colette by then and wash his hands of the entire affair knowing that she was safe, one way or another.

"It's a deal, Cousin." James held out his hand.

They shook to bind the wager, while Jeffrey ignored the uneasy feeling that crept over him. And it had nothing to do with the outrageously large sum of money he had just wagered on Yvette Hamilton's heart.

"This will be the easiest money I ever made." James continued to smile, as he pumped Jeffrey's hand with growing delight.

Withdrawing his hand from James's grip, Jeffrey advised him coolly, "Don't spend it yet, Cousin. You'd do well not to underestimate me."

4

September Rain

"Yes, *Maman*, of course, I'm ready," Yvette answered, adjusting the skirts of her new lavender gown. They were on their way to visit her sister Lisette and her new baby that afternoon. Yvette had intended to go riding in Green Park with Lord Shelley, but the drizzling rain had spoiled those plans.

"Then let us be on our way. I am weary of waiting for you. *Je suis fatiguée de t'attendre. Cela fait déjà dix minutes que j'attends. Dépêche-toi*," her mother, Genevieve Hamilton, said impatiently while pounding her ornate cane on the floor to enhance the emphasis of her words.

"Well, let's go then, shall we?" Yvette quickly ushered her mother into the waiting carriage, complete with the Sinclairs' liveried footmen, that would carry them the short drive to her sister's townhouse. Yvette would have preferred to walk there, but her mother was not able to make even such a short distance nor would she be able to tolerate the damp weather. There were a lot of things that Genevieve

Hamilton could not abide and she was quite vocal about them. All the time.

It was too hot. It was too cold. Too many people came to visit them. Not enough people came to visit them. Her tea was not strong enough. Her tea was too strong. Didn't anyone know how to make a proper cup of tea anymore? And what was the matter with the servants at Devon House? Didn't Colette know how to train them properly? No one knew how to take care of her the way she wanted. She missed Brighton. London was a horrid, loud, and dirty city. On and on it went. All day. Every day. Nothing pleased her. Nothing satisfied her.

Yvette had protested vociferously against having her mother come to stay with her while Colette and Lucien were away, declaring that she was quite able to manage on her own. However, neither her sister nor her brother-in-law would budge on this matter. It was final. Appearances must be kept up and she was not to be left unattended. Genevieve Hamilton came to Devon House. Yvette consoled herself that she had won the battle to stay in London and not go to America. At least she had that triumph!

So her mother, with the air of a great martyr, reluctantly left her cottage by the sea in Brighton and came to stay with Yvette at Devon House. Genevieve had only been there a few days and already Yvette was exasperated with her. Her mother always had that effect on her. She would be glad to get to Lisette's house and share the burden of her mother's draining presence with another sister for a while.

As the carriage wended its way through the wet London streets, Yvette blocked out the incessant French ramblings and complaints about the bumpy roads and dreary weather from her mother and thought only of William Weatherly, Lord Shelley.

Lord Shelley had invited her to go riding in the park with him!

Yvette had been more than pleased with her progress with him since the ball the night before last. He was showing a definite marked interest in her. Not only had he danced with her, but he had also walked her out to the terrace, where they had conversed. They had talked easily together about nothing of true importance. She had seen the signs before in other gentlemen, but Lord Shelley seemed quite smitten with her. If one could call a future duke smitten!

Everything was going according to her plan. She sighed heavily, looking out the carriage window. If only for the rain, she would be with him now!

Instead, she had been obligated to accompany her mother to her sister's home for the afternoon. Not that Yvette minded visiting her sister and her sweet little children. It was just that she would have preferred to be out in Green Park in Lord Shelley's carriage, where everyone could see her with him.

"Are you still disappointed that your plans were changed, Yvette? I can see that your eyes are sad. *Tu as l'air très triste. Je peux lire une certaine déception dans tes yeux.*"

Surprised, Yvette turned to her mother.

"You think I am a foolish old woman who does not know what is going on around me. But I know, Yvette, I know. *Je sais ce à quoi tu penses. Tu penses que je suis insensée mais je ne le suis pas. J'en sais quelque chose. J'ai raison. J'en suis certaine.* You were looking forward to being with a certain gentleman today, were you not?"

"*Maman*, please." The last thing Yvette wished to do was discuss her feelings for Lord Shelley with her mother.

"No need to say so. I am right, I know."

"Well, yes," Yvette admitted the truth with reluctance. "I

was supposed to go riding with a very nice gentleman this afternoon. Had he come to the house, I would have introduced you."

"Who is he?"

"Lord Shelley."

"Ah, yes. Of course you would rather be with a handsome gentleman than visit your sister. It is only natural. *Mais bien sûr que tu voudrais être avec un bel homme. Quelle femme ne le voudrait pas?* I knew the truth of it. Tell me about him."

"There's nothing to tell yet, Mother."

"Ha! That is a lie! Now, this gentleman is the reason you wished to stay in London and the reason I am here in London, a city I despise, and not in my comfortable house in Brighton, to watch over you. I am not a fool, Yvette. *Je ne suis pas dupe. J'insiste pour que tu m'en dises plus sur cet homme. Je saurai tout, tôt ou tard. Je le saurai.* I insist you tell me about him."

"It's nothing, Mother. Truly. There is nothing to tell at this point. He is a very kind gentleman who asked me to go riding with him. Because of the weather, we have postponed our outing. That's all there is to tell."

"I do not believe you. However if what you say is true, then you are a bigger fool than you think I am." Genevieve laughed. "You will tell me before long! Mark my words. *J'ai raison. J'en suis certaine.*"

Yvette was grateful when they finally arrived at the pretty townhouse where Lisette lived with Quinton Roxbury, her architect husband. The footman helped her mother into the house just as the autumn rain began to fall in earnest. Yvette hurried up the steps behind them, managing to escape most of the rain.

"Oh, such a downpour! It is lucky I am not drowned. *Je déteste Londres. Je n'en peux plus de toute cette pluie. If y fait si froid et si humide,"* Genevieve exclaimed bitterly as Lisette rushed to greet them in the wide entry hall.

Their mother was in one of her dramatic moods, as always, and Yvette was fast losing patience with her. Luckily, her sister Lisette was there to take over. With her caring nature and calm sweetness, Lisette was the only one of all the Hamilton daughters who had the power to soothe their fractious mother when she was in one of her disagreeable dispositions.

"Oh, *Maman*, come sit by the fire and dry off," Lisette exclaimed with worry, fussing over Genevieve and taking her cloak and handing it to her butler. "At least you aren't too wet."

"Ah, *ma petite fille,"* Genevieve murmured. "You look so well, so healthy, so beautiful. How is my newest little granddaughter, the sweet baby?"

Lisette beamed with pride. "Oh, Mother, she is absolutely perfect!"

Yvette hugged her sister, whispering low, "It hasn't even been a week yet and Mother is quite literally driving me mad."

"Of course she is," Lisette whispered back with a secretive laugh. "What did you expect?"

"How shall I ever survive this?" The months until Christmas yawned before Yvette much like a prison sentence.

"You will survive though." Lisette smiled at her in sympathy. Then she said loudly, "Come, both of you, and have some tea and visit with my daughter and me. Oh, and we have a surprise guest today too!" Lisette took Genevieve's arm in hers and led her into the drawing room.

"A surprise guest?" Yvette wondered aloud as she followed her mother and sister into the Roxburys' tastefully decorated parlor. A warm fire glowed in the grate to ward off the fall dampness, candles flickered brightly in the sconces against the rose-patterned wall paper, and an elegant table was set for tea with the finest china. It was a welcoming scene typical of Lisette.

Except for the sight of Jeffrey Eddington standing in the center of the room, with a baby sleeping peacefully in his arms.

She hadn't expected to see Jeffrey at Lisette's house today any more than she had at the ball the night before last. The memory of what he'd overheard her saying caused her cheeks to flush slightly. She still felt the shame of her words, even if she hadn't meant them the way they must have sounded to him.

Now, here he was, with his dark black hair brushed back from his clean-shaven and impossibly handsome face and his sky blue eyes dancing with merriment. He looked quite at home holding Lisette's infant daughter. In fact, he looked remarkably comfortable with a baby in his arms. The image stunned Yvette.

Surely she had seen him holding one of her nieces or nephews before! Hadn't he held Phillip or Simon or Sara when they were babies? Or Thomas or one of Lisette's twins? Why could she not recall a clear memory of that? Why did this scene, of Jeffrey holding baby Elizabeth so sweetly, unsettle her so much?

"Good afternoon, ladies," he whispered, as he continued to gently rock Elizabeth in his strong arms.

"Ah, *monsieur*, what a sight for sore eyes you are! *Je suis toujours contente de vous voir. Vous êtes un beau scélérat, Lord Eddington, c'est bien pour cela que je vous adore.*" Genevieve grinned broadly at Jeffrey, who had always been a favorite of hers.

Lisette escorted their mother to a comfortable chair near the fire and covered her lap with a blanket.

"I told you we had a surprise guest," Lisette explained, clearly delighted by the turn of events.

"What are you doing here, Jeffrey?" Yvette could not help but ask. She still had not moved from the doorway. At the sharp glance Lisette gave her, Yvette stammered, "What I meant was it's such a surprise to see you here. We weren't expecting you."

Jeffrey flashed her one of his best grins. "I've been away so long that I hadn't seen Quinton and Lisette's newest addition. I didn't know that you were going to be here today either, Yvette. Or you, Mrs. Hamilton. But I was delighted when Lisette said you would be joining us." He walked over to her mother and handed her baby Elizabeth.

Slowly, Yvette took a seat on the sofa across from her mother. Such a goose she was being! She had never felt uncomfortable with Jeffrey Eddington before. He was family. Surely it was because he had seen her with Lord Shelley the night before last. Jeffrey was not stupid. He must have noticed her interest in Lord Shelley.

She had hoped to keep her interest in him a secret until they were more definite, when she was sure of his intentions and she could present him to her family as a *fait accompli*. How surprised they all would be when the baby of the Hamilton family became a duchess! They would finally see that she had grown up. How she longed for the day when everyone in her family could see that she was just as important as they were.

However, at this point it was still quite tenuous with Lord Shelley, and if things did not end well, she could not bear for her family to think she had somehow *lost* the chance for a duke.

With things going so well, now she only hoped Jeffrey wouldn't give her away too soon. She wasn't quite ready to reveal the wonderful news that a duke was interested in her. Silently, she pleaded with Jeffrey not to mention a word.

Giving her a curious look, Jeffrey took a seat beside her on the small sofa. Had his eyes always been so blue?

"Oh, my granddaughter is beautiful! Quite beautiful!" Genevieve exclaimed with pride, looking down at the sleeping baby in her arms. *"Ma petite-fille est belle."*

"I think she looks like Yvette."

All three women stared at Jeffrey in surprise.

Genevieve looked down at the baby and then looked slowly back up at Jeffrey in astonishment. *"Quelle surprise!* I think you are right."

"Elizabeth has Yvette's fair coloring and blond hair," Jeffrey continued. "Look, especially around the eyes."

Yvette stared blankly at Jeffrey, then giggled. "That's ridiculous. All I've heard my whole life is how alike all we Hamilton sisters look. Of course Elizabeth looks like me! She's Lisette's daughter and I look like Lisette and Lisette looks like me. And we both look like Colette, Juliette, and Paulette too. We're all related."

Jeffrey, shaking his head, continued to press his point. "You all look alike undoubtedly. But each of you has something special about her that sets her apart from the others. Something unique. You have that too, Yvette. I see it in little Elizabeth too."

Genevieve smiled in delight. "You are a wise man, Lord Eddington, our darling Jeffrey. A most discerning gentleman. *Vous avez vraiment raison. Vous remarquez des choses que les autres ne voient pas. Vous êtes un homme sage.* He is right. Elizabeth favors her *tante* Yvette." She placed a kiss on the baby's forehead. "Yes, he is quite right. But then handsome gentlemen are usually right about matters concerning beautiful women."

"Mother!" Lisette scolded lightly. "What a silly thing to say."

Genevieve was insistent. "But it is true. *Ma petite-fille est belle. Quel beau bébé. Elizabeth ressemble vraiment à Yvette.* Elizabeth does look like Yvette! Our Jeffrey is quite correct."

"Thank you, Mrs. Hamilton." Jeffrey bowed his head gallantly toward Genevieve. He obviously loved being right.

Lisette was about to reply when she was distracted by the arrival of her towheaded twin boys. Accompanied by their nurse, the tiny duo toddled into the parlor and scampered to the sofa where Yvette and Jeffrey were seated.

"The boys are here!" Yvette exclaimed with gladness. She took a nearly two-year-old Christopher in her arms and pulled him up to her lap. She only knew it was him because his name was embroidered on his little blue jumper. "Hello, sweet boy! Oh my, Lisette, they get bigger every time I see them!" She rained kisses on the boy's little face, delighting in cries of "Auntie 'Vette."

It was quite remarkable that Lisette had once been worried that she wouldn't have any children and now she had three! In total Yvette was currently aunt to eight nieces and nephews. It would be great fun at Christmas when everyone arrived home again and all the children were together!

Smiling broadly, Jeffrey lifted Charles, the other twin, high up into the air, making the boy squeal with laughter. "What a little man you've become, Charlie!" He looked over at Lisette as he sat back on the sofa with Charles on his lap. "Now these two boys both favor Quinton, most definitely. But how you ever manage to tell either of them apart is beyond me. They truly are identical!"

Glowing with pride at her handsome little boys, Lisette admitted, "It hasn't been easy. I've started to let Christopher's hair grow a little longer so it's easier to identify who is who. I must admit that I live in dread of mixing them up."

"What does it matter if you mix them up?" Genevieve observed from her chair, airily dismissing her daughter's fear. "They know who they are. *Quelle importance si vous les confondez? Les jumeaux savent qui ils sont eux. Les garçons restent des garçons. Ils n'ont pas tant d'importance.*"

"Mother!" Lisette gave Genevieve a hard look of disbelief, her delicate brows furrowed in consternation. "How would you like it if someone always called you by the wrong name?"

Genevieve threw up her hand and waved it in the air. "Eh. I would not care. What does it matter? Boys are boys! *Je ne m'en inquièterais pas.*"

Lisette frowned in consternation. "*Maman*, you are being impossible."

Yvette tried to contain her laughter. Genevieve was in rare form today. Lisette, usually the picture of serenity, was already losing patience with their mother and they had only just arrived. Yvette fervently wished she could leave her mother here with Lisette for a few days.

Just then, Lisette's husband, Quinton Roxbury, entered the room. Quinton was tall with golden blond hair and most handsome. Yvette thought he was smart, funny, and kind too. As far as brothers-in-law went, she had acquired four good ones over the years. She wondered idly how Lord Shelley would fit in with her sisters' husbands. She tried to imagine him sitting here with her family and playing with the children, and she had a bit of difficulty doing so.

"Well, look who's here!" Quinton made a fuss over Genevieve, making her flush with happiness. He gave her a kiss on the cheek in greeting. "Hello, *Maman*. It's good to see you."

Quinton laughed when he saw Yvette and Jeffrey cuddled together on the small sofa with Charles and Christopher in their arms. "And don't you two look like a happy little family with my twin sons on your laps!"

Yvette caught Jeffrey's gaze at that moment and she held her breath. A dark intensity in his blue eyes held her spellbound. She blinked rapidly.

"They look adorable!" Lisette agreed, smiling at Yvette and Jeffrey with an amused expression on her face.

Genevieve joined in. "They do! How wonderful! They look like a lovely family. *Oh, ils forment une belle famille.*"

With her cheeks warming inexplicably, Yvette gave a nervous laugh and avoided Jeffrey's eyes. "As if the infamous Lord Eddington would ever settle down and raise a family!"

"You never know. I might." Jeffrey winked mischievously at them. "If I found the right woman."

"That's right," Lisette pointed out with her usual optimism. "Jeffrey will make a wonderful husband and father someday. I'm quite positive of that. He just hasn't met the right woman for him yet."

"Run while you can, old fellow. They're plotting your future," Quinton cautioned in a joking manner.

"If I recall correctly, you started this whole line of conversation, my friend." Jeffrey laughed as he handed little Charlie to his father.

Later that afternoon, after the children had been returned to the nursery and the adults had enjoyed their tea, Yvette noticed that the sky had cleared up considerably and the sun sparkled through the windows of Lisette's parlor. She frowned at the sudden change of weather, which had ruined her original plans with Lord Shelley.

"Why the sad face, Yvette?" Jeffrey asked, eyeing her intently.

Before she could respond, her mother answered for her. "She is disappointed because the rain ruined her plans for riding in the park this afternoon. And now the sun has come out. *Elle est déçue parce que la pluie l'a empéchée de voir un certain monsieur*."

"Oh, who were you to go riding with, Yvette?" Her sister's face suddenly lit up with interest.

"Oh, no one you know. It really doesn't matter," Yvette said hurriedly, eager to change the subject. She was simply not ready to discuss it with them now, and she wished her mother had kept her mouth closed. It was entirely too soon. Yvette was still not sure of Lord Shelley's intentions. "Would anyone care for more tea?"

Jeffrey eyed her with an amused expression, his blue eyes dancing. Yvette blinked.

"Are you keeping company with someone?" Lisette asked, her tone curious.

"No, I'm not keeping anyone's company at the moment," Yvette said through gritted teeth. "I assure you that when I am, I will let you know."

"Come, Yvette. I can take you riding now if you like," Jeffrey suggested brightly. "It's cleared enough and the sunshine might cheer you up a bit."

"Oh, yes! Thank you, Jeffrey. That would be lovely." Yvette rose from the sofa in eagerness to leave. Jeffrey. He understood how she needed to escape her mother and sister's prying. He was such a dear at times!

"Well, that might be just the thing she needs, Jeffrey. *C'est une idée merveilleuse, mon garcon! Emmenez-la se promener en voiture. Vous savez comment lui remonter le moral.* Good luck with her." Genevieve waved them off with a smile.

Oddly enough, it struck Yvette as quite humorous that she had begun the day thinking she would be riding with Lord Shelley and she was ending up in a carriage with Jeffrey Eddington instead!

5

Secrets

Once settled in his elegant black carriage, Jeffrey looked at Yvette with sympathy. "Where would you like to go, my girl?"

"Anywhere." She sighed heavily, resting her head against the cushioned leather seat. "Thank you for rescuing me from them."

"My pleasure." He gave instructions to the driver and sat back beside Yvette.

The carriage slowly made its way down the puddle-strewn cobblestone lane, toward the park, while the sun, hanging low in the September sky, peeked between gray clouds.

Jeffrey looked at Yvette, her cheeks flushed with a mixture of frustration and embarrassment. There was no need to pretend with her. She knew that he knew. "You shall have to tell them all eventually."

"I realize that and I can't wait to tell them," she said, sounding somewhat weary. "I truly wish to tell them. I do.

But I need to be certain I have something definite to share with them first."

"Something definite?"

She hesitated. "Yes . . ."

"You mean a proposal?" he asked, not really surprised. "From Lord Shelley?"

Yvette's soft cheeks turned a deeper shade of pink as she admitted, "Well . . . yes. Or at least close to a proposal."

"Do you think that is a possibility in your immediate future?"

She nodded firmly, her dainty chin resolute. "I have every indication that it is."

"Then why not tell them now? They are your family. Your mother. Your sister. They love you and only want the best for you. May I ask why you are keeping your interest in Lord Shelley such a big secret?"

Yvette's robin's-egg-blue eyes looked up at him, and for the first time, Jeffrey saw something in them he had not expected to see. They fairly glittered with determination, and something in his chest tightened at the sight.

She said, "I've had marriage proposals before and turned them down because I simply was not interested. This time is different. It may sound silly to you, but I don't wish to spoil anything by mentioning him too soon."

"But are you not completely certain of him?" He watched her carefully.

She grudgingly admitted, "There is one obstacle."

After a moment of silence, Jeffrey prompted her. "And who would that be?"

"Miss Jane Fairmont."

"Ah, so you do have some competition. . . ." He liked the sound of that, although for the life of him, he couldn't imagine any man choosing another woman when he could have Yvette Hamilton.

"It seems that way, yes." Her tone was depressed.

"I've met Miss Fairmont before. She's a very pretty girl. Good family."

Sounding a bit deflated, Yvette agreed with his compliment. "Yes. I know."

"Are you in love with him?" Surprising himself with the question, Jeffrey could not stop the words from escaping his mouth.

Yvette turned her gaze to the window. "I'm not sure yet."

Relief washed over him. She wasn't in love with Lord Shelley! This fact only hardened his resolve to dissuade her from marrying the man. "You don't love him, yet you wish to be his wife." He paused before pointedly adding, "His duchess."

She did not hesitate in her firm reply. "Yes."

"I see." But Jeffrey didn't see. He couldn't believe that his sweet little Yvette, now a grown woman sitting beside him, could be so deluded.

"Well then," he said. "It seems your mind is made up. Is there anything I can do to help?"

"It's too bad you couldn't marry Jane Fairmont and get her out of the way," Yvette remarked rather dryly.

Jeffrey laughed in spite of himself. He had to give her credit for determination if nothing else. "I'm sorry to disappoint you, Yvette, but the lovely Miss Fairmont is not my type."

Suddenly Yvette's expression grew quite mischievous and she regarded him steadily. "And just what is *your* type, Jeffrey?"

He took a deep breath. Now was the moment to begin his romancing of her, his first move. He needed to turn her head a little. "Well, you are."

Yvette burst into giggles. "What?"

Bristling somewhat at her reaction, Jeffrey stated, "Well, you asked. And you are my type. Or someone like you."

Yvette rolled her eyes merrily. "Oh, Jeffrey! That's the most ridiculous thing I've ever heard you say!"

He frowned at her. "Why do you say it's ridiculous?"

"Because, Jeffrey," she spoke to him as if he were a small child, "if someone like me were your type, you'd be a respectable married man with a large passel of children by now."

"Not necessarily."

"You only consort with actresses and dancers. Women like that."

He narrowed his eyes at her. He was not comfortable with the idea of Yvette knowing about his private affairs. "How on earth would you know whom I 'consort' with?"

She laughed again. "Women always know about these things even if we never mention them. Everyone knows. Everyone talks. Have you forgotten how long I've known you?"

"No, I hadn't forgotten, but you were a little girl. I didn't think you were aware of my private life."

"I was a child then, but I am not a little girl any longer, Jeffrey." She gave him an arched look that shook him to his toes and added, "In case you haven't noticed yet."

He held his breath for a moment. Yes, he'd certainly noticed. His little Yvette was now a strikingly beautiful woman. A woman who wanted only to be a duchess.

"Besides," she continued, "your private life is hardly private. Everyone talks about you."

"Enough about me." Jeffrey knew he had a reputation. In fact, he had done more to create it over the years than he should have. But for the first time in his life, he wished he had been more discreet with the ladies he'd romanced.

The idea of Yvette knowing about this aspect of his life did not sit well with him.

"Tell me, Yvette, just how do you plan to win over the future Duke of Lansdowne?"

She suddenly grew flustered. "I don't have a plan exactly . . . I just wish to . . . that is . . . I shall endeavor to convince him in my manner of behavior and dress that I am better suited to be his duchess than Jane Fairmont. I hope to make him fall in love with me."

"Yes, and of course he will." Jeffrey almost felt sorry for the man.

"It shouldn't be too difficult to do, I would think." Yvette gave a delicate shrug of her shoulders. "Other men have fallen in love with me when I wasn't even trying. Do you have any advice for me?"

He shook his head. "No, I believe you will do fine on your own. But may I ask you a question?"

She nodded. "Of course."

"Why do you wish to be a duchess?"

"What woman wouldn't want to be a duchess?" she asked incredulously.

"I know plenty of women who would not be interested in such a position. However, I'm posing the question to you, Yvette. Why do you want to be his duchess when you don't even love him?"

"I never said I didn't love him. I am still getting to know him, for heaven's sake!" She rolled her eyes in exasperation. "As it is now, I like Lord Shelley very much. He's quite handsome, well-mannered, distinguished, and gallant. And I shall come to love him in time, I'm certain. And if I were his duchess, I would be a very important and grand lady."

"You don't believe you are important and grand enough now?" he questioned.

She waved her hand airily. "You know what I mean.

I must say that I've grown weary of this conversation, Jeffrey. You used to be far more entertaining than this."

Reluctantly, he supposed she was right. He had not been at all amusing and teasing with her as he usually was. Now that he had a clearer perspective on the situation, he should refrain from criticizing her and make himself more appealing than the highly regarded Lord Shelley. In order to protect her, Jeffrey had to make her want him more than she wanted to be a duchess.

He groaned inwardly, hating himself a little for what he was about to do.

Flashing her his most engaging smile, he caught her gaze. He gave her a heated look he usually reserved for his most desired conquests and Yvette's eyes widened slightly in surprise. He noted that she caught her breath.

"Far be it from me to allow a beautiful woman to be displeased in my company."

She giggled, relaxing a bit. "Now there's the Jeffrey I've come to know and love!"

Yvette's words, said lightly with no hesitation on her part, should have made him happy, but instead left Jeffrey suddenly feeling very empty inside.

6

Autumn Days

William Weatherly, Marquis of Shelley, Earl of Cheshire, and the future Duke of Lansdowne, rode his horse across the fields that sprawled around his ancestral estate, Lansdowne Manor. He loved the fresh air and his horses. He was on a particularly fine mount today, a large black stallion named Charger. This was exactly where William wanted to be. Outside, feeling the bracing wind on his face, riding over his lands dotted with trees painted in autumn colors, watching the sun sink behind the distant hills. Not in some infernal drawing room at a musicale listening to a silly chit embarrass herself by thinking she could sing.

His entire afternoon had been wasted on such drivel.

He'd intended to take the enchanting Miss Hamilton for a carriage ride through the park, but the weather had not cooperated. Instead, his mother had cajoled him into attending the aforementioned dreadful musicale. Afterward, they had escaped to the relative serenity of his ancestral home. The sunset ride about the grounds had been good for him. Cleared the cobwebs from his head.

And so did Miss Yvette Hamilton. Now there was a lovely thought.

She was undoubtedly beautiful. And quite entertaining. She had a quick wit and had not fawned over him as the other females did. When William had asked to take her riding, she'd seemed reluctant to accept his invitation and, he had been on pins and needles for some moments waiting for her response. Finally, as if she had had a difficult time making up her mind, she had looked up at him with her incredibly blue eyes, and smiled enchantingly.

"Yes, I would be honored to go riding with you, my lord."

His heart had done a somersault at her acceptance. It was ridiculous! How could such a little slip of a girl have that effect on him? William was accustomed to ladies of all classes making themselves readily available to him. It had been that way his entire life, and at times it had been quite an asset and at others, just a boring reality. As the heir to a wealthy dukedom, he was more than sought after. He was also pursued, harassed, and harried by every female and their mother trying to arrange a marriage for him.

That was the reason William had gone abroad in the first place. Spending time traveling the Continent had removed some of the pressure and stress of his position and allowed him to be himself. For years it had been his escape. He knew one day he would have to return home and pick up the reins of his duties and responsibilities, but while his freedom lasted it was wonderful. He could admit that he'd had more time than most to enjoy himself before marriage, and enjoyed himself he certainly had!

However, it was the letter from Mother that had brought him back to London this summer. He'd been on a warm beach in southern Spain when he'd read her elegant script.

Dearest William,

It is with a heavy heart that I write these words, but I shall be brief. Your father has been stricken with an illness that has weakened his body and, most tragically, his spirit. In spite of excellent care from the best doctors, he does not seem to be recovering.

I implore you to come home. It is long past the time for you to marry and provide an heir. Your father may not have much time left with us. Please come back, my dearest boy, and assume your duties as son and future head of this family.

I await your speedy return.

Your with love,
Mother

Like any loyal son, William had left the arms of the Spanish beauty he had been attending, packed his bags, and begun the journey home to England that very day.

Seeing his father again had been a terrible shock, for his mother had greatly understated his condition. The man lay in bed, his seventy-year-old body withered and pale, unable to move or speak. It was as if he were asleep permanently. For all intents and purposes, William was now the duke in everything but name. It suddenly became William's responsibility to handle the affairs of the estate and all that that required. And as he'd neared his fortieth birthday, he'd realized that his mother was quite right. It was time he settled down properly and took up permanent residence on the estate. It was definitely high time to find a wife, someone to be his duchess, the mistress of Lansdowne Manor, and most importantly to provide him with an heir.

William pulled the reins of his horse and guided the

obedient animal to a stop at the crest of a high ridge. He looked back at the grand manor house that had been his childhood home. Generations of Lansdownes had lived there and pride swelled within his chest. The line would not end with him. He had given himself a deadline. He would choose a bride by Christmas.

He had spent the entire summer weeding through the scores of pretty debutantes angling for a chance to be his duchess. And as late in the Season as it was, there were scores of them, preening and prancing for his attention! He could have his pick of them without even trying. Spending his nights in crowded, noisy ballrooms with people who tended to bore him had quickly grown tedious and he longed to be done with the matter. However, choosing his duchess required a good deal of careful thought and consideration. Through all the contenders, only two ladies had stood out from all the rest.

Miss Jane Fairmont and Miss Yvette Hamilton.

He had narrowed his selection down to the two of them.

They both were beautiful, accomplished, and elegant ladies with much to recommend them. Yet they were vastly different.

Tall and slender, Jane Fairmont was very alluring with her wavy chestnut hair and dark green eyes, and William had always been more attracted to dark-haired beauties like her. She came from a long and illustrious family and had a hefty dowry, and he was quite attracted to her. He enjoyed her company and had a feeling she would be more than agreeable in the bedroom.

On the other hand, Yvette Hamilton was her complete opposite in looks. Fair and petite, with soft blond curls and pretty blue eyes, there was an elegance and delicacy about her, almost like that of a china doll, which he found most appealing. She was bright and vivacious and delightful company. She utterly enchanted him and he could not say exactly why that was. There was something about the shape of her sensuous mouth that drove him mad. He wanted desperately to kiss her full, pink lips. . . .

However, Yvette had been born the daughter of a shopkeeper! Although her uncle held a minor title, she had not been raised a daughter of the nobility but in a family that was in trade. It seemed her older sister had married quite well for herself, snaring the Marquis of Stancliff, and another sister had married an Irish earl. He'd discovered that Yvette had come to live at Devon House when her sister married Stancliff, and had acquired niceties and polish fine enough to make anyone forget her middle-class beginnings. But it still begged the necessary question. Could Yvette Hamilton be a proper duchess?

In all truth, he wasn't so much of a snob as to let her background spoil her chances with him. He simply needed to assure himself she was up to the task and the great responsibility that came with being his wife.

Yvette Hamilton or Jane Fairmont.

How would he know which lady would best fit him as his wife? He needed to spend a little more time with each one to become more familiar with them before making such an important decision.

He rode Charger back to the house, leaving the animal in the family's prized stables with one of the grooms. Once inside the manor house he found his mother. She sat at her oak desk in the study, penning a letter.

"Hello, William, dear." She glanced up from her papers. His mother, Wilhelmina Weatherly, the Duchess of Lansdowne, smiled, her face brightening at the sight of him.

On his return to England, his father's appearance wasn't

the only one that had surprised him. His mother had also changed while he had been away. Although well over sixty years old, Wilhelmina was still an attractive woman, thin as a reed and with only a touch of silver in her blond hair. Her fine features and pale green eyes had once made her a great beauty. But now he noticed a different change in her that made him quite anxious. The puffiness and redness of her cheeks and her frequently slurred speech were telltale signs. He hoped now that he was home again he would be able to control the situation and help her.

"Hello, Mother." He eyed her warily, noting the half-full decanter of wine on the desk near her. There was an empty crystal glass beside it.

"How was your ride, William?" she asked.

"Invigorating. It was good to clear my head."

"Are you spending the night here or are you going back to town?" she asked.

"I'd love to stay here, Mother, but I should return to London."

"Wait until morning?" Her sad eyes pleaded with him.

He could not deny her. With a heavy sigh he said, "Of course, I'll stay the night, if you wish." Although what difference it made to her, he wasn't entirely sure. After dinner his mother would more than likely hide herself in her room with a silver flask of wine for the remainder of the evening and believe that he hadn't a clue as to what she was doing.

"Oh, that's wonderful, William. I just feel better when you're in the house."

"You have an army of servants at your beck and call, Mother."

"Yes, but they're not family. They don't love me."

William sighed heavily. When had his mother become

so maudlin? "Well, I shall leave in the morning. I have business in London which needs my attention."

Wilhelmina suddenly giggled like a silly schoolgirl. "I know what that business is!"

Perhaps she'd already had more to drink than he realized. She'd certainly started earlier.

She gave him a slightly lopsided grin. "I'm delighted that you are serious about finding a wife and starting a family, William. I was beginning to have doubts about you. I feared that perhaps you were the type of gentleman who doesn't prefer women."

His mother had most definitely been dipping into the wine! She never would have uttered such an outrageous statement otherwise. If her remark had not been so appalling, he might have laughed.

Frowning at her, he said, "I can assure you, Mother, that is most certainly not the case. I immensely enjoy the company of women. And I promise that I shall be engaged before the year is out. However, I think it's time we dressed for dinner. I'll walk you to your rooms." He removed the wine decanter from her desk and set it on the far table.

Wilhelmina blithely ignored him. "Have you set your sights on a particular lady yet? Do I know her?"

"I have narrowed my selection down to two ladies. And no, I don't believe you know either of them. Come now." With a gentle touch he placed his hand on her arm and began to lead her from her desk. She followed obediently, like a small child. There was a frailty about her that twisted his heart.

He silently chided himself for waiting so long to provide grandchildren for his parents. They had never pressured him to wed, unlike the parents of so many of his friends who had been pushed into marrying before they wanted to. His mother and father had not been happy that he'd stayed abroad for such a long duration, but they had never reproached him for it. They had understood, as he had, that he would return and assume his role and take on his duties eventually. There had never been a doubt of that. They both loved him and had doted on him, their only child, his entire life.

When he had first come home, he'd been so preoccupied with his father's illness and throwing himself into the social Season to look for a bride that he had not given much attention to his mother. His mother should be bouncing the future heir to the Lansdowne dukedom on her knee, not drowning her sorrows in decanters of wine.

Now William regretted that he had waited so long to marry. He had been selfish and only thinking of his own desires. He was now forty years of age and his parents . . . well, his father was on his deathbed and his mother . . .

"Will you tell me who they are, William? Can I assist you in any way?"

He guided her from the room, unable to bear the look of longing in her hopeful expression. "Of course, you can assist me, Mother. I value your opinion and should like to know your thoughts on the woman who would be my wife. She will, of course, be filling your shoes as Duchess of Lansdowne, which will not be easy to do since you have done it so beautifully."

A genuine smile lit her face at his compliment. "Thank you."

They walked together and reached the grand staircase that dominated the front hall. As a young boy he had run up the curving oak steps and slid back down the wide banisters with reckless glee. Now, as he escorted his fragile mother up the stairs, he thought that if she had a wedding and grandchildren to keep her occupied perhaps she wouldn't drink so much.

"I promise you, Mother, I shall announce my engagement at the Duke of Rathmore's annual Christmas ball and be married before the spring. In the meantime, I shall invite the two ladies I have in mind to have tea with you, and together you can help me decide who would be a better duchess."

"Oh, William, assisting you in your choice of bride would make me so happy."

Oddly enough, it would also make him happy to have his mother's assistance. For who knew the role better than she? Since he was having such difficulty choosing between the equally lovely Yvette Hamilton and Jane Fairmont, he could use all the help he could get.

7

Pretty Packages

October 1878
London

Yvette Hamilton stood in front of the cheval glass mirror in her dressing room wondering if her new satin damask bustle gown might be a bit too low cut. She turned this way and that, regarding herself critically. The sapphire-blue color definitely complemented her eyes and complexion. She adored the elegant shape of the lace-edged sleeves and loved how the cut of the gown accentuated her narrow waist. Her seamstress had assured her the gown was the epitome of current fashion and her lady's maid, Maureen, told her she looked wonderful, yet Yvette felt slightly uncomfortable at the amount of her bosom that was exposed. Perhaps if she wore a shawl? But then the gown would lose its impact and no one would see the lovely sleeves.

Sighing heavily, she wished one of her sisters were here to offer advice. Juliette would no doubt tell her to wear the daring dress. Paulette would be uncertain. Lisette would probably tell her to change into something else. She wondered what Colette would say? It had been a month since Colette sailed to America and the house seemed too quiet. Oh, how Yvette missed her sisters!

One by one, each had married the man of her dreams and moved away from home. And now Yvette was all alone. From her earliest memories, her sisters had always been there, a constant presence in her little world. The five of them were intertwined with each other and she could not imagine a life without them. She had depended on them for everything and felt quite lost without them now.

She missed Paulette most of all, for they had been the closest in age. They had shared a bedroom and each other's secrets their whole lives, even though her sister had always been a little preoccupied with the bookshop and not as interested in society and romantic pursuits as Yvette was. She had always relied on Paulette's calm, rational approach to problems when she'd been upset. Now Paulette was married to an earl and living in Ireland for half of each year and Yvette missed her terribly. She could write to her sister more often, she supposed. But writing letters had never been Yvette's forte. However, soon Paulette and her husband, Declan Reeves, would return to London with the two children for Christmas.

Christmas. Two more months. That was when she and her four sisters would all be together again.

Yvette simply had to be engaged to Lord Shelley by then. She had to be.

All her sisters had experienced romantic adventures and been swept off their feet by handsome men who loved them. When would something wonderful happen to Yvette?

Why, her sister Colette's story was nothing short of romantic! Colette had been struggling to save their family from financial ruin and rescue their father's failing bookshop when the handsome and debonair Lucien Sinclair walked into Hamilton's Book Shoppe one day. Not only had Colette managed to make the bookshop an incredible success, but Lucien Sinclair had fallen as madly in love with her as she had with him. Now her sister was the Marchioness of Stancliff, who had cared and provided for all her younger sisters by bringing them to live with her and Lucien at Devon House when their mother moved away to Brighton. Colette was the only reason Yvette lived in such a grand and stately manner, had a debut Season, and possessed all her pretty clothes. The Hamilton sisters would all be lost if not for Colette and Lucien's love for each other.

And Juliette! Oh, how Yvette longed to have thrilling and daring adventures like Juliette had! Her audacious and slightly scandalous second oldest sister had been bold enough to run away to America. She'd secretly stowed away on the ship of the dashingly handsome and swashbuckling sea captain, Harrison Fleming, who had rescued her from danger. And as they'd sailed across the Atlantic Ocean, they had fallen madly in love with each other. A shipboard romance! Harrison and Juliette now spent their time traveling the world on his clipper ship, visiting exotic and foreign places, and living on their grand and beautiful seashore estate in America.

Oh, and sweet, romantic Lisette! While engaged to her childhood sweetheart, Lisette had accidentally collided with Quinton Roxbury one winter day and it had been love at first sight. But Quinton, a boyishly handsome and charismatic architect with political ambitions, had already been affianced to the daughter of a duke. Lisette had been torn between the love of two men! What could be more romantic? Lisette and Quinton had struggled and fought against their impossibly passionate feelings for each other, until their hearts could stand no more. Causing somewhat of a scandal, they'd both broken off their engagements and finally married each other. True love had won out.

Then Paulette, the most practical of the sisters, had surprised them all when she fell in love with a brooding and mysterious Irish earl. Declan Reeves, a handsome widower with a sweet little daughter, had been accused of murdering his wife in Ireland. Ignoring the rumors and whispers of his guilt, Paulette had been swept away by her love and infatuation for Declan, and they had set out to prove his innocence. Whoever would have guessed that Paulette would have the most romantic affair of all? And would become the Countess of Cashelmore on top of it?

So what was there for Yvette to do? She'd never liked working in the bookshop when she was a little girl and she did not possess any business sense or had a head for numbers like Colette and Paulette. Restless and easily bored, she had little interest in public works like Lisette and Quinton. She was not as wild and adventurous as Juliette, for she was too afraid to go away someplace on her own.

Yvette was simply the baby of the family, the youngest of the pretty Hamilton daughters, but altogether quite uninteresting and alone in London in the shadow of her more glamorous sisters.

Something exciting just had to happen to her too!

Studying her reflection in the mirror now, she saw only an impatient and eager face longing for a romance of her own. All she could do was try to make something happen. Which was why she was wearing the daring sapphire gown.

Attending a ball at Lady Abbott's townhouse this October evening, she would be sure to see Lord Shelley there. For the last month she had played her cards quite well and had most definitely caught his interest. Tonight, however, she intended to eclipse Jane Fairmont entirely. Tonight she would elicit some romance with the handsome future duke.

There was a gentle knock at her bedroom door and her mother entered, balancing on her elegant cane, which Yvette knew she did not truly need.

"Your aunt and uncle have arrived to escort you to the ball. They hate me and I detest the two of them. *Oh, comme je les déteste ces deux-là.*"

Yvette gritted her teeth in agreement. No one in their family was overly fond of their father's elder brother and his critical wife, but they were a necessary evil and had willingly agreed to escort Yvette to social events. She supposed they were better than dragging her mother along, even if Genevieve had agreed to go, which she would never do. Her mother hated leaving the house and had become somewhat of a recluse.

"You look lovely, *ma fille. C'est une robe exquise. Les hommes ne pourront pas s'empêcher de te regarder dans cette tenue.* That dress is stunning. The color is perfect on you."

"Thank you, *Maman*, but you don't think it's too low cut, do you?" Yvette asked apprehensively. When she looked down all she saw was cleavage. It worried her.

Genevieve Hamilton laughed gaily and waved her free hand. "Not at all. I used to wear lower! You would be shocked at my scandalous clothes back in the day. You would not believe such things of your mother. *J'ai porté des robes avec des décolletés encore plus profonds que celui-là. J'étais assez populaire de mon temps. Oh, qu'est ce que tu ne sais pas au sujet de ta propre mère!*"

"*Maman!*" Yvette could not help but giggle at the thought of her mother playing the coquette.

"We are not all that different, *ma petite*. You are more like me than you know. I wish you luck with your handsome gentleman this evening."

Yvette kissed her mother's cheek. "Thank you."

"Do not do anything foolish that you will regret, and"— Genevieve winked at her—"and do not settle for less than you deserve. *J'ai porté des robes avec des décolletés encore plus profonds que celui-là. J'étais assez populaire de mon temps. Oh, qu'est ce que tu ne sais pas au sujet de ta propre mère!*"

Yvette squared her shoulders. "It is not my intention to settle at all."

Her mother smiled proudly at her. "Oh, *mais oui*, you are my daughter."

"Good night, *Maman*. Don't wait up for me." Yvette kissed her mother's cheek. She then grabbed her black velvet cape and reticule and hurried down the stairs to greet her chaperones. She hastily buttoned up her cape to avoid her aunt's certain disapproval of her gown.

Lady Cecilia Hamilton was dressed fairly fashionably, if not severely, in deep purple. Her thin blond hair was pulled tightly from her pinched face, accentuating her perpetual frown. Lord Randall Hamilton, her father's half brother, was a tall, balding man with thick bushy eyebrows. When she was younger, Yvette had feared her aunt and uncle. For after her father died, they had always threatened to cast the Hamilton sisters into the street if the bookshop failed, and it very nearly did because their father had left the shop in dire straits and left them next to nothing to live on. Then Randall and Cecilia had tried to marry off Colette and Juliette, and they had been thrilled when Colette married Lucien Sinclair and they could claim a marquis in the family.

Just wait until they had a duke in the family!

"You're late, Yvette," Randall stated with a deep frown.

"Good evening, Aunt Cecilia, Uncle Randall. Please forgive me." She gave them each a perfunctory kiss on the cheek, marveling that her kind, bookish, absent-minded father had been related to this cold, stern gentleman. "Will Cousin Nigel be joining us?"

Cecilia and Randall exchanged an uncomfortable glance.

"Unfortunately not this evening," Cecilia said through tight lips. "He had a previous engagement."

Yvette knew that her only cousin was a troubled young man who favored gambling and drinking more than anything else. Her aunt and uncle had been attempting to get Nigel married and settled down for years, but to no avail. Their son had been an ongoing disappointment to them. Yvette knew that Nigel was supposed to attend the ball with them this evening, and she hoped that whatever had happened to detain him this time wasn't anything too scandalous. "Perhaps he'll be along later," she added to cheer them.

"I wouldn't count on it." Randall said tersely. He then escorted them to the door and the Devon House butler let them out.

"Thank you, Granger." Yvette smiled at the butler who had always been so kind to her.

"Have a good evening, Miss Yvette." He favored her with a wide grin.

Lady Abbott's townhouse in Mayfair was stylish and large enough to host a good-sized gathering and an orchestra, which was playing rather loudly when they arrived.

Once inside the house, Yvette quickly glanced around looking for Lord Shelley, wondering if he had already arrived. As she removed her velvet cape, she saw a deep frown of disapproval form on Aunt Cecilia's face at the sight of her gown.

"Really, Yvette," she muttered low. As she scowled, the lines on her face wrinkled in frustration. "How could your mother allow you out of the house wearing that?"

"Mother loved my dress, Aunt Cecilia. It is the height of

fashion." Yvette smiled brightly as if nothing were amiss. She would not let her aunt sour her good mood. She was at a party wearing a beautiful gown and about to see her future husband. What could be better? As she ignored her aunt, her attention was caught by a familiar grinning face.

"Miss Hamilton! They're about to begin the first set. Would you do me the honor of dancing with me?"

"Of course, Lord Calvert! I would be happy to dance with you!" Yvette glanced at her aunt and uncle with a smile. "Please excuse us." Gratefully, she took his arm as he led her to the ballroom.

Lord James Calvert was a good-looking younger son of the Earl of Campbell and had declared his love for Yvette on more than one occasion. She found him to be charming and funny and quite a good dancer, but had refused him most sweetly. Yet he still pursued her. As for tonight she was happy for his company and the immediate escape he provided from her aunt and uncle. He took her in his arms and they moved to the music of a quadrille.

"You look lovely this evening, Miss Hamilton. Your gown is most becoming."

Yvette noticed his eyes gaze briefly on her bosom and she laughed. "Lord Calvert, you've become an even finer dancer than I remember."

"That is only because I'm dancing with you." Lord Calvert flirted with her.

She smiled at him as they marked the steps in time to the music. Yvette enjoyed every minute of the dance, thanking him when it ended. She excused herself and headed to the ladies' retiring room, where she met her friend Lady Katherine Spencer and the two of them greeted each other with a warm embrace.

"Kate! Your gown is simply gorgeous!" Yvette exclaimed with excitement. "That color green brings out your eyes."

Her friend stared at her, open-mouthed. "Yvette," she whispered, "your gown . . ."

Already a bit self-conscious, Yvette worried. "Is it too low? My dressmaker and mother told me it wasn't, but now I feel overexposed, and—oh, Kate, what are you thinking? Please tell me the truth."

"The gown is very low cut, yes, but that's not all of it." Kate looked her up and down with an expression that bordered on awe. "It's everything together, Yvette. It's the deep blue color, the way it clings to you, the sleeves. I don't even know the word that would describe you. You look womanly and sophisticated. I've never seen you look better, to tell you the truth. The men will be falling all over themselves for you tonight."

"Well, I doubt that, but as long as you don't think I look too scandalous."

"It's almost scandalous," Kate added. "I think someone else wearing that dress could look unchaste and loose. But you . . . you don't. You make the dress look elegant and sophisticated and the dress makes you look stunning."

"Oh, Kate, thank you!" Relief flooded Yvette at her friend's words knowing that Kate would only tell her the truth. "My goal in wearing it is to outshine Jane Fairmont."

"I've no doubt that you will have accomplished that by the end of the evening!" Kate cried. "You will outshine every woman here. Has Lord Shelley seen you yet?"

Yvette shook her head. "No, not yet." If William Weatherly did not show up this evening, she would have worn this dress for nothing.

"Well, I promise that he won't be able to keep his eyes off of you, once he does see you!" Kate predicted with glee.

Giggling, she and Kate returned to the ballroom and

Yvette danced a few more dances before she finally saw Lord Shelley for the first time that evening. He looked tall and handsome, and he glanced around the room as if looking for someone. Was it her? Their eyes met briefly as she did the galop with a young baron. She gave Lord Shelley a light smile and continued dancing with quick, even steps.

When the dance ended Yvette did not rush to Lord Shelley's side. Not even when she saw Jane Fairmont do just that. Her rival looked very pretty in a demure gown of primrose with her dark hair cascading around her face. Smiling, Yvette turned and accepted another dance with the infamous Earl of Babey, who flirted with her outrageously. At the end of that dance, just as she thanked her partner, Lord Shelley suddenly appeared at her side.

"Good evening, Miss Hamilton. Would you honor me with this next dance?"

"Why, Lord Shelley, I would be delighted."

William Weatherly held her close as the orchestra played a familiar waltz, and they stepped in time to the music. Yvette was struck by a tension around his mouth. It seemed almost as if he were displeased with her.

"I have the distinct feeling, Miss Hamilton," he said in a low voice that was slightly scolding, "that you have been ignoring me this evening."

"Why on earth would I ignore you, my lord, of all people?"

"You seemed quite occupied with your many admirers. Especially Lord Babey. I saw you dancing with him."

Oh, my! He was jealous! Yvette hid the undeniable triumph that surged through her with a mask of calm. "I so enjoy dancing, my lord, and he was simply kind enough to ask me."

"I see." The tense lines around his mouth lightened and his hazel eyes raked across her chest, lingering above her décolletage. "Miss Hamilton, you look more beautiful than ever this evening."

Yvette flushed slightly at his bold gaze, knowing her gown was achieving its desired purpose. "Thank you, my lord. You look wonderful too. Have you been enjoying the ball?"

"Yes, now that I'm dancing with you, Miss Hamilton." His fingers pressed against her waist and she could swear he pulled her a bit closer to him. "You do seem to have many admirers, and I confess that I must count myself as one of them."

"You do me a great honor, Lord Shelley." Yvette cast her eyes demurely downward.

"Might I hold out a hope that I stand apart from your other admirers in your affections?"

Now her eyes met his, and Yvette was a little taken aback by the intense desire she saw within their hazel depths. "Yes, you might hope," was all she said.

An unexpected smile lit his face, making him look much younger than his years. His hazel eyes gleamed. "You've just made me very happy, Miss Hamilton. Very happy, indeed."

In spite of a giddy sense of victory at his words, Yvette still wanted to know if he had asked Jane Fairmont that same question. The two of them had danced together earlier, she had noted.

She wondered if he would attempt to get her alone this evening. She had not been alone with him since last month when they walked on the terrace together and even then there had been people about. They had followed this same pattern for weeks, where he sought her out at balls and parties and paid her compliments, but nothing definite progressed beyond that and he had never rescheduled their carriage ride. It was most frustrating! Perhaps she should endeavor to be alone with him this evening? And allow him to kiss her?

The music played on, and Lord Shelley moved and spun her about the dance floor with graceful ease. He was quite a good dancer and she always enjoyed dancing with him.

Yvette smiled, just as the music came to an end and he bowed to her. "Thank you for a lovely dance," she said.

They hadn't yet left the dance floor. Lord Shelley's hand still held her arm and he gazed at her longingly. "Miss Hamilton, would you care to go—"

"There you are, Yvette. I've been waiting for you to be free all evening. Come dance with me!" Jeffrey Eddington was suddenly at her side. "You don't mind do you, Shelley?"

His eyes said yes, he did mind, but Lord Shelley removed his hand from Yvette's arm with great reluctance and gave a brief nod of assent. "Eddington."

Yvette began to protest the interruption. "Why, Jeffrey, Lord Shelley and I were just about to—" Before she could continue, Jeffrey had her in his arms and was twirling her away to a waltz.

It had all happened so quickly that Lord Shelley was left standing alone with a somewhat stunned expression on his face.

"Really, Jeffrey, that was quite rude of you!" she scolded him in irritation. She was certain Lord Shelley had been about to ask her something important! Then Jeffrey had come along and spoiled it!

Grinning mischievously, he asked, "It was rude of me to ask the most beautiful woman in the room to dance with me?"

His charming, magnetic smile melted her, as she was sure he intended it to. Yvette shook her head in exasperation. It was impossible to stay angry with Jeffrey. And he was so handsome it was difficult to refuse him. He looked very dashing in his black evening clothes. But she was still piqued, for she was sure that Lord Shelley had been about to ask her to go outside for some air. "Thank you for the compliment, but I was in the middle of something with Lord Shelley."

"It's good to keep a man like him on his toes." Jeffrey winked at her. "You shall thank me for it later."

Perhaps Jeffrey, rogue that he was, was correct, she mused as they danced. Lord Shelley was already a bit jealous, so perhaps making him more so would spur him to greater action. All she could do now was hope that was the case.

Yvette began to enjoy the waltz and noted that Jeffrey did not hold her as tightly as Lord Shelley had, but he moved with greater confidence and she felt lighter and more secure in his arms. He guided her effortlessly across the floor in perfect time with the music. It suddenly occurred to her that she had never danced with him before. Why, Jeffrey was an expert dancing partner! Although it shouldn't surprise her that he was, oddly enough it did.

"I believe that this is the first time we have ever danced together, Jeffrey."

"Is it?" His expression was amused. "Then we must note the name of this waltz to remember the occasion and then it shall be our song."

Yvette laughed at his suggestion. "Do you do this with all the women you consort with? Have a special song with them?"

His blue eyes met hers directly. "No. I do not."

"Oh." Yvette felt suddenly awkward with him, not sure what he meant by that.

The waltzing was heavenly, she had to admit. She even

closed her eyes for a moment to enjoy it as she floated in his arms.

"Who the hell let you out of the house wearing this gown?"

Her eyes flew open to find Jeffrey's expression of displeasure. "Whatever do you mean?" Her reddening cheeks belied her words.

"You know exactly what I mean." He leveled her with his gaze. "It's no mystery you have men falling over themselves to dance with you this evening. Surely your aunt must disapprove?"

Yvette defended her wardrobe choice. "Mother said it was fine and my *modiste* told me it was the height of fashion. Besides, Aunt Cecilia didn't see it until we arrived here and I removed my cape." She smiled wickedly. "It was too late then."

He rolled his eyes at her.

"Don't you like it?" she asked.

He gave her a wolfish grin. "Oh, I like it just fine. That's the trouble. Because I'm certain every other man here tonight likes it as well. It's a beautiful gown and you look ravishing in it." The smile disappeared from his face. "But it's too low for you, Yvette."

"It's not that low!" she pointed out heatedly. "And I'm not the only one wearing such a neckline."

His eyes locked with hers. "I don't care what anyone else is wearing."

"I love this gown! It's beautiful and elegant. Stop acting like an overbearing older brother."

His blue eyes were piercing. "I am not your brother, Yvette. You'd do well to remember that."

"Then stop acting like one."

His eyes glittered. "So just what did your Lord Shelley say about your gown?"

She stiffened slightly in his arms. "He said I looked beautiful this evening."

"That you most certainly do."

Suddenly shy with him again, she glanced away. He continued to waltz with her and Yvette wondered why this dance with Jeffrey seemed longer than any dance she'd had so far.

8

Unexpected Surprises

When Jeffrey finally made it home that night, he poured himself a good long drink. He figured he deserved it. Sipping the bourbon, he closed his eyes, but it did not block out the memory that taunted him.

Once again he had spent yet another evening watching Yvette Hamilton. He'd spent the last month following her from party to party, and had managed to remain calm. But seeing Yvette in that blasted gown with every man in Lady Abbott's ballroom ogling her made him want to cover her with a blanket, throw her over his shoulder, and carry her out of there. What on earth had possessed the girl to wear a provocative dress like that? She was a walking temptation and he didn't like thinking of her in that way.

When he'd first seen her, he'd almost had heart palpitations.

Lustful thoughts about Yvette Hamilton were completely wrong. It was his job to watch over her, not lust after her. But that low-cut sapphire gown displaying her luscious breasts had made it impossible to think of anything else.

He hadn't been able to relax for one minute until he'd seen her safely leave the ball with her aunt and uncle.

Jeffrey had always regarded Yvette as a sweet young girl, as a little sister. The feelings he had while holding Yvette in his arms this evening had not been the least bit brotherly in nature. In fact they were quite the opposite and he had to fight them with all the power he could muster.

Blast Lucien Sinclair to perdition for making him promise to watch over the spoiled child!

But that was also the problem right there. Yvette Hamilton was no longer a child, but an extremely attractive woman. She looked like the goddess Venus herself in that dress. Radiant with her flawless skin and her golden blond hair cascading down her bare shoulders, that sapphire dress clinging to her every curve, she commanded the attention of every male in the room without even trying. She had, quite literally, taken his breath away.

And that Lord Shelley! The look on that man's face when he was dancing with Yvette had made Jeffrey want to punch him. It had taken all of his wherewithal to keep from knocking the future Duke of Lansdowne senseless.

It was only October. And Jeffrey had to see it through. He didn't know how he'd make it until Christmas when Lucien returned to London. Once again he pondered the irony of being cast into the role of her protector, when all he wanted to do was tear that gown from her body!

Jeffrey sighed heavily and took another drink of bourbon, thinking there wasn't enough liquor in his house to drown out the wicked thoughts he was having about Yvette Hamilton.

He heard his front doorbell ring and his heart sank at the sound. A brief glance at the clock over the mantel told him it was half past two in the morning. There was only one person who could be calling on him at this hour of the night,

and Jeffrey had completely forgotten he was supposed to go
to her. She would not be very happy with him. He heard the
voice of his butler, Dennings, low and muffled, and then
two pairs of footsteps as they made their way toward his
study.

Jeffrey braced himself as the door opened.

"I decided to come to you instead," a soft female voice
whispered from the doorway.

Reluctantly, he rose from his chair and faced the dark-
haired beauty who stood before him. Dennings, used to late-
night comings and goings, nodded discreetly at Jeffrey and
left the two of them alone, closing the study door behind
him.

"Jennie . . . what a wonderful surprise!" He mustered one
of his smiles for her, but it was half-hearted at best. At least
she wasn't angry with him. Jennie had a bit of a temper and
he was not in the mood to have a scene with her.

Wrapped in fur, she stepped toward him. Traces of the
heavy stage makeup she wore when performing were still
visible on her elegant face, but they did not mar her beauty.
"I waited for you, and then when you didn't show and there
was no note or message from you, I feared that something
terrible had happened to you."

She had been worried about him. He relaxed, then pulled
her into his arms and hugged her. Breathing in her familiar
rosewater scent, he whispered, "I'm so sorry. Forgive me."

Jeffrey wondered at his thoughtlessness. He'd never forgotten to meet a woman before. Especially one as desirable as Jennie Webb, with her long dark hair, deep green
eyes, and full red lips. He had met her while in Paris a few
months ago when she was acting in a stage show, and she'd
returned to London with him.

She pressed her lips against his and he kissed her back,

feeling a gnawing emptiness in his gut. Trying to ignore it, he kissed her harder.

Jennie pulled away and stared up at him, her green eyes wide. "What happened, Jeffrey? It's not like you to leave me waiting."

What the hell *had* happened to him? Jeffrey wasn't even sure. Seeing Yvette looking the way she had in that gown had addled his wits, and he'd spent the rest of the night brooding over it. He couldn't tell Jennie that though.

"I simply have a lot on my mind and at the risk of sounding like a cad, I have a splitting headache. I apologize for not sending you a message. It was terribly thoughtless of me." He gave her a rueful grin.

Jennie took his hand and led him to the leather sofa in front of the fireplace. "Come, darling. Let's sit and you can tell me all about it. Let's see if I can make you feel better."

Jeffrey sat obediently. Jennie let the fur wrap slip from her shoulders to reveal that underneath she was clad in only a red silk nightgown. The outline of her curvaceous figure usually aroused him in an instant. Tonight he didn't seem to care at all. She curled up beside him on the sofa and began to massage his head with her long fingers, running them through his hair and easing the tension and pressure from his neck. She placed soft kisses on his cheek.

"Now, what is it, Jeffrey?"

"I don't know. I'm just tired, I suppose." He sighed, relaxing a bit as her fingers worked their delicate magic on his scalp.

"So you're not hurt?"

"No."

"And nothing is wrong?"

"Not in the least."

"There was no emergency this evening?"

"No. Everything is fine, Jennie."

It wasn't as if he could tell her that he was thinking illicit thoughts about another woman. A woman he shouldn't be thinking of in the first place. His jaw grew slack and he closed his eyes as he lost himself to Jennie's wonderful massaging fingers. The woman did have a way with her hands, God love her. It was one of his favorite things about her.

Her soft voice whispered in his ear, "So you simply forgot to come see me even though we had arranged to meet at my house at midnight?"

"Yes," he admitted reluctantly, "I'm afraid so, darling."

The stinging slap that met his cheek shocked him. The abrupt change from pleasure to pain caused his eyes to fly open and he stared open-mouthed at Jennie, who now stood before him as angry as a fury. He sputtered, "What the hell—?"

"How dare you, Jeffrey Eddington?" she screamed, with her hands on her hips. "How dare you *forget* me? No man has *ever* forgotten to meet me! I have scores of men wishing they could be with me, begging to be with me!"

He rose from the sofa, still stunned by her violent mood swing. "Jennie, please calm down."

"Don't tell me to calm down!" she shouted, her voice wavering with emotion. "There's every reason for me to be angry with you!"

"It just slipped my mind. Honestly, I apologize."

"I'm not the type of woman who slips a man's mind, Jeffrey, if you hadn't noticed!"

He'd never seen Jennie this enraged, and he understood her feelings were hurt. "I know that and, again, I'm very sorry."

Her dark green eyes flashed at him. "The only thing that

would make me angrier right now is if I had discovered you with another woman when I arrived here. And knowing your reputation, that is exactly what I expected to find!"

"Then you should be relieved!" Jeffrey shot back, his own temper rising. "I'm not with another woman! I was here. Alone!"

"But don't you see?" she cried, nearing hysteria. "That makes it even worse!"

He bunched his fists at his sides. It made no sense. She made no sense. "Why?"

"Because you forgot about me!" She grew silent for a moment and her expression turned from anger to sadness. She then said wearily, "After all we've done together the last few months, I wasn't even a thought in your head tonight. You used to rush to be with me when we were in Paris, but you've changed. Very much so." She held up her hands to silence his protests. "Don't deny it. We've seen each other less and less since we came to London. You've become distant and preoccupied. And now you've forgotten about me. I'm not a fool and I don't appreciate being treated like one. This is just the beginning of the end and I detest long good-byes. It is over between us, Jeffrey." She reached down and picked up her fur wrap, allowing him a tempting view of her full breasts straining against the red silk as she did so.

"You are completely overreacting. Stop it." He offered his hand to her.

She slapped him away, her words like ice. "Don't touch me."

"Jennie, come now. . . . Please don't be this way. You know how I feel about you." He smiled at her seductively. "Let's go upstairs and forget all about this nonsense." Then he would make love to her and everything would be fine between them again.

"No." She draped the fur over her shoulders and walked to the door of the study.

"Jennie . . . don't leave like this. . . ." He took a step toward her, but he didn't try to stop her.

She looked back at him when she opened the door. Her green eyes were hard. "I don't wish to see you again, Lord Eddington. Good night."

The door closed with a final *click*.

Dumbstruck, Jeffrey scratched his head, trying to take in what had just happened with Jennie Webb.

Yes, he was supposed to have met her at her townhouse at midnight, but he had stayed later at the ball than he had intended because he could not leave Yvette alone in that damned dress with dozens of men ogling her. Once she had safely left with her aunt and uncle, he was free to go as well. But instead of going to Jennie's little townhouse, without thinking, he'd come straight home. He hadn't realized he'd spent two hours sitting here thinking so much about Yvette that he had completely forgotten about Jennie until she'd shown up on his doorstep.

Rubbing his cheek, Jeffrey sighed and flopped back down on the sofa.

It was over with Jennie.

Strange, he felt oddly relieved and not at all saddened by her unexpected departure. Was she right then? Had tonight just been the beginning of the end of things with her? Perhaps it was. Now that he thought about it, their relationship *had* changed once they had returned to London. Their time together was not as frequent or as passionate as it had been in Paris. Things had just run their course.

It was a damned shame though. He liked Jennie a great deal and could use the distraction of her considerable charms. He supposed he would soon find another mistress to keep him occupied. It wasn't as though he lacked other options.

But somehow he hadn't the heart for such matters now.

All he could think about was a petite, beautiful blonde in a sapphire gown waltzing in his arms.

And he shouldn't be thinking of her at all.

9

All That Glitters

November 1878
Lansdowne Manor

"Well, what do you think?" the Duchess of Lansdowne asked.

Yvette Hamilton smiled in awe as she gazed out the large glass window overlooking the rolling green fields that surrounded the grand manor house. "The view is simply breathtaking, Your Grace."

She had been invited to meet Lord Shelley's mother and asked to visit his ancestral home, Lansdowne Manor. Although Yvette had almost lost her mind the week before when she learned that Jane Fairmont had already been to visit William and his mother. Filled with despair, she had thought all her hopes to be the next Duchess of Lansdowne were dashed. She could barely get out of bed for two days so distraught had she been.

Then a letter had arrived at Devon House from William's

mother, Wilhelmina Weatherly, the Duchess of Lansdowne, inviting her and her mother to tea at Lansdowne Manor.

Genevieve, in her usual frustrating manner, had pled illness and headache and refused to venture from Devon House, leaving Yvette with her aunt for a chaperone. Aunt Cecilia had practically licked her chops at the possibility of Yvette snaring a future duke and jumped at the chance to accompany her to Lansdowne Manor that afternoon a week later.

So Yvette, dressed in her finest tea gown of rose damask, found herself seated in the formal drawing room of the Duchess of Lansdowne with Aunt Cecilia beside her. William's mother seemed a very sweet and charming lady and Yvette liked her immediately. The house itself was beautiful and grand on the scale that Yvette would have expected of such a distinguished family.

"When our little lake freezes over, we shall host a skating party," the Duchess said happily. "It's been so cold recently that it shouldn't be much longer until it's ready. You shall have to join us, Miss Hamilton."

"Oh, thank you, that sounds like such fun!" Yvette exclaimed with a smile. The Duchess liked her enough to invite her back! Yet she couldn't help but wonder if Jane Fairmont had also been invited to return to Lansdowne Manor.

"Good afternoon, ladies." Lord Shelley entered the drawing room. "How was tea?" He kissed his mother's cheek, greeted Cecilia Hamilton, and bestowed a smile upon Yvette, before sitting on the arm of the oversized chair upon which his mother was seated.

"We had a delightful time, William, dear," his mother said, her expression pleased. "Miss Hamilton was just telling me about her family. You must take me to visit one of their bookshops."

"Yes, they are quite innovative stores, Mother. I've visited both of them and I believe you would like them."

"You've been to our bookshops, my lord?" Yvette asked in surprise. He had never mentioned that before! When had he been to Hamilton's? Was he looking them over to see if her family was respectable enough?

"Of course I have." Lord Shelley laughed in amusement. "I do read books, Miss Hamilton."

"The Hamiltons seem like a charming family," the Duchess continued pleasantly. "I'm still trying to learn all of the sisters' names and who is married to whom. Imagine five sisters! I always wanted to have a sister." She turned to Yvette. "Are all of your sisters as pretty as you are, Miss Hamilton?"

"Yes, they are," Aunt Cecilia chimed in, pleased as punch that they were making such a good impression on the duchess. "They have varying shades of hair and eye colors yet all five girls look remarkably alike. So much so that some people have difficulty telling my nieces apart. Just wait until you meet them, then you shall see what I mean."

"That is something I am looking most forward to, I must admit." Lord Shelley's gaze lingered on Yvette.

She smiled warmly at him. "They should all be returning home for Christmas in a matter of weeks, my lord. Although I daresay, you might be overwhelmed when seeing all of us girls at once."

He laughed again. "I don't believe I would mind that experience!"

His mother swatted his arm and scolded him mockingly. "William! Really!"

Yvette marveled at how relaxed he was. Lord Shelley was usually quite formal and she found she liked this more casual side of him.

"Lady Hamilton, would you mind if I took your niece for

a short walk about the grounds before you take your leave?" he asked, quite solicitously.

Aunt Cecilia fairly burst with excitement. "I wouldn't mind in the least, my lord. Please enjoy yourselves."

He looked toward Yvette. "Miss Hamilton? Shall we get your wrap?"

Yvette nodded and followed him to the grand entry hall, where a footman was waiting with her fur-trimmed pelisse and matching muff.

It was an overcast day and the clouds hung low in the sky that November afternoon. A winter chill was definitely in the air and Yvette hugged the muff to her for warmth. They walked side by side along the garden path, the gravel crunching under their feet.

"Thank you for visiting with my mother, Miss Hamilton."

"It was an honor for me to visit with her and see your childhood home, my lord."

"Would you do me the honor of calling me by my given name? William? I don't wish to be so formal with you." His expression was soft.

"Why, yes. Thank you."

"And may I address you as Yvette? It's too pretty a name not to use." Again, he smiled so warmly at her that she barely felt the cold.

She gazed up at him as they walked the shrub-lined path toward the dormant flower gardens. "I would like that very much, William."

"It makes me very happy to hear my name on your lips, Yvette."

Yvette wanted to dance for joy. The day couldn't be going any better! His mother liked her and had invited her back to go skating and wished to meet her sisters. And now Lord Shelley had asked to use their given names. It was just too perfect. He was moving toward a declaration of his feelings for her and that could only lead to a proposal.

They continued walking the length of the garden, the chilly November wind buffeting them along the gravel path.

Lord Shelley began, "I didn't intend to drag you out here in the cold, but I did wish for a few moments alone with you, Yvette. There is something I would like to discuss with you."

"Yes, William?" Yvette held her breath in excitement. Her heart was about to burst from her chest. Was he going to declare his love for her right now?

"It cannot have escaped your notice that I have singled you out with my attentions of late."

She laughed a little. "No, it hasn't escaped my notice."

He laughed with her for a moment. He then stopped walking and turned her so they faced each other. His tone grew serious. "Are you also aware that I am seeking a wife and that you have emerged as my chosen favorite?"

She nodded somberly. "You do me a great honor, William." Oh, heavens! He was going to propose now! It was happening! Yvette imagined announcing the news to her sisters. They would be so surprised!

"I find you irresistibly beautiful, Yvette." With his deep hazel eyes on hers, he stepped closer, his arms encircling her shoulders. He leaned down, his mouth near her cheek, and whispered, "May I?"

"Yes." Yvette tilted her face to his to allow him to kiss her, thrilled at this sudden development. For weeks she had been waiting in vain, hoping he would try to steal a kiss from her at one of the balls or musicales they attended, but he had always been too proper. He'd never even made an attempt to get her alone. And now . . . now she was about to get a kiss from him. Finally!

Yvette had been kissed before, of course, but she just

knew this kiss from Lord Shelley would be different. Special. Magical. And most romantic. It would be from the man who would be her husband. William.

When his lips finally met hers, Yvette found them to be surprisingly warm and soft. He smelled good too. Like good clean soap. It was a nice kiss. Nicer than any she had ever had before. She felt cozy and warm in his embrace and didn't mind being close to him. He pulled her tighter to him, and in a daring move on her part, she placed her hands around his neck. He growled low and kissed her harder. Yvette felt power surge through her own body and with her gloved fingers, she touched his hair and stroked the back of his neck. She didn't know why she did it, she just thought he might like it. His reaction startled her because his kissing became more insistent. She suddenly felt as if he would devour her. Her body grew warm and she didn't feel the cold as she did before. His mouth grew more demanding over hers and the tip of his tongue was at her lips, forcing her mouth open. What was this? His tongue! Reluctantly, she opened her mouth and his hot tongue slipped inside moving and touching her own tongue. It wasn't entirely unpleasant, but it was quite strange.

It felt as if they kissed for quite a long time, and she was beginning to wonder just how long it would last, when suddenly William pulled away from her, murmuring her name.

He hugged her tightly against his chest and her cheek pressed up against the buttons of his wool coat. "My sweet, sweet Yvette. Please forgive me. I got carried away."

"It's all right," she murmured.

"I should have taken more care with you. You haven't been kissed before, have you?"

"No." She didn't know why the lie flew from her lips like that. She supposed it was only a half-truth. She had been kissed before by boys her own age, but never had she been kissed like this. By a man. Frankly, the whole experience surprised her. She wondered what her sisters made such a fuss about. There was no swooning and weak-kneed light-headedness as they had foretold.

He smiled proudly. "I'm glad you have only been kissed by me, Yvette."

"I am too, William." Would he propose to her now? Oh, hurry up already! It was nearing the time she and Aunt Cecilia must return to London. And she was beginning to grow cold again even though she was still wrapped in his embrace.

"Yvette, my feelings for you are . . . well . . . they are quite passionate."

Yes, she had gathered that already from his kiss. Could he get on with it and ask her already? She bit her lip to keep her teeth from chattering.

He asked, "Is it too presumptuous of me to assume that you harbor some feelings for me as well?"

Yvette shook her head, staring at his handsome face. "You are not assuming. I do have feelings for you too, William."

He smiled down at her, obviously thrilled with her response. They stared at each other for a moment.

"You're shivering, you poor girl. Let's get you back inside and warmed by the fire before you head back to London." He cupped her chin in his hand, making her look up at him. "You've made me very happy today, Yvette." He kissed her forehead, smiled, took her arm, and led her back to the house.

Feeling slightly deflated and bewildered, Yvette chided herself. She had hoped for too much and now she was disappointed. He hadn't proposed to her when it felt like he was going to. She'd been certain. And then . . . nothing.

She shook herself from her disappointment. But he *had*

just given her all the more reason to believe that he *would* propose to her soon. He had asked to address her by her given name and had just kissed her passionately, and she'd met his mother. Yes, all signs pointed to an engagement. Maybe he was waiting for a more romantic setting than a freezing cold garden on a gray afternoon? Yes, that had to be the case! For he surely had feelings for her and by all accounts he was as pleased with the progress of the day as she was.

Still, she couldn't help the niggling little feeling inside her that all was not as it should be.

"You should know, Yvette, that I am really looking forward to meeting all of your sisters when they return," William said as they continued walking back to the house. "In the meantime I would love to call on you and your mother at Devon House sometime next week. I'm sorry that she wasn't feeling well enough to make the journey to Lansdowne Manor with you today."

Oh, so that was it! He wanted to meet her mother and sisters before he offered for her. Of course! It made perfect sense now. He wanted to be sure of her family before he married into it. Yvette suddenly felt much better. There were no worries on that score. William would adore her sisters. Everyone did.

"I would be delighted to have you come by, William. My mother is anxious to meet you, too, and deeply regrets not being able to join us this afternoon."

"Then you may count on my visit." He squeezed her arm lightly and stopped to look at her. "You have grown very special to me, Yvette."

For a brief moment, Yvette thought he was going to kiss her again, but he did not.

"You are too kind, William."

"Come. I'm sure my mother and your aunt are impatiently

awaiting our return." They quickened their steps and went inside the house.

"There you two are. We were beginning to worry." The duchess smiled indulgently at them as they entered the parlor. "Did you have a nice walk, Miss Hamilton? It wasn't too cold?"

"It is getting a bit chilly out there, but we managed quite well, Your Grace," Yvette said. "Your son took very good care of me."

William gave her a heated look for her eyes only and then smiled.

After saying their farewells and making promises to return, Yvette and her aunt left Lansdowne Manor. Once they were in the carriage on their way back to London, Aunt Cecilia could not contain her excitement any longer.

"Yvette, my girl, I believe you've done it! You are on the brink of becoming the next Duchess of Lansdowne! I can feel it in my bones!"

"Do you truly think so? Sometimes I have my doubts." Yvette's heart filled with uncertainty and worry as soon as the carriage drove away from the estate.

"Why, yes!" Cecilia's thin lips spread into a most joyful grin. "It's obvious to me that the man is smitten with you! His mother approved of you too. And why wouldn't she? You're a beautiful girl from a good family. They should be lucky to have you!"

"Thank you, Aunt Cecilia."

She patted Yvette's shoulder. "You're the smartest of all your sisters, you know. You've done well, girl, you've done well. Landing a duke! I could cry with happiness for you." Her aunt sighed deeply.

Yvette stared out the window.

"I was there for your sisters' debuts," Aunt Cecilia continued. "They couldn't have cared less about marrying well.

Colette was lucky to catch Lucien Sinclair, who was in line to inherit his father's marquisate, because she was not the least bit interested in a title. All she cared about was that infernal bookshop of your father's. Then Juliette wasted the money we spent on her and ran away and married a sea captain! An American sea captain! Heavens, what a shame! When I think of the brilliant matches I could have made for her! But at one point I feared both their reputations would end up ruined by associating with Lord Eddington, that handsome rapscallion! But he turned out to be a decent fellow, didn't he? Although he is definitely not marriage material. Illegitimate sons rarely are."

Cecilia paused for a breath before continuing on. "Then Lisette and Paulette both turned up their noses at a Season. Imagine! They refused to have one. How your mother allowed such a thing, I'll never understand. Those two deliberately squandered their resources and excellent connections. Just like Juliette. And it was a fluke that Paulette ended up a countess. But an Irishman? Honestly." Her aunt shook her head in disbelief.

Yvette turned from the window and looked at her aunt. "In any case, my sisters are all quite happily married to very fine men, Aunt Cecilia."

"I daresay that might be true," Cecilia said. "But out of all your sisters, you are the only one who had a proper come-out and, oh, Yvette, just think of it! You shall be a *duchess!* It's simply too marvelous to believe!"

Yvette pinched herself. Her aunt was saying all the things she had wanted to hear. She wanted her family to be overjoyed and to think her clever and successful for marrying a future duke. Still, nothing was definite yet.

"Your uncle and I are quite pleased with you. And I know

your father, God rest his poor soul, would be proud of you too, Yvette."

Proud. Yes, Yvette wanted her family to be proud of her. And they would be when she was engaged to the future Duke of Lansdowne at Christmastime.

10

Glad Tidings

Jeffrey Eddington walked up the steps to his father's London townhouse, just as his cousin, James Granger Eddington, was exiting the front door. Both men stopped midway on the stairs when they were at even heights with each other.

"Good evening, Jeffrey."

"James."

"How are things?"

"Good. And you?"

"Just fine." James took a step down, as if to continue on his way. Then he suddenly turned and came back up, until he was a step above Jeffrey. "Oh, by the way, how goes our little wager?"

"Swimmingly."

"Really?" James's face filled with smugness. "It seems to me I heard that the Duchess of Lansdowne invited Yvette Hamilton to tea this week. Rumor has it that Lord Shelley is on the brink of proposing to her. Once she agrees to marry him, and you know she will, I win!"

"That means nothing." Jeffrey gave a careless shrug. "The Duchess of Lansdowne also invited Jane Fairmont to tea as well."

"Oh, come now, Jeffrey!" James laughed wickedly. "If you had to choose between having Jane Fairmont in your bed or Yvette Hamilton, who would it be? You'd better hurry up, Cousin. Time is ticking away. You'll be paying off our wager before you know it!"

Jeffrey ignored his cousin's obnoxious laughter as he continued down the steps. Not sure if he was more infuriated by James's pompous predictions or the thought of Lord Shelley bedding Yvette Hamilton, he stormed up the stairs and flung open the door to his father's house.

"Hello, my boy!" Maxwell Eddington, the Duke of Rathmore, greeted his only son with a smile when Jeffrey entered his father's private study. He sat before a roaring fire, drink in hand. "Fix yourself something. Have a seat."

Without a word, Jeffrey went to the sideboard, where he poured himself a tumbler full of whiskey from the crystal decanter.

"You just missed James," his father said affably.

"Oh, no," Jeffrey replied after he took a swig of whiskey. "I caught him on the steps on my way in. Wished I could have knocked him down." He sat on one of the leather chairs opposite his father before the fire.

Maxwell Eddington laughed, his blue eyes alight with merriment. "I wish you had knocked him down. The man can't wait for me to die. I swear he stops by to see me only with the hope to find me on my death bed."

Jeffrey shook his head, not finding the humor in any of it. He sipped his whiskey. "Don't say such things."

"Well then." Pausing for a moment, the duke changed the subject. "Your mother sends her regards."

Almost choking on the liquor, Jeffrey didn't think he

heard correctly. He sputtered, "Wh . . . what? When did you see my mother?"

"That got your attention, didn't it? I thought it might." His father chuckled. "Yes, I went out to visit her last week. We had a good long talk, she and I."

"You went to see Mother? My mother?" Jeffrey asked again. As far as he knew, his mother and father had not spoken in years.

"Yes. She looks just as beautiful as I remember, too. She was always a lovely woman, your mother. It's a shame the way things worked out between us."

Stunned at this development, Jeffrey shook his head. "I'm afraid I don't quite understand."

"What's to understand?" Maxwell asked. "Janet Rutherford was the only woman I ever cared about. And she gave me the greatest gift of my ill-gotten life." Maxwell paused and stared at Jeffrey. "That would be you, my boy. Yes, she gave me a son. The finest son any man could ever ask for. Something my wife, God rest her soul, was unable to do."

Jeffrey stared at his father. "I'm still shocked you went to see her."

"We thought you might be."

"We?" Jeffrey questioned, growing more confused by the minute.

"Yes, your mother and I thought you would be surprised. We had a very nice visit together, as I said. Very nice indeed."

"So you did." What were his parents doing together? It confounded him.

His parents had caused quite a scandal when he was born. Jeffrey's mother, a beautiful and acclaimed ballerina, had had an affair with the dashing Duke of Rathmore, who had already been married to the quite respectable, Lady Georgia Grant, daughter of an earl. Their adulterous affair had resulted in the birth of Jeffrey Maxwell Eddington. The beleaguered duchess had bravely ignored all of her husband's many affairs, including the one with Janet Rutherford. But when the duke publicly claimed Jeffrey as his son, Georgia could do nothing but bear it with her innately bred stoic and quiet dignity.

Jeffrey had been well provided for and spent most of his early childhood with his doting mother and summers with his father at Eddington Grove, one of the smaller estates. He had then been sent to Eton and educated as most aristocratic children were, and had even attended Oxford. His father, thrilled to have a handsome and healthy son, had managed to grant him the courtesy title of Lord Eddington, but as far as claiming him as his heir, that was quite impossible. Illegitimate sons did not inherit their father's title. As it stood, his distant cousin, James Granger Eddington, was legally next in line. As Jeffrey grew older, he had spent the majority of his time in London with his father, but he'd visited his mother often. His father had purchased a pretty house for her just outside the city and seen to it that she wanted for nothing.

When the duchess, who had always been very kind to Jeffrey in spite of the awkwardness, finally passed away a number of years ago, he'd thought for sure that his father would remarry and try to produce a legitimate heir to the dukedom. Yet he did not. He busied himself with a string of gorgeous mistresses instead.

"Why do you not just marry again, Father?" Jeffrey posed the question to him yet again. "I know there are plenty of young women willing to be your bride. You could have a passel of children if you wanted."

Maxwell shook his gray-haired head. "My marriage to Georgia was not a happy one by anyone's standards. In fact, it was a disaster from the start and it is not something I am eager to repeat. But I am getting on in years and having a wife whose company I enjoy might be a comfort. Who knows? Besides, I don't need any more children. I have a fine son sitting here in front of me."

"Father." Jeffrey gave him an exasperated look. "You know what I mean. You could have an heir of your own and James would get nothing, as he deserves."

"Yes, I do know what you mean and I just told you. I haven't married again because I was pressured into an arranged marriage when I was young and it ruined so many lives. Georgia and I were terribly unsuited for each other. As I strayed, she became consumed with jealousy, and the fact of her barrenness tormented her. I think she died of bitterness, yet it was a relief for me and I think it was for her as well. We were finally rid of each other. So, I didn't have a favorable view of marriage after that. I've been quite free as a widower and I'm more than content with my life as it is."

Jeffrey's eyes narrowed. "So then why were you visiting my mother?"

Maxwell smiled sheepishly. "I hadn't seen Janet since before Georgia died, although we correspond regularly, mostly about you. I was coming back from my estate in Sussex and stopped by to see her for a few days."

"A few days?" Jeffrey asked, incredulous at this news. "You stayed with my mother for a few days?"

It almost looked as if his father was blushing. "Yes. We had a lot of catching up to do."

The conversation made Jeffrey undeniably uncomfortable. He did not wish to think of how his mother and father spent their time alone together. "I see."

"She and I talked about you at great length," the duke said pointedly.

"Oh?" Jeffrey rose to refill his glass, slightly amused at

the idea of the two of them discussing their grown son. He held up the decanter of whiskey. "Would you like another drink?"

"Yes, please." Maxwell handed Jeffrey his glass. "Your mother and I both think it's time you married."

Jeffrey raised a brow as he filled his father's glass and handed it back to him. "It's perfectly fine for me to marry, but not you?"

"Touché." The duke laughed heartily. "But you see, I was already married once. Now it's your turn."

"I suppose you both have someone in mind for me as well?" Jeffrey asked with not a little sarcasm as he walked back to his seat.

"Well, no. Of course not," his father protested, looking a little abashed. "I would never presume to choose for you, Jeffrey. I've been on the receiving end of meddling parents and an arranged marriage and know how terrible it can be. But yes, I do have ideas, of course." He paused expectantly.

"I don't wish to hear them."

"Well, I'm going to tell you anyway. You've missed your chance with those pretty Hamilton sisters you're so involved with. But the youngest one is still unattached, and you spend an awful lot of time in her company or so I hear. Do you not?"

"Yes, but . . ." Was his father actually suggesting that Jeffrey marry Yvette Hamilton? The idea was preposterous.

"But what?" His father eyed him intently. "Don't let this one slip through your fingers like you did the others."

"I wasn't interested in marrying the others," Jeffrey shot back.

"But you are interested in marrying the youngest one?"

Jeffrey remained silent, unsure how to respond to that. He didn't wish to discuss Yvette with his father.

"All I'm saying is that I happen to like her and her sisters. They're a wonderful family and they've been good to you. I believe you'd be happy with her, my boy." He paused before adding, "I just think it's time for you to think about marrying and having children of your own."

Marry Yvette and have children? Jeffrey shook his head in disbelief. She would never have him. He wasn't half good enough for her. "Have you forgotten that even if he is the son of the Duke of Rathmore, no respectable woman wants to marry a bastard?"

His father's face looked stricken. The room grew silent.

Jeffrey immediately regretted his words. He sighed in remorse. "Forgive me, Father."

"No. It is I who should beg your forgiveness, Jeffrey. I'm the cause of the terrible situation you're in." Maxwell sighed heavily, a sudden sorrow in his eyes. "I wish things had been different for you. I was so pleased when you were born, but saddened by the circumstances that surrounded it. You've done nothing but make me proud of you each and every day. I wouldn't have wished this label of illegitimacy on you for all the world, Jeffrey." He mumbled under his breath, "That accursed marriage to Georgia. I should have run away rather than marry her." He looked sadly at Jeffrey. "I just wish I could have given you more."

"You've given me a great deal, Father. More than most fathers give their sons."

"No. I wish I could give it all to you, Jeffrey. My land, my title, my money. There were times I thought perhaps I should not have acknowledged you and let you live your life in relative peace and obscurity. But I wanted to acknowledge you. I was always filled with pride that you were my son."

Jeffrey was touched by his father's words. "Thank you.

I've always been proud to be your son. Even when I got the stuffing beaten out of me for it."

"It builds character," the duke said with a grimace.

Jeffrey gave a rueful laugh, recalling his tumultuous years at school. "Well, then, I have character in spades."

"But you've done quite well in spite of it. You've made your own fortune in your shipping business with Lucien Sinclair and Harrison Fleming. You don't even need my money. You've made me quite proud of you, my boy."

"Thank you. I'm glad of that."

"You've done more with your life than that half-wit, James." Maxwell shook his head in disgust. "You deserve to inherit more than he does. Why, with all the work you've done for the government alone, that should make them grant the title to you!"

Jeffrey laughed at his father's outrageousness. Leave it to his father to think that the British government owed him a favor, a debt. "Honestly, Father." He sipped his drink.

"Am I wrong?" Maxwell asked. "Have you not provided them with an invaluable service with your spying? Don't they rely on the work you do for them in Europe? In France especially? You've spent the last year there, gathering sensitive information for our government, risking your life, and what have they given you in return? I ask you, Jeffrey?"

"One has nothing to do with the other, Father."

Very few people knew of Jeffrey's secretive dealings with the government. Only his father, Lucien Sinclair, and Harrison Fleming. That was it. He preferred it that way. Everyone in London thought him to be a careless rogue, a playboy bastard, and a charming rake who spent all his time in pleasurable pursuits with beautiful women. Over the years, he had cultivated that image, part of which was true, because it detracted from anyone questioning what he really did. No one took Jeffrey Eddington seriously and that suited him just fine, because he knew better.

After he graduated from Oxford, Jeffrey had been approached by one of his father's friends, who worked for the government. He had asked Jeffrey to go to France, just before the Franco-Prussian War of 1870, to gather some sensitive information. With nothing else to do, Jeffrey had agreed. He'd been such a success that they had sent him to a few more countries. Spain. Germany. Italy. Even America. He had contacts in most every city in Europe. And no one suspected him in the least. He actually enjoyed the work he did. With his easy charm and careless manner, he was able to get people to tell him things they shouldn't. It was almost like a game. And he always won.

This past year in France, he'd been working on a highly sensitive case. It had ended quite well and he was glad to have some time off to simply enjoy himself. That was until he took on another highly sensitive matter for his friend Lucien Sinclair.

Keeping an eye on Yvette Hamilton.

"Yes, but Jeffrey, it is time you started thinking of yourself," his father pressed on. "You're thirty-three. Life goes by faster than you think. You're going to wake up suddenly one day at sixty years old, finding yourself all alone and it will be too late."

Jeffrey sighed heavily. "You're not alone, Father."

"And neither are you, my boy."

"Perhaps you should rethink your views about marriage," he suggested.

"Perhaps. I will if you will," Maxwell said slowly.

"Deal." Jeffrey winked at his father.

11

Those Who Are Dear to Us

Yvette wanted to crawl under the carpet. She wanted to jump out the window. Or run away and never come back. The afternoon couldn't possibly get any worse or be more mortifying.

Yvette was rendered speechless as her mother embarrassed her in front of Lord Shelley.

The visit had started pleasantly enough, but then Genevieve had grown more and more fractious. First she had complained of a headache, her usual affliction, then she had become nothing short of disagreeable. She interrupted William every time he spoke, asking him questions that made no sense, and then she outright insulted him. Her mother could not have done a better job of it if she was deliberately trying to ruin Yvette's chances with him. Yvette simply couldn't understand what was the matter with her. Genevieve was acting so strangely and Yvette was helpless to stop it.

"C'est un imbécile s'il ne veut pas de toi!" Genevieve said to her.

Praying that William's French was not up to par, Yvette cringed. With another anxious glance at the clock on the mantel, she hoped that it was time for William to take his leave and finally end this humiliating visit. Never had time passed so slowly!

Although Lord Shelley remained unfailingly polite, Yvette could tell he was just as taken aback by her mother's increasingly bizarre comments and rude behavior, even before Genevieve began speaking entirely in garbled, nonsensical French.

The visit grew more awkward and uncomfortable by the minute and she felt her cheeks burn scarlet with embarrassment. She apologized to William with her eyes, hoping he understood, as her mother continued to babble in French.

"Pourquoi est-ce que ma fille voudrait épouser un crétin pompeux comme lui? Je ne comprends pas. Il n'y a qu'un idiot pour porter un tel chapeau. Regarde ses chaussures. Pourquoi est-il içi? Je ne l'aime pas. Je n'ai aucune intention de lui parler. C'est un âne! Un idiot. Fais-le partir. Oh ce chapeau! Il est horrible!"

"Please forgive my mother, William," Yvette murmured in utter mortification. "She doesn't seem to be herself today." Her mother, aside from being insulting, was making no sense! "Mother, please," she hissed furiously at her.

"Me pardonner mais pour quoi? Je n'ai rien dit qui ne soit pas la vérité! Tu es une petite idiote." Genevieve stared at them.

William looked as confused and embarrassed as Yvette felt. "I think that perhaps I should—"

At that moment Granger came in the room and announced that a visitor had arrived. Yvette was delighted for the distraction, whoever it might be, but her jaw dropped slightly when Jeffrey Eddington entered the drawing room, where she sat with her mother and Lord Shelley.

"Jeffrey!" she exclaimed in surprise, rising to her feet. "What brings you here this afternoon?"

"I just stopped by to say hello to the two prettiest ladies in London, but forgive me, I did not mean to intrude." He glanced coolly at Lord Shelley. "I wasn't aware you had company."

"That's quite all right, Eddington," Lord Shelley rose hastily to his feet as well, obviously grateful for an excuse to leave. "I was just making my farewells. I have a previous engagement I need to attend to."

"It was kind of you to visit, William." Yvette gazed at him worriedly, apologizing with her eyes. He must think her mother was a witless fool. Or even worse, a drunkard! She whispered to him, "I do apologize. My mother has not been well for some time and I don't know what has gotten into her today."

He looked rather embarrassed as he whispered back, "There is no need to apologize. It was a pleasure, as always, Yvette, to see you." He turned to her mother, speaking loudly. "Thank you for an enjoyable visit, Mrs. Hamilton."

Staring blankly at him, Genevieve babbled something in unintelligible French.

"Merci," Lord Shelley responded with utter politeness to her incoherent ramblings. He thanked Yvette once more, promising to see her again soon, and nodded to Jeffrey, and then Granger escorted him from the room.

"Mother!" Yvette cried when William Weatherly had left. "Why would you behave like that? How could you do this to me? I am humiliated! Oh, what Lord Shelley must think of us!"

Genevieve did not react to her daughter's obvious distress. Instead, she stared mutely at the teacup in her hand, her eyes unfocused and blank.

"What is wrong?" Jeffrey moved quickly to Yvette's side, whispering, "You look ready to cry."

"It's Mother." Yvette blinked back hot tears of frustration and disappointment. "She has completely disgraced me, and our whole family, in front of Lord Shelley. He will never wish to marry me now."

"I'm sure it's not as bad as all that." Jeffrey attempted to comfort her. "He did not seem that dis—"

The shattering of china caught their attention and they turned to stare at her mother. The teacup now lay in scattered pieces on the floor.

"Maman?" Yvette asked, an uneasy feeling growing within her.

After another string of slurred and incomprehensible French, Genevieve, her mouth slack and her face ashen, suddenly slumped from her chair to a heap on the floor.

Stunned, Yvette gasped, while Jeffrey rushed to her mother's crumpled form and dropped to his knees beside her.

"Mrs. Hamilton!" he called tensely. "Mrs. Hamilton!"

"What happened?" Yvette cried, hurrying to them. Panic raced through her at the sight of her mother lying lifeless on the floor. After years of listening to her mother's imaginary ailments and complaints, Yvette had never expected her to be seriously ill. "Did she faint?"

"I don't know," Jeffrey murmured, his voice anxious. He gently tapped the woman's cheeks and called her name again. When she did not respond, he looked up at Yvette with worried blue eyes. "I think it might be more serious than a fainting spell though, Yvette. Have Granger send for the doctor right away. I'll carry her upstairs."

As Jeffrey lifted Genevieve in his arms, Yvette called frantically for Granger.

The Devon House butler, immediately taking in the gravity of the situation, moved faster than Yvette had ever seen him move. "I shall send for Dr. Carlisle right away! Then I'll have Fanny come up with the medicine chest."

Hurriedly, Yvette guided Jeffrey up the grand staircase to her mother's suite of rooms. He gently laid her on the bed and still she had not revived. When Jeffrey stepped back, Yvette sat beside her mother on the bed. Fanny Reed, the woman who acted as companion to their mother at her little cottage in Brighton and had accompanied her to Devon House, hurried into the bedroom.

"What has happened to Mrs. Hamilton?" asked Fanny, her round face wrinkled with worry.

"We're not sure yet," Jeffrey answered.

"Oh, Fanny, she just crumpled to the floor and now she won't wake up!" Yvette cried.

"Oh, dear lord!" the woman exclaimed, moving to the other side of the bed.

"Mother? *Maman?* It's Yvette, *Maman*. Can you hear me?" Tears welled in Yvette's eyes. She had been so angry with her mother just a few moments ago; now she wished desperately for her to awaken. *"Maman!"* she called softly. "Please, please wake up." She brushed the soft gray hair from her mother's forehead and kissed her. Taking Genevieve's soft, wrinkled hand in hers, she held it tightly, willing her mother to be well.

Yvette had no idea how long she sat there until Jeffrey, placing his hand on her shoulder, whispered softly to her that the doctor had arrived.

Dr. Carlisle bustled into the room and quickly opened his black leather medical bag. "Luckily for you, I happened to be across the street with the Deane family. They have a touch of fever over there. Now what seems to be the matter with Mrs. Hamilton?"

Yvette scooted out of his way. "She was fine one minute and then just fainted away, Dr. Carlisle."

The doctor leaned over the bed and examined the unresponsive form of Genevieve Hamilton. Her breathing was shallow and she had very little color to her skin. Her face looked slack, as if she had no muscles underneath. "Was there any change in her behavior before she fainted?" the doctor asked.

"Well, she wasn't making any sense when she spoke, now that you mention it," Yvette explained. "She'd been complaining of a headache, but that was not unusual for her. She was chattering and using a mix of French and English that made no sense. It all sort of slurred together at one point. And then she dropped her tea cup on the floor."

The doctor pondered this bit of information. "Hmmm. She might have had an apoplectic fit." He turned and looked at Yvette kindly. "Now Miss Hamilton, please wait outside and let me examine your mother here."

Yvette refused to go, shaking her head. "No. I wish to stay with her."

Dr. Carlisle gave her a disapproving frown. "Now, now. Please let me try to help your mother. It would be best if you left, Miss Hamilton."

Gently, Jeffrey placed his hand on her shoulder again. "We should listen to the doctor. Come with me, Yvette."

"Will she be okay?" she asked the doctor.

"I hope so." Dr. Carlisle smiled at her, but his eyes looked worried.

The knot in her stomach tightened.

"Come with me now," Jeffrey whispered low and took her hand in his.

Reluctantly, Yvette let him lead her from the bedroom, leaving Dr. Carlisle and Fanny to care for her mother. In mute obedience, she followed him to the small, rarely used sitting room across the hall from Genevieve's bedroom, where Jeffrey guided her to the large chintz-covered sofa. The room was dark and cold.

"Sit here," he ordered. Taking a wool blanket that was folded on a chair, Jeffrey wrapped it around Yvette's shoulders carefully, trying to warm her up. She watched as he pulled the service bell, then he sat down beside her. In a swift movement, Jeffrey encircled her in his arms.

Leaning gratefully into the warmth and strength of his body and drawing comfort from him, Yvette once again felt tears well in her eyes.

"No crying," Jeffrey admonished gently, handing her his handkerchief. "There's nothing to cry over at the moment and hopefully there won't be. We don't know anything yet. But I do know that your mother is a strong and spirited woman and will most likely be better before we know it."

Sniffling, Yvette dabbed at her eyes, feeling foolish for overreacting, and nodded. "Yes. I suppose you're right. It was just so frightening to see her like that."

Jeffrey hugged her close. "I agree. I was frightened by it myself."

"You didn't seem frightened." She had marveled at his quick control of the situation while she simply stood there, horrified and helpless.

"Well, I assure you that I was." He flashed her a warm smile.

One of the housemaids hurried into the room and Jeffrey removed his arms from Yvette, rose to his feet, and gave the girl instructions. "Let's have the fire lit since it's like an icebox in here and we're likely to be here for a while. Then have the cook send up some strong tea and something to eat for Miss Hamilton and myself. Also please have Granger send a footman with a message for Lisette Roxbury right away. She'll want to know about her mother."

"Yes, sir." The girl left hastily and moments later one of

the footmen came in with wood to light the fire. In no time, a bright fire was blazing and a few lamps were lit, making the seldom-used room instantly seem cozier.

"Thank you, Jeffrey," Yvette said, grateful he was there with her and she was not alone. She pulled the blanket tighter around her shoulders.

"No need to thank me." He gave her a small smile and stepped toward the door.

Fresh panic surged within her. "You're not leaving me, are you?"

He paused, gazing at her with understanding eyes. "I was only going to let the doctor know that we are just across the hall in case he needs us. But no, I was not planning to leave you, Yvette. Unless you wish for me to go."

Oh, how she wanted him to stay! She could not face whatever might happen alone. "Please stay with me?"

There was an intense flickering in his eyes that sent a strange flurry of feelings through her as he said, "For as long as you need me."

"At least until Lisette gets here," she murmured thickly. Oh, if only Lisette were here now! Yvette would feel much better if one of her sisters were with her.

Jeffrey went and spoke to the doctor, and after a tray with biscuits, fruit, and tea was sent up, they were alone in the sitting room again, which had finally grown a bit warmer.

Yvette whispered her greatest fear. "Oh, Jeffrey, you don't think she'll die, do you?"

He came and sat beside her on the sofa once more. With a long sigh, he said, "I wish I could tell you that I didn't think so, but I am worried about her too."

Yvette caught her breath as he echoed her own thoughts. "I don't know what I'd do if I lost her. Especially after all the horrid things I was thinking about her earlier. I had no idea she was truly ill!"

He took her hand in his and squeezed tightly. "Your mother has never made things easy. But let's just keep good thoughts, shall we?"

Yvette nodded, thinking his hand felt warm and strong. "I wish Colette or any of my sisters were here. I feel like I don't know what to do. They are all so much more capable than I am. They always know what needs to be done."

"Yvette, dearest, you are more than capable and there's nothing to handle at the moment. We sent for the doctor immediately and got your mother settled upstairs. We sent a message to Lisette. Dr. Carlisle and Fanny are in there with her now. There's nothing more for you to do but wait."

"I hate waiting."

"I do too." He gave her a halfhearted smile and squeezed her hand again before releasing it. "Come, have a bite to eat with me. This could be a long night."

12

By the Firelight

Yvette looked at the little ormolu clock on the mantel. It was nearing eight o'clock already. Jeffrey was right. She should eat something. But after a failed attempt at a few mouthfuls of food, all she could manage was to sip some tea. She had no appetite, but having Jeffrey there beside her was more comforting than anything else.

Granger came into the sitting room, his kind face worried. "Miss Yvette, Davies the footman has just brought a message from your sister. It seems Miss Lisette's baby daughter is quite ill with a terrible fever and she can't leave her right now. She sends her regrets and said she will come over just as soon as she can."

"Oh." Yvette's heart sank at the news. Poor little Elizabeth. Of course Lisette should stay with her baby. Yvette wouldn't have it any other way. Still, she had been counting on her sister to come to Devon House. To help their mother. To help *her*.

Jeffrey's face looked grim. "Thank you for letting us know, Granger."

Granger looked toward Yvette once more. "Can I get you anything, miss? Anything at all?" he asked with concerned eyes.

"No, thank you."

The butler nodded. "Please let me know if I can assist in any way," he offered before leaving the room.

Again tears welled in Yvette's eyes. Lisette would not be coming to Devon House tonight. Now Yvette was left to care for their mother on her own, without even one of her sisters there to help her. She had no choice but to handle it alone. She whispered a silent prayer not to let her mother die. She couldn't bear to think of *that* happening while she was all alone.

Barely able to breathe, she gazed at him. "Oh, Jeffrey, Lisette's not coming. . . ."

Without a word, Jeffrey drew her into his strong arms. "I'm here and I won't leave you, Yvette," he whispered as he stroked her hair in a soothing motion.

"I miss them all so much," she sobbed, clinging to him. She missed Colette and Lucien and her darling nephews, Phillip and Simon. The house had seemed too empty without them the last two months. She couldn't remember a time when at least one of her sisters hadn't been with her. And since she had moved into Devon House, there had always been *someone* there. Now everything was different.

She had never felt so lost and alone in her life.

"I know you do, sweetheart," he murmured. "I miss them too."

Jeffrey held her for some time as Yvette soaked up his strength. He understood how she felt because, in a way, they were his family too. Slowly, she pulled away from him and took a deep fortifying breath to steady herself. "I'm sorry. I don't usually act like a watering pot. Thank you."

Jeffrey gave her one of his signature heart-melting smiles. "Anytime."

He looked so incredibly handsome when he smiled like that, that she almost forgot what was happening. Closing her eyes for a moment, she settled back against the cushions with the blanket wrapped around her for warmth and propped her feet on the sofa beside him.

"Before you know it your mother will be well and all your sisters will be home for Christmas and everything will be right with the world," he said as he slowly took her right foot in his hands. Carefully he unlaced the ties of her little black boot.

"I hope you're right." Surprised by his actions, Yvette held her breath as he gently slipped the boot from her stocking clad foot, watching in fascination as he did so.

"Of course, I am," he said. "I am always right." He then removed her left boot in the same manner, leaving her feet resting on his lap.

It was a shockingly intimate thing for him to do, but she permitted it. On this unexpectedly frightening November evening, she allowed Lord Jeffrey Eddington to remove her boots. She felt taken care of, cherished even, by this man who could so easily make her comfortable and safe.

"Do you remember the first time I met you, Yvette?" he asked, while he rather absently massaged the bottoms of her stocking clad feet. He pressed his thumbs against the insteps of her feet, rubbing and squeezing all the tension from within her.

No one had ever touched her feet before and the sensation was almost too heavenly to bear. It took all her wits to form an answer to his question. "It was at the bookshop, as I recall."

He continued to leisurely massage her feet as he spoke. "I'd met all of your older sisters before I ever met you.

But I remember you were in a red dress that day, climbing a ladder in the shop, looking most adorable and trying so hard to act like a little lady."

"It was a navy dress with red stripes and red ribbons and I loved that dress!" Yvette smiled, oddly touched that he would remember such a trivial detail about her.

"You were just a slip of a girl, but I knew even then that you were the prettiest of the Hamilton sisters."

A warm blush crept in her cheeks. "Jeffrey."

"It's true." He winked at her.

"I remember I thought you were most dashing. You bowed over my hand like a knight!"

Jeffrey laughed. "I did?"

"Yes, you did and I almost swooned. Then Juliette sent me from the room. But you had a terrible cut on your face that day, didn't you?"

"Oh, yes." He grinned, rubbing a spot under his eye in remembrance. "I'd forgotten about that. Lucien had hit me."

"Lucien?" Yvette cried in astonishment. "Why on earth would Lucien hit you?"

"It's a long story, and not mine to tell, but suffice it to say that Juliette and I were meddling in his romance with Colette. I deserved no less. But how old were you then, Yvette?"

"I was thirteen the year Colette met Lucien and we all met you."

"And now?" He continued to rub her feet.

"I shall be twenty-one in January."

"Why, you're all grown up now!" His blue eyes gazed steadily at her. "And I was right."

"About what?"

"You are the most beautiful of all your sisters."

Her breath caught for an instant. All she could manage to say was, "Oh."

"It's nothing but the truth."

Her heart flip-flopped at the intense look in his blue eyes. Slowly, she pulled her feet away from his hands, tucking them under her as she huddled on the sofa with the blanket still wrapped around her. "And how old are you now?"

"Thirty-three."

"And you are still a bachelor! You ought to be married by now. Lucien married Colette years ago and he's your age. How do you manage to stay unattached, Jeffrey, when all the women are mad for you?"

His expression grew somber. "Not many wish to marry an illegitimate son. You know that as well as anyone, Yvette."

"That's not true."

"Would *you* marry me?"

She giggled uneasily at his question, which seemed to have some deeper meaning that she didn't quite understand. "Well, no, of course not. I could never marry you. But not because of the illegitimacy."

"The fact that I can't inherit my father's dukedom wouldn't stop you from marrying me?" He eyed her carefully, almost with skepticism.

Feeling oddly defensive, she hesitated before responding. "No . . . I couldn't marry you because I know you too well, Jeffrey."

His brows furrowed. "What does that mean?"

"I know how you are."

"No." He gave her a lopsided grin. "You only *think* you know how I am."

"You've been part of this family for eight years, Jeffrey, I do believe I've learned a thing or two about you."

"Pray, go on." His eyes danced in amusement at her comment.

"I am aware of your . . ." Yvette struggled to find the

proper words to describe what she was trying to say. "I'm aware that you have many dalliances with certain types of women."

"And to exactly which types of women are you referring?"

She waved her hand dismissively. "We've discussed this before. Actresses. Dancers. That sort."

"Yes, that's true," he admitted frankly, with a shrug. "But do you know why I 'dally,' as you so eloquently phrased it, with that type of woman?"

Yvette found that she was oddly fascinated by their conversation. "Why?"

"Because they don't care that I'm a bastard. It doesn't matter to them in the least. They love me for myself."

"I love you for yourself." The words bubbled out before she realized what she was saying. Because they were true.

The room grew silent and they stared at each other for a long moment. Yvette blinked first.

Jeffrey continued, "Do you think I don't know that mothers warn their daughters to stay away from me? That your Aunt Cecilia warned Colette and Juliette away from me when I first met them?"

"But that's because you're an outrageous flirt and a charming rogue, Jeffrey!" Yvette laughed in protest. "Your reputation precedes you."

"No, it's because most mothers deem me not worthy enough for their daughters to marry. Which is fine with me, for I've no wish to marry most of them anyway. There are some benefits to being a bastard son. There is no lineage I'm required to maintain, therefore I am not hounded and pressured to marry and produce an heir."

"But don't you wish to have children someday? To have a family of your own?"

"I suppose so . . . yes." Jeffrey grew quiet, almost pensive.

"I've never given it much thought before now, to tell you the truth. However, it seems to be on my mind frequently of late."

She suddenly recalled the day at Lisette's house when Quinton Roxbury remarked that Yvette and Jeffrey looked like a family while playing with her nephews, Charles and Christopher. "You seemed very comfortable with Lisette's children."

"Oh, I love other people's children." Jeffrey's expression softened. "I just hadn't thought of having any of my own. You wish to have children though, don't you?"

"I seem to be gaining nieces and nephews at an alarming rate and I don't think I'd want as many as my mother had, but yes, I'd like to have children of my own someday."

"Legitimate children," he pointed out dryly.

She eyed him with sympathy. It was such an unusual conversation and she had never seen Jeffrey so contemplative. "It bothers you much more than you let on, doesn't it?"

"It bothers me much less than it did when I was a child and tormented by the other boys at school. Children can be vicious to each other. I was lucky Lucien Sinclair befriended me when he did."

Full of curiosity about him, Yvette asked, "How did the two of you meet?"

"At Eton. We were ten or eleven years old, the youngest ones there. He overheard another boy, named Walter Brockwell, call me a bastard. Lucien punched Walter in the face and almost got expelled for doing so. None of the other boys said anything to me after that, at least not within my hearing. Years later Lucien told me he didn't know what 'bastard' even meant at the time, he only knew that boy was taunting me. He earned my undying loyalty that day and we've been friends ever since."

"I never knew that story." Yvette tried to imagine Jeffrey

as a young boy, away at school, being teased for reasons that were not his fault. She could almost picture him, a handsome little boy with black hair, those impudent blue eyes, and fair skin, sad but smiling to act as if he didn't care. He acted cavalier, pretending those taunts didn't hurt him. Just as he did now.

"But my becoming friends with Lucien, who has been like a brother to me," Jeffrey continued, "had added benefits I didn't foresee as a child. It's through Lucien that I met all the Hamilton girls. You became the family I never had. The family I think I always wanted."

Yvette thought back over the years. Yes, Jeffrey had been present at every one of their family gatherings and at the holidays. He'd won over all of them. Even Genevieve adored him. Indeed, he had become a member of their family, but she'd never given much thought to his family. Of course Yvette had met Jeffrey's father, the Duke of Rathmore, on more than one occasion. He was just like Jeffrey, handsome and charming, which is why everyone accepted Jeffrey as his son. But no one ever mentioned his mother. Yvette had heard rumors, but she realized she had never heard Jeffrey talk of his mother.

"What about your mother, Jeffrey?"

"What about her?"

"Well, do you see her often? What is she like? Are you close to her?"

"She's a wonderful person, and yes, I see her often. She lives just outside of London." He paused before asking, "Would you like to meet her some day?"

Yvette was momentarily stunned. "Well, yes, of course, I would like to meet her." And she realized she really did wish to meet the woman who had borne Jeffrey and created such a scandal.

"I've told her all about you," he said.

"You have?"

"Oh, yes, she knows all about the Hamilton girls. And how much you mean to me."

"Well, you mean a great deal to us as well, Jeffrey." Yvette stressed the word *us*, but she really wished to tell him just how important he was to her in that moment. But she suddenly felt very shy about doing so. Instead she asked, "Jeffrey, I've been wondering about this. . . . What brought you by to see us this afternoon? We weren't expecting you."

He shrugged casually. "I hadn't seen you in a few days, and I thought I'd stop in and say hello, see how you and your mother were doing. That's all."

Yvette had seen more of Jeffrey Eddington in the weeks that Lucien and Colette had been in America than she'd ever had. He seemed to be turning up everywhere she happened to be. Her suspicions finally bubbled over. "Did Lucien or Colette ask you to watch over me?"

He gave a noncommittal smile. "Perhaps."

That was answer enough for her. In truth, it didn't surprise her that he had been asked to keep an eye on her. "Well, they needn't have bothered to ask you. But thank you for taking time out of your schedule to play nursemaid. I assure you that it isn't necessary."

His voice grew lower. "I don't mind looking out for you, Yvette, and I would have done it even if Lucien hadn't asked me to. I've rather enjoyed it. In fact, spending time with you has been my pleasure."

"Truly?"

"Yes." He looked deep into her eyes and Yvette felt an odd sensation rush through her.

This whole evening had an unreal quality to it. The hours ticked by with just the two of them, cozy and confiding in each other before the fire. She had never been so intimate with a man before.

It was near to midnight when the door to Genevieve's bedroom opened and Dr. Carlisle walked into the sitting room at long last.

Yvette fairly flew off the sofa at the sight of him. "How is she?"

"Your mother is resting comfortably now, I believe, Miss Hamilton. I've given her some laudanum to help her sleep. It seems that she did have a mild attack of apoplexy. We won't know the full effects until she awakens tomorrow. There may be partial paralysis on her right side and some impairment of her speech. It's difficult to know for certain at this point. However, she will need plenty of rest for a while."

"But she will be all right, won't she?" Yvette asked in a small voice that squeaked. "She won't . . . die?"

He shook his head in sympathy. "No, my dear, I doubt she will die from this. Now, there's nothing more you can do until the morning when she wakes. Her lady's maid is in there with her and I have left instructions with her. So I suggest you both get some sleep. Tomorrow could be a difficult day, I imagine. I'm going to take my leave now and I'll be back by noon tomorrow to check in on Mrs. Hamilton."

Yvette wrung her hands. "May I go see her now?"

"Yes, of course, but she's heavily sedated and won't even know you're there."

"I just need to see that she's all right. Thank you, Dr. Carlisle," Yvette said.

"I understand. Good night, Miss Hamilton. Lord Eddington." The doctor tipped his hat to them and made his way out of the room.

With a backward glance at Jeffrey, who sat back down

on the sofa and nodded at her to go, Yvette hurried in her stockinged feet to her mother's bedroom. Except for a small lamp burning on the nightstand, the room was shrouded in darkness. Yvette stepped softly across the carpet to the large four-poster bed. Genevieve looked quite small and frail lying there, her gray hair spilling around her on the pillow, her complexion ghostly pale.

Gently, Yvette held her mother's limp hand, whispering, "Oh *Maman*, I'm here. I'm here if you need me. Everything will be all right. The doctor said you shall be well again soon." Not knowing if her mother could hear or understand her words, she said them anyway.

Fanny, her mother's devoted servant, said to her, "Now, Miss Yvette, you get yourself to bed. It's late. I'll sleep on this little sofa here, in case anything happens, so don't you worry. She'll need you tomorrow when she wakes."

"Yes, I know, Fanny. And thank you. It's a comfort to know that you are here with her."

"We'll get Mrs. Hamilton as right as rain again. You'll see."

"Sleep well, *Maman*." Yvette pressed a kiss to her mother's cheek. She then turned to Fanny. "Good night. I hope you can get some rest too, Fanny."

"Oh, I will. Don't you worry your head about me. Good night, Miss Yvette."

With a heavy heart and reluctant feet, Yvette returned to the sitting room, where Jeffrey waited for her expectantly. He met her at the door and walked her back to the sofa.

"How is she?" he asked.

"She's sleeping now, but just as the doctor said, we won't know how she really is until tomorrow. Dear Lord, I hope she's not paralyzed." Yvette slowly sank down on the sofa, her legs too weak to hold her any longer.

"You should get to bed," Jeffrey suggested.

"No. I think I'd prefer to stay here a little longer, in case she wakes and calls for me." Feeling guilty that she'd taken up Jeffrey's entire evening, she looked up at him. "You don't have to stay with me any longer, Jeffrey. You've been so wonderful to me, but I think I'll be fine now. You can go home."

"You are my home and I'm not leaving until you go to sleep."

The utter sweetness of his words was her undoing, and Yvette couldn't stop the tears that slowly rolled down her face.

In an instant Jeffrey was beside her, taking her in his strong arms once again. He whispered soothing words. "Shhh, Yvette, it's all right."

Weariness overwhelming her, Yvette placed her head on his shoulder and let him pull her close again. This time she sobbed like a baby. The myriad of emotions she had held in check all night spilled forth in the strength, warmth, and safety she found in the arms of Jeffrey Eddington.

13

The Coming Dawn

Jeffrey knew the minute Yvette fell asleep in his arms. Her whole body relaxed against his and her breathing slowed. Holding a sleeping Yvette gave him the most beautiful feeling of peace and a sense of home he'd never experienced before. She had cried herself out, and then grown quiet, just snuggling against him, while he stroked her back in a soothing motion. Little by little, they had shifted themselves so he was reclining on the sofa with Yvette in his arms, her head resting on his chest. She fit him perfectly.

It was ridiculously improper and scandalous of them to be lying in such a position together. But he didn't care. There was no one to see them anyway. The servants were all asleep by then and nobody would ever know.

He should wake her and send Yvette to her bedroom, to go to sleep properly in her own bed. But he was loath to rouse her. And he was too selfish. He wanted to stay here on the sofa in the little sitting room in front of the dying firelight, and hold her close to him a little longer, her heart beating slow and steady, close to his. She felt so good in his arms, cuddled warmly against him. It was as if he held the world's most priceless treasure.

He had felt powerless to help her this evening. The stricken expression on her beautiful face when Genevieve Hamilton collapsed was too much for him to bear. Yvette looked so fragile and frightened and he wanted to protect her. Now she looked like a sleeping angel in his arms. Unable to stop himself, he pressed the softest of kisses to her smooth cheek and breathed in her floral scent. She smelled of gardenias, and he knew he would forever associate that heavenly scent with Yvette.

Never had Jeffrey felt so content and so utterly tortured at the same time.

Had they really spent the entire evening alone together, just talking to each other? To his great surprise, he discovered that he enjoyed being with her and listening to her soft voice. He had confided in her too. He'd never done that with a woman before. Actually spending time talking, confiding, sharing all night without it leading to bed sport. Yvette had the strangest effect on him and he didn't know quite what to do about it.

What he did know was that there was no way in hell he was going to let her marry Lord Shelley.

When Jeffrey had inadvertently learned that Lord Shelley was visiting Yvette and her mother that afternoon, he'd rushed right over to Devon House. He'd had no real reason for being there. He'd just known that he could not let her marry a man she didn't love.

It also had not escaped his notice that she had not mentioned Lord Shelley's name once all night.

Wouldn't a woman in love mention the man she was supposedly in love with? Wouldn't it come up in a conversation naturally? Especially when they spoke of marriage and children? But Yvette had not even uttered his name.

To Jeffrey, it was further proof that he was doing the right thing in protecting her. Now he simply had to do something dramatic to sweep her off her feet. And very soon. Before the man proposed to her, which he seemed very intent on doing.

But what? What could he do to stop her? How could he get her to see that Lord Shelley was not the right man for her? The thoughts circled around and around in his head, exhausting him.

Later, Jeffrey didn't recall falling asleep that night on the sofa with Yvette, but he recalled perfectly the minute he awoke. Something caused him to stir at the exact same moment Yvette did. The room was dim in the predawn light, the candles having burned out and the fire was just embers. In the surrounding cold and silence, they shared the warmth of their fully clothed bodies covered beneath a soft woolen blanket. Blinking, they stared into each other's eyes, more than a little bewildered to find themselves in such a position.

"Hi," she whispered softly, her blue eyes heavy lidded and sleepy. Her long blond hair was slightly tangled around her face.

His heart flipped over in his chest. The urge to kiss her mouth roared through him. She was achingly close, softly tousled and tempting in the dim light, and it would be so easy to kiss her lips, to taste the sweetness of her. She was so close. . . . With a gentle caress, he brushed a stray curl from her cheek with his finger. "Hi."

"We slept here together all night?" she asked in wonder.

"It seems that way." And strangely enough he'd slept like a baby, in spite of being in his clothes on an uncomfortable sofa. "I'm so sorry. I should have awakened you and sent you to bed."

"Don't be sorry." Her voice was the faintest whisper. "It was lovely to be held like this. Thank you for staying with me when I was so worried and frightened."

"I would never leave you if you needed me, Yvette." Jeffrey hadn't intended to say those words to her, but he meant them. Lately he would act less and less like his usual self when he was with Yvette.

"I knew you wouldn't leave me."

She gazed at him with large blue eyes, and for a moment he couldn't breathe.

The length of her luscious body was pressed intimately against his. All he could think about was how close his mouth was to her lips. They were soft and inviting. He could lose himself forever in those lips. It would be so easy to kiss her and the urge to do just that overwhelmed him. How would she respond to his kiss? He wasn't sure he was ready to learn the answer to that question just yet.

With great reluctance, he gently eased his arms from around her and inched his way to a sitting position, assisting her as he did so. The air chilled him immediately, as the warmth that had cocooned them all night melted away when they moved apart. They sat there in the silence, still for a few moments.

Finally Jeffrey said, "You should try to get some more sleep before your mother wakes. I shall go home and return later."

"Yes, that would probably be best," she agreed, rising slowly to her feet.

He glanced down at her stocking-clad toes, her feet so small and dainty. Had she really allowed him to take off her boots? It had been quite bold of him to remove them, let alone massage her feet as he had.

Jeffrey remained seated, but as she stepped away from the sofa, he reached for her hand.

She stopped and looked back at him. Her hand was warm and soft in his. He felt as if he should say something to her but didn't know what to say. They had spent the night together and he had not even kissed her, yet it felt as if they had been incredibly intimate with each other and he should offer some words of comfort or . . . something. But no words would come. As he gazed up at her standing before him, he saw a look on her sweet face that he'd never seen before. An expression of longing, an intense yearning that surely mirrored his own. Jeffrey forgot to breathe.

"Yvette . . ."

"Jeffrey?" she whispered, her voice full of expectation.

Yvette squeezed his hand. He squeezed back. For the briefest instant, he imagined pulling her back down to the sofa and making love to her then and there. He feared that if he kissed her, he would never let her go. He wanted her so much it terrified him. Instead, with great reluctance, he released her hand.

Yvette turned and quietly left the room and Jeffrey was alone.

14

Comfort and Joy

Lisette Hamilton Roxbury, her auburn hair swept from her face in a careless bun, looked exhausted when she entered their mother's bedroom later that same morning. Dark circles lined her blue eyes.

Yvette rushed to greet her sister at the doorway and they hugged tightly.

Lisette said in a frantic whisper, "I'm so sorry I couldn't get here sooner. How is she?"

"We're still not sure since she hasn't woken up from the laudanum yet," Yvette said in a hushed tone, thankful her sister had finally arrived. She'd been sitting by her mother's bedside for the past hour. "How's Elizabeth?"

"Better. Her fever broke last night and she's sleeping peacefully now. It was terribly frightening to see her that way. I can only stay a little while, since I must get back to her." She squeezed Yvette's hand. "Now, please tell me what happened to Mother."

"The doctor said she had some sort of attack. She

had been acting strangely all yesterday, complaining of a headache, but you know Mother." Still not quite sure if their mother could hear them or not, Yvette lowered her voice. "She is always saying she has a headache, so naturally I assumed it was nothing. But then her words were slurry and she was speaking in French and nothing made sense. Before we knew it she had collapsed on the floor in a dead faint."

"How awful!" Lisette cried, grasping Yvette's hand in hers. "Oh, poor *Maman*."

"Jeffrey carried her upstairs and we sent for the doctor and you."

Lisette's brows rose in surprise. "Jeffrey was here with you?"

"Yes, he stayed with me all night."

"Oh, thank goodness!" Lisette cried in relief. "I felt terrible thinking you were here all alone."

No, Yvette had not been alone. Dare she tell Lisette how she spent last night? Sleeping in Jeffrey Eddington's arms? Probably not. "I wasn't alone. Jeffrey was with me until the doctor left and he was wonderful."

Lisette nodded emphatically. "Yes, Jeffrey is very good in a crisis."

He certainly was! Last night he had made Yvette feel safe and cared for, taking charge of the situation and comforting her at the same time. She didn't know how she would have survived the night without him.

Talking with him had been a wonderful revelation as well. They'd spent hours alone on the sofa together, just the two of them. They had never passed that much time in each other's company alone before, simply discussing their lives and memories. How she had fallen asleep in his arms, she had no idea! But it had been nothing short of heavenly to sleep beside him. Never had she felt so warm and safe, so cherished.

The whole evening with Jeffrey had been such an unexpected turn of events, even setting aside her mother's condition. And it would be quite scandalous if she had spent the night with anyone other than Jeffrey. Then again, she couldn't imagine doing something that intimate with anyone *but* Jeffrey.

In fact, she had thought of nothing except him since she'd awoken in his arms Opening her eyes and seeing his handsome face so close to hers had filled her with a sense of wonder. He'd looked boyish and immensely appealing. She'd had an overwhelming sensation that he was going to kiss her. And most unexpectedly, she had found herself hoping that he would kiss her. She had almost longed for him to do so.

Imagine being kissed by Jeffrey Eddington!

The idea of it left her a little weak-kneed.

Something had seriously shifted and changed between them last night and she couldn't quite define what it was. Still, she could not stop herself from thinking about kissing him. It was too delicious a thought not to consider.

What would have happened if he *had* kissed her?

"What do you think about that?"

Blinking, Yvette stared at her sister. "Excuse me?"

"I asked if we should try to wake Mother." Lisette gave her a curious look. "Didn't you hear me?"

"I'm sorry," Yvette said, a bit embarrassed to be caught daydreaming. About kissing Jeffrey Eddington, no less! She struggled to explain her lapse in focus. "I'm just overtired. I was up very late last night and I did not get much sleep."

"Good morning, ladies." A familiar low voice said from behind. "May I come in?"

Yvette froze in place, her heart suddenly pounding in her chest.

Lisette grinned and cried with gladness, "Oh, Jeffrey! You're here!"

Slowly, Yvette turned around to face the doorway, where Jeffrey hugged her sister and they spoke softly of Genevieve and baby Elizabeth.

He looked impossibly handsome and refreshed, not at all as if he had spent the night before on an uncomfortable sofa. He was clean-shaven now, although earlier this morning she had seen the dark stubble on his cheek and had been tempted to touch it.

"Good morning, Yvette," he said, his blue eyes on her.

Yvette couldn't keep from smiling. "Good morning, Jeffrey."

"I trust you slept well last night?" The corners of his mouth twitched as if he held back a secret smile.

Indeed, they shared a secret, for whom could they possibly tell what had happened? Even her sisters would be shocked. Yvette had spent the night sleeping beside Jeffrey Eddington. It was scandalous and yet innocently sweet and wonderful. "Yes, I slept surprisingly well considering the circumstances."

"I am very glad to hear that." His blue eyes danced and he walked toward her. "Now, how may I be of help today?"

She fought an irresistible desire to throw herself into his arms, wanting to feel his warmth and strength. Mentally, she shook herself. It was ridiculous. What would William Weatherly think of her having thoughts like these?

Lord Shelley!

Goodness, gracious! She had completely forgotten him! She'd been so preoccupied with her mother and wild daydreams of Jeffrey that she hadn't given William a thought at all! She must remember to send him a note explaining that her mother had suddenly taken ill after his visit, which would hopefully excuse her erratic and disgraceful behavior during tea yesterday.

Lisette answered Jeffrey for her, "Well, it seems we don't know much. She still hasn't wakened. Perhaps the doctor will know more when he sees her. When will Dr. Carlisle return, Yvette?"

"He said sometime around noon."

"Well, that's good. He should be here any moment now."

Jeffrey, looking between the two sisters, said, "Then perhaps I should take my leave. It seems you have matters well in hand. I didn't know if you had arrived yet, Lisette, and I wanted to make sure Yvette wasn't here alone."

He had come to make sure she was all right. How sweet of him. Then Yvette's heart sank at the thought of Jeffrey leaving. It wasn't as if he could do anything to help their mother, but just his being there made her feel infinitely better.

"Oh, but I shan't be staying very long, Jeffrey," Lisette explained. "I must return to my daughter. She's still not well. It will be a great comfort to me to know that you're here with Yvette and Mother. If you can stay . . ."

Jeffrey gazed at Yvette. She smiled hesitantly at him. "Will you stay with me?"

He grinned back at her. "Of course."

Yvette ignored the unexpected fluttering of her heart at his response.

15

The First Frost

"I shall let Miss Hamilton know you are here, but I am not sure if she is receiving visitors today," the Devon House butler told him.

"I believe she will wish to see me," William Weatherly, Lord Shelley, answered with confidence as he was led to the same drawing room he'd been in the day before.

He had read Yvette's brief note, which had been delivered by one of the Devon House footmen, with great interest and not a little relief. So Genevieve Hamilton had been taken ill yesterday. Well, that explained a good deal. What a dreadful scene that had been. From the start Mrs. Hamilton had behaved most oddly; then, little by little, she had degenerated into incomprehensible speech in both English and French. It had been quite disturbing. Along with his own discomfort, Yvette's horrified embarrassment had been almost palpable.

Still, the situation had alarmed William. He had been so close to making a final decision about Yvette, but her mother's behavior had given him good reason to be cautious. Was it a mental deficiency? Was it hereditary? He wondered how ill the woman was, since Yvette had given no other details in her note. That was when he decided to pay her a visit.

Although he had already promised to call on Jane Fairmont that afternoon, he felt he needed to see Yvette Hamilton as his first priority.

He had worried about Yvette, for she'd seemed most distressed when he left the day before. How he had longed to take her in his arms and kiss her! Ever since he'd kissed her that day in the gardens at Lansdowne Manor, he had thought of little else but his desire to kiss her again.

He yearned for her desperately.

After her visit to Lansdowne, his mother had given her approval of Yvette and that had pleased William greatly. He had wanted his mother to like Yvette Hamilton. And he wanted to like her family too. But he still needed to meet her sisters and their husbands before he could propose to her. It surprised him how much he wanted to like and approve of them. He hoped fervently they were suitable. He was a bit worried about the sister who had married the American. He'd heard some stories regarding that affair.

If all went well when he met her sisters, William would ask her brother-in-law, Lucien Sinclair, for her hand in marriage before Christmas. He had come to his final decision gradually. He feared Miss Fairmont would be quite disappointed in the end, but he could not ignore that his true desire was for Yvette.

"William!"

He rose to his feet when Yvette, looking quite charmingly disheveled, hurried into the room. She was wearing a plain navy dress with a smock-like apron over it. Her long golden-blond curls, usually perfectly and most-fashionably coiffed, were rather askew, hanging loose down her back.

He'd never seen her in such an informal state and he found her even more attractive than the night she'd worn that damned sapphire gown. Her surprised delight at his presence was written all over her pretty face, her luscious mouth opened slightly in undisguised astonishment.

Oh, how he wished to kiss those full lips of hers!

"I wasn't expecting you," she murmured nervously, her blue eyes wide. "Please forgive my appearance. I've been attending to my mother."

"It is I who beg your forgiveness, Yvette. I didn't mean to intrude. It's just that after I received your note, naturally I became very worried about you. And your mother. I came to inquire after her health and I apologize if I am interfering. But I thought seeing you would be the best way to allay my fears." Smiling, he stepped toward her and took both of her small hands in his. "And indeed it has."

"Oh, William. How sweet of you!"

"Now please tell me, how is your mother faring?"

Her face clouded over with worry. "Well, it seems she had some sort of apoplectic attack. She's awake now, but she's having difficulty speaking and moving her right arm. The doctor left a little while ago, but he said she was fortunate that her attack was a mild one. He suggested we keep her spirits up and try to encourage her to move and speak as much as possible." She grimaced slightly. "That will not be an easy task."

"Oh, my poor, sweet Yvette." He gave her hands a gentle squeeze. "This has had to be a frightening and trying experience for you."

She nodded in agreement, the weariness in her expression quite obvious. "Yes, it has. More than I can say. But at least my mother is alive. All last night I feared we would lose her, but Dr. Carlisle has since assured me that she will recover."

"Thank heavens she will be well again. I understand how difficult it is to see your parents suffer. My father still has not recovered from his illness last year."

"Oh, I had quite forgotten about your father, William." She flushed prettily. "I'm so sorry."

"There is no reason for you to be sorry, my sweet Yvette."

"Good afternoon, Shelley."

Surprised, William looked up to see Lord Jeffrey Eddington standing in the drawing room. What on earth was the man doing at Devon House again? William had been a bit put out by his appearance yesterday afternoon, but had been so rattled by Mrs. Hamilton's odd behavior, he'd quite forgotten about Lord Eddington. Yvette often explained that Jeffrey was a close family friend, like a brother. However, he seemed to hover around Yvette like a guard dog. It was most annoying.

Looking at him now, William couldn't help but wonder what the man was really up to. With his shirtsleeves rolled up and his hair tousled, Jeffrey Eddington appeared entirely too comfortable at Devon House. Just how long had he been there?

Somehow it seemed altogether improper, bordering on scandalous, that this handsome rake, a bastard no less, with a roguish reputation should be on such familiar terms with his future bride.

Frowning, William released Yvette's hands from his own. "Eddington. This is a surprise."

The man gave him a smug look. "It's not a surprise at all to see you here, Shelley."

"Lord Shelley was worried about Mother and me and came by to see if he could be of assistance in any way." Yvette took a step away from him, looking quite flustered. "Wasn't that thoughtful of him?"

"It is kind of you," Eddington said, displeasure clearly written on his face. "But we have the situation in hand now." Turning to Yvette, his expression changed entirely. "Fanny asked me to tell you that she thinks we're overtiring your mother and that we should let her rest for the evening. She has tossed us out!"

Yvette smiled at him in amusement. "Yes, Fanny can be quite the little despot. But I suppose she's right. Mother had stopped laughing at your antics already, Jeffrey."

"Dr. Carlisle had said to keep her spirits up, so that's merely what I was doing." Jeffrey grinned mischievously. "It was good for her to laugh. Besides it was a funny story. Even Fanny was laughing."

"I grant you, your story made Mother laugh, but that was because it was entirely inappropriate!" Yvette giggled charmingly.

William listened to their easy conversation and suddenly felt the odd man out. The strong familiarity between the two of them was revealing. Lord Eddington was on more intimate terms with the family than he'd realized, if he'd spent the day in the sickroom with Yvette's mother, as it appeared he had. Was he here with Yvette alone in the house? Was one of her sisters here with them?

This did not sit well with William in the least. He had not been overly fond of Eddington when he'd first met him, but hadn't thought him a bad sort of fellow. He had dismissed him and thought him rather harmless and good-natured. Now, however, William felt Eddington was intruding on his territory. Yvette Hamilton belonged to him now, not Eddington. He had kissed her quite passionately! He would be the one marrying into this family, *not* Eddington.

A strong sense of enmity surged from deep within him. When Yvette became his wife, this man would certainly not be allowed such familiarities with her and her association with this so-called "brother" would be severely curtailed.

Watching the interplay between Yvette and Jeffrey, William got the distinct impression that Jeffrey harbored more than brotherly affection for Yvette. Without thinking, William stepped closer to her. Yvette glanced up at him and smiled enchantingly, and that mollified him somewhat.

"Oh, William, forgive us," Yvette apologized. "Jeffrey has been so sweet to spend time with Mother today. She just adores him. And he was such a great help to me after Lisette had to return home to care for her baby daughter, who is very ill."

So, Yvette had been alone with him! William watched as Eddington made himself comfortable in one of the armchairs, propping his feet upon a footstool and folding his arms behind his head. It appeared the man was not planning on leaving Devon House anytime soon either.

William rested his stare on Eddington's smug expression and fought the urge to toss the man out of the house. He managed to mutter, "Yes, I've gathered that Lord Eddington has been quite indispensable."

"Would you care for some tea, William?" Yvette asked. "Or something to eat? It just occurred to me that I haven't eaten all day."

She looked so lovely standing there, gazing up at him with her pretty blue eyes. William wished they were alone so he could have a chance to kiss her again. As much as he wanted to be with Yvette, he wasn't about to spend another minute in this man's insufferable company.

With a disapproving glance at Eddington, William frowned. "I'm sorry, Yvette, but I must take my leave as I have another appointment. I only wanted to reassure myself that all was well with you and your mother."

"I understand, William, and it was very kind and thoughtful of you to stop by and see me. Thank you."

Her sweet smile turned his heart upside down. William longed to pull her into his arms and dishevel her appearance even more. Instead he made his farewells and stepped out into the cool November air, feeling quite unsettled by the jealous feelings that had been aroused in him by Lord Jeffrey Eddington.

16

Making Spirits Bright

Jeffrey watched Yvette's expression carefully as Lord Shelley left. Did he see relief flicker briefly in her eyes? She flopped into the armchair across from him and grinned happily. In that simple navy dress, with her golden hair falling softly around her face, Yvette looked more appealing to him than ever. The naturalness of her beauty and the graceful ease with which she stretched her arms over her head caused his heart to somersault in his chest.

"He came to see me!" she squealed with childish delight.

Catching her gleeful enthusiasm, Jeffrey couldn't help but smile back at her. "Why wouldn't he come to see you, my dear girl?" The man would have to be made of stone not to be attracted to the likes of Yvette Hamilton. Although there were times he wished the old fellow *were* made of stone.

"Yes, but he came after Mother's humiliating behavior."

"That wasn't your fault, Yvette. He can't possibly hold that against you."

"Oh, but you don't know how dreadful yesterday was.

I was afraid William would wish to never see me again." Her expression grew serious. "You have no idea how bad things were with Mother before you got here, Jeffrey. She insulted him! I thought I would die of mortification."

Feeling relaxed, he crossed his feet on a footstool, curious to know more about what happened yesterday. "What could your mother have said that was so awful?"

"She called him a pompous ass, among other disparaging remarks. It was in French, of course, but we both knew what she was saying, although William was too polite to acknowledge her words and pretended she didn't say them."

Jeffrey grinned broadly, settling back in the comfortable chair once again. He'd always known he liked Mrs. Hamilton, in spite of her dramatics. He wished he'd been there to see the expression on the face of the "pompous ass" when Yvette's mother said such a shocking thing. He tried not to laugh. "Well, old Shelley seems to have forgiven and forgotten. Your mother was not well and he understands that now."

"I certainly hope so," she said with a little sigh.

"You're on a first-name basis with him now?" The use of their given names had not escaped his attention. Neither had the sight of Shelley holding Yvette's hands when Jeffrey entered the room. He'd had to fight the urge to deck the man for touching her.

"Yes!" Yvette looked thrilled. "Ever since my visit with his mother. It's quite encouraging, don't you agree? I believe he may propose to me as soon as Lucien and Colette return."

"Quite encouraging, yes."

There was a comfortable silence between them. After a worrisome night and an exhausting day, they were both too lethargic to move. The two of them just sat there, across from each other, as the late afternoon turned to twilight. A fire burned low in the grate to ward off the chill.

Jeffrey spoke up again. "However, I did notice that you didn't mention 'William's' name once last night."

Yvette's delicate brows drew together in confusion. "Didn't I?"

"No. Not once. With all we talked about marriage and children, you never made mention of Lord Shelley."

"Oh." She gave him an odd look. "I suppose I was distracted with all that happened with my mother."

"I see." He didn't believe that was the reason. No, not in the least.

Another long silence followed. Neither of them made a move to leave the room. Jeffrey was certain he knew the answer, but he couldn't stop himself from asking the question anyway. "Have you fallen in love with him yet?"

After a brief hesitation, she admitted in a small voice, "No, but I've given it some thought and I suspect it will come with time and marriage."

Irrationally happy with her answer, he smiled in spite of himself. He'd known she wasn't in love with the man. No, Yvette definitely wasn't in love with Lord Shelley.

With a look of hope, Yvette added, "But from the way he kissed me, I believe he may be falling in love with me."

Jeffrey's heart skipped a beat. He could barely make his mouth form the words. "He kissed you?" He hadn't thought old Shelley had it in him to make a move like that so soon.

"Yes, of course, when I was at Lansdowne Manor," Yvette stated matter-of-factly, as if it were an everyday occurrence. "I don't see why you should be so surprised, Jeffrey. I am almost twenty-one."

"I'm not surprised." But he was. And he did not like the idea of his Yvette being kissed by this future duke. "I'm sure that you are well aware that you are quite kissable, Yvette."

She smiled, genuinely touched by his words. "I am?"

"Yes." And never more so than at that moment. With that look of delight on her face, he wished he could kiss her himself.

"Well, I suppose that's very good information for a woman to have."

He laughed at her logic. "I suppose it would be."

"Oh, it helps to know that gentlemen find me desirable. I've not kissed that many men, and never one quite like William, but I was never sure if I were doing it properly."

If he'd had a drink he would have choked on it. "And just how many men have you kissed, Yvette?"

Her cheeks suffused with color. "I'm not sure I should talk to you about such things, Jeffrey."

"Why not? We've been talking about everything else."

Her brow arched in question. "Well, in that case, how many women have you kissed?"

He would have laughed if he hadn't wanted her to answer his question so desperately. Just who had Yvette been kissing and when? And why did it bother him so much to think of her kissing anyone but him? It was the oddest conversation to be having in the Devon House drawing room, her mother ill upstairs, and her almost fiancé having just left them alone. Things seemed to have changed so suddenly between them since last night. But Yvette deserved an answer from him. And if he expected an answer from her, it was only fair to reciprocate. Honestly.

"Over the years, I've kissed more women than I could possibly count."

Her blue eyes widened in astonishment. "Oh my."

He irrationally wished he could have given her a different

answer. One that wouldn't have shocked her. "And you?" he prompted.

"Not nearly as many as you. There have been three, if I count Lord Shelley."

He imagined they were brief, stolen kisses by the young bucks in town, who were half mad with wanting her. They couldn't have been very memorable. But a mature man like Lord Shelley . . . he would be quite experienced and know how to kiss a woman like Yvette. At least as experienced as Jeffrey was. That thought made his stomach roil. "Did you like kissing Lord Shelley?"

"Yes." She nodded her head slowly, as if giving the matter some consideration. "It was nice."

"Oh, I see." Jeffrey struggled to contain his laughter. *Nice*. Lord Shelley's kisses were merely *nice*. Filled with relief, he now knew with 100 percent certainty that Yvette was not in love with Lord Shelley nor had she been properly kissed by him. Jeffrey also thought smugly that if *he* had been the one to kiss Yvette, she certainly wouldn't describe his kisses as *nice*. Oh, no. He would kiss her so thoroughly she wouldn't be able to—

"Have you ever kissed any of my sisters?"

Startled out of his thoughts of kissing Yvette, Jeffrey sat bolt upright in his chair, his feet planted on the floor. "What did you say?"

"While we were on the subject of the thousands of women you've kissed, I just wondered if any of them were my sisters."

"I never said I kissed thousands."

"Hundreds then."

"Yes, that's more accurate." He nodded. "I don't think I've hit the five-hundred mark yet." He winked at her.

She rolled her eyes heavenward. "Well?"

"Well what?"

"You haven't answered my question and I've answered yours."

He was evading her question. He sighed reluctantly, grateful for the darkening room as the sun set outside and returned to his comfortable reclining position on the chair, propping his feet up once again. "Yes. I kissed Colette many years ago."

"Colette?" Yvette couldn't contain her surprise at his revelation. "You kissed Colette? She's the last one I would have guessed."

He nodded, not willing to divulge more. His one kiss with Colette Hamilton had been before she'd married his best friend and it had been a mistake.

"Oh," Yvette said, realization suddenly dawning. "Is that why Lucien hit you?"

Again he nodded at her. "Partly, yes."

"I never knew that." She looked deep in thought, her expression pensive and almost amused. "We always suspected there was a romance between you and Juliette."

Jeffrey laughed at that. "Good God, no! I love your sister dearly, but Juliette and I have never been anything other than the best of friends."

"And you haven't kissed Lisette or Paulette either then?"

"No." He laughed ruefully. "I hate to disappoint you, Yvette, but I don't go around kissing every woman I happen to know. You Hamilton sisters are exceedingly beautiful, but alas, your sisters were already in love with someone else and not me."

"Have you ever been in love, Jeffrey?"

"No."

She paused in thought. "So you have no more experience in the area of love than I do."

"I suppose that's true." Surprisingly, he didn't mind admitting that to her.

Jeffrey had never been in love with a woman. In lust, yes, and there were one or two occasions when he thought he might be in love. But as for true love and wishing to marry and spend your life with one woman . . . no, that he had not yet experienced. Over the years he'd watched his friends declare themselves in love and marry, one by one. First Lucien, then Harrison and Quinton. They all seemed happy enough. Hell, they seemed ridiculously happy with their wives and then their children.

Once in a while he wished he'd had someone to love. Someone who belonged just to him, someone who could love him in return. So far, that hadn't happened. Certainly not with Jennie Webb. Or Olivia Trahern. Or any of the other beauties he'd bedded over the years. And now he looked at Yvette Hamilton sitting in the chair across from him and remembered the feel of her sleeping in his arms last night. A knot tightened in his stomach at the memory. There had been something very right about holding her so close to his heart.

A silence grew between them as the shadows began to lengthen across the room. Jeffrey found it quite peaceful sitting there with Yvette, talking quietly in the dimness.

"Do you ever wish to be in love, Jeffrey?"

"Doesn't everyone?" he answered, feeling a strange flutter in his heart.

"I suppose so."

"You don't think you should be in love with William Weatherly before he proposes?"

"I shall be in love with him at some point, I would imagine."

"I don't believe you can plan something like that, Yvette."

"Why not?" she asked. "People have arranged marriages all the time and grow to love each other afterward."

"Yes," he admitted, "but those are the exception and not the rule. Arranged marriages are basically cold and distant contracts and they don't always end happily. In fact, they can end quite disastrously and my father can attest to that. You used to be the most romantic little girl, Yvette. I'm surprised to hear you say these things."

Yvette remained silent.

Jeffrey added, "I would rather experience the thrill of falling head over heels in love before asking a woman to marry me."

"I know my sisters had that experience," she said, a touch of wistfulness in her voice.

"Don't you wish to feel that way about the man you marry? Don't you believe you deserve to be in love, Yvette?"

"Yes. I believe it would be wonderful."

They grew quiet, each in their own thoughts. Again, he wanted to ask why she would marry Lord Shelley when she was not in love with him, but he already knew the answer to that. Yvette wanted to be a duchess more than she wanted to be in love with her husband.

"Jeffrey," she interrupted his thoughts, changing the subject completely. "May I ask you a question?"

"Of course."

"What is it that you do?"

His brows furrowed. "I'm not sure I understand what you're asking, Yvette."

"I mean, what is it that you do when you're away? Traveling? When you went to France, you said it was partly business." She sat up and looked at him curiously. "What business do you do?"

He had not been expecting that question from her at all, and he was uncertain how much of the truth to tell her. "Well, I have various business ventures that need my attention, my shipping enterprise, for one."

"Yes, but I thought I overheard you and Lucien talking once about the government and I was wondering if you did something in that capacity."

"Are you asking if I do work for the government?"

She nodded. "Yes. Do you?"

"From time to time," he admitted reluctantly. "When they need me."

Her face lit up with wonder. "Is it secretive?"

She looked so excited he wanted to kiss her. "Yes. Very. And I don't wish for anyone else to know about it."

"Your secret is safe with me." She paused. "Is it dangerous?"

"Sometimes."

"Are you careful?"

"Very." He winked at her.

"Excuse me, Miss Yvette?" Granger entered the room, which had grown dark since the sun had set in the late autumn sky. He lit one of the gas lamps on the wall, casting the room in a yellow glow.

"Yes, Granger?" she asked.

"Will you and Lord Eddington be having supper in the dining room this evening?" he asked solicitously. "Or shall I bring something up to the small sitting room again?"

"Are you staying for supper, Jeffrey?" Yvette asked him softly from the depths of her chair. "Please don't feel obligated to stay because of me. You were here last night and all day today. I'm sure you must have other engagements and things to attend to rather than staying here with me."

"I can't think of anywhere else I'd rather be than here, dining with you, Yvette."

Jeffrey did have any number of obligations that needed

his attention, but her smile of pure delight was his reward for ignoring them.

"We shall dine in the sitting room upstairs again, Granger," she said. "To be near my mother."

Jeffrey couldn't have been happier. He was going to spend an evening alone with Yvette. Again.

17

Westward Leading

November 1878
Fleming Farm
Rumson, New Jersey

Colette Hamilton Sinclair read Yvette's most recent letter with growing alarm, while trying to ignore her younger son's impatient tugging on her skirt.

"Mama! Come with me! Please . . ."

"I will, Simon, I promise. Please be patient for just a moment, darling," she murmured absently, staring at the words scrawled across the page in Yvette's careless script. Mother had suddenly taken ill and Yvette seemed more than a bit frantic. Her youngest sister wasn't known for her correspondence so the fact that she'd written such a detailed and lengthy letter caused Colette's heart rate to increase.

"But Mama," Simon wailed again with mounting urgency. "Phillip and Sara are hiding and I can't find them anywhere. Please help me."

"Oh, all right, Simon," Colette said with a sigh. His green eyes were too much like his father's to be ignored.

Folding the letter and tucking it into the pocket of her gown, Colette took her five-year-old's little hand in hers. The children had been cooped up inside the house all day due to the rainy weather and were apparently wearing on each other. "I've already told them once to stop hiding from you, Simon. Come now, let's go find them again, shall we?"

Once she had rounded up the errant and giggling Phillip and Sara from behind the long, velvet drapes in Juliette's bedroom, Colette brought the three children to the nursery, under strict instructions not to hide from each other again.

"Now play nice," she admonished, trying to appear stern and not laugh. Especially at her pretty dark-haired niece, whose impudent face was so much like Juliette's that it brought back memories of her own childhood. She then left the children to quietly assemble a wooden puzzle before bed, with their nanny looking after them.

Colette then found her husband with her sister Juliette and her brother-in-law Harrison in the main drawing room of their beautiful New Jersey estate. The three of them sat talking and drinking coffee before a cozy fire as the cold rain continued to come down outside.

"I think we should sail back to London right away," Colette announced to them as soon as she entered the room. "Maybe before the end of the week."

Lucien, taking in his wife's worried expression, set down his cup and asked, "What on earth for, sweetheart?"

"This letter from Yvette that came today," Colette explained walking toward them. "It seems Mother is very ill."

Juliette, her blue eyes flashing, laughed dismissively and waved her hand. "Oh Colette, when has our mother ever *not* been ill?"

Colette shook her head. "No, this is quite serious and

different from anything that has happened in the past. She had some sort of apoplectic attack and fell to the floor. This is real and not imaginary. Yvette seems terribly distraught and said she feared that Mother might die . . . that first night." Colette blinked back tears. "The doctor has been there and he's afraid that Mother might have lost the ability to speak or to move the right side of her body."

The room grew silent and the sardonic amusement completely vanished from Juliette's expression. "Truly?"

"That's what Yvette has written." Colette held the letter in her hand. "So I think we need to go home as soon as we can."

She moved to sit on the sofa beside her husband. He took her other hand in his and Colette instantly felt calmer. Just his presence had that effect on her, even after eight years together. His green eyes filled with concern as he lifted her hand to his lips and kissed it. Oh, how she loved this handsome man!

"It sounds very similar to what happened to my father," Lucien said. "He suffered an apoplectic attack that left him paralyzed and his speech impaired. And I agree with Colette that we should leave right away." He looked to his brother-in-law. "Is that possible, Harrison?"

"Of course it is. I can have the *Sea Minx* ready within a day. If we pack tonight, we can leave for New York tomorrow afternoon and sail the day after." Tall and blond, with a rugged handsomeness that came from years of sailing his beautiful clipper ship, Captain Harrison Fleming was a strong and charismatic man.

Although relieved to be returning to London a little earlier than planned, Colette felt a bit sad to be ending their holiday. It was their first visit to America, and they had enjoyed their time in Juliette's home. But their mother and sister needed them now.

"That's settled then?" Juliette asked. "We are leaving right away?"

"Yes. Mother's illness sounds quite serious and I'm very worried," Colette said. "And poor Yvette. She also wrote that Lisette has been occupied tending to baby Elizabeth, who's been quite ill as well, leaving Yvette to care for Mother on her own."

"I assume she let Paulette know. Won't she and Declan come back from Ireland sooner now?" Juliette asked hopefully. "They should be there before we arrive, certainly."

"I suppose so," Colette said with a weary sigh. "Yvette said she'd written to Paulette as well, and I'm positive Paulette would rush back to London with Declan and the children as soon as she learned of Mother's condition. Still, I feel terrible that Yvette is there alone. We should have insisted that she come with us."

Shaking his head, Lucien pointed out, "No, because then all of this would be on poor Lisette's shoulders alone and she's just had a baby. It's good that Yvette has been there with your mother. I'm confident that she can handle things well enough."

"Yes," Juliette agreed. "She's not a child anymore, Colette. I'm sure she's managing better than you give her credit for."

Colette glanced around the room. "She said Jeffrey's been there with her and been very helpful."

Juliette smiled. "Jeffrey is helping with Mother? How wonderful."

Colette nodded. "Yvette says that Jeffrey has been a great comfort to her. She speaks very highly of him, in fact."

"Yvette and Jeffrey. Now there's a match made in heaven."

Three pairs of eyes stared at Harrison Fleming.

"What did you just say?" Juliette asked, looking at her husband in disbelief.

Harrison looked bewildered by their surprised expressions. "Why are you all staring at me like that? It's not that far-fetched of an idea, is it? Think about it for a moment. The two of them would be perfect for each other."

"Yvette and Jeffrey?" Juliette asked in confusion, her brows drawn together.

"Yes. Yvette and Jeffrey," Harrison defended his point with a smile at his wife.

"I'm sorry to dash your hopes, Harrison," Lucien said, "but I have it on the highest authority that Yvette has her sights set on someone else."

"How do you know something like that?" Colette asked, her curiosity piqued. Lucien hadn't mentioned anything about her sister before this. How would he know whom Yvette was interested in romantically?

"Jeffrey wrote to me," Lucien explained. "He's been keeping an eye on our little Yvette since we've been away."

"Do you mean to tell me, Lucien Sinclair, that you've had Jeffrey spying on the comings and goings of my little sister and report back to you all this time?" Juliette demanded to know, crossing her arms over her chest. Clearly, she was irritated.

"Yes, as a matter of fact," Lucien said with his brows furrowed, glaring back at Juliette. "Did you honestly think I was going to leave Yvette unattended and unmarried in London and with no one but your mother looking after her?"

Juliette laughed lightly and shook her head. "I was only teasing you. Oh, I can still ruffle your feathers so easily, Lucien. I wouldn't have expected any less of you. I'm very glad you had Jeffrey watching out for Yvette, although I can't imagine it has been easy on him."

Lucien grinned at her wryly. "I'm so relieved to have met with your approval, Mrs. Fleming."

"That's enough needling, you two," Colette said, swatting her husband playfully. "Lucien, tell us what you know about Yvette. I made her promise to write to me, but this is only the second letter I've had from her since I arrived and I had no idea she'd set her sights on someone. I can't believe you've kept this from me, Lucien."

He gave a helpless shrug. "I was going to let you know eventually."

"Oh, tell us already," Juliette prompted him with mounting impatience.

"Well, I've been informed that Yvette might be very close to getting a proposal from none other than the future Duke of Lansdowne." Lucien looked around for the reaction to his impressive news.

"Of course she is," Juliette said, rolling her eyes. "I'm not the least bit surprised. Our Yvette wouldn't settle for anything less than a duke."

"Yvette would make a perfect duchess," Harrison pointed out.

"Do we know him?" Colette asked, trying to put a face with the name. "I can't recall who he is."

"I believe he's been away traveling and has only just returned to London. I'm sure I've met him once or twice. From what I recall he's not a bad sort and is apparently quite taken with Yvette," Lucien said. "He's much older than she is. Jeffrey mentioned that too."

Unable to shake a sudden uneasiness, Colette frowned at the thought of her sweet little sister with some old duke. "Oh, I don't know. I think I liked the idea of Yvette and Jeffrey together better."

The three of them turned to stare at her again.

"What?" Colette asked. "Harrison's right. I think they'd

be perfect together and then we could keep Jeffrey in the family."

"Jeffrey is already a part of our family," Lucien pointed out.

"See? Colette agrees with me," Harrison chided his wife.

"Well, Lucien and I think it's a terrible idea. Don't we, Lucien?" Juliette looked to her brother-in-law for support.

"It's rare that you and I are in agreement on anything, Juliette"—Lucien flashed her a conspiratorial grin—"but I happen to agree wholeheartedly with you on this point."

"Why would it be so terrible?" Harrison asked, his gray eyes questioning.

"I don't even want to go into it," Lucien said, dismissing the subject and rising to his feet. "I do think, however, that if we plan on leaving tomorrow morning, we should start getting ready as soon as possible."

"He's right," Harrison agreed as he stood also. "We have a lot to do if we're going to set sail in a day or two. Let's go, girls."

As they walked from the room, Juliette pulled Colette aside. "You don't truly believe that Yvette and Jeffrey together is a good idea, do you?"

"Yes, I do actually. But there's no reason for you to be worried. According to Lucien and Jeffrey, Yvette's practically engaged to the Duke of Lansdowne."

"Thank goodness for that!" Juliette exclaimed in relief.

Still Colette couldn't help but think about her sister and Jeffrey together. She smiled at the thought.

18

And Winter Came

December 1878
Lansdowne Manor

Yvette Hamilton squealed with delight as she flew across the frozen lake, the cold wind stinging her cheeks. Not very steady on her new pair of ice skates, she clasped Lord Calvert's gloved hand in hers as he guided her along. She wished fervently that it was Lord Shelley holding her hand, but William had declined to skate and stood in the stone gazebo, watching the fun on the lake at Lansdowne Manor from afar.

"Oh, please don't go so fast!" Yvette cried out.

"If we don't go fast, we'll both fall down," Lord Calvert said with a jovial laugh.

A winter or two had passed since Yvette had skated last and she was none too confident on the ice, but she was desperately trying to make a good impression on Lord Shelley. She even wore her new red coat trimmed with white fur and matching white fur hat that she thought was so stylish. He was certainly watching her and she did not wish to fall on her bottom in front of him.

It was the first time Yvette had left Devon House since her mother had fallen ill. She had been loath to leave her mother for the past two weeks, but the invitation from William Weatherly to join him and some friends at a skating party at Lansdowne Manor had been impossible to resist. It had been freezing cold for days and a recent light dusting of snow covered the ground, making conditions perfect for skating. So with Fanny and Lisette by her mother's side for the day, Yvette had been free to ride off with her friend Lady Katherine Spencer to Lansdowne Manor, determined to make up for lost time with William.

When she'd arrived, he had seemed quite happy to see her again. He had clasped her hand in his and said how pretty she appeared and how much he had been looking forward to seeing her again. William had encouraged her to skate with the others even though he had declined, so she had ventured to the ice without him.

"Shall we take a break?" Lord Calvert asked.

"Yes, please," Yvette answered, eager to return to William's side. There was so much romantic possibility in a day like today. She didn't wish to squander a minute of it. Perhaps he would propose this afternoon?

She allowed Lord Calvert to guide her back toward the shore. Laughing, Yvette stumbled as she reached the bank, but James Calvert steadied her with his arm. Grinning in triumph, she had succeeded in staying on her feet and had not fallen once. However her smile disappeared completely when she looked up and saw none other than Jane Fairmont sitting in the gazebo with Lord Shelley.

He had invited her as well! Crushed with disappointment, Yvette was so stunned, she couldn't move for a moment. She had hoped she and William would find an opportunity to be alone together and he might kiss her again. Seeing Jane Fairmont there had not crossed her mind.

"Are you all right, Miss Hamilton?" Lord Calvert asked in concern.

"Yes, thank you." But Yvette still did not move.

She had been certain that she had gained in favor with William, so why on earth would he include Jane Fairmont on this outing? Had that visit with her mother been so dreadful that she lost preference with him? Did he not understand that her mother had been stricken with illness that day? Had he not forgiven the episode? Did he hold it against her?

True, Yvette had not been very social as of late, as busy as she was caring for her mother. She assumed William understood her duty lay with her mother, but perhaps he was put out by her lack of attention to him?

She sighed and let Lord Calvert, who was a terribly kind and charming gentleman, escort her to the small stone bench, where she removed her skates.

"Do you mind if I go back out on the ice?" he asked her.

"Not at all." Yvette smiled. "Thank you for helping me. I'm sorry I slowed you down."

"It was my pleasure, as always." He tipped his cap to her and returned to the lake.

She watched Lord Calvert skate expertly across the ice and saw that her friend Katherine was skating with her fiancé. With a heavy heart, Yvette then trudged through the snow toward the gazebo, not quite ready to face William and her rival.

Most of the guests were on the ice and some had gathered along the banks of the lake to watch. But in the large gazebo, which had been equipped with a fire to keep them warm and a table with hot tea and refreshments, there were only two people. William had been sitting on one of the cushioned benches with Jane Fairmont. He stood when he saw her walking toward them.

"Yvette, please come join us! You skate quite well! I am impressed with your skill. Did you enjoy yourself?" he asked.

"Oh, yes, William, it was wonderful." Yvette smiled at him and then turned to the woman who still sat on the bench. "Good afternoon, Miss Fairmont."

Jane was dressed just as fashionably as Yvette in a brown coat with black fur trim. Her brunette hair was hidden under her fur hat. She smiled at Yvette, her green eyes glittering. "Good afternoon, Miss Hamilton. It's such a surprise to see you here."

Jane was surprised to see *her*? Yvette fumed silently and flashed a glance of annoyance in William's direction.

"Don't you wish to skate, Miss Fairmont?" Yvette asked, for want of something better to say. Feeling terribly awkward, she wished she knew where she stood with William and what Jane's presence here today meant.

"Oh, no," Jane said with a gentle shake of her head and a pretty pout. "I am afraid I never learned how to skate. Besides, I couldn't leave William sitting here all alone with no one for company." She smiled coyly up at Lord Shelley.

So William and Jane were on a first name basis as well, were they? A terrible knot formed in Yvette's stomach at the thought. How had she been such a fool as to think she had gained in his favor? He had misled her! She did not know what to think of William now. Although a twinge of anger was beginning to bloom in her chest.

How dared William hint that he was going to propose

to her and then invite Jane Fairmont to Lansdowne Manor again!

"You ought to learn how to skate someday, Miss Fairmont. It's great fun out on the ice," Yvette said to her with a bright, forced smile.

Jane turned up her nose in derision. "I don't think it's for me. Skating is only for athletic girls."

Bristling at her comment, Yvette opened her mouth to reply, but William spoke before she had a chance.

"Yvette," William began, "you must be cold. Have some hot tea and there are blankets too. Come sit by the fire and warm yourself." He quickly guided her to a seat beside Jane. After wrapping a thick blanket around her shoulders, he brought her a piping cup of tea.

Yvette's anger simmered. She and William hadn't seen each other in weeks and she'd thought for certain that he would be thrilled to see her and endeavor to spend a moment or two alone with her this afternoon. Jane Fairmont's presence had put a damper on those hopes.

Now she was part of this tense little trio in the gazebo, huddling under her blanket and listening to the shouts of delight and carefree laughter from the others down on the lake. With a little shiver, she sipped her tea. It seemed much colder out now than it had been when she was skating.

In vain, she wished Lord Calvert, or her friend Kate, or anyone for that matter, would return from the lake and break up the awkward silence between the three of them.

More than anything, she wished Jeffrey Eddington were there at Lansdowne Manor with her. His breezy charm and engaging manner would lighten the mood and he would surely say something witty or amusing to make them all smile. She knew he would have said something remarkably clever to put Jane Fairmont in her place.

Darling Jeffrey.

They had spent a great deal of time together during the past few weeks. Since her mother had taken ill, Jeffrey had come to Devon House every single day, helping in any way he could. Sometimes he would read to or talk with Genevieve, trying to make her laugh and usually succeeding.

He'd lifted Genevieve's spirits and engaged her in conversation daily, and indeed her speech and movements had improved considerably. Jeffrey had patiently walked Genevieve along the hallways for exercise, while she leaned on him for support. The doctor had been most impressed with her recovery, stating that Yvette, Lisette, Jeffrey, and Fanny had done remarkable work in getting Genevieve to speak and move by talking to her and encouraging her to exercise her right arm and leg. Her mother could already stand on her own, although she truly had to rely on her gilt cane now. It was no longer merely ornamental. Her speech had steadily improved and for the most part, she could be understood when she spoke.

Yvette felt comforted just by Jeffrey's presence. She had come to rely on him and looked forward to his visits each day and their private dinners together each night.

The fact that her mother was recovering so well was the only reason she had agreed to come to Lansdowne Manor today. And now that she was here, Yvette found herself longing to be back at home with Jeffrey.

The thought startled her.

Longing to be at home with Jeffrey?

What a surprising thing to want. But she supposed it was true. After spending so much time together she missed his company. His handsome smile. His comforting presence.

Something had changed between them since the night she had slept in his arms. They talked more, confided in each other more. And there was something else. Something she couldn't quite define. A shift, a change, a spark. There was an excitement within her whenever Jeffrey was near. She found herself anticipating his visits and when he did arrive at Devon House, she enjoyed their time alone together more than anything else. Especially since they had taken to having supper together each night.

She didn't think it was her imagination that things had changed between them. He was behaving differently toward her. He no longer treated her as a little girl, but more as an equal. She noted he found excuses to be near her, to touch her arm or her hand, and she didn't mind in the least. She half expected Jeffrey to kiss her. She was both dreading and wishing for that moment to happen. For kissing Jeffrey was an intriguing prospect and she found herself thinking about it more often than was decent.

What would it be like to have a man such as Jeffrey kiss her? He had kissed so many women he must be quite skilled at it. Her heart started racing at the thought of his lips on hers.

Heavens! She should not be thinking about kissing Jeffrey Eddington! Her attention and thoughts should be completely on Lord Shelley.

William. Who sat here with his two prospective brides! Surely he should have made up his mind by now! Yvette almost wanted to slap him.

"Is it too cold?" he asked both ladies. "Should I escort you back to the house where you can get properly warmed?"

"Whatever you think best, William," Jane Fairmont said with a dainty toss of her head. "If you are staying out here, I shall be happy to remain here with you."

Yvette knew the girl had to be feeling quite chilled and was only making a point to stay because William was. Yvette tried to work the situation to her advantage. She needed to get William alone for a little bit and if Jane was staying put, then Yvette would leave.

"Are you staying out here, William?" Yvette asked softly, using his first name to show Jane that she could.

He nodded. "Yes, as host I feel I should be out here with my guests."

"Of course you should remain with your guests," Yvette agreed. "But would you mind terribly walking me to the house? I am quite chilled." She smiled prettily at him.

William must have been as anxious to end this little threesome as she was for he immediately rose to his feet. "Yes, of course I shall walk you to the house, Yvette. Would you mind waiting until I return, Jane?"

"Not at all." She grinned through clenched teeth.

Yvette smiled back in triumph. Jane could stay here and freeze. Yvette was going inside to get warm and having a private walk with William after all. She took his arm as he led her down the steps of the gazebo and along the snow-swept path to the manor house.

The December wind swirled snow around them and Yvette shivered in spite of herself and hugged her fur muff closer to her chest. They were in a copse of thick evergreen trees about halfway to the house when William spoke.

"I'm so pleased you were able to come skating today, Yvette. I was worried you wouldn't be able to leave your mother," William said.

"Yes, so was I, but she's much recovered now. And I find that it's wonderful to be out with people again," Yvette responded with a smile. "Thank you for inviting me."

"I'm very happy to see you. I've missed you very much, Yvette."

"Thank you. It's good to see you again too, William."

"I shall be attending Lady Deane's party tomorrow. Will you?"

"Yes, I believe I will be able to attend." Yvette hadn't left her mother alone at night yet, and going to the ball would mean missing one of her dinners with Jeffrey, but she had to make more of an effort if she wanted Lord Shelley to propose.

"Then I shall look forward to seeing you there." He hesitated a moment before saying, "Yvette, I feel I owe you an apology."

"An apology?" she asked, a bit confused.

"Yes." Clearing his throat, he looked into her eyes briefly before continuing. "I would like you to know that I was not expecting to see Jane Fairmont today. In fact I did not invite her here."

Yvette came to a halt. She turned and faced him. "Didn't you?"

Looking rather embarrassed, he said sheepishly, "No, I didn't. My mother invited her without checking with me first. I've a feeling it's been terribly awkward for you with Jane here and I'm very sorry about that."

Yvette did not know what to say. She stared mutely at him, a sense of triumph flooding her. William wanted her after all! He still preferred her to Jane! Why, Jane Fairmont, sitting alone in the cold gazebo, was someone William hadn't wanted there! A slow smile spread across her face.

"You take my breath away, Yvette."

"Do I?"

"Yes, most assuredly. I had hoped I was clear in my feelings for you."

"I admit I felt quite uncertain when I saw her here with you today," she said softly, searching his hazel eyes for confirmation of his feelings.

With a most serious expression, he took her in his arms and the warmth of him surrounded her. "May I make you perfectly certain of my feelings now, Miss Yvette Hamilton?"

It was evident that William intended to kiss her, so Yvette lifted her face to him. She stood perfectly still as his mouth covered hers. He pulled her closer to him and his lips pressed against hers. She wondered if he was going to put his tongue in her mouth as he did last time and she wasn't sure she wanted him to. Aside from the thrill of victory at winning him from Jane Fairmont, Yvette felt oddly . . . empty while kissing him. He was her future husband and she had hoped she would feel something more momentous when he kissed her. Oh, it felt nice to be held by strong arms, which shielded her from the cold wind. And the kissing wasn't unpleasant, but it wasn't at all like the kisses her sisters had described to her.

"Oh, Yvette," William murmured against her lips before plunging his tongue in her mouth.

She allowed him to do so, even lightly touching her tongue against his. The kiss seemed to last a very long time. Yvette put her arms around his neck, remembering that he liked when she did that. How odd that he seemed to find their kisses so wonderful and she did not. She kissed him back a little, waiting patiently for it to be over.

After what seemed like an eternity, he pulled away from her. "You have no idea how you make me feel, Yvette."

William hugged her tightly and she rested her head against his chest, snuggling against the thick wool coat for warmth, wishing she could feel that warmth within her own heart.

19

The Comforts of Home

When she returned to Devon House after skating later that day, Yvette knew she should be happy. William had declared his feelings for her quite clearly, and he'd kissed her. She should be thrilled. Instead she felt inexplicably out of sorts and irritable.

Jeffrey was waiting for her when she arrived home. His handsome face lit up when he saw her. "There's my girl."

She smiled in spite of herself at his sweet greeting and she instantly felt better. There was something special about being called *his girl*. With his black hair combed back and his blue eyes twinkling, he looked remarkably gorgeous in his dark dinner jacket. She found that she liked looking at him. "Hello, Jeffrey."

Giving her a wink, he held out his arm. "Granger has kept supper waiting for us. So let's go upstairs, shall we?"

They had continued the habit of taking their evening meal together in the little sitting room across from her mother's bedroom. Holding his arm, Yvette walked beside Jeffrey up the wide marble steps. She asked, "How's Mother today? How long have you been here? I didn't expect to be out quite so late."

"Apparently, Fanny wore your mother out this afternoon. She could barely keep her eyes open to talk to me when I arrived about two hours ago and she's already asleep for the night. Lisette just went home. And you are not late at all. You deserved a day out."

Relieved that her mother was well, Yvette knew that Genevieve had been in good hands with Fanny, Lisette, and Jeffrey. Idly, she wondered when her sisters would finally return home. It could be any day now. Part of her wished for them to hurry and a part of her had grown to enjoy having the run of the house. She had been in charge of her mother's care and had truly managed Devon House on her own since Colette and Lucien had been gone.

She and Jeffrey arrived at the little sitting room, where a fire burned cheerily and the table was elegantly set for two with tapered candles flickering in the center. He held out her chair and she took a seat. This intimate setting had been their private retreat each evening and Yvette found herself looking forward to spending her evenings with Jeffrey this way. However, they had never spent all night together again. Jeffrey always left at a respectable hour.

He sat across from her now and lifted his glass in a toast.

Yvette raised her glass of red wine as well. "What shall we drink to tonight?"

His blue eyes questioned her. "Well, how did your outing go?"

"Fine."

Jeffrey sensed her reluctance to discuss the day's events at Lansdowne Manor and expertly changed the topic. "Let's drink to us, then, shall we?"

"To us?" she asked, a flutter of excitement welling within her at his use of the word *us*.

"Yes. The past few weeks we've grown to be very close friends." He gave her a knowing glance.

"We have, indeed." She smiled, filled with unexpected joy. "To us."

"To us."

They sipped their wine and enjoyed their supper together, speaking of her mother's improvement and discussing whether Colette and Juliette might arrive from America before Paulette returned from Ireland.

"Are you not going to tell me?" he finally asked.

Yvette looked up from her roast beef. "Tell you what?"

"What happened at Lansdowne Manor today? You did not seem happy when you came in." His eyes stayed on her.

Yvette set down her fork with a sigh. "Jane Fairmont was there."

"Ah. The rival."

"It upset me, even though William assured me that he was not the one who invited her."

Skeptical, Jeffrey raised one dark eyebrow.

She ignored his dubious look. "His mother invited her without telling him."

"So what is the problem then?" he asked.

"Nothing. It's just . . ." She shook her head.

"It's just what, Yvette?"

"It's not what I thought it would be, I suppose."

His gaze was very intent on her. "I thought this was what you wanted?"

"Yes, I know, but none of it is how I imagined it to be. . . ." She felt her cheeks redden as she pushed her food around on her plate with her fork, no longer hungry. An odd feeling settled in her stomach. It was so difficult not to confide in Jeffrey when she longed to know his thoughts on the subject.

"Out with it," he commanded with his most charming smile. "If you can't tell me, who can you tell?"

Yvette sighed. "Well, it's rather personal and normally I would discuss something such as this with one of my sisters." She sipped her wine.

"They are not here. And I am."

She looked into his eyes. Yvette's heart fluttered at the intensity she saw within them. "Yes, you're here."

"So tell me. Or let me guess." His expression suddenly turned dark. "Did old Shelley kiss you again?"

"He's not that old." Her face burned and she glanced away. "And yes, he did."

"Then what's the problem?" he asked politely, but there was an edge to his voice. "Isn't that what you wanted him to do?"

"Well, yes of course." She paused before adding, "It's just that kissing him is not what I imagined it would be like."

"What do you mean?"

Yvette took another sip of wine before making her confession. "My sisters described kissing a man as something quite extraordinary, and exciting . . . magical even, and . . . well, I just don't feel anything special when William kisses me."

"You're disappointed." He half smiled at her.

"Yes," she blurted out, staring at his mouth. She wondered what Jeffrey's lips felt like. They looked most appealing. She had the wildest impulse to reach across the table and touch them with her fingers. But of course, she did no such thing. "I expected so much more. I expected to be swept off my feet or to feel like I would swoon. You know what I'm talking about, don't you?"

He answered rather slowly. "I suppose I do."

"Don't you feel that way when you kiss a woman? Don't you feel something special?"

Jeffrey shook his head, suddenly looking a little uncomfortable. "What I feel when I kiss a woman is desire. I think the feelings you are describing are part of being in love."

"But I felt nothing," she said in a small voice. "Nothing at all. Shouldn't I have felt *something* when William kissed me?"

"You're not in love with him, Yvette."

She remained silent. Her feelings for William were confusing. He was a good man, an attractive man. She wanted to be his wife and she wanted desperately to be in love with him. All signs pointed to him being in love with her, which is exactly what she had wished for. Then why wasn't she happier about it? Perhaps it would be easier if she knew what being in love was supposed to feel like.

With a heavy sigh Yvette rose from the table and walked to the fireplace. "Perhaps there's something wrong with me," she murmured, biting her lip.

Jeffrey watched her for a moment. "There's absolutely nothing wrong with you, Yvette." He rose to his feet also and moved to stand beside her. Gently, he placed a hand under her chin, tilting her face to his. "Absolutely nothing wrong with you."

At his touch, Yvette's pulse began to quicken. Her heart fluttered for a moment as she looked into his eyes. They were so blue and piercing, as if he could read her very thoughts. Her fingers itched to run along the length of his jaw, to feel the slight stubble on his cheek. What would it be like to kiss his lips? What would it feel like to be kissed by Jeffrey Eddington? For a wild moment she wished he *could* read her thoughts.

They continued to stare at each other. His blue eyes glittered and his expression was unreadable. He stood so close Yvette could smell the now-familiar scent of him. Masculine. Clean. Sandalwood. A sudden crackle of excitement filled the air around them.

Her voice whispered so low she could barely hear herself, "Jeffrey, would you kiss me?"

Yvette held her breath, watching his reaction to her startling request. She had surprised herself by uttering her thoughts out loud. At that moment she so desperately wanted him to kiss her that she couldn't prevent the words from tumbling out of her mouth.

For a split second, his eyes widened. Then they darkened with what could only be desire. She recognized the yearning in his eyes, for surely she felt the same way. Jeffrey wanted to kiss her! The revelation filled her with excitement and longing for him to kiss her passionately. Her heart raced and she took a big breath.

He still held her chin in his hand, and somehow moved even closer to her. His voice was low and husky. "Yvette . . . if I kiss you now, I don't know that I could ever stop."

His words filled her with a wild desire that left her breathless with anticipation. They were so close.

"Please, Jeffrey . . ."

Her whispered plea seemed to unlock something in him, for in the next instant he lowered his head and she closed her eyes, the sense of expectancy almost too great to bear. When his lips finally met hers, Yvette thought she would perish from the sheer pleasure of it. Warm, soft, and firm, his lips possessed her mouth thoroughly. Sensations she had never known existed washed like waves through her body, warming her from head to toes. She pressed herself closer to him, wanting to feel his body next to her own.

Falling, falling . . . she felt as if she were drifting outside of herself as the blood rushed hot in her veins and her heart beat in triple time.

His kiss grew in intensity and her mouth opened eagerly, hungry for more. Sleek and hot, their tongues met and Yvette sighed as an incredible pleasure blossomed within her. Wrapping her hands around his neck, she slid her fingers into his thick, black hair. It was so much softer than she had expected.

Gently, his hands slid from her face, along her shoulders and down her back. His touch, sensual and slow, fanned a growing flame within her. She could barely breathe, so consumed was she with these new sensations that were overwhelming her with their force. Her knees weakened and she trembled as Jeffrey continued to kiss her with an increasing passion that demanded she respond.

Oh, *this* was a kiss! A real kiss! One that made her feel hot and weak and wild. One that sent a rush of fervent feelings through her all at once. Breathless. Dizzy. Excited. Terrified. Thrilled. Satisfied. Yearning. Of course only Jeffrey could kiss her and make her feel this way.

It was heaven.

Filled with a feverish excitement, she kissed him back, wanting more from him than she ever thought possible. She clung to him, pressing herself against his muscular, male body. His hands stroked her back, moving up and down. And still they kissed, barely taking the time to breathe. Suddenly his hands were in her hair, carefully removing the pins that held her curls in place. As her hair fell in waves around her shoulders, this newfound passion and excitement grew within her, threatening to overwhelm her.

Yvette was kissing Jeffrey Eddington. Jeffrey was kissing *her*! It was ridiculous. It made no sense! She had known him for years and had never thought of this happening between them. Yet it seemed so natural and so *right* to be in his arms. And so wickedly delicious. She never wanted to stop. Her heart pounded frantically and she could barely breathe, but she didn't care.

This, this was what her sisters had been talking about. Yes, Yvette now understood exactly what they'd meant. This was an earth-shattering kiss. This was something special.

Lost in increasing desire and passion, Yvette and Jeffrey continued to kiss. With her long hair now completely undone and hanging loose, she clung to Jeffrey, wishing she could stay with him like this forever. She had no idea how long they kissed like that and she didn't care because she didn't want it to end. Time seemed to melt away and nothing mattered but the two of them.

Her fingers still played in his thick hair, and his hands slowly moved along her back, along the curve of her hips. Oh, goodness, every time he touched her she became more aware of her own desire.

Suddenly Jeffrey broke away, ending their passionate kiss.

"Good God, Yvette," he murmured low.

Finally coming up for air, her breath came in shallow gasps. The pounding of both their hearts echoed around them. He stroked her hair, holding her close.

"Oh, Jeffrey," she whispered against his cheek, still trembling with unfulfilled desire. "That was . . . that was . . . I . . ." Rendered speechless, she could not find the words to describe what had just happened between them.

He groaned and looked down at her. He pressed his forehead against hers, his hands bracing her shoulders. "Oh lord, Yvette. There is absolutely nothing wrong with you. You're perfect."

Tears inexplicably welled in her eyes and spilled down her cheeks.

He cupped her face in his hands once more, staring hard at her. There was so much raw emotion on his face, Yvette didn't know what to think. She'd never seen Jeffrey in such a state.

"Yvette, you have no idea . . . You have made me feel . . . I think that I—"

Suddenly there was a bit of a commotion in the hallway outside the sitting room. Footsteps. Voices. Stunned, Yvette and Jeffrey stared at each other in confusion for a split second as the enormity of the situation hit home. They managed to step away from each other just as the door to the sitting room flew open.

"We're home!"

20

Home for the Holidays

Dumbfounded into silence for the first time in his life, Jeffrey was left wondering what to do as Paulette Hamilton Reeves, the Countess of Cashelmore, entered the sitting room.

"Paulette!" Yvette fairly flew across the room to her sister's outstretched arms amid squeals of delight. They hugged each other tightly. Jeffrey moved toward them, attempting to shake off what had just happened between Yvette and him.

And not succeeding.

He'd kissed Yvette Hamilton, for Christ's sake! He'd only meant to romance her a little, sweep her away from Lord Shelley, to make her see how wrong the man was for her. He hadn't meant to take advantage of her in any way. But when the moment happened he had been powerless to stop it. Not when she looked up at him with her big blue eyes, her lips trembling, and *asked* him to kiss her. God, but she was a tempting sight. No man on earth could have refused her.

The kiss they had just shared had been like no other. It had left him feeling . . .

But Yvette was not for him! He had promised to watch over her, to protect her, and keep her safe. He had no business at all kissing her as passionately as he had!

Never had he felt so elated and so terribly wretched at the same time.

Not that he *had* thought of anything else but kissing her during the last few months since Lucien and Colette had been away. At times, all he could think of was kissing her. And Yvette had *asked* him to kiss her. God help him, how could he refuse such an offer? Christ, but she looked so irresistible when she had asked him. And he had wanted to make her feel *something*. Something, anything, she hadn't felt when she kissed Lord Shelley. A girl like Yvette deserved to be kissed passionately.

And she had been astonishingly warm and sensuous, seductively responsive to him. She had fit so perfectly in his arms, he never wanted to let her go.

But what stunned him more than anything else was how *he* had felt while kissing her. He had grown weak-kneed and breathless. It had been an earth-shattering kiss for *him*, something he'd never felt before and he didn't know what to make of it. He'd kissed dozens and dozens of beautiful women in his life and never had one affected him like Yvette Hamilton.

The tears in her eyes almost undid him and he had been on the verge of confessing his feelings for her. Feelings he hadn't known he had until he'd kissed her. Crazy, wild, tumultuous feelings. Feelings that had him reeling and left him worried. What did Yvette think of him now? Had this kiss changed everything between them? How could it not?

It had been a blessing in disguise that Paulette arrived when she had, for he did not know what would have happened had they been left alone together any longer. It was far too tempting and far too dangerous. For both of them.

"Jeffrey! I'm so glad you're here too!" Paulette called to him with a big smile.

The fourth of the Hamilton sisters was blond and blue eyed like Yvette. And Paulette also happened to be one of the smartest women he'd ever known. Marriage, motherhood, and life in Ireland agreed with her because she had grown even more beautiful.

Jeffrey wrapped her in a big hug. "Oh, how I've missed you, Paulette!" And he had. These Hamilton sisters were his family. Which made his current state of affairs with Yvette all the more confounding.

Declan Reeves, the Earl of Cashelmore, moved forward to hug Yvette and shake Jeffrey's hand. Jeffrey had grown to like Paulette's husband, in spite of being the most suspicious of Declan at the start of his romance with Paulette.

"Jeffrey, good to see you again." Declan smiled in warm greeting.

"You too, Declan. It's wonderful to have you both back," Jeffrey said.

Paulette said, "We arrived in London just at sunset, dropped the children off at our house, and came right over to see Mother, but Fanny told us she's asleep already and that you two . . . were in here?" Paulette, never one to miss a trick, eyed them most curiously.

Yvette, with her golden blond hair undone and hanging tousled about her shoulders, her soft cheeks suffused with color, and her full lips swollen from kissing him, looked wide-eyed, panic-stricken at Paulette's insinuation. It was obvious that she and Jeffrey had been dining alone together and Yvette's disheveled appearance made them look just as guilty as they were. God only knew what Paulette was thinking! The last thing Jeffrey wanted was for Yvette to be embarrassed. The kiss they had just shared was too special to be ruined. He had to salvage the situation as best he could.

"Your timing couldn't be more perfect." Jeffrey smiled at Paulette and Declan. Nonchalantly, he ran his hand over his own hair, smoothing it down where Yvette had run her fingers through it just minutes ago. "Yvette was just crying to me about how much she missed her sisters. Look at her, the poor thing. The stress of taking care of your mother has been wearing on her."

"I'm afraid I've taken terrible advantage of poor Jeffrey, crying like a ninny in front of him." Yvette flashed a grateful look in his direction as she dabbed her watery eyes with a handkerchief. "He's been so wonderful to me. He's been here every day, helping me with Mother." She sniffled and tears welled again.

Jeffrey knew she wasn't just crying about her mother. Yvette was overwhelmed with emotions, partly due to him, and his heart flipped over in his chest. He longed to pull her back in his arms and kiss away her tears, comfort her and protect her. He wanted to make her smile. He wanted to make her happy. He wanted her in his bed. He wanted to kiss her until she was breathless and wanted to make love to her for days on end and . . .

Jeffrey's thoughts startled him. This was *Yvette Hamilton* he was lusting after and imagining naked, for crying out loud! Not some stage actress. Not some chorus dancer. Not just any woman. This was his sweet little Yvette. She'd been like a little sister to him for years. It was wrong, wrong, wrong. But it didn't feel wrong when he held her. The feelings he was having for her were all over the place. What the hell was the matter with him?

"Oh, I'm sorry, Yvette." Paulette's expression changed

from suspicion to sympathy and concern. She placed her arm around her younger sister's shoulders. "I had no idea it has been so trying for you, and you here all alone. Thank goodness Jeffrey has been with you. Declan and I came just as quickly as we could after we received your letter, but I was ill myself and we had to wait until I was well enough to travel. Come now and sit down. And tell me about Mother and everything that's happened."

The two sisters moved to sit on the sofa. The very same one where Jeffrey had spent the night sleeping with Yvette in his arms. He could still recall the soft feel of her, the light gardenia scent of her, the utter sweetness of her, as he'd held her close to his heart. Never had he felt so content. That night with Yvette was seared into his memory.

The enormity of his feelings suddenly hit him like a ton of bricks.

Good God.

He was in love with Yvette Hamilton.

The revelation stunned him. But it was true. He was in love with her. He loved everything about Yvette. The last few weeks of spending so much time alone just the two of them, being with her so intimately and seeing all the different sides of her personality, their constant talking and laughing together, and their confiding in each other, had awakened something deep within him.

He knew what made Yvette laugh, what made her cry. He loved the soft sound of her voice, the sweet smell of her perfume, and how she grew cross at her mother's dramatics. He loved how she adored pretty things, how her incandescent smile lit up any room she was in. He loved the way her golden hair fell around her face. He loved the shape of her luscious mouth. He loved how she sashayed when she walked across the room. He loved her honest admission that she was completely disinterested in the family bookshop. He loved how she giggled at his jokes and teased him back when he teased her. He loved how she looked up at him with her big blue eyes.

More than anything, he loved how she felt when he kissed her and held her in his arms. It felt as if she belonged to him.

Jeffrey Eddington stood there, immobile, staring at the woman he loved as she sat beside her sister. Tears streamed down her pretty face and he was powerless to help her. Hell, he was more than likely the cause of her distress, for all that she was pretending he wasn't. He wanted to be the one to comfort her. He wanted to hold her, and kiss her, and tell her that everything would be all right, that he would make it all right.

Somehow he had fallen in love with Yvette Hamilton, and God help him, he didn't quite know what to do about it. Yvette couldn't love him. She certainly didn't want to marry him and he had nothing but a scandalous past to offer her. He was nothing but a rogue and an illegitimate son. He couldn't make her a duchess as she deserved to be. He was not good enough for her. It was a hopeless situation. Even if there was the slightest chance that she loved him back, her family would never understand or approve of such a *liaison* between them. Why, Lucien would surely kill him for taking advantage of his wife's little sister! And rightfully so.

What a god-awful mess he had made of things!

He was a complete and utter fool. An idiot. An infamous rogue caught in his own trap.

How the hell had he fallen in love with Yvette Hamilton?

"Jeffrey, why don't you and I go downstairs and have a drink?" Declan Reeves asked, with a wry grin. "We'll leave the two girls here alone to talk. I know I could use a drink and by the look of you, I'm sure you could use one too."

Jeffrey, glancing at the pair of sisters on the sofa, now both crying, readily agreed with Paulette's Irish earl.

A strong drink was most desperately called for about now.

21

In the Spirit

"Let's see you stand, *Maman*," Colette Hamilton Sinclair coaxed her mother gently, as she held on to her arm.

Genevieve stood, her thin body shaking, and clutched her ornate gold cane tightly. She looked up at her daughter proudly. "See? I can do it. I can stand on my own. *Regarde-moi. Je suis là debout sur mes deux pieds. Je me sens mieux, n'est-ce pas?*" Although slightly slurred, her words were understandable.

"That's wonderful!" Colette clapped her hands in delight, relief flooding through her.

Genevieve was so much better than she had feared while sailing home. Colette had imagined all sorts of dreadful prospects and luckily none of them had come to pass, but still the dramatic change in Genevieve's appearance was shocking nonetheless. Her mother was not completely bedridden and her speech was intelligible, but she looked much thinner and frailer and there was something different about her face. All things considered though, Colette was more than relieved at seeing her mother again.

"Oh, Mother, you are doing so well!" Juliette said, watching with bated breath.

Genevieve suddenly stumbled, about to topple over, and Colette reached out to catch her, just in time.

"Oh, let me help you!" cried Colette. Then Fanny rushed over to assist her in getting Genevieve settled safely in her bed once again.

"I am happy you are both home," Genevieve said. *"Je suis ravie que vous soyiez revenues."*

"We are happy to be home with you, *Maman*," Colette said, smoothing her mother's hair.

Genevieve frowned. "I have a headache. *J'ai besoin de me reposer. J'ai mal à la tête. Je n'aime pas ça.*"

"Yes, it is time for her nap now, girls." Fanny looked at both Juliette and Colette, dismissing them with her eyes.

"I suppose you shall make me live here with you now," their mother said, closing her eyes in weariness. *"Je suppose que tu vas m'obliger à rester à Londres maintenant. Est-ce que j'ai le choix?"*

Colette sighed. "We'll talk about that later, *Maman*."

As bossy as ever, Fanny pushed them out. "Your mother is tired and needs her rest. Come back in to see her after supper."

"Yes, of course, Fanny. Oh, Mother, we're so happy to be home again and to see you so improved! This is going to be a very happy Christmas, with all of us together. We'll let you sleep and visit you later." Colette kissed her mother's cheek, as did Juliette.

They both left the bedroom, slowly walking down the long upstairs hall of Devon House together.

"She looks much better than I expected from Yvette's letter," Juliette remarked.

"Yes, thank goodness," Colette agreed. "But I'm wondering what we shall do about her. She's right, you know. She'll have to stay here. We can't have her go back to Brighton and continue to live in that cottage alone. Not anymore."

"She'll never agree to live in London again. She hates the city."

"She has made that fact quite clear over the years, but I'm afraid she won't have much of a choice in the matter, just as she said. Lucien and I would gladly welcome her to stay with us, where she can be looked after properly with a trained nurse, not just relying on Fanny."

Juliette shook her head ominously. "I agree with you, Colette, but you know how Mother is. She will be very difficult to persuade."

"Perhaps not now that she's ill. All of her care cannot rest on poor Fanny's shoulders. She must realize that. I'm going to employ a trained nurse to help out immediate—"

A sudden high-pitched scream from the nursery caught their attention. The two sisters exchanged knowing glances. More shrieks ensued, followed by some very irate shouting.

"That sounds like my daughter," Juliette said, looking weary. "I'll go see what trouble she is causing this time. Perhaps while you're looking for a nurse for Mother, you could find a very strict governess who can handle little Miss Sara Fleming for me?"

Colette laughed at her sister. "I shall see what I can do. You run along and solve the problems in the nursery, and I'll go downstairs to see if the rest of our trunks have arrived from the ship yet."

Grumbling in annoyance, Juliette continued on to the nursery. She called back, "I know she's my retribution for all the heartache I caused our parents."

"I know you're absolutely right about that!" Again Colette laughed, knowing that Juliette's high-spirited daughter had indeed inherited not only her mother's looks, but also most definitely her personality. The three children, Sara, Phillip, and Simon, had grown weary of each other's company after months together in New Jersey and a week crossing the Atlantic in close quarters on the *Sea Minx*. They had all just arrived at Devon House earlier that day and were still unpacking and settling in, and the children had been sent to the nursery. Obviously things were not going well.

"Paulette and Lisette will be here later, so there will be some new children for them to play with. Console them with that thought," Colette called after her sister, before making her way down the massive staircase.

It was good to be back home again. Colette had missed her beautiful house. But most of all she missed the bookshops! It was the longest she had ever been away from them. Her plan was to visit them first thing in the morning. However, she still had the great tasks of unpacking and readying Devon House for Christmas ahead of her yet. Not to mention the dilemma of what to do with their mother.

As she reached the bottom of the staircase, Granger was opening the front door for Jeffrey Eddington. Colette broke into a smile at the sight of him looking as debonair as ever.

"Jeffrey!" she called in delight.

He looked up at her in surprise. Then his expression turned to joy and he grinned broadly. "Colette!" He rushed to meet her with a warm embrace. "When did you return home?"

"This morning!" Colette hugged him tightly. "Oh, it's so good to see you! I wasn't expecting to see you here so soon!"

"I was coming to see Yvette." He paused at her confused expression and added hastily, "And your mother. I check in on them both every day."

"Oh, how sweet of you!"

"How was your crossing?" he asked. "Did you enjoy America? Where is Lucien? And Juliette and Harrison?"

She rolled her eyes. "Oh, we have so much to talk about! Harrison is still at the dock with his ship, Lucien's in his study, and Juliette is upstairs, trying to wrangle her daughter."

Jeffrey laughed. "I saw Paulette and Declan last night when they arrived, so now everyone is home again."

"Yes, we're all home for Christmas this year! Isn't it wonderful?" Colette took his hand in hers, happy to see her friend again. "Come sit with me while I rest for a moment, have some tea, and figure out which tasks need my attention first. Lucien is in his study, going through piles of correspondence. You can go see him only after you've had a good long talk with me."

"It would be my pleasure." Jeffrey followed her to the drawing room.

"So, tell me everything," she said to him when they were alone.

Jeffrey, frozen in his tracks, looked quite panic-stricken for a moment, almost guilty. "What do you mean?"

Perplexed, she stared at him. How odd! Why would Jeffrey look guilty? She could not recall ever seeing him look anxious about anything before. "I want to know all about what happened with Mother. Yvette told me that you were an immense help to her."

His brows furrowed and his eyes glanced at her questioning. "Where is Yvette this afternoon? Is she upstairs?"

"She ran out for a fitting at her dressmaker. You know how Yvette is. Your father's annual Christmas ball is coming up and she wants to make sure her new gown will be perfect. We're all going to be there. I think it may be the first time ever that all five of the Hamilton sisters will be attending the same ball together."

He relaxed considerably at her words and smiled again. "Now that fact alone will ensure that my father's Christmas ball will be a resounding success."

"I'm rather looking forward to it myself. It's so nice to be back home." Colette sat upon a chair. "Now, tell me everything."

"I'm sure you know all of it by now," he said, taking a seat near her. "You have seen your mother, of course? Don't you think she looks well?"

Colette sighed. "Yes and no. She's not as bad as I imagined, but not as good as I had hoped."

Jeffrey's expression turned grim. "You've no idea how bad it was that first night, Colette. Your mother gave Yvette and me quite a fright."

"They were both fortunate you were there when it happened. Mother and Yvette have been singing your praises. Especially Yvette."

He grew almost bashful at her compliments. "Thank you, but I did nothing anyone else wouldn't have done given a similar situation. I care deeply for her."

"Her?" Colette raised a brow.

"Your mother," he amended hastily. "I care for your mother and for your sister."

"Of course you do. We all care for you too, Jeffrey. I hope you know that." She nodded, but kept an eye on him. Jeffrey was acting quite peculiar this afternoon. "And I am most grateful to you for all that you did for us while we were away. I think Lucien was only able to enjoy our trip because he knew that you were watching over Yvette."

Jeffrey looked a bit sheepish. "He told you about that, did he?"

"Yes. My husband usually tells me everything. Sooner or later." She smiled at him and paused before adding, "Yvette told me all about Lord Shelley this morning, although we already knew from your letters to Lucien. Do you really think he's going to propose to her?"

Jeffrey's expression darkened. "Yes. Lord Shelley seems quite set on her."

"What is he like?"

He shrugged. "He's a nice enough fellow. There's nothing wrong with him at all. In fact, he has much to recommend him. It's just . . ." He shook his head.

"You don't like him, do you?" Colette asked.

"No, it's not that. Whether or not I like the man has no bearing on the situation in the least. However . . ."

"However," she prompted him. It wasn't like Jeffrey to hold back on giving his opinion.

"Well, I don't think Yvette will be happy if she marries him."

"Why ever not?"

"It's just a feeling I have."

"Have you mentioned this to Yvette?"

He seemed a bit reluctant to admit it, but he said, "Yes, I have."

"Well, what did she say to that?"

He shrugged casually, although he looked a bit pained. "She is still intent on marrying him, regardless of what I say to her."

"I see." Colette had the oddest feeling that there was more to the story than Jeffrey was admitting. "She's attending Lady Deane's ball with him this evening."

"Is she?"

Again, there was a distinct look of displeasure on Jeffrey's face. Surely Colette was not imagining it! He certainly did not care for the idea of Yvette being with Lord Shelley. "Yes, she mentioned that she wouldn't be dining with us this evening, because she had promised Lord Shelley that she would attend the ball."

"I see."

Colette hesitated. She knew her younger sister quite well.

"It would be just like Yvette to think that being a duchess would make her happy. Yvette said Lord Shelley is quite anxious to meet all of us and now I must say I'm most eager to meet him. He's coming to Devon House for tea tomorrow afternoon. I will let you know what I think after I see them together. But if any of my sisters was born to be a duchess, it's Yvette."

Jeffrey did not say a word, but his expression grew grim.

Colette shook her head at his gloominess. "Come now, Jeffrey. You've known Yvette and her romantic notions since she was a child. Becoming a duchess is romantic to her. I'm sure she will be fine."

"I'm not so sure about that," he muttered rather ominously.

Colette's heart skipped a beat as a reason for Jeffrey's reluctance to accept Yvette's choice occurred to her. "Is there something you're keeping from me? Do you know something we don't about Lord Shelley? You don't think he'd be the type to strike her or anything like that, do you?"

"No, of course not!" he protested heatedly. "I would lock her up in her room if I thought she was placing herself in that kind of danger."

Colette relaxed, however she was still puzzled by Jeffrey's demeanor. "Then whatever could be the matter with him? From everything we've heard about him, Lord Shelley is a very nice gentleman from a fine family. Yvette tells me that he's good looking, titled, wealthy, and mad about her. What more could any girl wish for in a husband?"

Jeffrey opened his mouth, on the verge of saying something, but stopped himself at the last second. He shook his head. "You're absolutely right. My opinion is of no value in this instance. It's Yvette's wishes that matter the most. Lord Shelley is everything a girl could wish for in a husband. She should marry him and she will no doubt be quite happy."

Something about his answer struck Colette as odd. In fact, Jeffrey's whole manner seemed peculiar this afternoon. Granted, she had not seen him in months, but she'd known the man long enough to know when something was amiss and he was certainly not acting like himself in regard to Yvette. She was about to question him further when Juliette burst into the drawing room.

"Jeffrey!"

"Juliette!" Smiling, he rose to his feet and they rushed to embrace each other. "You beautiful girl! It's been almost two years since I've seen you!"

Colette watched him carefully and wondered. He seemed quite like his usual old self now with Juliette, teasing and laughing with her. But something was definitely different about Jeffrey Eddington. Somehow she couldn't shake the feeling that it had something to do with her youngest sister.

22

Christmas Season

"How do you manage to always look more beautiful every time I see you, Yvette?" Lord Shelley flirted with her as they waltzed about the spacious ballroom in Lady Deane's townhouse.

"And you look most dashing, William," Yvette answered with a bright smile that for some reason she did not entirely feel. She was wearing another new gown, this one cut in the same daring style as the sapphire gown, but in a rich shade of gold.

"You must be happy all your sisters are home again," William said. He moved her expertly to the music.

"Yes, I am. I'm always happy when my sisters are together." And she was glad. Mostly.

Devon House was now bursting at the seams with the hustle and bustle of her family and little nieces and nephews once again. She loved having them all home, but strangely she also found that she missed the peace and quiet of having the house to herself. She had grown quite used to it during the past three months.

But more than anything, she would miss the time she'd had alone with Jeffrey over dinner each evening. Their little interlude together had come to an abrupt end with her sisters' homecoming. She had not seen Jeffrey since the night he kissed her. That kiss, which had sent shivers of delight through her entire body, had been all she could think about.

Yvette wondered if he felt as awkward as she did after their kiss. Had it changed things between them? She thought it might have, for how could it not? The kiss they'd shared had left her most unsettled and she had been unable to focus on anything else clearly since it happened. That kiss had made her *feel* things she hadn't felt before.

Things she had certainly not felt with William Weatherly.

Jeffrey's kiss had left her breathless and dizzy and longing for more. She had wanted the kiss to go on and on and on. Surprisingly, she had wanted even more from him. She had wanted him to touch her, craved for him to touch her. It was more romantic and passionate than she imagined a kiss could possibly be.

"I'm happy that you're happy, Yvette." Lord Shelley beamed at her.

Yvette stared at the handsome man dancing with her, wondering why she felt nothing when he kissed her, when she wanted to feel something most desperately.

The waltz ended and Lord Shelley escorted her from the dance floor. The Earl of Babey, a handsome and notorious rake, smiled wolfishly at her as they approached him. Yvette had a feeling it was due to the daring cut of her gold gown.

"Lord Shelley!" Lord Babey called, shaking hands with

William. "It's good to see you." He turned his attention to Yvette. "And Miss Hamilton. You're looking ravishing this evening."

"Why, thank you, Lord Babey!" Yvette smiled back at him.

"Please don't tell me a beautiful girl like you is falling for this old man!" he teased, inclining his head toward William.

"Better she falls in love with me, than an inveterate gambler like you, Babey!" William shot back with a wicked grin.

Yvette laughed at the two men's banter, but inside she felt a twinge of guilt. Naturally, William thought she was in love with him. Yet she wasn't.

"So I take it you have heard about my newest business venture, then, eh, Shelley?" Lord Babey asked, his face alight with excitement.

William looked somewhat amused, nodding his head a little. "Yes, yes, I have."

Lord Babey laughed loudly. "And you know no good can come of that!" He winked broadly at them before continuing on into the ballroom.

William raised an eyebrow at the notorious earl's departure. He whispered low to Yvette. "It's amazing how society always overlooks Lord Babey's outrageous behavior. The man knows no bounds. The word is he has now become an impresario and has even opened a new gaming hall."

"Well, I think he's most charming," Yvette murmured absently, as William continued to walk with her. In spite of what everyone said about Lord Babey, she found him to be quite amusing.

"Have you spent much time in his company?" William asked.

"Not overly much. He is a friend of Jeffrey's. But he always makes me laugh." Yvette added, "And he's a good dancer."

William eyed her with an amused smile. "But not as good as I am, I hope?"

"Of course not." She shook her head, wishing to soothe his vanity. Neither of them was as good a dancer as Jeffrey. But she kept that thought to herself.

Anxiously, Yvette scanned the crowded ballroom for Jeffrey, wondering if he would be in attendance this evening. She missed his smile and their long talks and his comforting presence, and she could not stop reliving their wonderful kiss and her wanton response to him.

The more she thought about it, the more embarrassed she became. Yvette had *asked* him to kiss her. She had let him undo her hair. She had run her fingers through his hair. Like some sort of loose woman, she had pressed her body against his, and sighed and groaned into his mouth. Oh, his mouth! His mouth, his lips, his tongue had been—

Yvette shook herself from her errant thoughts. She had behaved scandalously with Jeffrey. She was grateful that she had been at the dressmaker when he'd come by Devon House earlier that afternoon and had been spared facing him.

"I am very much looking forward to meeting your sisters tomorrow, Yvette."

She glanced up at William, who smiled at her so sweetly. "And they are quite eager to meet you too. I've told them all about you."

Colette had invited Lord Shelley to tea tomorrow, and all four of her sisters would be there with their husbands.

Yvette felt surprisingly nervous about it and wasn't quite sure why.

When her sisters had all arrived at Devon House, she had confessed to them her courtship with Lord Shelley and his intentions toward marriage. They had all seemed very happy for her. Yet for some reason, telling her sisters that she was about to become a duchess hadn't felt as dramatic and important as she had imagined. She felt oddly deflated and not as happy as a girl ought to be, all things considered, when she had a future duke practically offering for her hand!

She could not help but believe that her intense reaction to Jeffrey's kisses and her complete indifference to William's kisses had something to do with her sudden state of confusion. Both men were very experienced and rumored to have been with many women, and their friendship with Lord Babey was further proof of that. But could it be that Jeffrey was somehow more skilled in the area of kissing than Lord Shelley? It was a distinct possibility and one that she had been pondering ever since it happened.

What else could be the difference between them?

With Jeffrey, everything had been most unexpected. His kiss had taken her by surprise, because she had not been expecting to have those wild, passionate feelings with him, whereas with William she had wished for his kisses to be something special. Perhaps her expectations with him had been too high? There was no element of surprise. She needed for William to kiss her again, when she was not expecting anything to happen.

She suddenly noticed that Lord Shelley had led her from the ballroom and they were now walking along a quiet corridor. So lost in her thoughts had she been, that she had not realized where she was.

"Where are we going, William?"

He patted her arm in reassurance. "Lady Deane invited me to view a new painting she acquired last week. I thought you might like to look at it with me."

"That would be lovely," she answered with a smile. He was arranging for them to be alone! How convenient! If William tried to kiss her, Yvette would simply relax and let the mood take over.

They entered a small, elegant parlor with rich scarlet wallpaper and a thick, flower-patterned rug. A fire had been lit earlier, so the room was very warm. A few sconces flickered on the walls.

"I believe this is it." He guided her to the marble fireplace, where a pretty oil painting was mounted above the mantel. It depicted a summer scene of elegantly dressed people on the shore of a lake. "Yes, this is it. It's by a French painter. A fellow named Renoir. Do you like it, Yvette?"

"Yes, it's very pretty." Yvette was not in the mood to concentrate on a picture at the moment. She found the painting pleasant enough, but did not care about it one way or another. "The colors are quite nice. Especially the greens."

"Yes, aren't they? I had an opportunity to buy it, but I turned it down and let Lady Deane have it. Now I'm wondering if I made a mistake. Would you care to have something like it in our home one day?" He turned his attention from the painting to her.

Yvette stared up at him. "In our home?" she echoed his question.

"Forgive me for thinking aloud." He shook his head in disbelief, smiling warmly at her. "Oh, Yvette, when you are near me, I can't think straight and I lose all restraint. I should not have even brought you in here."

"I . . . I don't know what to say," she murmured. Her cheeks suddenly burned.

"There's no reason for you to say anything, my dearest."

William pulled her into his arms and before she knew it, he was kissing her. He didn't ask permission this time, and for that she was most grateful. Now he was kissing her! She closed her eyes in an attempt to relax and let the feelings just come to her.

His mouth moved over hers and his breathing became more rapid. Yvette turned into his embrace, waiting in anticipation for the dizzy, breathless sensation to come over her as it had with Jeffrey, certain it could happen this time with William. She waited. William's kissing became more insistent and he held her tighter. His tongue entered her mouth and she kissed him back, but those wild feelings didn't come over her. The kiss went on and on and she put her arms around him, waiting, hoping.

But that wild, passionate, dizzying sensation never came.

William moved from kissing her mouth to her cheek and his lips began sliding down, kissing her neck, all the while he murmured her name as he pressed his lips to her bare flesh. She ought to be feeling something by now! She sighed in growing frustration.

"Oh, Yvette," William moaned against her throat, nuzzling her and lowering his head toward her chest.

Recalling that she was wearing the low-cut gold gown and realizing where his mouth was moving, instinctively Yvette pulled away from him. "William, please."

At her words, he stopped abruptly. Coming to his senses, he stared at her, his hazel eyes blazing. "Forgive me, Yvette. You make me forget myself."

Yvette wished fervently that she felt for him even half of

what he obviously felt for her. What on earth was wrong with her? "I forgive you, William. And I—"

Their attention was suddenly caught by a sound at the door. "Ahem." A male voice cleared its throat purposely. Loudly. "Excuse me."

"Jeffrey." Yvette's legs trembled at the sight of him.

"Eddington," William muttered through clenched teeth. He took a step away from Yvette and adjusted his jacket somewhat nervously, but he looked very sure of himself.

"I'm sorry to interrupt." Jeffrey's deep blue eyes settled on Yvette for an instant, then turned to William. "Lady Deane is looking everywhere for you, Shelley. There's been a message from your mother. You're wanted at Lansdowne Manor right away. There is some sort of emergency."

William's face paled at the news and Yvette's heart went out to him. "Oh, William."

"Oh. I see. Thank you, Eddington, for letting me know." He looked to Yvette, his expression pained. "Forgive me, Yvette. I must go."

"Of course you must, William. I understand. I do hope it is nothing too serious."

Jeffrey spoke up. "You'd best hurry. Don't worry, Shelley, I'll see that Miss Hamilton is looked after."

"Thank you." William looked torn. He took Yvette's hand in his and raised it to his mouth, pressing a light kiss to her fingers. "I hope I shall still be able to visit you tomorrow and meet your sisters, Yvette."

"So do I."

"I shall send you a message as soon as I can. Good night." He released her hand and hurried from the room, leaving Yvette and Jeffrey very much alone in Lady Deane's little parlor.

They stared at each other in silence.

As usual Jeffrey looked incredibly handsome in his black evening suit. Tall and broad, he filled it out most impressively. He really was the most handsome man she had ever known.

With deliberate slowness, he closed the parlor door and walked toward her. Yvette's heart quickened and a shiver raced over her, in spite of the warmth of the room. She unconsciously backed away from him until she found herself against the wall.

"Jeffrey."

"Yvette." He stopped mere inches from her, leaning one hand on the wall beside her head.

"It's good to see you again." She licked her lips. "I haven't seen you since . . . since we . . ."

"Since we kissed?" he asked, his eyes fixed on her.

"Mmm hmm," she murmured like a witless fool. He smelled so good and he was so close to her she couldn't think clearly.

His head lowered toward her. "And what have you been thinking about our kiss, Yvette?" He reached out gently and brushed a stray curl from her face.

She almost gasped at his touch. "It was . . ." She fumbled for the words.

"Yes?" he prompted her, his eyes narrowing.

Feeling a little breathless, she said, "I . . . I can't stop thinking about it. It made me feel quite faint."

He smiled then, a heart-melting smile that left her a little breathless. "And here I was afraid you might be upset with me for kissing you."

"Why would I be upset with you, Jeffrey?" Again, he flashed her a smile that made her knees a bit weak. Why did Jeffrey suddenly have this strange effect on her? Nothing made sense anymore. "But I was feeling that I should apologize to you for my behavior."

"Apologize for *your* behavior?" He looked incredulous.

"Yes, I acted a bit brazenly and I want to apol—"

"No." He shook his head, holding up his hand. "Do not apologize to me, Yvette. There's nothing at all for you to be sorry for last night. You were perfect."

"But, Jeffrey, I wasn't. I asked you to kiss me!"

"If anyone should apologize, it should be me. But I'm not going to."

"You're not?" It was her turn to be incredulous.

His expression suddenly darkened. "No, not if you're allowing Lord Shelley to kiss you as you just did."

A little embarrassed that he had seen her kissing William, she lifted her chin defiantly. "I merely was experimenting."

"Experimenting? Pray, go on. . . ."

"Yes." She swallowed nervously, as she looked into his fathomless blue eyes. "You see, I . . . I felt . . . something when you kissed me."

He grew silent and stared at her. His words were ever so soft. "What did you feel when I kissed you?"

Yvette's heart began to race. "Everything. Feelings I didn't know existed."

His eyes bored into her, but she could not read his expression, his thoughts.

"And when Shelley kissed you just now?" he asked again.

She stared back at him and confessed. "I still felt nothing."

He exhaled as if he had been holding his breath. "Nothing?"

"Nothing at all." She shook her head in confirmation.

Suddenly the air around them fairly crackled with heat

and tension. He placed his hands possessively on her shoulders and drew her closer to him, his arms holding her tight.

"I want you to feel something only when I kiss you, Yvette."

Yvette sucked in her breath. Her whole body was on pins and needles in anticipation. "Jeffrey, I . . ."

Before she could utter another word, his mouth came down over hers and a thrill swept over her at the contact. And in that instant, she was lost. Completely and utterly lost in his kiss. All rational, coherent thought scattered like leaves in the wind. This, *this* is what she had been craving. Jeffrey's warm lips on hers. Oh, and this time was even better, if such a thing were even possible.

This kiss carried her into a state of bliss she had not known existed. Jeffrey's very touch melted her. His strong hands. His warm mouth. His fervent tongue. Yvette had never suspected such feelings of desire dwelled within her, but Jeffrey seemed to awaken them. Her breath grew shallow and faint. Her legs trembled and her knees weakened. She clung to him as if she were drowning in a deep and endless pool of water and he was the only steady thing in her world.

Jeffrey. Jeffrey. Jeffrey.

His name, his being, consumed her, left her filled with an incredible yearning and longing for something more, much more, from him.

Slowly, his hands slid from her shoulders and roamed across her back, stroking her, caressing her until she thought she would faint with the pleasure of it. The feel of his skilled fingers against the bare skin of her shoulders and back filled her with little quivers of desire. Shivers of need ran up her scalp and she ached for him to remove the pins in her hair and let the tendrils fall loose again. She couldn't get close enough to him. Her clothes felt restrictive and hot, almost suffocating. She longed to remove them, wished that *he* would remove them for her. Never had she wanted anything in her life more than she wanted Jeffrey Eddington to touch her at that moment.

Sighing heavily, she ran her fingers through his thick, black hair and breathed in the deep, spicy, woodsy scent of him. She longed to lie with him on the sofa again, to feel the masculine weight of his body on top of hers. She murmured his name and unconsciously pressed her breasts against his chest.

Jeffrey groaned low as if in pain and held her tighter. His hot tongue plundered her mouth and she surrendered eagerly, giving and wanting more each second. With her heart pounding against his, she felt she would perish from pleasure and passion at the same time. His hands moved even lower, cupping her bottom and pressing her against his hips. A sudden thrill raced through her at the contact.

Their kiss deepened, if such a thing were even possible.

And his hands . . . his hands were everywhere as the heat grew between them. One hand cupped her breast through the material of her gown. She sucked in her breath, arching her back. Her body tingled with pleasure, desire, anticipation, yearning. For Jeffrey.

"Oh, God, Yvette," he murmured hoarsely.

"Jeffrey." Oh, how she wanted him, ached for him. She'd do anything he wanted.

His mouth continued to cover hers, their passion intensifying.

Suddenly he let go of her, releasing his hold on her.

Stumbling back against the wall, Yvette wanted to cry with the loss of him, and stinging tears welled within her eyes. She gazed up at him, emotions raw and hot warring within her in tumultuous confusion.

"Jeffrey?" she whispered, her heart still racing.

Placing both of his hands on the wall on either side of her face, he leaned in close. His gaze penetrated her very being, his blue eyes full of desire, perhaps even a touch of anger. "You wanted to experiment, Yvette? No one will ever kiss you like I can and what you felt just now with me you will *never* feel with him. Consider your experiment complete."

Before she could even respond, Jeffrey placed one fast, hard kiss on her lips, which took her breath away, before he abruptly turned and stalked from the room.

23

Be of Good Cheer

The Devon House butler escorted Lord Shelley along a hallway to the formal parlor and he noted that the house had been decorated for Christmas. He was amused at his own feelings, for in spite of the fact that he was the one looking them over for their suitability as potential in-laws, William was a little nervous. He wanted to approve of them for he truly wished to make Yvette his wife.

The staid butler opened the double doors and William was greeted immediately by Yvette. She looked quite fetching in a simple gown of dusky pink.

She placed her hand on his arm and guided him into the room. "Good afternoon, William. I'm so happy to see you! I was pleased to receive your note this morning that your mother is well and I'm so glad all is fine at home after all."

"Yes, I am too."

William had fled the ball last night panic-stricken at his mother's urgent message, believing that his father had finally passed away. When he had arrived at Lansdowne Manor he'd discovered that his mother, after having drunk entirely too much wine, had fallen and hit her head on an end table. She had a nasty bruise and a raging headache this morning, but she was perfectly fine. The entire incident irritated him, for he had been enjoying the ball and Yvette's delightful company and did not desire to leave when he had.

And having to leave Yvette alone with Eddington hadn't sat well with him either. He'd been in a foul mood all last night because of it. The proprietary look in that infernal man's eyes had raised his hackles. He hated the idea of Yvette alone with Jeffrey Eddington for any reason.

But being here with Yvette now almost made up for it. Her sweet smile worked wonders to soothe his jealous feelings.

As he lifted his gaze from Yvette to the rest of the room, William came up short. "Oh, my!" he muttered in surprise.

A small crowd awaited him. He had known she had four sisters, of course, but seeing them all at once was rather astounding. He had heard that they looked remarkably alike and were quite stunning. But in person they were almost overwhelming. He didn't know how he would be able to hold a coherent conversation with such a sight before him.

And then there were the husbands. They were very handsome fellows all around. William suddenly felt a bit lacking in the face of these younger men.

Yvette laughed at his expression and teased, "It doesn't seem quite fair meeting them all at once, does it?"

William rolled his eyes in amusement. "I should say not!" This was not what he had been expecting at all.

Yvette made the introductions nicely, and William hoped he could remember each of their names correctly. They all took their seats about the room and he sat beside Yvette on a blue damask sofa.

She grinned at him. "So this is my family."

William said, "I am pleased to finally meet all of you. I've been looking forward to it for some time now." In fact, he had grown quite impatient waiting for Yvette's sisters to return from their travels. He was anxious to propose to her and the only holdup was meeting her family. He had checked their backgrounds very carefully and on paper the family seemed respectable enough. Still, he had his doubts. There seemed to be a hint of a scandal surrounding each of them.

However, if all went well this afternoon, he would ask Yvette to marry him next week and they could begin planning their wedding. The sooner they were married, the sooner he could have Yvette in his bed. That thought alone kept him up at night in anticipation, especially after last night's kiss.

"We are just as glad to meet you, Lord Shelley." The oldest sister, Colette, a beautiful brunette, poured him a cup of tea and handed it to him with a warm smile. He knew Yvette's sister was now the Marchioness of Stancliff and he had met her husband, Lucien Sinclair, once before many years ago. One would never know to look at her that she had been raised above a bookshop. She was quite elegant and refined, a perfect marchioness.

"Lady Stancliff, Yvette tells me that you have two young sons?" he asked her. It was amazing how much she looked like Yvette, only with darker hair.

Colette's face lit up at the mention of her children. "Yes, Phillip is seven and Simon is five. They are both wonderful little boys."

"I assume that they accompanied you on the trip to America?"

"Yes, and they had a grand time, didn't they, Lucien?" She turned to her husband.

Lucien Sinclair, the Marquis of Stancliff, was a handsome

man and a financial force to be reckoned with about town. He had amassed a fortune in the shipping trade since he had taken over his father's estate and had more than tripled his assets and properties. He was a fine man, but there had been a terrible scandal years ago involving Lucien's mother and an Italian count. Much had been swept under the rug and he was under the impression that Lucien's parents had reconciled before his father passed away.

"We all had a fine time visiting America. The boys especially loved being on board ship. Have you ever had occasion to travel to the United States, Lord Shelley?" Lucien asked amiably.

"No, I can't say that I have, although I would like to one day." William sipped his tea. "I've spent most of my time in France, Italy, and Spain during the last ten years or so."

"Have you been to the Orient?" The one called Juliette looked at him with frank interest, her blue eyes glittering.

William was most curious about this sister, for he had heard that she was wild and had run away to America against her family's wishes. With her dark hair and fair skin, she was quite a beauty too, and he sensed an innate impulsivity about her that made him feel slightly uneasy in her presence.

"No, I haven't been there either, Mrs. Fleming. Although I should like to visit there as well."

"Oh, if you enjoy traveling you must visit the Orient. Harrison and I have traveled all over the world together and have seen so many incredible places, but China is the most exotic," she said, her sharp eyes still resting on him, as if she were sizing him up.

William looked to Juliette Hamilton's husband, the sea captain, with surprise. He had expected someone swarthier, more pirate-like, but Harrison Fleming was an attractive man with blond hair and gray eyes. He looked very fit and had an athletic build, but he could easily pass for a gentleman in spite of being American. And a sea captain. Juliette and her husband both appeared more than respectable. Besides, they didn't reside in London and spent most of their time in the States.

Harrison Fleming gave him a friendly smile. "You have an open invitation to visit us in America any time, Lord Shelley."

"Why, thank you very much. I may take you up on that!"

Then another sister, Lisette Roxbury, the one married to the renowned architect and member of Parliament, gazed at him sweetly. Her hair had a hint of red in it, but she looked just like the other sisters. It was uncanny, the resemblance they shared.

Lisette asked him, "Lord Shelley, are you looking forward to being home for Christmas?"

He nodded. "Yes, I must admit I am. It's been years since I've been able to do so. Our Christmas celebrations will be scaled back of course, due to my father's condition, but it will be a happy holiday nonetheless."

The middle sister and her husband had a bit of a scandalous beginning to their relationship. He'd discovered that Quinton Roxbury had first been engaged to the Duke of Wentworth's only daughter. Then the wedding had been suddenly called off, and Roxbury had quietly married Lisette Hamilton a few weeks later. William hadn't been able to uncover the reason for the sudden shift in plans, except that the duke's daughter had changed her mind and hadn't wished to marry him. He suspected there must be more to the story, but there hadn't been a whiff of scandal about the couple since. By all accounts, they were a generous, well-respected couple. And Roxbury was doing fine architectural work about the city and was well regarded in Parliament.

"Will you be attending the Duke of Rathmore's annual Christmas ball?" Paulette asked him.

Ah, the fourth sister intrigued him also. She looked the most like Yvette, since they had the same blond coloring. But Paulette Hamilton had married an Irish earl, who had been suspected of ridding himself of his first wife in a fire. Turned out, it had been a relative of the earl's who had done the deed and Declan Reeves had been exonerated, but still there was a sordidness about the entire affair that William didn't wish the Weatherly name to be associated with.

"Yes, my mother and I will be in attendance," William said. "I am looking forward to it, as I haven't been to one of his parties in years."

Paulette smiled at him. "We are all going as well! It should be great fun. The Duke of Rathmore's annual Christmas ball is considered to be the most lavish."

"Yes, it will be the first time that our entire family will be there together," Lisette added, happily. "The five of us have never attended the same ball before."

"That sounds like it will be a wonderful time. Undoubtedly I shall have some good news to share that evening." William glanced to Yvette, his meaning quite clear. Her cheeks reddened prettily.

"William," she whispered low.

"I'd love to know more about the family bookshops." William looked to her sisters with interest. "I know Yvette here is not overly involved in them, but I've only heard excellent things about your stores. In fact I've bought a number of books from the shops recently. How often are you there?"

As he listened to Colette and Paulette describe how they had transformed the small shop of their father's and managed to create an expanding and successful business, his respect for them increased.

He had worried about Yvette's family background and the fact that they were in trade particularly had concerned him. And women running a business was always slightly scandalous. No hint of scandal had ever touched the Weatherly family before and he didn't wish to start now. But William found her sisters to be absolutely charming and elegant ladies. He could find no fault with them.

And then there was the French mother, Genevieve La Brecque Hamilton. Although her lineage was acceptable and her atrocious behavior on the day of his visit could be excused by the onset of her apoplectic attack, William had gotten the distinct feeling the woman didn't like or approve of him. He was quite relieved that she had been unable to attend today's tea.

As the afternoon progressed, he found he liked the Hamilton sisters very much in spite of his initial skepticism. And their husbands too. He had to give them all credit for showing up to meet him that afternoon, for he had not formally offered for their sister as of yet, although it was implicitly understood why he was there.

He noted that Yvette was quieter than usual during his visit, although she looked lovely. Everything about her was perfect. Her disposition suited him and it was obvious that she would make a wonderful duchess. With her beauty, style, and graciousness, Yvette would be an asset to him and his estate. And seeing as her four sisters had procreated with seeming ease, all things considered, Yvette should also be able to provide him with an heir without any difficulty at all.

Yes, indeed, not only was Yvette perfect for him, but also he was wildly attracted to her. So much so that he had lain awake at night dreaming of making love to her. And their kiss last night! His increasing desire for her had almost made him lose control. He had come quite close to taking advantage of her. Yes, they would marry just as soon as they possibly could.

Satisfied at last that the Hamilton family would not bring any scandal to the Lansdowne name, William finally relaxed and enjoyed the remainder of the afternoon with them.

"It was delightful meeting you, Lord Shelley," Colette said to him when it was time to take his leave. "We look forward to seeing you again very soon. Perhaps you and your mother could join us for dinner one evening?"

"Thank you, Lady Stancliff, I would enjoy that and I'm sure my mother would too." Once his mother recovered, it would be good to have her meet Yvette's family. He felt sure she would like them very much.

After his farewells to the others, William turned to Yvette, who looked quite pleased. She walked with him to the front hall and they paused by the door. The Devon House butler hovered nearby.

"Your family is charming."

"Oh, thank you, William. I'm so happy that you like them." Yvette's face brimmed with satisfaction. "I'm positive they think you're wonderful."

"It's all working out quite well, isn't it, Yvette? Then I shall see you at the theater tomorrow night," William said. He had plans to escort her to see a show. Perhaps that would be the night he would formally propose to her. He took her hands in his and gave them a squeeze, wishing he could kiss her good-bye.

"Yes, that would be lovely." She smiled up at him, looking so appealing it took his breath away.

"Good afternoon, Yvette."

"Good-bye, William."

He left Devon House feeling much better than he had

before he'd arrived. Yes, all in all, it had been quite a successful afternoon. He must get his mother's engagement ring ready to give to Yvette. It was a very beautiful emerald ring set with a circle of diamonds and it had been in his family for generations. He knew Yvette would love it.

As William made his way down the front steps toward his waiting carriage, another carriage pulled up in front of the house. Curious, he paused to watch. The now-familiar figure of Lord Jeffrey Eddington leapt from that carriage to the sidewalk and headed up the steps of Devon House.

"Eddington," William greeted him coldly.

"Shelley." Eddington tipped his top hat genially, a slow smile spreading across his damnably handsome face. "Just leaving, are you?"

"Yes." It annoyed William that Eddington was at Devon House yet again. He felt slightly mollified knowing that Yvette was no longer alone in the house. Nothing untoward could happen with her entire family watching over her. Could it? With Eddington's reputation it would be difficult to say.

"So you finally met all the sisters?" Eddington asked.

William nodded. "Yes, they're a wonderful family."

"Aren't they, though?" Eddington winked at him and continued up the steps. The butler opened the door in welcome. Before he entered the house as though he lived there, he called back carelessly, "See you around, Shelley."

William walked with reluctant feet to his own carriage, unable to shake the heavy feeling of unease at the thought of Jeffrey Eddington in the house with Yvette. The man's constant presence in Yvette's life troubled him. He would have to have a talk with her about it. Once he married Yvette, that bastard Eddington's visits with his wife would be severely curtailed. Of that William was quite certain.

24

Christmas Shopping

With hurried steps, Yvette walked into the Hamilton Sisters' Bookshop, the little bells over the door jingling as she entered. She didn't often venture into the family business, leaving the running of it to her better-suited sisters, but today she desperately needed advice from one of those sisters. This newer store, now decorated for Christmas with cheery red ribbons and Christmas card displays, she was most unfamiliar with, since it was not the one she had grown up knowing.

Of all the five sisters, Yvette had the fewest memories of bonding with their father in the shop and had never been as enamored of books in the way Colette and Paulette were. Still, she was inordinately proud of the work her sisters had done to build the new store and to maintain the great success of the original shop as well. Paulette had even opened yet another Hamilton's bookstore in Dublin, which was proving just as successful as the two shops in London.

As Yvette now looked around at the bright, inviting

space, skillfully designed and well organized, she wished fleetingly that she had been a part of creating it. She really longed to have something of her own to be proud of. Maybe that was what was driving her to be a duchess.

"Good afternoon, Miss Hamilton." One of the well-trained female staff members, wearing Hamilton's signature dark green aprons, greeted Yvette with a warm smile. "Are you doing some Christmas shopping today?"

Yvette nodded, thinking of the gifts she had purchased earlier that afternoon that were now in the waiting carriage out front. "Yes, I have, and I thought I'd take a break and visit with my sister."

The girl smiled. "Oh, she's upstairs in her office now, going over the books. You can go right up."

"Thank you." Yvette made her way up the wooden staircase to Paulette's office on the second floor. She tapped on the door lightly before entering.

Paulette looked up from one of the thick ledgers on the mahogany desk in front of her. "Yvette! What a surprise to see you here! I thought you were shopping today."

"I was, but I'm all finished now. And I wished to talk to you about something. Am I interrupting you?"

"No, you're not interrupting at all. I could use a break from all these numbers. My head is spinning." Paulette sighed with a rueful smile and pointed to a pretty chintz-covered sofa. "Sit down there."

Yvette removed her coat and gloves and sat on the sofa, glancing around at her sister's elegant office. "How are you feeling?"

Paulette smiled, placing her hand protectively over her abdomen. "I'm tired, but I feel wonderful now. I haven't been sick in days, although Declan insists that I rest and barely lets me do anything."

Paulette was expecting another baby. She had confided in Yvette the night she returned from Ireland, explaining that it had been the reason for their delay in coming back to England to help with their mother. She had simply been too ill with morning sickness to travel.

"I'm sure Declan is right to insist that you rest. You work too much, Paulette."

Paulette rolled her eyes. "I'll pretend you didn't say that. So, what did you wish to talk to me about?"

Yvette hesitated. She was not sure how to phrase what she had to say.

"Is something the matter?" Paulette's expression grew concerned, as she closed the heavy ledger.

"Something is the matter, but I don't quite know what." Yvette looked helplessly at her sister.

"Is it about Lord Shelley?" Paulette asked. "You know we all liked him. Are things not going well with you two?"

"No, it's not that. Everything is going as well as I could have hoped for with him." Yvette paused, still not sure how to begin. Oh, what would Paulette think? "Well, yes, I suppose it has everything to do with William, but not in the way you think. Something else has happened and I am unsure how best to handle it."

"Well . . ." Paulette prompted, her blue eyes curious.

"It concerns Jeffrey." There she'd said it. Aloud. To her sister. Yvette almost wished she could take it back and flee the store. But she had to tell someone what was happening or she would go mad. Paulette was the only one she could confide in.

"Jeffrey?" Her sister looked confused. "What has Jeffrey to do with you?"

Yvette took a deep breath and squeezed her hands together. "He kissed me."

"What?"

"Twice now."

"What?"

"Jeffrey kissed me. Things have changed between us since everyone went away and I don't know what to do about it."

"What?"

"Paulette . . . I beg of you . . . please don't make me say it again."

Her sister was astonished. "Forgive me. I just can't quite believe it." Paulette shook her head in disbelief. "Jeffrey kissed you?"

"Yes," she said with a quick nod.

"Not merely a peck on the cheek, but a true passionate kiss?"

"Yes."

Suddenly Paulette rose from her desk and moved to sit beside Yvette on the sofa. Her face was alight with curiosity. "You must tell! How was it?"

"Kissing Jeffrey?"

"No, flying to the moon!" Paulette rolled her eyes in exasperation. "Of course, kissing Jeffrey! What was it like?"

Yvette placed her hand over her heart. "Oh, Paulette . . . it was breathtaking. I can't stop thinking about it."

Her sister let that bit of news sink in. "Oh, my."

"I know. You see my dilemma now?"

Paulette's eyes narrowed. "Why did he kiss you? How did it happen? I thought there might be something happening between the two of you the night Declan and I returned to Devon House."

"That was the night he first kissed me," Yvette confirmed, nodding her head. "But it's been more than just the kisses. He's been so sweet to me and since Mother fell ill, he has been with me every single night until you came back. We even slept together."

"What do you mean!?" Paulette's eyes widened with shock.

Yvette hurried to explain. "Just that we fell asleep together and spent the night on the sofa while we waited to see how Mother fared."

"Oh." Her sister looked somewhat relieved but perplexed. "But I still don't understand any of this."

"Neither do I. That's my dilemma and the reason I need to talk to you. I don't understand what's happening with Jeffrey and me."

Paulette grew pensive. "He must have feelings for you, because I cannot imagine Jeffrey would trifle with you, of all people. Has he said anything?"

"Nothing at all."

"So he simply kisses you and that's it?"

"Well, yes—no, it's just that. . . ." Yvette stammered. "We talk all the time. In truth he's been quite wonderful. The kissing only came about because I told him I felt nothing when William kissed me and we were sort of experimenting. At least I was."

"You were experimenting with Jeffrey?" There was shock and disbelief in her sister's voice.

"I wanted to know what it felt like to kiss him, that's all," she answered a bit defensively, if not entirely truthfully.

She wasn't just experimenting. She had wanted Jeffrey to kiss her and that's what frightened her more than anything. That night in Lady Deane's little parlor she had come dangerously close to doing things with Jeffrey she knew she shouldn't do.

They had both been swept away by their wild feelings. And they hadn't been able to discuss it since. Although Jeffrey had come to Devon House for supper last night after

Lord Shelley had left, her entire family had been there and there hadn't been a chance for them to talk privately. She had caught his eye a few times during dinner, but his expression had been unreadable.

No, Yvette had no idea what Jeffrey felt about her.

"I suppose no one can fault you for wanting to kiss Jeffrey. He has that way about him that makes women want to do things they shouldn't," Paulette murmured in understanding. "I'm just surprised that he wanted to kiss *you*."

"That's not a very nice thing to say."

Paulette laughed a little. "I'm sorry, that didn't come out how I meant it. Of course any man would *want* to kiss you, Yvette. It's the fact that Jeffrey is just so protective of the five of us that makes it hard to believe. You have no idea how angry he was with Declan for becoming involved with me at the beginning. Jeffrey is like our older brother. He would never do anything to hurt one of us."

"I know that. The problem is," Yvette began, "that when William Weatherly kisses me I feel absolutely nothing. And when Jeffrey kisses me . . . I forget to breathe, I can't think, I can't see. All I want to do is drown in his kisses and forget about everything else."

Paulette let out a long breath. "Oh, Yvette, that is a problem."

"What am I going to do?" Yvette wailed in desperation. "How can I feel nothing with the man I'm supposed to marry, yet feel everything with the man who is supposed to be like an older brother to me?"

"He's not really our brother," Paulette pointed out softly.

"Yes, I am very much aware of that fact, thank you."

Paulette gave her a long look. "Do you love Jeffrey?"

"Of course I love Jeffrey! I have loved him for years. He's always been so good to me. He's funny and charming and handsome. I adore him."

"That's not what I meant." Paulette shook her blond head. "I love Jeffrey too. We all do. But are you *in love* with him?"

"The thought of marrying Jeffrey is ridiculous. He'll never marry anyone. He has said so himself. Besides, I'm going to be the next Duchess of Lansdowne." Yvette suddenly wondered if she had said those words aloud to convince her sister or to convince herself.

"Yes." Paulette nodded slowly. "So you say. But do you think it's possible that Jeffrey has romantic feelings for you?"

"I don't know."

Yet she recalled the sweet words he had said to her that had tugged at her heart. *There's absolutely nothing wrong with you, Yvette. You're perfect. I want you to feel something only when I kiss you.* There was the tender way he cared for her. How he had held her in his arms and comforted her when she cried and slept beside her all that long, terrible night. *Could* Jeffrey have feelings for her? Lord knew the feelings she had for him were more than a little confusing and unsettling.

Was it possible he felt the same way about her? Confused and conflicted? Surely not! Jeffrey was not the type to lose his head over a silly girl like her. He was simply quite skilled at kissing women and had worked his brand of magic on her. He did not possess romantic feelings for her. The thought was utterly ridiculous.

"Are you certain?" Paulette asked once more.

"Yes," Yvette answered her sister with more conviction than she felt, but she spoke the truth. Jeffrey hadn't said he was in love with her. He hadn't declared any feelings for her in words. None whatsoever.

"Then if you are still intent on marrying Lord Shelley, there's only one thing for you to do, Yvette."

"What's that?"

"You must stop kissing Jeffrey."

Yvette grew quiet.

"You mustn't kiss him again," Paulette advised. "You must think only of Lord Shelley."

Her sister was quite right. It would solve all Yvette's problems if she simply steered clear of Jeffrey. She needed to cease playing these silly games with him and focus on her future husband. She was about to be engaged to the future Duke of Lansdowne and he deserved better from her than how she had behaved so far. Cringing at the thought of William's reaction if he found out she had been kissing Jeffrey, Yvette agreed with her sister's straightforward plan. "Yes. That would be best."

"At least we are all home now and there is no reason for you to be alone with Jeffrey again." Paulette pointed out this fact with her usual practicality.

"No, there's no reason at all." There was not a single reason for her to be alone with Jeffrey Eddington again. No reason, except that she wanted to be alone with him. At times it was all she could think about.

But kissing Jeffrey was wrong and it could not happen again. She was so close to achieving her dream of becoming a duchess. She couldn't squander it all on kisses with Jeffrey Eddington, no matter how wonderfully delicious and breathtaking those kisses were.

No, she would not be alone with Jeffrey again.

Suddenly a great sadness filled her heart at such a prospect.

25

Twelve Days of Christmas

Jeffrey Eddington smiled, outwardly calm, yet he continued to look at the large grandfather clock at the end of the spacious and comfortable library in Devon House. It was only three minutes past nine. It would be a few more hours before Yvette returned home and he didn't know how he would stand the wait.

"Shall we shoot some billiards?" Lucien Sinclair asked.

"No," Declan Reeves said, his Irish brogue quite strong. "I'd prefer to sit here a while before the girls come back and force us to play charades."

Quinton Roxbury laughed at that. "Then I suggest we have another drink."

"I agree with Quinton," Harrison Fleming said. "While you're up, will you get me one?"

"Would you like another as well, Jeffrey?" Quinton asked.

"Yes, please." Jeffrey glanced at the clock again. It was now four minutes past nine. He had joined the family for supper that evening, hoping to see Yvette. When he'd arrived, he'd discovered that she'd gone to the theater with Lord Shelley and her aunt and uncle and his heart sank, fearing that William Weatherly would propose to Yvette before he had time to intervene.

He had to do something soon, although just what that something was, he wasn't sure. And after his behavior with her the other night, he didn't know if Yvette was even speaking to him.

Jeffrey could barely keep his mouth closed throughout the meal as Yvette's sisters and brothers-in-law all raved about how wonderful Lord Shelley was and how lucky Yvette was to have made such a match. Everything had gone so well when they'd met him and all seemed to be going along swimmingly.

Jeffrey felt sick to his stomach.

He simply couldn't let Yvette marry the man. He had to alter their course. If she came home this evening, announcing that Shelley had proposed to her and she accepted, Jeffrey didn't know what he'd do.

Taking the glass filled with fine bourbon from Quinton, Jeffrey looked to the other men. "So, what did you all really think of Lord Shelley?"

The four Hamilton brothers-in-law exchanged covert glances.

Quinton spoke first. "I thought he was nice enough, if a little formal."

"There's nothing to fault the man for," Declan added softly. "He seems a good sort."

Harrison sighed. "I don't think I know him well enough yet to decide if I like him or not."

"As long as Yvette is happy with him, that is all that matters," Lucien said resolutely. "We must simply get accustomed to having him around."

Jeffrey was relieved to hear that his friends were not

overjoyed about Yvette's prospective husband. Yvette's prospective husband . . . Lord Shelley could have already proposed to her. He took a swig of his bourbon.

"Well, as the only single man left among us, Jeffrey, how is life treating you?" Harrison asked, a mischievous smile on his face.

Jeffrey glanced at the clock—seven minutes past nine. "What do you want to know, Harrison?" He took another sip of his drink.

Lucien laughed heartily. "Harrison wants to know who your current mistress is."

"Yes, it's difficult to keep up with your women, Jeffrey," Quinton pointed out, returning to his seat by the fire. "So tell us, who is your latest?"

"He's seeing the lovely actress Jennie Webb. He brought her back with him from Paris," Lucien stated. "Or at least that's who it was before I left for America."

"Oh, an actress again, is it?" Declan asked, with a raised brow.

Jeffrey looked blankly at the other four men. He had completely forgotten about Jennie Webb and how things had ended between them. He hadn't even entertained the idea of another woman since the night she left. All he could think about was Yvette. And those were thoughts he should not be having.

"Jeffrey?" Harrison called to get his attention.

"Oh, I ended things with her a while back." Jeffrey sipped his bourbon, feeling the burn in his throat.

"Well, who is it now?" Quinton asked.

With another quick glance at the clock, Jeffrey shook his head. "No one."

All four men echoed him in utter disbelief. "No one?"

Jeffrey shrugged. "Not at the moment, no."

"Oh, Jeffrey, you disappoint me," Harrison laughed.

Lucien gave him a curious look. "It's really so unlike you."

"I've been preoccupied."

"With what?" Quinton asked.

At that moment, the door to the library opened and Paulette and Juliette entered.

"Good evening, gentlemen." Juliette, looking lovely in a gown of amber, announced with devilish glee, "Colette's quite anxious for a game of charades when she comes back downstairs."

Declan Reeves groaned audibly. "Must you torture me?" he asked while the others laughed.

"Oh, it will be good for you," Paulette called to her husband with no mercy. "Try to have fun, Declan!"

Jeffrey watched the clock. It was twelve minutes past nine. He would go mad if Yvette didn't come home soon. Then again, he would most likely go mad when she did come home. He looked up as Paulette Hamilton Reeves, now an elegant countess, came to sit beside him on the large leather sofa. The others were engaged in a conversation on the far side of the room.

"Jeffrey," Paulette began softly, "I feel I haven't really had a chance to chat with you since I arrived in London. I wanted to thank you for taking such good care of our mother while we were away."

"It was my pleasure." He hadn't minded helping at all. It was the least he could do for this family who had given him a home to belong to. "I'm just happy that she's recovered so well. And so quickly."

"Yes, Dr. Carlisle is quite optimistic. He thinks she will be well enough to join us for Christmas dinner."

"That's what I'd heard from Juliette earlier." He grinned at her. "It will be nice to see Mrs. Hamilton at dinner again."

"And thank you for being so good to Yvette while we were gone. She spoke very highly of you."

"Did she?" He liked hearing that Yvette talked about him when he was not there. And apparently she said good things about him. He wasn't sure she would still say good things after the way he'd kissed her the other night.

"Yes." Paulette arched a knowing eyebrow at him. "*Very* highly."

Jeffrey blinked. Had Yvette told her sister that he had kissed her? Was *that* what Paulette, ever the little imp, was referring to?

"Oh, yes," Paulette continued with a secret smile. "She said you were quite skilled."

Christ! Yvette had definitely told Paulette. Jeffrey suddenly felt a bit embarrassed, knowing that Paulette knew he had kissed Yvette

"Listen, Paulette, I don't know exactly what your sister told you, but I never—"

"Jeffrey." Paulette placed her hand on his shoulder and gave him a meaningful look. "You must know by now that we sisters tell each other everything eventually. You've helped me when I needed you and I would do anything for you, which is why I'm giving you this advice now."

"What advice?"

Paulette looked at him with her pretty blue eyes, which were so like Yvette's, yet not the same at all. "If you want her, you had better hurry and do something, or you're going to lose her." She leaned over and kissed his cheek very sweetly.

Jeffrey grew silent. Never had he felt in such a quandary as this. "What exactly did she tell you, Paulette?"

"Enough for me to have an idea of what's going on between you two. I must say that I'm not sure what to make of it."

He sighed heavily in resignation. No secrets were kept

for long in this family, except the ones that Jeffrey kept for them. "Who else knows?"

"Just me. I think." She gave him a guilty smile. "You know how sisters are."

"What are you two whispering about over here?" Juliette Hamilton Fleming stood before them, an amused expression on her face and her hands on her hips.

Hastily, Paulette removed her hand from Jeffrey's shoulder and sat up straight. "Nothing."

"You never were a good liar, Paulette," Juliette pointed out.

Jeffrey glanced up at the first Hamilton sister he had ever met. He and Juliette had been through some memorable adventures together, but he wasn't at all sure how she would feel about his newfound affection for her youngest sister.

He gave Juliette a teasing glance. "Not every conversation needs to include you, Miss Master Plan."

Juliette laughed in delight. "You haven't called me that in years, Jeffrey!"

"Is that what you call her?" asked an inquisitive Paulette.

At that moment, Yvette walked into the library. Dressed in a sumptuous gown of deep amethyst and still wearing a black evening cape, she was a vision of loveliness. Elegant and sophisticated, her golden hair styled prettily atop her head, she stood in the doorway. Jeffrey had to stop himself from rushing to her.

"You're home early," Juliette remarked with a quizzical look.

Yvette remained still, an odd expression on her face. "Lord Shelley was suddenly taken ill and we had to leave the theater before we could see the show. Uncle Randall just brought me home."

"Oh, that's terrible. Will Lord Shelley be all right?" Paulette asked, her brows drawn together in concern.

"I hope so," Yvette murmured absently, her eyes on Jeffrey.

"You must be disappointed," Jeffrey said, staring back at her. Something flashed between them. Was it relief he saw in her blue eyes?

"Yes, very much so," she said to everyone, but her gaze remained on Jeffrey.

"Well, why don't you go change and join us, Yvette? We were just going to have a bit of dessert and then play charades," Paulette said. "Granger brought in a lovely tray of cakes. Colette and Lisette are upstairs with Mother and will be right down."

"Yes, that sounds fine." Yvette nodded a bit absently. "I shall be back in a few moments." She gave Jeffrey one last look before she turned and left the room.

"I guess old Shelley didn't get a chance to pop the question yet," Lucien said to the room once Yvette had left.

Harrison chuckled and shook his head in pity. "Poor fellow. I hope he's all right."

"I'm certain Lord Shelley will plan another occasion to ask for Yvette's hand soon enough," Juliette added.

Jeffrey exhaled deeply. He was more relieved than he'd realized. For the first time that night he relaxed a little. He still had time.

Slyly, Paulette whispered in Jeffrey's ear. "I think you just got granted a reprieve."

"I think you may be right." He smiled at Paulette, his little co-conspirator.

Declan Reeves came to stand at the end of the sofa near his wife. "What are you two whispering about over here?"

"That's what I wanted to know too," Juliette remarked with a laugh. "They are up to no good, Declan, but I can't figure out what it is. I think they are plotting something."

"Yes, that's what we're doing. Plotting. It's Christmastime. We're allowed to have secrets." Jeffrey smiled smugly at Juliette.

"Yes, it's almost Christmas and we're allowed to have some secrets," Paulette chimed in. With that, she rose to her feet and moved to the dessert table, leaving Jeffrey alone on the sofa.

Jeffrey sat there, not moving at all. His mind was on Yvette and the fact that she was still not engaged to Lord Shelley. Paulette was correct. He had to do something quickly or Yvette would end up married to another man. Quite frankly, he was terrified.

After kissing Yvette the other night, he'd feared he had gone too far with her. It was seeing her in Shelley's arms that had made him act so recklessly. He had wanted to teach her a lesson, let her know what experimenting with him would get her. The moment his lips had touched hers he had forgotten where they were, forgotten everything. He'd almost devoured her. He had been on the verge of sliding that low-cut gown from her shoulders, when somehow an alarm bell had rung in his addled brain, and he'd stopped himself before he'd done anything irresponsibly foolish with her.

What he had truly wanted to do was make love to her for days.

Yvette had been so willing, so eager for more, so hungry for his kisses, it had surprised him. Caught off guard by her amorous response, Jeffrey almost gave in to his own desires, her desires, their desires. She tasted like heaven and he had wanted more, much more from her. But he didn't dare.

But he now regretted treating her so brusquely.

Yvette was not one of his seductive and skilled ladies eager for a quick tumble with him. No. Not at all. Anything he did with Yvette could not be entered into lightly or carelessly. Nothing could be done in his usual fashion, for Yvette was a sweet innocent and deserved the greatest respect.

This was all new territory for him.

Jeffrey had never been in love before.

Part of him wanted to leave London. Return to Paris, find a bevy of beautiful women to console him, and forget any of this ever happened with Yvette. The smartest and best thing he could do for her was to leave her alone and let her marry the future Duke of Lansdowne. He certainly didn't have to look after her anymore. Lucien and Colette were back from America. She was no longer his responsibility.

It was not his duty to watch over Yvette Hamilton and he should let it go at that.

But it was as if he were paralyzed. He couldn't leave her and he couldn't stay away.

He was in love with her. Hell, he was thinking of marrying her. But even though he could tell she enjoyed kissing him, he knew Yvette Hamilton had no wish to marry him.

Jeffrey looked around at her family. His family. Colette and Lisette had since returned from upstairs, and now all the people he loved were in this room. What would they think? What would they say if he were to tell them he was in love with their sister and wanted to marry her? Would they be happy for him? Would they be shocked? Would they disapprove of him being with her?

If he married Yvette, these four women would truly become his sisters. Lucien would really be his brother, as would Harrison, Quinton, and Declan. All of that would just be an added bonus, of course. The real prize would be having Yvette by his side for the rest of his life.

If he could have her. That was the question. How could he persuade her to marry him instead of the future Duke of Lansdowne when she wanted so desperately to be a duchess?

It always came back to that.

He pondered this over and over, unable to sleep at night for thoughts of her.

"Don't you want some coffee, Jeffrey?" Colette offered him a cup and he took it, thinking he'd prefer a much stronger drink instead. He'd finished the bourbon.

"Thank you, Colette."

"Anything for you, Jeffrey." Colette paused in thought. "You're awfully quiet this evening."

"Just tired, I suppose," he remarked, and lifted his cup. "This ought to perk me up though."

"Good. I want you to play on my team for charades later." Colette winked at him and returned to the dessert table.

Jeffrey glanced up as Yvette returned to the library in much more casual attire. Wearing a plain dress of dark green wool, with a soft white shawl covering her shoulders, her blond curls hung down her back, tied loosely with a green ribbon, she was even more beautiful and much more tempting than she had been in her sophisticated gown moments before. Quietly, she took a cup of coffee and looked around for a place to sit.

Their eyes met again and Yvette walked slowly to him before taking the seat beside him on the sofa. Everyone was talking and laughing with each other, enjoying their dessert, paying no attention to the two of them. Jeffrey could think of nothing but how much he wanted to take Yvette in his arms and kiss her.

"Your evening didn't go as planned," he said. "I'm sorry."

She looked at him. "It's not your fault William took ill."

"No, but I'm sorry the evening didn't work out as you

thought it might." His gut tightened at the reference to her engagement.

She sighed lightly. "It will eventually, I'm sure."

He whispered so the others wouldn't hear. "So you told Paulette about us?"

Her eyes widened, and he could tell she was a bit annoyed that Paulette had mentioned it to him. "Well, yes, I did. . . ."

He kept his voice low. "We need to talk, Yvette. Privately."

"Do you really think that's wise?" she asked softly. "Especially after the last time we were alone together?"

"That's exactly why we need to talk."

Yvette hesitated. "I . . . I don't know if that's such a good idea."

"Jeffrey, you've been doing quite a lot of whispering with my little sisters this evening." Juliette was standing in front of them, her eyes watching them both curiously.

"I'm not a little girl anymore," Yvette said heatedly, as she rose from her seat.

"You'll always be my little sister," Juliette stated firmly, grinning.

"Come on, everyone! It's time!" Colette called to them with enthusiasm. "Let's choose teams for the game!"

Jeffrey, ignoring a questioning look from Juliette, watched Yvette cross the room away from him, and his heart pounded in his chest so loudly he thought everyone could hear it.

He had never been at such a loss in his life as to what to do about a woman.

26

Two Turtle Doves

Yvette held her breath and banged the knocker on the front door, which was bedecked with a large Christmas wreath. She had only been to Jeffrey Eddington's townhouse once before, years ago when she had needed his help with Paulette. She hadn't been at all nervous then. Now she was shaking like a leaf. Doubts about her last-minute decision to talk to him plagued her. She should forget this foolishness and go home before he saw her!

The bright red door opened and it was suddenly too late for her to run away.

The tall butler, Dennings, eyed her with surprise and ushered her in quickly. "Please wait here, Miss Hamilton. I'll let Lord Eddington know you're here. He wasn't expecting you and he has company at the moment."

Yvette's curiosity was piqued. Jeffrey had a visitor? She wondered who he was entertaining. Was it a woman? More than one? Her imagination was running away with her. And she wondered how he would react upon learning that she was waiting for him in his front hallway. Would he be happy to see her? Or would he be irritated by her unexpected and highly unusual appearance at his house?

Yvette caught her reflection in the large gilt-framed mirror above the marble table and smoothed a few stray curls that had escaped from her fur-trimmed hat. She looked quite fetching this afternoon in her new gown of dark blue and white stripes. It was too bad she had to cover it up with her heavy pelisse.

At the sound of footsteps she turned around. Jeffrey strode toward her, his expression worried. "Yvette! What are you doing here? Is anything wrong? Is everyone all right?"

Her heart raced at the sight of him. She was touched by his obvious concern. He must think she was only there because there was some sort of family emergency.

"Everyone is fine," she explained hurriedly. "Everything is fine. I only came because . . ."

He stopped inches from her. "What?"

Warmth spread across her cheeks. "You . . . I said . . . you needed . . . to talk . . . so, well, I . . ."

"You came here alone?" He looked completely and utterly stunned by her presence. "To talk with me about us?"

She nodded, feeling quite foolish.

He ran his hand through his hair, giving him a rakish, devil-may-care look. "Yvette, you said you didn't want to be alone with me again. I thought . . ."

Her heart sank. Suddenly, coming to see him seemed like a terrible idea. She had told her sisters that she was going shopping for the afternoon. No one even knew she was at Jeffrey's. After lying in bed all night, sleepless, she realized that Jeffrey was right. They needed, *she* needed, to understand what was going on between them. How on earth could she accept an offer of marriage from Lord Shelley while craving the kisses of Jeffrey Eddington? It wasn't right and she had to do something about it.

William becoming ill last night had been a blessing in disguise for it had bought her a little more time to figure out what was going on in her mind and in her heart. It was then she'd known that she had to come see Jeffrey. They would be able to talk this afternoon and lay to rest any doubts and worries she had about her choice of husband. Then she could accept Lord Shelley's proposal with a clear conscience when he asked her.

But now, the shocked look on Jeffrey's face made her regret her impulsive decision to come to his house. She pressed her hands together tightly. "I'm so sorry. This was a mistake."

"No, no, it's not," he protested. "Yvette, I would love to talk with you. In fact I'm very pleased that you came to see me." Jeffrey gave her one of his smiles and took her gloved hands in his, squeezing lightly.

At his touch, Yvette began to relax, not realizing just how tense she'd been. Jeffrey looked so incredibly handsome and his warm smile made her heart race.

He continued to explain. "It's just that it's not the best time for me to talk with you right now. I have company. Guests who surprised me this afternoon as well, and I'm not sure how long they will be here."

"Forgive me," she began. He had visitors and it wouldn't do to have her reputation tarnished by being seen here. She should slip out right away. "I should have sent word to you first, Jeffrey. I apologize for interrupting. It's quite all right. We can talk tomorrow perhaps. I shall simply leave—"

"You shall do no such thing, Miss Hamilton!" a booming voice rang out.

Yvette startled at the sound, then smiled when she saw the Duke of Rathmore. Jeffrey's father was a larger, grayer, and more mature version of Jeffrey, but just as handsome and charming. Yvette adored the duke, for he always treated her most gallantly.

"Your Grace!" she cried in delight. "It's wonderful to see you!"

Releasing her hands, Jeffrey stepped back and gave a resigned sigh. He muttered low for Yvette's ears. "Yes, my father's here."

The duke engulfed Yvette in a bear hug. "It's delightful seeing you, Miss Hamilton. Always a pleasure! And look at you, getting prettier all the time!"

"Oh, thank you, Your Grace!"

"Well, this is a great surprise," the duke said with a laugh. "You must come in and sit with us, my dear. Take the afternoon chill off you and warm up by the fire. There's someone very special I would love for you to meet."

Yvette looked toward Jeffrey for guidance, even as his father was leading her into the drawing room.

With an expression of disbelief, Jeffrey shrugged helplessly in surrender, following behind. "I was trying to spare you, Yvette."

The three of them entered Jeffrey's large drawing room and Yvette was surprised to see a woman seated in an armchair by the fire. Dressed elegantly, she was very beautiful and vaguely familiar, with dark hair that slightly grayed at the temples. As soon as she smiled, Yvette knew exactly who she was, for the resemblance was startling. She had the same amazing smile as Jeffrey.

Jeffrey made the introductions. "Mother, may I present Miss Yvette Hamilton? Yvette, this is my mother, Miss Janet Rutherford."

Yvette shook her hand eagerly. "It's a pleasure to finally meet you, Miss Rutherford. Jeffrey has told me so much about you."

Yvette was so excited to be meeting Jeffrey's mother that she couldn't stop smiling. And seeing both his parents together! She had never imagined that!

Miss Rutherford looked quite pleased. "And I've heard so much about you, Miss Hamilton. Jeffrey talks about you and your family all the time. Please sit and join us, won't you?"

"Thank you." With a nervous glance at Jeffrey, who seemed completely dazed, Yvette removed her coat, handed it to Dennings, and took a seat in an overstuffed armchair. "I didn't mean to intrude on your visit."

The Duke of Rathmore laughed jovially. "Oh, you're not intruding, my dear. Jeffrey wasn't expecting us today either. We surprised him this afternoon by our arrival."

Yvette glanced again at Jeffrey, who seemed not at all himself.

"Oh, they surprised me all right," Jeffrey said sardonically, folding his arms across his chest. "Today must be my lucky day for surprises."

"Well, it's a wonderful surprise to see you here, Miss Hamilton," Janet Rutherford said, ignoring her son's remark. "You're even prettier than I've been told."

"I told you she was beautiful, didn't I?" the duke asked, quite gleeful in his manner. "And there's four more of them! Each one a beauty."

"That's very kind of you to say about my sisters and me," Yvette murmured to the duke before turning her attention to Jeffrey's mother. She was quite curious about this woman. "Are you in town long, Miss Rutherford? Jeffrey mentioned that you live outside London."

Janet Rutherford hesitated before answering. "Actually, I've been in town all week."

"And she'll be staying permanently," Maxwell Eddington added with an emphatic nod. He looked happy enough to burst, his face beaming. As he moved to stand beside Jeffrey's mother, he took her hand in his. "Janet has agreed to marry me. We were just telling Jeffrey the good news."

Yvette was speechless. She stared at them and then dared a glance at Jeffrey.

"Yes, it seems my parents are getting married." Jeffrey smiled in spite of himself.

Astonished at the unexpected news, Yvette cried, "Oh, how wonderful! Congratulations to you both!"

"Now that Miss Hamilton is here, we must have a proper celebration! A little party! Come, Jeffrey, let's go to your wine cellar and choose the best bottle of champagne you've got!" Maxwell Eddington moved toward his son, prompting him to follow.

"Isn't it a little early in the day for champagne?" Jeffrey asked.

"Nonsense!" Maxwell winked at them. "It's never too early for champagne."

Jeffrey looked helplessly at Yvette. "You'll stay?"

"Of course." She grinned at him, enjoying that Jeffrey wasn't in control of the situation for once. "I wouldn't miss it for the world."

"We'll be right back," he called over his shoulder.

The two men exited the room and Yvette was left alone with Jeffrey's mother. Even though no one could dispute that Jeffrey was Maxwell Eddington's son, for they were spitting images of each other, something about Janet Rutherford's expression reminded Yvette even more of Jeffrey than his father did.

"So, while the boys are seeking some champagne, we can have a nice little chat alone, Miss Hamilton," Janet Rutherford said lightly.

"Yes, I'd enjoy that," Yvette responded with enthusiasm, instantly liking the woman. Her earnest and friendly manner made Yvette feel comfortable. Yvette had a dozen questions at least that she wanted to ask about Jeffrey's childhood and what he was like as a little boy. But first things first. "This is such exciting news about your marriage to the duke. You must be very happy."

"I am. Quite happy." The woman sighed. "It's been a long time coming for Maxwell and me and it's rather late to right such an old wrong. Better late than never, I suppose." She paused and gave Yvette a knowing look. "I'm sure you've heard the whole story by now."

Yvette nodded her head in sympathy. "Well, one does hear things, but Jeffrey doesn't talk very much about himself. I only know that he cares deeply for you and his father. I'm sure your marriage will make him very happy."

"If the shock of it doesn't kill him first." She laughed, a winsome smile on her elegant face. "But the reasons that kept his father and I apart all those years ago no longer exist or no longer matter so much at our age. Oh, some people will still be outraged by our decision, of course, and our marrying will revive the old scandal, no doubt. But Maxwell is determined to wed me at long last. Once that man makes up his mind, it's difficult to sway him, and at our age we don't have time to waste."

"Well, I think it's lovely," Yvette said. "And very romantic."

"It wasn't romantic at the time, I can assure you, my dear," Janet said with a regretful sigh. "There was much damage done to innocent people. But it's been over thirty years now and Maxwell is still the greatest love of my life . . . and I am his. We're simply a couple of old fools."

"Oh, I don't think so at all!" Yvette thought it was sweet that they were finally able to marry now that the duke's wife had passed away. There was something oddly poetic about it. "You are Jeffrey's parents and it's right that you should be married."

"Yes, I'm happy for Jeffrey's sake, although he is more surprised than I expected him to be. I'm afraid our situation has been much harder on Jeffrey than on anyone else even though he'd never admit it."

"Yes, I've thought that as well," Yvette agreed with her. She believed the shame of illegitimacy had hurt Jeffrey in ways she couldn't even begin to imagine. "Please tell me, Miss Rutherford, what was he like as a little boy?"

"Oh, he was simply adorable!" Janet Rutherford's face lit up while talking about her son. "A handsome little scamp he was, but so loving and dear too. Everyone loved him. It was impossible to ever scold him when he misbehaved, because he inherited all of his father's charm and could smile his way out of anything."

Yvette gave a little laugh. "That's exactly how I imagined him to be!"

"Yes, he was quite special. It's a miracle he turned out as fine as he did with how terribly we spoiled him as a child. But in spite of all the heartache and dreadful scandal surrounding his birth, I never regretted having him for one second. He's been the joy of my life." Janet paused and gave her a meaningful look. "And I wish to thank you and your sisters."

"Thank us?" Yvette was confused. "Whatever for?"

"Yes, I thank you. For you and your sisters have given Jeffrey a sense of family that his father and I were never able to give him. He adores all of you girls. He's very protective of you."

Touched by her words, Yvette had never quite realized how much her family meant to Jeffrey before. "Well, he is wonderful and we all adore him. We treat him like he is our brother."

Janet looked pensive. "Jeffrey is a very sensitive and thoughtful man, in spite of his rather careless demeanor."

"Yes, I think I've learned that about him." Yvette nodded in agreement. "He never lets on that things bother him, but I believe he feels things quite deeply."

"Yes, he does," Janet Rutherford said pointedly, "and Jeffrey is very much in love with you, my dear."

Yvette almost fell out of her chair. "I beg your pardon?"

His mother looked apologetic and asked softly, "Oh, you had no idea, did you? I can tell by your expression."

Rendered speechless, Yvette tried to catch her breath. Jeffrey? In love with her? Well, they kept kissing each other lately and it had been most passionate between them. They had become very intimate during the last weeks, certainly. But in love? With her? Her head spun and she gripped the arms of the chair for support.

"I see the surprise on your face, my dear, but yes, I believe I'm certain of this. He talks about you all the time," Janet explained. "And I saw it quite clearly on his face when you arrived just now. It's most obvious."

"No, he can't be." Yvette's stomach somersaulted. It was impossible and she refused to believe it. Jeffrey could not be in love with someone like her. She was not at all like the sort of woman he romanced.

"Yes, he is." Janet Rutherford gazed at her in sympathy. "He's never been in love before and I don't think he knows what to do about it. You've won his heart and you must treat him gently."

In shock, Yvette stared at Jeffrey's mother, still uncomprehending what she was saying to her. *Won his heart? Treat him gently?*

"From what I gather, my dear, you are about to be engaged to someone else?"

Yvette nodded mutely in response.

"Jeffrey is not happy about that at all, and he thinks you are making a dreadful mistake." His mother gave her a knowing look. "He says this only because he's in love with you."

With her heart racing, Yvette finally opened her mouth. She closed it. Then she opened it again. "Oh, Miss Rutherford, do you think it is possible that—"

Their intimate conversation abruptly ended as Jeffrey and the duke returned to the parlor. Dennings, the butler, trailed behind them, carrying a silver tray with four crystal champagne flutes.

The duke held up a green bottle in triumph. "I knew my son would have the finest champagne in town!"

They popped the cork and set to filling the flutes with the sparkling wine. Breathless, Yvette took a glass when it was handed to her, still stunned by Janet Rutherford's revelation. She rose to her feet when the others stood to make a toast to Jeffrey's parents and lifted her glass as if in a trance. His mother said Jeffrey was in love with her. Was he? Her heart raced wildly in her chest.

"To my mother and father." Jeffrey made the toast. Then he shook his head in disbelief. "After all these years."

"Hear, hear!" the Duke of Rathmore called as they clinked their glasses together. "Better late than never."

Yvette sipped the cool champagne and met Jeffrey's questioning gaze over the rim of the glass. She gave him a tentative smile and stared at him in wonder. Could his mother be right? Was Jeffrey Eddington in love with her? Her head spun.

"And to my beautiful bride who changed all my thoughts about marriage," the duke added, kissing Janet Rutherford on the cheek. Janet blushed, her expression joyful.

"I still can't believe this is happening," Jeffrey muttered with a wry smile.

In an attempt to rejoin the conversation, Yvette managed

to ask, "So when is the wedding to take place?" Yet her voice sounded hollow and far away.

"We are going to marry the day after tomorrow. Then I shall announce our marriage at my annual Christmas ball this Friday." Maxwell laughed in gleeful delight. "It will cause quite the stir, don't you think?"

"Yes, it will, Father. Quite a stir." Jeffrey's eyes flickered in droll amusement.

"It will be a small and very private ceremony in the chapel at Eddington Grove in Berkshire, with just Jeffrey, Maxwell, and me." Janet Rutherford suddenly looked inspired, asking, "Oh, Miss Hamilton, will you please join us? I'm sure Jeffrey would love for you to be there."

Yvette almost choked on her champagne. She dared a glance at Jeffrey. His handsome face was frozen, his expression unreadable.

"Oh, Mother, I'm sure Yvette doesn't wish to travel all the way out there at this time of the year." Jeffrey sounded a bit panic-stricken. "Besides, I'm certain she has other plans."

The three of them turned their eyes to Yvette, waiting for her response.

Without even questioning why, Yvette instantly knew she wanted to be there with Jeffrey. Oh, there would no doubt be questions from Lucien and Colette that she did not wish to answer before she would be given permission for such an excursion, but she wanted to go anyway. A trip to Berkshire would mean a long journey out to the country with Jeffrey. They would surely have an opportunity to be alone together there for they would be away one night at least. Perhaps even two. But it was reckless of her to even consider such an invitation.

Yvette took a deep breath. "I would be honored and delighted to attend your wedding, Your Grace."

Jeffrey's jaw dropped.

"There! See? She does want to come." The Duke of Rathmore kissed Yvette's cheek. "I knew you were a smart girl as well as beautiful. It's all settled then. I will make the necessary arrangements with Lucien Sinclair for you, Miss Hamilton. We shall leave together first thing tomorrow morning."

Taking another sip of champagne, Yvette glanced nervously at Jeffrey. She suddenly had a feeling that she had just made an irrevocable decision.

27

A Winter Wonderland

A light snow began to fall as the carriage transporting Jeffrey Eddington, Yvette Hamilton, Janet Rutherford, and the Duke of Rathmore arrived at Eddington Grove. It was one of the smaller of Rathmore's many properties, on a lush, wooded estate in Berkshire. They had left early from London that morning and reached the picturesque little house just at dusk.

"And here we are!" Maxwell Eddington exclaimed. "My favorite home."

A second carriage that also conveyed their valets and ladies' maids, pulled up behind them. As their luggage was being unloaded and taken inside, Jeffrey escorted Yvette into the charming stone cottage that was covered in green ivy. He had spent a great deal of time at Eddington Grove when he was a child and he had always preferred this place to the very grand but rather cold Rathmore Castle.

"Oh, it's enchanting!" Yvette cried in delight at the cozy atmosphere and the warm and inviting rooms.

"Isn't it perfect?" Janet Rutherford asked in agreement.

"Maxwell and I spent some wonderful times together in this little house so many years ago. That's why we wanted to be married here."

Jeffrey still could not believe that his parents were getting married the next morning. Nor could he believe that he had Yvette Hamilton there to share the momentous event with him. Why she had even agreed to come along with them was still a mystery. But then nothing had made sense since his parents had showed up together at his townhouse yesterday with their astonishing announcement about marrying, followed by Yvette's surprise visit.

There had been a bit of explaining to do and some hasty arrangements to be made before Colette and Lucien gave their consent for Yvette to accompany them to Eddington Grove. But Jeffrey's father was quite persuasive when he wanted to be, and when he explained how much he wanted Yvette to be there, Lucien and Colette could hardly refuse, although they did seem a little bewildered by it all. Jeffrey had ignored the questioning looks Lucien cast in his direction and the oddly satisfied expression on Colette's face as Yvette and her lady's maid were bundled into the Rathmore carriages that morning.

During the journey there, Jeffrey could think only of how happy he was to have Yvette with him.

And Jeffrey found himself alone with Yvette much sooner than he had expected to. The four of them had shared a lovely supper, talking easily and laughing together. Then, after dessert, his parents excused themselves and retired for the evening, leaving Yvette and Jeffrey together in the small but comfortable study by themselves. They sat beside each other on the plush velvet sofa. A fire blazed in the charming stone hearth while the snow fell outside the pretty mullioned windows.

"So here we are at last. Do you wish to tell me now why you came to see me yesterday?" Jeffrey asked finally.

"Yes . . ." Yvette gave him a shy glance. "I changed my mind and thought you were right and that perhaps we should talk about that night."

"I was afraid you would never want to talk to me again after that, so I was overjoyed to see you yesterday."

"Were you?" she asked, her blue eyes intent on him.

"Of course. I was a little distracted by my mother and father, but I was so happy you came to see me and even more pleased that you agreed to come along on this little trip with us today."

"As I said yesterday, I wouldn't have missed it for anything. Besides, I had the feeling that you needed me here."

"I do need you here." He nodded, surprised he had admitted this to her. He needed her there for more reasons than he could say.

The circumstances that defined his whole life were changing and he wasn't sure how to handle it. His mother and father's sudden decision to marry after all this time transformed everything, yet nothing. Because of their actions in the past, he had been branded, living his life as an outsider, never truly belonging anywhere. And now, they were altering those circumstances and his world was upside down. He felt a little lost. Having Yvette with him at his parents' wedding in the morning meant more to him than she could possibly know.

"Jeffrey, I can only imagine how strange all this must be for you." Yvette's voice was quiet. "I thought you needed a friend to be with you."

He looked into her pretty blue eyes and his heart flipped over in his chest. Perhaps she knew him better than he realized. "Thank you, Yvette."

"You're most welcome. It's the least I could do after you've been so helpful to my mother and me."

He arched a brow at her words. "Is that the only reason you're here with me, Yvette?" He reached out and took her hand in his. Gently he squeezed her fingers.

"No." She squeezed his hand back.

He didn't release her hand and they sat in silence for a moment as the fire blazed warmly and the snow swirled outside the windows. "It's almost like we're back in the sitting room at Devon House."

She smiled at the memory and still held on to his hand. "Yes, it is. Those were lovely nights we spent together."

He lifted her hand to his lips and kissed her fingers very lightly. Her slight intake of breath caused his heart to race. "Yes, and here we are alone together again. After the last time I kissed you, I'm surprised you want to be anywhere near me, Yvette."

"But that's the other reason I came here with you." Her voice trembled.

"So you could be alone with me?" His eyes locked with hers.

"Yes."

The longing and desire he saw burning in her eyes almost undid him. Slowly, he closed his eyes and then re-opened them. "Yvette, you cannot marry Lord Shelley."

Yvette grew very quiet and the silence echoed through the room. Jeffrey held his breath and waited, pressing her hand to his lips. The fire crackled and the snow continued to fall silently outside.

After what felt like an eternity, she finally whispered, "I know I can't marry him. I'm not going to accept his proposal."

"You're not?" His heart skipped a beat and relief flooded

through him. Yvette was not going to marry Lord Shelley. It was almost too good to be true.

Her expression was full of sorrow. "No. I can't marry William. I've really tried, but I don't love him enough."

"I've known that all along."

"You have, haven't you?" She looked at him intently.

"Yes." He continued kissing her fingers, quite slowly, quite gently.

"How did you know?" she murmured, staring at his mouth.

"I just know these things." He shrugged lightly. "The most telling was that you felt nothing when he kissed you. You can't be in love with a man who leaves you feeling nothing."

"But I feel something when you kiss me."

He almost couldn't breathe. "What do you feel when I kiss you?"

Her cheeks reddened. Her voice was so soft he could barely hear her confession. "I feel hot and shivery . . . and I never want you to stop."

Never in his life had a woman's words had such an effect on him. Her sweet and honest answer left him speechless. He turned her hand over and placed a kiss on her palm.

"Did you feel something when you kissed me, Jeffrey?" Yvette asked softly.

"Oh, yes." He looked in her eyes. "Like nothing I've *ever* felt with any other woman."

She was in his arms in an instant and he was kissing her mouth. He didn't know who had moved forward first, him or her, but it didn't matter. His lips met hers, eager and hungry. They kissed and kissed, their lips pressed together, their tongues in each other's mouths. He was lost in the utter sweetness of her. He could drown in her. He *was* drowning in her.

An intense heat blossomed between them, stirring them.

Jeffrey forgot to breathe. He had Yvette in his arms again, where she belonged. And she wanted him.

His fingers slid into her silky hair, loosening the pins and setting her golden curls free to spill around her shoulders. The scent of gardenias enveloped him and he pulled her tighter to his chest. She sighed and clung to him. Losing himself in the feel of her body, his hands grew bolder in their caresses, moving over the flare of her hips and cupping her breasts over the fabric of her pretty green gown. She arched her back and leaned into him as he touched her. And still they kissed.

He stroked her back, slowly unfastening the hooks down the back of her high-necked dress, wishing for the first time that she were wearing that infernal low cut gown, so he would have easier access to her breasts. He was ready to tear the many layers of clothing to shreds to get them off her. Instead he ran his hands over her bare shoulders, nuzzling kisses against her smooth neck, her soft throat.

She tugged at his jacket sleeves and he removed it, flinging the jacket to the floor. Next, she undid his neck cloth and the top buttons of his shirt. She pressed her mouth to his bare neck, kissing the base of his throat. He groaned with the pleasure of it. His mouth returned to her mouth for more of the kisses that he craved.

Gently, he eased her back onto the sofa, until he was lying on top of her, the length of her curvaceous little body beneath his. One hand ran the length of her leg, slowly pushing the skirt of her gown up as he went.

He wanted her. All of her. And he was absolutely terrified. He could take her now and she would willingly let him. He had never been more certain of anything in his life. Yvette Hamilton wanted him as much as he wanted her. And he wanted her desperately. Wanted to remove every inch of her clothing and make love to her slowly, over and over, for days and days on end.

But this wasn't just any woman. This was Yvette Hamilton.

He groaned as he broke off their kiss. He cupped her face with one hand.

She cried out in protest.

He soothed her, whispering. "We can't do this, Yvette. Not here. Not now. When it happens, I want you in my bed, all night. Not like this."

Her breath was shallow and rapid, her arms still wrapped around his neck. "But Jeffrey, I . . ."

"No." He shook his head, wondering if he had lost his mind. He'd never been this close to making love to a woman and stopped.

"Why not?" Her question was filled with confusion and disappointment.

"Because I want to marry you first."

He waited, holding his breath. She didn't move. She didn't say a word. When he felt her tears on his hand, saw them glistening on her cheeks, he thought he would die.

There, in the flickering firelight, he should have confessed his love to her, but he couldn't. He simply could not bring himself to say the words aloud. "Yvette, I want you to marry me."

"Oh, Jeffrey," she sobbed.

He pressed his forehead against hers, kissing her tears. "Say you will marry me."

Jeffrey didn't care what anyone else thought. He didn't care that he was twelve years older than she was. Or that he'd once thought of her as his younger sister. Because she wasn't a little girl anymore. She was a beautiful, intelligent woman who had become his closest friend. He enjoyed being with her, from simply sitting and talking together all night, to flirting and dancing at a ball, to dealing with the unpredictability of both their families. He loved this woman and he wanted her with him for always. He wasn't half good enough for her, but he wanted her anyway. If she didn't say yes, he wouldn't be able to go on.

The silence between them grew.

"Yvette," he whispered her name like a plea.

Her hand reached around to the back of his head, her fingers splaying through his hair. Her gentle touch made him tremble. She leaned up and kissed his mouth, and he could taste her tears. The sweetness of her made him want to cry.

"Yes."

"Yes?" Had he heard her correctly? Had she just agreed to marry him?

She kissed him again. "Yes, Jeffrey, I'll marry you."

He sat up in disbelief. "You will?"

She sat up too, wiping at her tears with her hands and nodding her head. "Yes."

Jeffrey stared at her. She'd said yes. Yvette Hamilton had agreed to be his wife. Filled with relief, he pulled her into his arms and she rested her head against his chest. "What about becoming a duchess?" He waited with bated breath for her answer.

"I'd rather be with you."

His heart flipped over in his chest and he squeezed her tighter to him. "You have no idea how happy that makes me."

She looked up at him, her eyes still wet with tears, her long hair tousled around her. "It's strange, isn't it?"

"What?"

"That of all the people in the world, I'm ending up with you. Someone I feel I've known my whole life."

He smiled at her words. "Yes, here we were under each other's noses the whole time. I suppose we were just waiting until you grew up." He kissed her again, the sweetness of her mouth almost undoing him. "What do you think your sisters will have to say about us?"

Her expression was thoughtful. "I don't know exactly what they will think, but it's safe to assume they will be surprised. Except maybe for Paulette. They've always thought of you as a brother, and now you will be their brother. Mother already loves you so I can't imagine that she'd object."

He figured her mother and sisters would be fine with them being together, but Lucien Sinclair had given Jeffrey more than a questioning look when he came by Devon House that morning to gather Yvette and her things for their trip to Berkshire. In fact, he'd looked a little suspicious. "Lucien might hit me again."

Yvette laughed and kissed his cheek. "No, he won't. But if he does, you just go right ahead and hit him back this time."

"Thank you for your permission." He smiled at her, loving that they could tease each other.

"What will your parents say?" she asked.

"They will be wildly happy. I think my mother asked you here with this purpose in mind and my father has wanted me to marry one of you Hamilton girls for years."

"I'm so glad." Yvette sighed and snuggled into him.

He kissed her again and she kissed him back. His tongue slid into her mouth and she leaned back into the pillows once more, drawing him down on top of her. God, but he wanted to melt into her, kiss every inch of her. The desire to make love to her then and there on the velvet sofa was too tempting.

"Come, Yvette. Let's get you upstairs to bed," he whispered thickly. With great reluctance he withdrew his arms from around her warm body and slowly stood up. He smiled ruefully and held his hand out to help her to her feet.

But she refused and stared at him with a mutinous expression. "Jeffrey."

Shaking his head, he reached out and took her hand to help her off the sofa. Then he turned her around and slowly began to refasten the back of her dress.

"Your bedroom is right next to mine," she whispered suggestively to him. "No one would have to know but us, Jeffrey."

His hands froze on her back. He'd like nothing more than to scoop her up in his arms and carry her to his warm bed for the night. "You're staying in your room and I'm staying in mine." He placed a kiss on the back of her neck and continued fastening her dress.

"Who knew you were such a gentleman?" she muttered ruefully. "Honestly, Jeffrey, I'm beginning to wonder about all I've heard of your powers of seduction."

Jeffrey spun her around and kissed her mouth hard, leaving her breathless. He then cupped her face in his hands. "I can have any woman I want. And I have had more than my share. But you are the only woman I want now, Yvette."

She blinked at him in surprise.

"I can't make you a duchess, but I can certainly treat you like one. We're waiting until we're married."

"Oh, Jeffrey . . ." Her eyes welled up with tears again.

He kissed her cheek softly and took her small hand in his. "Come now. Let's go up to your room."

She followed him obediently, out of the warm study and up the stone staircase of the cozy house. He stopped in front of the door to her bedroom. Yvette looked at him with longing.

He gave her one of his most seductive smiles. "I promise I will make it up to you."

"None of my sisters waited until they were married, you know," she said rather petulantly.

"Unfortunately, I do know."

"You do?" she asked, her face incredulous.

"Yes. But you are not your sisters. You're different and you mean more to me than you know." He grinned at her before kissing her senseless once more and sending her to bed without him.

28

My True Love Gave to Me

Yvette stood beside Jeffrey in the little stone chapel at Eddington Grove the next morning, while Maxwell Eddington, the Duke of Rathmore, married Janet Rutherford, the mother of his only child, thirty-three years after the fact.

As the chaplain spoke the ceremonial words, Yvette felt Jeffrey slip his hand into hers. At his touch, warmth flooded through her. She glanced at him next to her, so handsome and sweet. Last night she had told him that she would be his wife.

She was really going to marry Lord Jeffrey Eddington! She bit her lip to keep from giggling nervously at the thought of it. It was so preposterous, yet so perfectly right at the same time. *Jeffrey.* Jeffrey, of all people! Jeffrey must be in love with her to want to marry her.

Over the last three months, her feelings for him had changed so gradually, so slowly that she had not quite realized them. It wasn't until she'd felt utter relief that William Weatherly had been taken ill and could not propose to her that she'd known something was wrong. Whenever she was with William she found herself comparing him to Jeffrey and longing to be in Jeffrey's company instead. She simply could not marry Lord Shelley once she'd realized her feelings were all for Jeffrey.

Last night it had become quite clear to her that she was in love with Jeffrey. Perhaps she had been in love with him for weeks but had been too blind to see it? In either case she was deliriously happy now. She loved Jeffrey!

That morning they had told his parents of their plans to marry and she'd thought the Duke of Rathmore was going to burst with happiness at their news.

"Well, that just makes this day even more special!" He'd kissed Yvette soundly and pinched her cheek. "I'm delighted to have you as a daughter and I'm relieved my son wised up and grabbed one of you Hamilton girls. I was afraid he'd wait too long and lose you to some other fellow!"

"I'm grateful that she accepted me," Jeffrey said in a somewhat serious tone.

"Oh, my dear, I'm so happy for both of you!" His mother hugged her tightly and whispered only for Yvette to hear, "I told you he was in love with you, didn't I?"

Yvette smiled at her, too emotional to say more.

"Well, we shall have another wonderful announcement at our Christmas ball this Friday!" Maxwell exclaimed. "Both Eddington bachelors finally getting married!"

Now they stood quietly in the little chapel, as the chaplain declared Maxwell Eddington and Janet Rutherford to be man and wife. Becoming almost teary, Yvette listened to the familiar words, thinking she would be saying them to Jeffrey soon.

After their heartfelt congratulations and a hasty breakfast, Jeffrey and Yvette left Eddington Grove to begin their journey to reach London by nightfall, leaving the new Duchess and Duke of Rathmore to honeymoon alone. The second carriage followed behind transporting Jeffrey's valet and Yvette's lady's maid.

With Jeffrey's strong arms around her to keep her warm, Yvette sat beside him in their carriage. She felt so happy, just being with him, resting her head on his shoulder as the carriage swayed along the road to London. Never had she known such complete and utter happiness.

"It was a lovely ceremony," she said. "Quite romantic."

"I'm happy for them, that it worked out in the end," he said quietly. "But I don't think I would call any of it romantic."

She frowned. "Why not?"

"Their affair caused a great deal of pain to a lot of people and ruined his marriage."

"Yes, but that is all in the past now," Yvette reasoned.

Jeffrey's expression was somber. "Yes, it's all in the past now, I suppose."

Yvette lifted her head from his shoulder and stared at him, noting the pained look on his handsome face. She touched his cheek gently. "But if it were not for their affair, you wouldn't be here and I should be devastated without you."

He smiled at her words and her heart melted.

"You were the good that came out of bad circumstances," she whispered, placing a kiss on his cheek. "You made it all worthwhile, Jeffrey."

He cupped her face in his hands and looked deep into her eyes. "I need you to know that I am not like my father. I will never go outside of our marriage, Yvette. You are the only woman for me. In spite of my reputation with women, I swear to you, I will always be faithful to you."

Overwhelmed by the intensity of his feelings, she whispered, "I know you will."

They kissed then, and that slow, now-familiar heat

flamed between them once more. She slipped her tongue into his mouth, hungry for more. She loved kissing Jeffrey, loved being held by him. Loved him. Loved everything about him. He pulled her across his lap and kissed her deeply. Yvette sunk into him and sighed with pleasure.

Wrapping her arms around his neck, she wished they weren't wearing their heavy coats and scarves. "Let's take these off," she whispered seductively in his ear.

In an instant, she was placed back on her own side of the seat.

"Are you trying to kill me, Yvette?" he demanded with a strained laugh.

"No. Not at all. I just want to be with you." She wanted him so desperately and didn't know how he could be so controlled. She'd barely slept the night before because she was too filled with excitement. She had been giddy with desire for him and stunned that he wanted to wait until they were married. She had been willing to do anything with him on the sofa last night, surprising herself with her own wantonness.

He shook his head firmly. "I told you. Not until we're married. No illicit encounters. No illegitimate children. I don't want to start off that way with you, no matter how much I want you." He smiled at her wolfishly. "And believe me, I want you."

Yvette stared at him, suddenly understanding why he wanted to wait. "Oh, Jeffrey." She placed a kiss on his lips. "Then we better marry right away."

Giving her a pointed look, he said, "I believe you ought to have a little chat with Lord Shelley first."

Her stomach lurched at the thought. That was a task she was not looking forward to, but it must certainly be done. William was going to be terribly disappointed in her. "Yes. As soon as I can, I shall tell him. Tomorrow."

"Good." He leaned over and kissed her deeply.

"Oh, how soon can we marry?" she asked breathlessly.

He eyed her with all seriousness. "I thought you would wish to have a big, lavish wedding, Yvette, with a beautiful gown and anyone who is anybody in London in attendance. The social event of the Season?"

"Is that what you want?" she asked softly.

"I want whatever will make you happy."

Yvette grew quiet. There had been a time when all of that was quite important to her. The big society wedding had been her dream for years and years. To be a stylish and important duchess, to be admired and even envied by everyone, to wear the finest clothes, to host the most sought-out parties, and to have the best of everything had been what she thought would make her the happiest. But somehow when she was with Jeffrey, none of those things mattered at all anymore. When she was in his arms, she had everything.

"I just want you, Jeffrey. Being with you makes me happy."

Relief filled his eyes and the smile he gave her made her heart flutter. "Then I'll obtain a special license tomorrow and we can get married whenever you want."

"Oh, thank heaven!" she cried.

Jeffrey drew her into his embrace again, holding her close against his chest.

Yvette snuggled into him, breathing the masculine woodsy scent of him and closing her eyes. She sighed deeply. "I wish you could have married me today in the chapel, when your parents wed."

He chuckled at her impatience. "Had I known you didn't want a grand wedding, I would have."

With her head against his chest, Yvette listened to his heartbeat as she drifted off to sleep with Jeffrey's strong arms holding her tight.

Sometime later, Jeffrey kissed her cheek and whispered, "Wake up, darling. We're here."

Rising slowly, she stretched and peeked out the carriage window. It was dark out but the lights from Devon House cast a warm glow on the winter street. It was time to face her family and break the big news to them.

Yvette took a deep breath and looked at Jeffrey. "Are you ready?"

"Are you?" He countered with a wink.

"Let's go tell them." Filled with more nervousness than she'd expected, she entered the house with Jeffrey, greeted first by Granger.

"You've just missed supper, Miss Hamilton. Shall I bring you and Lord Eddington something to eat?" he asked them.

"Yes, thank you," Yvette answered. "That would be heavenly. We're both famished, aren't we, Jeffrey? Where are they all, Granger?"

"Everyone is in the large drawing room, decorating the Christmas tree," he told her. "They even managed to bring Mrs. Hamilton downstairs and she's with them, too."

"Thank you, Granger."

Mother was there! She gave Jeffrey an anxious glance and her stomach tightened. What would they all think? What would they say? Would they be happy for her?

Yvette and Jeffrey walked the hallway toward the drawing room and they paused in front of the closed door. From within came the sounds of conversation, laughter, children's voices, and Christmas carols.

Jeffrey took her hand in his and kissed her mouth briefly. "Do you want to tell them or should I be the one?"

"You tell them, Jeffrey," she whispered back. "I doubt they'd believe me."

"Be brave."

"I will." With her heart fluttering, she opened the double doors to the grand drawing room.

Her entire family was there. Her mother. Colette and Lucien. Juliette and Harrison. Lisette and Quinton. Paulette and Declan. Colette's two sons, Phillip and Simon. Juliette's daughter, Sara. Declan's daughter, Mara. The youngest of the children, Lisette's brood of three and Paulette's son, must be up in the Devon House nursery. They were all gathered together, enjoying the carols that Lisette was playing on the grand piano, and decorating the enormous evergreen tree that dominated the room with its height and rich pine scent.

"Yvette! You're back early!" Paulette called out to them, the first to notice their arrival, of course. Paulette never missed anything. "And you've brought Jeffrey with you! How was the wedding?"

Yvette hesitated before she entered the room, but Jeffrey still held her hand and pulled her forward.

Lisette suddenly stopped playing the piano and they all turned to look at Yvette and Jeffrey. Surprise registered on their faces; the fact that Jeffrey held her hand possessively was not lost on any of them. The room grew quiet except for the children, squealing and running around the Christmas tree.

Jeffrey gazed at Yvette's sisters and brothers-in-law before pulling her closer to his side. He flashed his signature smile. "We have some good news to share with all of you."

Juliette, who had been sitting beside their mother on the sofa, suddenly rose to her feet, her expression wary. Paulette grinned broadly in anticipation. No one else moved and Yvette could hear her own heart beating.

Jeffrey wasted no time. He cleared his throat and announced

clearly, "Yvette has agreed to be my wife. We're going to be married."

Juliette gasped. Paulette squealed in delight. Lisette looked utterly baffled. A slow smile spread across Colette's face. Lucien's brows drew together in a confused frown. Harrison looked vastly amused. Quinton stared at them in disbelief. Genevieve appeared quite pleased.

Out of all of them, Yvette was surprised that Declan Reeves was the first to speak. In his soft Irish accent, he said, "Well, I think that's just grand. We should celebrate!"

All hell broke loose then.

"You can't be serious!" Juliette cried, staring angrily at Jeffrey. "You cannot possibly marry my little sister!"

"What is going on here?" Lucien demanded, his expression a little reproachful.

"But what about Lord Shelley?" Lisette asked, her face a mask of confusion.

Colette rushed over to them, placing her hand on Yvette's shoulder. "Is it true?"

Yvette finally spoke up, knowing her cheeks were scarlet. "Yes, it's true. Jeffrey and I are going to be married."

"Oh my!" Her eldest sister was surprised, but obviously delighted. Colette declared, "I had a feeling about this, but I think you both have some explaining to do."

Paulette hurried to their side, hugging both Jeffrey and her in turn. "I knew it. I knew it!"

"You knew what?" Juliette asked in an incredulous tone. Her face was a strange combination of astonishment and distress.

"I knew they were in love with each other." Paulette smiled in triumph.

"When did all of this happen?" Lisette asked in wonder, gathering around them as well.

Yvette exchanged a glance with Jeffrey. "I'm not sure exactly. It just . . . happened."

"Yvette, *ma fille,* come here." Genevieve Hamilton's hoarse voice silenced all but the children, who were happily oblivious to the family drama unfolding around them.

With Jeffrey still holding her hand, the two of them walked over to her mother. She looked up from her perch on the sofa, staring first at Yvette, and then her gray eyes settled on Jeffrey. Still weak but having lost none of her fierceness, she asked, "You wish to marry my daughter? My baby? *Ma fille bébé?*"

Jeffrey answered, "Yes, Mrs. Hamilton, I do want to marry her. Very much."

"This makes me happy. *Je suis enchantée de ces nouvelles.* You are a fine man, *monsieur.* I knew it. I knew you would marry one of them! *J'ai toujours su que vous finiriez pas épouser une des mes filles. Vous avez bon goût, mon garçon. Mes félicitations.*" She smiled as Jeffrey leaned down and kissed her cheek.

Pleased that her mother was happy, Yvette looked up at the others for their blessings.

At that moment Granger entered the room with supper trays for her and Jeffrey, although Yvette had completely lost her appetite from all the excitement.

"Oh, Granger!" Colette called excitedly. "You must bring some champagne for us. We are going to have a little celebration. Yvette and Lord Eddington are engaged to be married!"

The old butler didn't blink an eye at Colette's announcement, perhaps because he'd served them alone in the sitting room for too many nights to count. He'd obviously suspected something all along. He smiled broadly at her and Jeffrey. "That's wonderful news! I shall return with champagne for everyone."

"Well now, I'd love to hear how all this came about between the two of you," Colette said to them. "And I'm sure I'm not the only one curious!"

"I'll take the children upstairs now," Juliette announced, her eyes dark. "It's time they were in bed." She hurriedly gathered the four children, who were quite reluctant to retire, and left the room, her discontent clear.

Yvette's heart sank at Juliette's reaction. She hadn't expected her sister to be so displeased with the news.

"I don't think Juliette's taking this very well," Jeffrey remarked wryly.

"I daresay she'll get over it," Paulette chimed in, ever the pragmatist.

"Well, I think it's wonderful!" Colette drew them to the sofa and everyone gathered around. "Now let's hear what happened while we were away."

"I still don't understand how this transpired right under my nose and I didn't notice anything," Lisette said, shaking her head.

Yvette, suddenly shy, looked to Jeffrey and then back at her family. "I don't know quite how it all happened."

"It's all Lucien's fault, really," Jeffrey said with a grin, looking at his friend most pointedly.

29

December Night

"I asked you to watch over her, not marry her, Jeffrey."

Later that evening Jeffrey finally found himself alone with Lucien Sinclair, his oldest friend, in Lucien's private study. Paulette and Declan had returned to their London townhouse, as had Lisette and Quinton. Mrs. Hamilton had been brought back upstairs to her rooms. Juliette and Colette were putting their little ones to bed. Yvette, exhausted from the long carriage journey that day, had retired for the night as well. Drinks in hand, Jeffrey and Lucien sat before the fire in the large leather armchairs, just as they had back in September.

Jeffrey shook his head. "I assure you, it was not my intention to marry her at the outset."

"What the hell happened?" Lucien asked. He still looked baffled by the news.

"I don't know. I simply fell in love with her. I can't explain it."

"I don't understand it. She's just a girl."

"She's almost twenty-one and quite grown up, Lucien. You know that as well as I do."

"I can't get my head around it."

"Neither can Juliette, apparently."

Lucien chuckled with glee. "It's a rare treat to see our Juliette so rattled."

"Isn't it, though?" Jeffrey grinned in agreement. Then he grew thoughtful. "I wish she had taken it better."

"To think the whole thing was Harrison's idea," Lucien said absently, shaking his head. "Juliette and I were against it from the beginning."

"What?" Jeffrey was thoroughly confused.

Lucien laughed again. "While we were still in America, Colette read Yvette's letter about their mother being ill and said what a comfort you'd been to Yvette. Then Harrison remarked, wouldn't it be perfect if you and Yvette married?"

Stunned, Jeffrey said, "He didn't!"

"Yes. Looking back now, it was quite a prediction on his part." Lucien drank his bourbon. "Colette was in favor of such a match, but Juliette and I, in a rare show of solidarity, were against it."

Jeffrey grew quiet before asking, "May I ask why you're against Yvette marrying me?"

Lucien tossed his friend an apologetic look. "I can't really say. There's truly nothing I have against you, Jeffrey, you know that as well as I do. You're a good man, a fine man, and my closest friend. I'd trust you with my life. It was just my initial reaction, perhaps because I still think of Yvette as a child and I'm protective of her."

"I can understand that. And I expected you to feel this way, to tell you the truth. I even told Yvette you'd more than likely hit me."

"What did she say?" Lucien raised a brow.

"She told me to hit you back."

Lucien laughed again. "That's my little Yvette."

"She's my Yvette now," Jeffrey pointed out.

"Yes, I suppose she is," Lucien said thoughtfully. "I'm happy for you both. Honestly."

"Thank you." Jeffrey felt relieved. Lucien's acceptance meant a great deal to him. Now he only had to contend with Juliette.

Lucien continued, "You and Yvette marrying is actually a good thing, the more I think about it. Now I don't have to make friends with old Shelley."

It was Jeffrey's turn to laugh. "I almost feel sorry for the man."

"Me too."

Jeffrey sipped his drink. "So why is Juliette so put out?"

Lucien sighed. "Probably not for the same reasons I was. But give her time. It's an unexpected adjustment. You'll have to talk to her about it, smooth things over. I'm sure she'll come around. You know Juliette."

"Yes, I know Juliette." Jeffrey smiled wistfully, thinking back on all the time he had spent with her that summer, once he'd finally caught up with her in New York after she had run off. They had had their fair share of heated arguments as well. But that was the nature of his friendship with Juliette Hamilton.

"I thought I'd find you two still in here." Colette smiled at them as she slipped quietly into the study. She walked over to Lucien and he pulled her onto his lap.

"Colette might know," Lucien said, hugging his wife.

"Colette might know what?" she asked with a light laugh.

Jeffrey answered, "Why Juliette is so put out with me for wanting to marry Yvette."

Colette gave him a warm smile. "I don't know, really.

You'll have to ask her that. As I said earlier, I couldn't be happier for you both."

"Thank you." It meant a great deal to him that Colette was pleased by his love for her sister.

"Now we get to keep you in the family, Jeffrey," Colette declared happily.

"Was I going somewhere?" He arched an eyebrow.

"No, but if Yvette married Lord Shelley and then you eventually married someone else, then naturally you'd spend more time with her family and we wouldn't get to see you anymore."

He quipped wryly, "I can see you've thought this through a great deal." Still, he was touched that she wanted him as a permanent member of the family. That inclusion mattered more to him than anyone knew. Except maybe Yvette.

"I have. And now you will truly be our brother and we won't lose you to someone else! It's perfect. I said so from the start, didn't I, Lucien?"

"Yes, you did," Lucien agreed. "Juliette and I were the holdouts."

"Did I just hear my name?" Juliette asked.

Jeffrey looked up to see that Juliette and Harrison stood in the doorway of the study.

"Come in and join us." Lucien waved his hand. "We were just talking about you, Juliette."

She and Harrison took seats on the sofa. "Yes, that's what I heard."

"Jeffrey and I want to know why you're so upset about him and Yvette." Colette folded her arms across her chest and gave a questioning look to her sister.

"I can't explain it," Juliette said rather mutinously.

Jeffrey arched a brow at her. "Do try."

Juliette looked with an appeal toward Lucien. "A little help here?"

"Oh, no. Don't look at me to save you," Lucien said with a shake of his head. "I've already thrown in my cap and made peace with it all."

"Traitor." Juliette frowned at him.

"Come now, Juliette," Harrison chided his wife lightly. "What's so bad about it? We love Yvette and want the best for her. We all love Jeffrey. The two of them together make perfect sense."

"Thank you, Harrison." Jeffrey grinned at his old friend, grateful for his support. He and Lucien had become friends with Harrison Fleming over ten years ago when they had gone into the shipping business together. Never could they have imagined then that they would each marry into the same family. Three sisters. It was almost ridiculous.

"I'm sorry, Jeffrey," Juliette began rather haltingly. "It's just that you were *my* friend first. Yvette's just a child and I—"

"She's not a child anymore." The heat in his own voice surprised Jeffrey. "And I love her."

The room grew silent.

"Yes," Juliette said softly at last, her eyes wide. "You're quite right. She's no longer a child. But it's just that I've known you a long time and I happen to know a little about the women you have known in the past and I . . ."

"Don't, Juliette." Jeffrey stopped her from saying any more. "They can't even compare to your sister, so don't do it."

"I wasn't comparing, I just don't see why . . ." Juliette's voice faded. "Never mind."

"Jeffrey, as you well know, my wife can be a little possessive in her friendships," Harrison pointed out in a conciliatory tone. "I think she may be afraid of losing yours."

Jeffrey stared at Juliette. "Did I lose your friendship when you married Harrison?"

"No," she admitted. "But you were ours and now you'll be Yvette's."

"Yes," he said, liking the sound of that. Belonging to Yvette.

"I don't know about anybody else, but I'd like another drink." Lucien stood and went to the bar, refilling his glass with bourbon.

"I'll take one of those while you're up," Harrison called out.

While Lucien fixed the drinks, Jeffrey caught Juliette's eyes again.

"I'm sorry, Jeffrey. I've been a terrible brat tonight, haven't I?" Juliette asked.

"Well . . ."

Harrison chimed in. "Yes, you have."

Colette laughed a little. "Harrison's right, Juliette. You behaved dreadfully."

Looking almost defeated, Juliette hung her head. "I don't know why you're so happy about it, Colette. Don't you think it's a little . . . uncomfortable?"

Jeffrey stared at her. "The fact that I am marrying your sister is uncomfortable for you, Juliette?"

Juliette remained silent.

"Well, I think it's perfect, Jeffrey." Colette smiled. "And I had my suspicions that something was going on between the two of you that first afternoon I came home. You acted so funny when I mentioned Yvette."

"Did I?" Jeffrey had not realized he had been so transparent.

Colette laughed. "Oh, yes. But the best part of it all is now we get to keep Jeffrey as one of our own."

"And we don't have to entertain Lord Shelley," Lucien added with relief.

Colette eyed her husband carefully. "You really didn't like him, did you?"

"I don't *not* like him," Lucien amended. "But I'd rather have Jeffrey as my brother-in-law than William Weatherly."

"I heartily agree," Harrison added. "I think it's a wonderful turn of events."

"I suppose it will just take some getting used to," Juliette said slowly. "Again, I'm sorry for how I acted, Jeffrey."

"You're forgiven." Jeffrey had to forgive Juliette. After so many years, he knew her too well and loved her too much to hold anything against her.

"Thank you." Juliette gave him an apologetic smile.

"It's going to be quite an eventful Christmas ball, what with your father's momentous news and your engagement to Yvette," Colette said with excitement.

"I don't usually enjoy those types of social affairs, but I wouldn't miss this one for the world," Juliette added.

Jeffrey wondered just how much of the old scandal his parents' marriage would resurrect. People didn't tend to forgive and forget as easily as his father would like to think. He doubted his mother would be welcomed into society with open arms either. It would not be easy, but his father didn't seem to care. Neither did Jeffrey, for his part. He did worry what effect the scandal would have on Yvette. She could marry the very respectable Lord Shelley and live a life in the upper echelons of society as an elegant duchess. Instead, Yvette was marrying the scandal-ridden bastard of a duke.

He wished he could do better by her.

"Well, I think it's time we all go to sleep," Colette announced with a little yawn. "It's past midnight. Are you coming up with me, Lucien?" she asked her husband.

"Yes, I am," Lucien said. "I'm quite tired myself." They rose and said their good nights, leaving just Harrison, Juliette, and Jeffrey in the study.

"It's still such a surprise to me Jeffrey . . . you and Yvette," Juliette remarked with a heavy sigh. "When are you planning to marry?"

"We're not sure yet, but sooner rather than later," Jeffrey answered. "I'm getting a special license tomorrow and we might wed as soon as next week."

"Next week?" Juliette suddenly looked horrified. "Oh God, you're not in a hurry to get married because the two of you . . . Yvette isn't—"

"No," Jeffrey interrupted. He shook his head emphatically. That was not a rumor he wanted bandied about. "Absolutely not. I have not touched your sister."

"Good lord, Juliette!" Harrison exclaimed, laughing in amusement. "You give yourself away asking such questions! Please forgive my wife, Jeffrey. She often speaks without thinking first."

"Well, what was I to think?" Juliette protested. "I'd have thought Yvette would have wanted an extravagant and grand wedding with all the world invited. Besides, Jeffrey somehow knows everything about all of us. He understands why I'd ask such a question, don't you, Jeffrey?"

"Yes. Yes, I do." Jeffrey nodded with a slow, secret smile. He knew entirely too much about the Hamilton sisters, all because he'd been trying to protect them. Still, he didn't feel comfortable talking to Juliette about his personal relations with her sister.

"You're a good man, Eddington." Harrison lifted his glass in tribute. "I wish you all the best with *your* Hamilton sister."

Jeffrey raised his glass as well. "Thank you, and I wish you the best of luck with *yours*. You need the luck more than I do." He winked at Juliette and she rolled her eyes at him.

The door to Lucien's study opened again. This time Yvette walked in. She was dressed in a white silk nightgown, with a long fur-trimmed robe wrapped around her. Her blond hair hung completely loose. She looked like an angel, all ethereal and soft. Jeffrey's mouth went dry at the sight of her.

"I thought I heard your voice, Jeffrey." She hesitated before stepping farther into the room.

"Yvette." He set his drink down on the end table, rose to his feet, and walked to her. "I thought you'd gone to bed." He took her hands in his, fighting his desire to wrap his arms around her and carry her back upstairs.

"I did, but I couldn't sleep at all." She looked up at him, her eyes luminous.

"You must be exhausted," he said.

"We were just talking about you, Yvette," Juliette called to them.

"You were?" Yvette asked, as Jeffrey took her hand and led her back toward the sofa.

Juliette continued, looking somewhat contrite. "Yes. I was just telling Jeffrey how sorry I am for how I behaved earlier when you first told us your wonderful news."

Yvette looked to Jeffrey, her eyes questioning, and she asked in a whisper, "Did she really?"

He nodded, glad to see the relief on Yvette's face. He knew that Juliette's reaction had upset her just as much as it had upset him.

"Yes, I really did," Juliette added. She rose from the sofa and hugged Yvette tightly. "I am happy for you. And I apologize for being such a horrid brat." She then hugged Jeffrey. "And I'm so thrilled that you'll always be a part of our family, Jeffrey. I love you both very much."

"Oh, thank you, Juliette," Yvette cried. "It means so much to me to have your blessing."

"It's still hard for me to imagine my little sister with Jeffrey, but you couldn't have chosen a better man to marry," Juliette said, becoming a little teary in spite of herself.

"Well, now, on that happy note," Harrison began, rising to his feet, "I think it's well past time to call it a night. Let's go upstairs, Juliette."

"All right, Harrison," Juliette said, wiping her eyes. "I'm turning into a watering pot anyway."

"We'll leave you two to say your good nights in private," Harrison said before dragging Juliette from the study.

When they were alone, Yvette asked, "Did everything go well?"

"Everything went great."

"Lucien didn't hit you?" she asked, her eyes twinkling.

"No, he didn't even come close. Apparently, the more everyone thinks about us together, the more they like it. Even Juliette."

She smiled happily at him. "Even Juliette."

"So now everyone is happy for us." He eyed her carefully. "Except poor old Shelley."

Yvette frowned at him, her eyes reproachful. "He's not that old. And he's going to be terribly hurt when I tell him about us. I feel very badly about it all, as if I've led him on."

"There's always Jane Fairmont, but that's poor consolation for losing you. I do feel badly for him too."

"I know you do."

"You'll tell him tomorrow?"

"Yes. I'll send a message to ask him to come to Devon House for tea."

"I don't like the thought of you seeing him again, but I suppose it can't be avoided in this case."

"I owe him that much at least. He can't just hear about our engagement at your father's Christmas ball. That would be cruel."

"You're right."

She smiled. "I know."

"But do you know how beautiful you look right now?"

"Jeffrey . . ."

"Just one kiss before I leave . . ." He drew her into his arms, and kissed her. The feel of her body beneath the thin silk material, free of all the heavy layers of her usual dress, was intoxicating.

She melted against him and it took all his self-control not to take her to the sofa and have his way with her right then and there. But he was determined to do right by her.

"Good night, Yvette," he whispered in her ear.

"Good night, Jeffrey."

30

Five Golden Rings

Yvette was worried. The letter she held in her hand did not hold good news.

She had been trying for three days to talk with Lord Shelley and now she had received yet another letter telling her that he was still suffering from influenza and not well enough to come to tea at Devon House or receive visitors at his home. He hoped to be sufficiently recovered in time to attend the Duke of Rathmore's Christmas ball tomorrow evening and was greatly looking forward to seeing Yvette then.

"Just go to his house and tell him what happened, whether he's ill or not," Paulette advised as she and Lisette sat together in Yvette's bedroom discussing the situation.

Yvette shook her head. "Even if I were daring enough to go over there, how can I see him when he is not receiving visitors?"

"It is a tricky problem," Lisette added.

The Duke of Rathmore's Christmas ball was tomorrow night and Yvette simply had to speak to William before then. She could not let him find out she was marrying Jeffrey Eddington in such a publicly humiliating manner and she couldn't write the news to him in a letter either. He deserved the decency of her telling him in person that her feelings for him had changed.

And changed they certainly had.

It was then that Colette entered the bedroom, joining the three sisters. She asked Yvette, "Have you decided what gown to wear to the ball?"

"No. I keep changing my mind." Yvette shook her head, and gestured to the two sumptuous gowns that were hanging from her wardrobe doors. "I can't decide between the red silk or the emerald."

"I think I like you in the emerald silk best," Paulette chimed in from where she rested on the velvet chaise. "But can I borrow your beaded wrap, Yvette? I left my favorite one in Dublin and I need something to cover up my expanding waist."

"I have a pretty one you can wear," Colette offered. "But one could hardly notice that you're expecting at all, Paulette."

"Do you really think so? I feel quite round already." Paulette rested her hands protectively over her midsection.

"Honestly, Paulette, you haven't the faintest hint of a belly," Lisette said from her perch on the window seat. "Are you wearing your gold satin, Colette?"

"Yes, I think so, because my new blue gown with seed pearls won't be ready in time." Colette frowned in disappointment.

"Can you please tell me what I ought to do?" Yvette cried from where she sat at her writing desk. She still held the letter from Lord Shelley in her hand.

Just then Juliette entered the bedroom. "What are you all doing in here?"

"Talking about gowns," Lisette said. "Do you know what you're wearing tomorrow night?"

"I have a burgundy silk and black lace dress I had made in New York by a seamstress from Paris. It's beautiful. Wait until you see it!" Juliette said, her eyes twinkling.

Lisette smiled with glee. "I'm so excited that we shall all be attending the same ball together. And the Duke of Rathmore's Christmas ball is spectacular. Do you remember when Jeffrey escorted me to his father's ball? That was the first time I went."

"Oh, yes, I remember because I went with you too," Juliette said with enthusiasm. "It was the first time we ever met Quinton."

"I've never been able to attend before," Paulette said. "That's why I'm so excited."

"I believe Aunt Cecilia and Uncle Randall will be there as well," Colette pointed out to them.

"Oh, wonderful!" Juliette rolled her eyes, never having been fond of their aunt and uncle. "We get to spend the evening with Uncle Randall watching over our every move and criticizing our behavior."

"Do you think Cousin Nigel will be there?" Lisette asked. "I haven't seen him in ages, but I've been hearing some rather scandalous things about him."

Juliette asked, "Such as?"

"Nothing as scandalous as it will be if I jilt a future duke at the Christmas ball!" Yvette cried in an attempt to catch her sisters' attention. They turned to stare at her.

"Whatever on earth is the matter, Yvette?" Colette asked in dismay.

Paulette answered for her. "She still hasn't been able to see Lord Shelley to tell him about her engagement to Jeffrey. He's too ill to pay calls or receive visitors."

"Yes," Yvette continued, her frustration growing. "And I

simply must tell him before the Duke of Rathmore announces it at the ball tomorrow night."

"I told her to go right over to his house and just insist on seeing him," Paulette added emphatically. "She has to let him know!"

"She can't do that if he's too ill to see her!" Lisette cried.

"No, she can't do that," Colette agreed with Lisette, while taking a seat on the edge of the four-poster bed.

"So what should I do?" Yvette asked again. Tomorrow night would be absolutely dreadful if she did not tell William Weatherly that she had promised to marry Jeffrey Eddington.

"Well," Juliette began slowly, "maybe you could arrange to see him as soon as the ball begins and tell him before they announce it."

Yvette was almost ready to cry. "I can't do that either. I should let him know before we're at the Rathmore town-house."

"You could postpone the announcement of your engagement," Lisette suggested softly from the window seat.

"Yes, I could . . ." Yvette said with reluctance. "But I don't wish to do that either. Jeffrey's father is so looking forward to announcing both his marriage and our engagement. It is his Christmas ball and he's so happy about Jeffrey and me."

"It's going to create another scandal, the two of them marrying after all these years," Colette said.

"Yes, and so will the fact that the infamous rogue Lord Eddington is finally settling down and marrying the youngest of the Hamilton sisters!" Paulette exclaimed.

"I still don't know how I missed a romance between the two of you," Lisette marveled aloud. "Especially when I was here with you both for most of the time!"

"It's understandable considering you were preoccupied

with the baby and worried about mother," Colette said kindly.

"I suppose." Lisette sighed heavily with a little shake of her auburn head. "Yvette is marrying Jeffrey."

Juliette added, "It's so strange."

"It's *not* that strange," Yvette retorted. Honestly, they acted as if she were marrying a man with two heads. "Please, what shall I do about Lord Shelley?"

"I'll see what Lucien can do to help," Colette said. "Perhaps he could send word to Lord Shelley?"

Yvette glanced back at the letter in her hand. "Yes, perhaps."

"She said Jeffrey is quite skilled at kissing." Paulette's words from the depths of the chaise brought the conversation about Yvette's dilemma with Lord Shelley to a standstill.

"Well, that's not surprising in the least," Colette said with a little smile.

Yvette eyed Colette in amusement. Her sister would certainly know if Jeffrey was a good kisser, but she kept her thoughts to herself.

Lisette giggled like a schoolgirl. "You must tell us, Yvette. We're all dying to know."

"I think I may already know the answer to this, but—" Juliette, who still stood near the doorway, stepped back and quickly closed the bedroom door. She joined Colette on the edge of Yvette's large four-poster bed. "Now we can talk."

With her four older sisters staring at her, Yvette suddenly didn't know what to say. She had always been the one asking them the questions!

She knew about relations between a man and a woman, of course. Yvette had secretly read the medical text in their father's bookshop, just as her sisters had. She had overheard them whispering about it when she was younger for it was the worst kept secret in the family. They had all furtively read *A Complete Study of the Human Anatomy and All Its Functions* by Doctor T. Everett. Although the book described events in great detail, Yvette longed to know how it felt to actually do those things with a man. From what she had gathered from her sisters, the experience was incredibly wonderful. And judging by the way they were looking at her right now, they assumed that she had already done with Jeffrey those things depicted on page 232 of the book.

Slowly, Yvette shook her head. "I'm sorry to disappoint you, but there's really nothing to tell. Jeffrey has been a complete gentleman."

Paulette sat up on the chaise, her face registering her disbelief. "With his infamous reputation with women, you mean to say he hasn't seduced you yet?"

"No."

"Not even while we were all away and you were alone in the house together?" Colette asked, quite incredulous.

"No."

"I thought for sure something must have happened then." Colette eyed her with some suspicion.

"No," Yvette repeated with conviction.

"And nothing happened when you went to his father's estate in Berkshire for the wedding and were gone overnight?" Lisette asked eagerly.

"And came home engaged?" Colette added.

Again Yvette shook her head. "No."

"Oh, I don't believe it!" Paulette cried out in astonishment.

"Yvette's telling the truth," Juliette said softly. When they all looked at her in awe, she added, "As shocking as it may sound, Jeffrey said as much to me the other night. He hasn't touched her. And Jeffrey never lies."

"What did Jeffrey say to you?" Yvette's heart raced.

"He said nothing untoward had happened between you and him," Juliette explained, "when I suggested that the two of you were marrying quickly because something *had* happened between you."

Yvette lifted her chin. The way that Jeffrey treated her made Yvette feel wonderfully cherished. "He wants to wait until we're married. He's being quite proper because he doesn't want a hint of scandal."

"Oh, my," Lisette murmured softly.

Paulette giggled in amusement. "Well then, we must be quite a scandalous bunch, because that is more than any of us can say."

Lisette added, "I think it's very sweet of him."

"Everything he is doing shows how much he cares for you, Yvette." Juliette looked at her in admiration. "I'm sorry I doubted the two of you."

"Thank you, Juliette." Yvette smiled at her sister, glad that all was well between them again.

"But he's kissed you certainly?" Colette asked.

"Oh, yes," Yvette said, her cheeks reddening helplessly. Every time Jeffrey kissed her, it just became better and better. She didn't know how she could bear the wait until she was married to him. His kisses drove her mad with desire.

"So is Jeffrey as swoon worthy as the rumors say he is?" Lisette asked, her face alight with curiosity.

With a telling gleam in her eyes, Yvette looked at each of her sisters. "Oh, he is so much better."

The five of them squealed with laughter.

Then Yvette made a confession. "I don't know how either of us will be able to resist temptation until we get married. That's why we wish to marry right away."

"Well, I applaud both of you. It's right that you should wait until you are married." With a somewhat abashed expression, Lisette confided to them, "I surrendered to Quinton's considerable charms not even a month after I met him. I was completely helpless against his kisses."

With an understanding nod of her head and a reticent smile, Colette said, "I must admit that Lucien swept me off my feet not much longer than that after I met him in the bookshop."

"And it's not a secret that I yielded to Declan's powers of persuasion well before we were married," Paulette said guiltily, holding up her hand and pointing to her belly.

"I have no idea what wanton behavior you all are referring to," Juliette said, her eyes flashing mischievously. "I must say I am quite appalled!"

"Come now, Juliette!" Paulette admonished her, eager to know the truth. "Not one of us believes you waited until you married Harrison!"

Juliette glanced at each one of them in turn. "Mere days."

The sisters all shrieked at Juliette's daring revelation, staring at her in awe.

"You had only known Harrison for a few *days* when it happened?" Yvette cried in astonishment.

Juliette shrugged helplessly, not in the least bit embarrassed. "Close quarters on a beautiful ship, locked in a sumptuous cabin with a very handsome and dashing captain with an enchanting American accent had an extraordinary effect on me. The romance of moonlight and the sea air and all of that . . ."

The four sisters stared at Juliette with wide eyes.

"It was the same with Mother, you know," Paulette stated calmly.

"What?" the other four exclaimed in unison.

"When the reason that Declan and I needed to marry quickly was quite obvious, Mother confessed to me that it had been the same with her and Father," Paulette said.

"She never did!" Colette cried.

Yvette said, "I don't believe it!"

"It's true," Paulette confirmed. "She told me."

Lisette murmured, "I'm stunned."

"Well, I'm delighted to hear it," Juliette said with a nod of her head. "It just confirms my theory that it's always been that way and it's part of life. We are all swept away by our feelings sometimes. There's nothing to be scandalized about."

"It's nice to think of them that way," Colette agreed slowly. "Their marriage was not happy in the end, but it's good to know that they were wild about each other at least in the beginning. . . ."

"Please don't mention it to *Maman*." Paulette looked a little guilty. "She made me promise not to tell you, but I thought you would like to know."

"As if I would ever bring up such a topic with her!" Juliette laughed.

The five sisters grew quiet, each lost in their own thoughts about themselves and their parents.

"Well, if Yvette and Jeffrey can wait until they are married, I think it's lovely," Lisette finally said.

"But I don't wish to wait!" Yvette exclaimed with a giggle. "I keep trying to convince Jeffrey otherwise, but he won't hear of it."

"He's getting a special license, so you won't have to wait too much longer." Juliette smiled at her.

"Yes, I know. But I still have an even bigger problem." Yvette held up the letter from William Weatherly. "What do I do about Lord Shelley?"

The bedroom door flew open and a gaggle of children charged in the room: Phillip and Simon Sinclair; Mara Reeves, dragging her younger brother, Thomas; and Sara Fleming, attempting to carry one of Lisette's twins and holding the other by the hand.

"Oh, goodness," Juliette cried in amusement, as the little tribe descended upon them. "Who let all of you out of the nursery?"

Sara, the image of Juliette with her dark hair and flashing eyes, looking quite outraged, spoke for the group. "Phillip said Christmas is the day after tomorrow, but that's not right, is it, Mama? I told him he was wrong, but he won't believe me."

With a laugh, Lisette gathered her blond twins, Christopher and Charles, from their older cousin. They were covered in cookie crumbs and pudding. "What have you two little scamps been up to?"

"Now, Phillip, don't go telling stories to your cousins," Colette scolded her son lightly. "You know very well that Christmas is not the day after tomorrow. Now behave yourself, because Santa Claus doesn't visit naughty children."

Paulette rose with great reluctance from the divan, scooping up her son, Thomas, in one arm and taking little Mara's hand in the other. "Come on, you two. It's time we were heading back home anyway."

Yvette watched her sisters, who minutes ago had been discussing the intimacies of their relationship with their husbands, instantly revert back to being the caring mothers that they were. She smiled to herself, thinking how much she loved each of them, and their husbands, and all their children.

But she still hadn't solved her problem of how to tell Lord Shelley that she was marrying Jeffrey Eddington!

31

Ladies Dancing

The night of the Duke of Rathmore's annual Christmas ball had finally arrived, as hundreds of invited guests filled his massive London townhouse. Decorated with festive pine wreaths, evergreen garlands, and boughs of holly leaves tied with red and gold silk ribbons, the rooms sparkled with hundreds of flickering beeswax candles and golden gaslights. A giant noble fir tree stood majestically in the center of the hallway and reached almost to the top of the twenty-foot ceiling, filling the air with its fresh pine scent. Adorned with tiny candles and crystal and colored-glass ornaments, the tall Christmas tree glistened with bright cranberry garlands and red silk ribbons.

Liveried servants scurried about, serving punch and champagne and an endless supply of delicious delicacies prepared by Rathmore's famous French chef. An orchestra played Christmas carols while anyone who was anyone in society gathered in the main hall to greet their host. More than the usual buzz of excitement was in the air as rumors swirled that the duke was planning to make an important announcement at some point during the evening.

The Duke of Rathmore, looking dashing and elegant, shook hands and met his many honored and distinguished guests. No one seemed to notice the lovely dark-haired woman who hovered quietly in the background, dressed in a gown of midnight blue, looking on the proceedings with a sparkle in her eyes.

As Yvette Hamilton entered the grand hall with all her sisters and brothers-in-law, her heart was in her throat. Leaving her sisters behind as she brushed by elegantly attired people and made her way deeper into the hall, she glanced about the crowd anxiously, searching for a sign of either Jeffrey or William. She had hoped to arrive earlier, but their carriage had been stuck in the crush of other guests outside and it had taken her almost a half an hour just to get into the house. Panic-stricken, she wondered if William Weatherly had already arrived. As she peered through the throng of guests searching for the sight of his fair hair, she said a little prayer that she would have a moment to speak to William alone first.

"Yvette!" Lady Katherine Spencer called to her with a little wave.

"Kate!" Yvette maneuvered her way through the crowd to her friend. "You look so pretty tonight!"

"Why, thank you." She preened in her deep pink gown. "Your dress is lovely too!"

"Thank you." Yvette nervously smoothed the shimmering emerald silk she'd finally decided to wear instead of the red. It fit her to perfection. "Kate, have you seen Lord Shelley?"

"No." Her friend shook her head. "At least not yet."

Yvette frowned. "I must speak with him right away. If you see him, will you please let him know I am looking for him?"

"Is something the matter?" Kate asked, her brown eyes concerned. "You look a bit distressed."

"Yes, there is something the matter. In fact, more than I can say at the moment." Yvette felt ready to cry.

"I'm so sorry, Yvette. I hope you kn—oh, here comes Lord Eddington," Kate squeaked. "My, my. Doesn't he look handsome tonight!"

Yvette turned around. There he was, making his way through the crowd toward her. The man she loved and was going to marry. Her heart skipped a beat, and for a moment she suddenly forgot all about finding Lord Shelley and everyone else standing around her. Her gaze was fixed on the gloriously handsome man staring at her with a devastating smile. Jeffrey.

"Good evening, beautiful ladies. It's so nice of you to come to my father's little party," he greeted them most gallantly. "Lady Katherine, you are a vision in pink."

"Thank you, Lord Eddington." Kate giggled at his compliment and his reference to the duke's "little" party, for the ball was anything but.

Jeffrey then rested his blue-eyed gaze on Yvette, grasping her hands in his. "Yvette, you take my breath away."

Out of the corner of her eye, Yvette saw Kate's face register her surprise at Jeffrey's familiarity with her.

"Lady Katherine, do you mind if I steal Yvette away for a moment?" he asked, his eyes still locked with Yvette's.

"No, not at all," she murmured in confusion as she watched Jeffrey escort Yvette away from the crowd and into a small chamber off the main hallway. Yvette knew she would have to do some explaining to her friend later.

Jeffrey quickly slid the double doors closed behind them. They were alone in an antechamber to the main drawing room. The noise of the crowd and the music could still be heard.

"Jeffrey," Yvette protested lightly as he drew her into

his warm embrace. "Anyone could have seen you take me in here!"

He lowered his mouth over hers, kissing her quite thoroughly. "I don't care. I've missed you too much." With a wicked smile, he kissed her again. His hands skimmed across her back, pressing her against him.

Breathless, Yvette lost herself to the sensations of his kiss, not caring that he was rumpling her new emerald gown or mussing her carefully coiffed hair. She was just happy to be with him, thrilled that she was soon going to be his wife and would be able to kiss him all day every day if she wanted to.

As their kiss deepened and their passion for each other increased, he finally broke away from her.

"Jeffrey." Her heart beat wildly in her chest.

"I know," he whispered in her ear. "I have the special license. Whenever you say the word, we can marry. Tomorrow, if you wish."

"Everyone will talk if we marry so quickly."

"Once we're legally wed, I don't give a damn what anyone says."

She thought for a moment. "Well, then . . . how about Christmas Eve?"

"Christmas Eve it is."

She smiled, warmth flooding her at the idea of being his wife in just four days. "I should think we can manage an elegant Christmas wedding, with just our families, on such short notice."

He looked at her intently. "We can wait and have a large fancy wedding if you've changed your mind. Are you sure this is what you want? A small wedding?"

Staring into his blue eyes, she whispered, "I've never been more sure of anything in my life. I want to marry you just as soon as we can."

He hugged her tightly to him. "Oh, Yvette." Then he reached into his pocket and retrieved a small box. He opened it and presented it to her somewhat nervously. "I have an engagement ring for you."

Yvette looked at the large, sparkling diamond that he held out to her and squealed with delight. "Oh, Jeffrey, it's beautiful!"

"I've never bought a ring before and I wasn't sure if you would like it."

"Like it? I love it!" With her hand trembling, she allowed Jeffrey to slip the gold ring with a square-cut diamond on her finger. It fit perfectly. "Oh, Jeffrey, thank you!"

"It looks beautiful on you."

She stood on tiptoes and kissed him, feeling tears in her eyes.

"I've never been happier in my life," he said.

"Me either. But we should get back to the others before I start crying," she said with a sniffle. Her sisters would be wondering where she was. And, oh heavens, she still had to talk with William!

"My father will be making the announcement in a little while and everyone will know that you're mine." He winked at her. "So the fact that we were in here kissing right now won't matter at all."

"Oh, Jeffrey!" she cried in sudden panic. "Your father can't make our engagement announcement just yet!"

He frowned and his expression darkened. "You still haven't told him about us?"

Sensing his disappointment, Yvette tried to explain. "Lord Shelley has been very ill. I've tried to see him, but he wasn't paying calls or receiving visitors. Lucien even went to see him this morning and tried to speak to him. Please. You must let me tell William first before your father announces our engagement."

"Yvette, even if I tell my father not to make an announcement tonight, it doesn't mean that he won't. You know my father."

"But it's not fair to Lord Shelley. I haven't seen him in a week, since the night he fell ill at the theater. I have to let him know that everything has changed between us. He deserves that from me."

"I thought you had taken care of this." His blue eyes flashed.

She looked up at him helplessly. "I tried. Honestly. Then my plan was to arrive early and speak to him as soon as he got here, but I haven't been able to find him in the crowd. And then you . . . brought me in here."

"You've put me in a terrible position, Yvette." He was upset with her and she couldn't recall ever seeing Jeffrey angry before.

"I'm sorry," she said. "I'm going to find William right now and tell him."

He glared at her. "Not if I find him first."

"Oh, no, you mustn't do that!" she protested. "I have to be the one to tell him."

Jeffrey walked to the door. His voice was cold as he said, "Let's go back to the party."

Yvette stood there staring at him, growing quite angry herself. None of this was her fault. She hadn't intended to disappoint Jeffrey or his father, but she had to do the decent thing and tell William Weatherly to his face that she had no intention of marrying him. "Don't you dare tell him, Jeffrey!"

He suddenly turned to her, his gaze frosty. "Have you not told him because you don't really wish to end it?"

Her mouth dropped open. "How can you even think such a thing of me?"

"It only stands to reason."

"No, it doesn't!" she exclaimed. "I'm going to tell Lord Shelley that I am marrying you the moment that I see him!"

His expression grew somber and Yvette suddenly felt that there was something terribly wrong.

"I hope that's true, Yvette. But I swear to you that if you don't tell him, I will." With that he left the room.

Yvette felt like screaming in frustration. Jeffrey was behaving like a jealous fool. She stormed out of the room after him.

"Come, Mother, it's this way." William Weatherly led his mother through the crowd of people in the front of the Duke of Rathmore's townhouse. The place was a mass of guests trying to enter the house. Already weary of the evening, William tried to suppress the hacking cough that had consumed him for a week. He simply could not shake this damned cough that had him bedridden and had ruined all his plans!

He held his mother's arm as he escorted her up the steps and into the great hall. Through the sea of faces, he searched for one face in particular. It had been a week since he had seen Yvette Hamilton and he missed her terribly. The notes he had received from her had been most insistent in declaring that she needed to speak with him as soon as possible. He was very curious to know what she wanted.

William was able to leave his mother in the company of a few of her friends while he went in search of Yvette. He hoped his mother wouldn't imbibe too freely of the champagne this evening, but he could not stand by her side and watch her all night either. He moved through the crowd, greeting numerous friends, before he finally caught sight of one of Yvette Hamilton's sisters. It was the one married to the American sea captain, who also stood beside her. She looked quite beautiful in a gown of burgundy trimmed with black lace. The look suited her remarkably well. He called to both of them.

"Mr. and Mrs. Fleming!"

Juliette smiled and stepped toward him. "Why, Lord Shelley! How nice to see you again. I do hope you are feeling better?"

"Yes, I am. Finally." He took her hand. "It's quite a crush in here, is it not?"

She laughed lightly. "Yes, it is. But then Lord Rathmore's Christmas ball is always like this."

"Good evening, Lord Shelley," Harrison Fleming, dashing in his formal evening clothes, greeted him.

"Captain Fleming. It's good to see you again as well." William looked toward Juliette. "I have yet to see your sister this evening. Do you happen to know where she is?"

An amused smile suddenly played across her face, as if she knew something he did not. "I'm afraid I lost Yvette in the crowd some time ago, Lord Shelley, but I know she is quite anxious to see you. If I see her, I will be sure to tell her that you are looking for her."

"Thank you very much, Mrs. Fleming. I do appreciate it." With that, he excused himself and moved through the crowd, trying to make his way to the ballroom. If he knew anything about Yvette, it was that she had many admirers and loved to dance. He would more than likely find his future wife waltzing with a young man who had already lost his heart to her.

* * *

Paulette Hamilton Reeves, feeling a bit more weary than usual, had decided to rest in a quiet alcove bedecked with poinsettia plants, while her husband went to find her something to drink. This pregnancy, although still in its early stages, was quite different from her first and she grew tired much more easily. So Paulette sat peacefully and listened to the lovely music the orchestra was playing. She hadn't the energy for dancing this evening and would probably make an early night of it, but she had never been to the Duke of Rathmore's Christmas ball before and wished to stay as long as she could. She had never seen such beautiful Christmas décor!

"Miss Hamilton?"

Paulette was startled out of her thoughts by the short, balding man standing in front of her. He held a glass of champagne in his hand and stared at her intently.

"Forgive me for disturbing you," the gentleman said, looking a little embarrassed. "My name is James Granger Eddington and you look so much like Yvette Hamilton that for a moment I thought you were her, but I see now that I was mistaken. You are one of the Hamilton sisters though, are you not?"

Paulette nodded in understanding. It was not the first time that evening that she had been mistaken for Yvette. People often confused the two of them, especially people who didn't know them very well.

"Yes, Yvette is my sister. I am Paulette Hamilton Reeves, Countess of Cashelmore. And you must be Jeffrey Eddington's cousin."

Paulette had heard about Jeffrey's cousin, the one who would inherit his father's title and estate, but had never met him. Seeing him now she had to admit they looked nothing alike. She never would have imagined that this man was related to Jeffrey!

"I am quite pleased to make your acquaintance, Lady Cashelmore. And may I say once again, that you and your sister, aside from looking remarkably alike, are both very beautiful."

"Why thank you, Mr. Eddington. That's very kind of you to say."

"And I see that you are acquainted with my cousin Jeffrey as well." His bushy eyebrows furrowed.

"Oh yes, my sisters and I all adore Jeffrey." Paulette smiled at him.

"Yes, I believe that I've heard that." He looked somewhat displeased. "Are you enjoying the ball, Lady Cashelmore?"

"Yes, my husband and I are having a wonderful time. Everything is so beautiful."

"I'm glad to hear it. My uncle does know how to throw a party, does he not?" He glanced around as if looking for something. "Have you happened to have seen my cousin this evening?"

"No, I haven't. But I am certain Jeffrey is here somewhere. It is his father's house, after all." Paulette did not know why she felt the urge to point that out when the man clearly knew whose house he was in. But something in the man's manner put her off. He had obviously been drinking. Feeling a little uncomfortable, she wondered what was taking Declan so long to return to her.

James Granger Eddington laughed a little at her remark, nodding his head. "It's funny, you see. I was looking to find Jeffrey because we had a little wager regarding your sister. And I believe he has lost and he now owes me a great deal of money."

"My sister?" Paulette echoed in surprise. What on earth was the man talking about?

He grinned rather smugly. "Yes, you see, I've heard that your sister is about to be engaged to Lord Shelley."

"Well . . ." Paulette hesitated, unsure what to say next. She supposed it was not her place to inform this man that Yvette was actually going to marry his cousin.

"Jeffrey and I had a wager about that engagement."

"You did?" Now very curious, Paulette eyed him carefully. She truly did not like James Granger Eddington, but now she had an uneasy feeling that she should listen to his story.

"It's quite amusing actually. I bet him that Yvette Hamilton would be engaged to Lord Shelley by Christmas and he bet me that Yvette would be engaged to him by then. And well, now it's almost Christmas and I believe my cousin owes me one thousand pounds!" He held up his glass of champagne and took a sip.

Paulette was stunned. What on earth was going on? Had Jeffrey only wanted to marry Yvette to win a bet? That simply couldn't be! Nothing James Granger Eddington said made sense at all!

"Please sit down, Mr. Eddington." Paulette motioned to the empty side of the velvet settee upon which she sat. "I must admit that I'm curious to know more about this bet you made with Jeffrey regarding my sister."

"Please, Father, just hold off announcing my engagement until the end of the evening." Jeffrey had finally managed to get his father alone. "All I'm asking of you is not to do it until later tonight."

Maxwell Eddington looked confused and not a little disappointed. "I don't see why. It's such perfect timing. I wanted to share your good news when I shared mine."

Jeffrey hesitated, hating to dash his father's plans. It was something he rarely did. "Please, you have to trust me on this. Could you just wait until I tell you it is okay?"

Crestfallen, the gray-haired duke reluctantly agreed. "But that means I have to wait to share my news as well."

"No, no, not at all. Go ahead and announce your marriage to Mother. That's fine. You just can't tell anyone that I'm marrying Yvette Hamilton until later."

His father looked at him curiously. "Why on earth not?"

Jeffrey gave a heavy sigh. "Because Yvette still has to inform Lord Shelley that she is not marrying him after all."

"Oh, I see now." Maxwell Eddington winked at his son conspiratorially. "I didn't know the way of things. I always believed that Yvette Hamilton was a little heartbreaker. You stole her away from old Shelley, eh?"

"I wouldn't put it quite that way, but yes, in a manner of speaking. So will you wait?"

"I will wait only until midnight. Will that give her enough time?"

"Yes, I think so. Thank you, Father."

"Then we shall all meet in the gallery at midnight for the announcement," Maxwell Eddington declared. "And don't be late!" He patted Jeffrey on the shoulder before returning to his guests.

Jeffrey was flooded with relief. Now he just had to find Yvette. He felt dreadful about how he'd left things with her. She was right, of course. Yvette should be the one to tell Lord Shelley, not him. He had reacted jealously and now he felt like an ass.

As he walked to the ballroom, he ran into his cousin, James Granger Eddington.

"Jeffrey! I've been looking for you, old boy!" James called to him.

The last person he wished to speak to this evening was his cousin, who sounded as if he'd been drinking. Jeffrey had much more pressing matters to deal with. Pretending as if he hadn't heard him, Jeffrey continued to make his way through the crowded ballroom. But James followed him.

"Did you forget about our little wager regarding Yvette Hamilton?" James whispered furtively. "I certainly didn't! You've lost, Cousin! And you owe me money!"

Jeffrey came to an abrupt halt. He turned around and stared at his cousin in bewilderment. Good God! He'd completely forgotten about the idiotic bet he'd made with James. He had a sudden sinking feeling in his gut that this evening might not end well at all.

32

Lords a'Leaping

"We are so pleased to meet you again, Lord Shelley!" Lady Cecilia Hamilton fairly glowed with happiness and pride, as she stood beside her husband. She had stopped William Weatherly on his way to the ballroom. "It's good to see you looking well again."

"Thank you. It's nice seeing you both as well." William answered her somewhat distractedly. His eyes were busily scanning the crowd for Yvette's pretty face.

"Your mother seems to be looking remarkably well this evening too," Cecilia Hamilton continued, eager to maintain any type of conversation with him.

"Yes, she's feeling much better, as am I," William said.

"Glad to hear it," Lord Randall Hamilton said. "We were a bit worried about you that night at the theater."

"Thank you for your concern." William paused before asking, "Do you know where Yvette is?"

Cecilia Hamilton looked confused. "Haven't you seen her yet tonight?"

"Not yet, I'm afraid." William shook his head in frustration. It was the damnedest thing. He still had not laid eyes on Yvette Hamilton all evening. "I think we may be walking in circles around each other."

Cecilia Hamilton laughed rather shrilly. "You must be! I just saw her not two minutes ago in the hallway. And I must say my niece is looking exceptionally lovely. Would my husband and I be presuming too much if I were to inquire if you will be asking a certain question to my niece this evening?"

William smiled kindly at her. "You are not being at all presumptuous, Lady Hamilton. As you know, my illness has preempted my plans for your niece. I am hoping to rectify the matter as soon as possible. Hopefully this evening."

"Oh, that is the most wonderful news!" Her thin smile beamed with delight.

"Yes, well if you will excuse me, I would like to find Yvette somewhere in this crush," he said. With a smile, he left her aunt and uncle and went in search of Yvette Hamilton in the ballroom.

Yvette stepped through the crowded hallway after leaving the ballroom, her frustration growing. She still couldn't find Lord Shelley anywhere. Where was he?

"Yvette!" Lisette called to her, with a wave of her hand. "Come here!" Her sister motioned for her to follow her.

She left the hallway and caught up with Lisette. "What is it? Have you seen Lord Shelley? I still haven't been able to talk to him."

Lisette took hold of her arm and pulled her into a small anteroom. Paulette was already inside. Lisette said, "Never mind about Lord Shelley right now. We have to tell you something."

Yvette looked between both sisters and their worried

faces. Something was obviously wrong. "Well, what is it? What is the matter?"

Paulette hesitated, her eyes worried. "I learned something tonight that I found a bit unsettling. At first I wasn't going to tell you, but Lisette thinks you have a right to know."

"I have a right to know what?"

Paulette looked quite reluctant, sitting there in her red silk gown, her hand over her midsection. "I'm sure it's some sort of silly joke. You know how Jeffrey is."

"It's about Jeffrey?" Yvette was confused and she didn't have time for this right now. She must go find William! She wasn't sure when the Duke of Rathmore was going to make his announcement, but she had a feeling she was fast running out of time.

Lisette prompted, "Tell her already."

Paulette began slowly, "I learned something about Jeffrey, and I don't think you're going to like it."

A thousand thoughts flooded Yvette's mind and her heart began to race. What could Jeffrey have said or done that she wouldn't like? Her first reaction was a gut one. "Is it another woman?"

"No." Paulette shook her blond head, looking more than a little grim. "But you should definitely ask him about this matter."

"What matter?" Yvette was quickly losing all patience with her two sisters.

Paulette exchanged a pained glance with Lisette before beginning. "Well, I was talking to Jeffrey's cousin, James Granger Eddington, a little while ago. And he told me that he and Jeffrey had wagered a bet for a large sum of money on who you would marry."

Yvette suddenly felt dizzy. "What?"

"Yes." Paulette's voice was quite low. "It seems James

bet that Jeffrey couldn't get you to marry him instead of Lord Shelley and Jeffrey bet that he could get you to marry him by Christmas."

The room spun around her and Yvette's legs grew weak. She closed her eyes. Surely it was some kind of prank? Clearly her sister was confused and must have misunderstood what Jeffrey's cousin had said. Jeffrey would never wager on her in such a way! Would he? She touched the diamond ring that adorned the finger on her left hand. He did love her, didn't he?

"Help her to sit down!" Paulette cried to Lisette.

Yvette was aware that Lisette guided her to a chair and she sat down woodenly, but she still could not speak. She could barely take a breath.

Jeffrey had wagered that he could get her to marry him by Christmas?

Her mind raced wildly, filled with doubts and confusion. Was it all just a bet? Did he really love her?

Jeffrey's mother had told her that he was in love with her. But Jeffrey had never actually said the words to her. He'd never said that he loved her, but he was quite insistent that she not let Lord Shelley propose to her.

Was that how he planned to win the bet?

Had he any intention of marrying her at all? With his reputation, it wouldn't be difficult to believe. It was a shock to everyone that Jeffrey wanted not only to marry Yvette, but that he wanted to marry at all! How could a man like him ever settle for one woman? Was he going to beg off at the last minute? How did she know if he had really obtained a special license? Had that been a ruse to get her to say yes? Was that also the reason he wouldn't bed her? Because he knew he was not going to go through with it and was never planning to actually marry her?

Terrible, terrible doubts and fears now tormented her.

Had Jeffrey only wanted to marry her by Christmas to win a wager?

Yvette didn't know what to think anymore. She was in love with Jeffrey and thought he was in love with her. Now she didn't know what to believe. There had to be some logical explanation. Perhaps his cousin was lying. But Paulette must have found a ring of truth to it and seen reason enough to be concerned or she wouldn't be sitting here now.

She could not have been that big of a fool! Jeffrey would not do that to her. She could not have lost a chance to become a duchess for the humiliation of being merely the instrument of winning a wager?

"Are you all right, Yvette? Can we get you some water or anything?" Lisette gently patted Yvette's shoulder and glanced at Paulette. "She's so pale."

"I'm so sorry, Yvette, I didn't mean to upset you with this." With regret written all over her face, Paulette looked on the verge of tears. "Lisette and I thought you should ask Jeffrey about it."

"It can't be true," Lisette said, with a shake of her head. "There must be some misunderstanding. Jeffrey would never wager on you!"

"Not about something as important as marriage!" Paulette agreed.

Yvette stared at her sisters mutely. She took a deep breath.

"Please say something, Yvette," Lisette begged.

"You're right. There must be some mistake," she finally murmured. Once again, she stared at the diamond ring on her finger.

"That's what we thought too." Paulette nodded her head emphatically. "You must speak to him and clear up this matter."

Yvette rose to her feet, trembling. Torn between a growing anger and a deep hurt, she held her head high. "There had better be some mistake, or Jeffrey Eddington is going to be very sorry he ever met me!"

With that declaration, Yvette stalked from the room intent on locating her fiancé, leaving her two sisters standing there open-mouthed.

Jeffrey finally caught a glimpse of Lord Shelley's fair-haired head on the other side of the ballroom. Yvette was not with him and he doubted she had been able to talk to him yet, judging from the contented expression on his face. Lord Shelley stood chatting with the Earl of Babey, a glass of champagne in hand.

Jeffrey knew he had to find Yvette right away and tell her about that ridiculous bet he made with his cousin months ago. James had consumed more than enough liquor for one evening and heaven only knew to whom he had been shooting off his mouth. If Yvette had even caught one whiff about his wager to marry her, she would be utterly devastated. Where was she? He hadn't seen her since their little encounter when she'd first arrived.

Then he saw her, heading away from him. He hurried in pursuit, catching up to her at the end of the hallway. "Yvette!"

She turned to stare at him, her expression furious. He knew at that moment she understood all about the wager with his cousin and he felt like the biggest fool.

"Yvette, I'd like to speak to you in private."

Giving him a hard stare, her blue eyes glittering, she said, "I'm sure you would."

With a sinking heart, he guided her to the small room they had been in earlier. After he slid the double doors closed, he faced her, the beautiful woman he wanted to spend the rest of his life with.

"I'm so upset," she began, her voice tremulous, "I don't even know what to say to you."

"Yvette, whatever you have heard, you have to hear my side of the story first," he said.

"Yes, I would have preferred to hear it from you rather than my sisters." Yvette crossed her arms in front of her chest.

"So you have heard about the wager with my cousin, James?" A knot tightened in Jeffrey's stomach. It was such an unfortunate set of circumstances. He'd forgotten all about the foolish bet weeks ago, when he'd fallen in love with Yvette. However, he knew it didn't look good and it was quite clear that she did not find it the least bit amusing. He had the hope, however farfetched, that she might see some humor in it. But in fact, it was the opposite. Her face was too pale and she looked stricken.

She whispered low, "Then it is true? You did wager on me? About . . . marrying me?"

He gave her one of his best smiles, hoping to soften the words. "Yes, but it's not at all what you think—"

"Don't think you can smile your way out of this, Jeffrey Eddington!" Her anger was suddenly palpable. "How dare you do this to me?"

"Yvette, I'm trying to explain to you—"

"What can you possibly say to make it better? You wagered an outrageous sum of money on marrying me before Christmas, on winning me away from Lord Shelley! And you did it. You won. Your skills of seduction are unmatched. Unparalleled, in fact! I fell for them completely. Congratulations! You don't have to bother with me anymore. You are free."

She slid the diamond ring from her finger, tears in her eyes, and handed it to him.

"Oh, Yvette, no . . . no. I won't take the ring back."

Jeffrey's heart pounded like thunder in his chest. Oh God, she believed the worst of him. Refusing to take the ring from her trembling hand, he shook his head. "You don't mean that. It's not at all what it sounds like. I didn't seduce you to win a bet, I swear. Perhaps I did try to seduce you a little in the beginning, yes, but only because I wanted to keep you away from Lord Shelley. I knew you didn't really love him and you would be making a terrible mistake in marrying him. But, Yvette, I do want to marry you. You're the only woman I have *ever wanted* to marry. I know it looks bad, but please believe me that it was never my intention to hurt you."

Blinking back tears, she remained immobile, staring up at him with her big blue eyes.

Jeffrey stepped toward her, longing to take her in his arms. He gently reached out and took hold of her shoulders, grateful that she didn't resist him. Drawing her into his embrace, he breathed deeply of her sweet gardenia scent and held her tight against his chest. He whispered, "You have every right to be angry with me. But I only had the best intentions, I swear to you. My cousin is an idiot and when he made the wager I only agreed because I wanted to protect you. I think I loved you—"

The double doors to the room suddenly slid open and Lord Shelley entered, looking positively thunderous upon seeing the two of them together. For a moment Jeffrey wanted to gloat that old Shelley found Yvette in his embrace. But he fought the urge to do so for now was not the time, nor did he know if in fact he had anything to gloat about.

Slowly he and Yvette disengaged, even though he was reluctant to let her go. She still clutched the diamond ring in her hand.

"I thought I saw you both come in here. Alone." Lord

Shelley's usually calm face was a mask of fury. He scowled at them in complete disdain. "Yvette, I have been looking for you all evening, and this is where I find you? In the arms of Lord Eddington?"

The man uttered Jeffrey's name as if he were a contagious disease. If it had been any other time Jeffrey would have made a biting retort in response, but now . . . now he was too upset with himself and too frightened of losing Yvette, to think of anything but the beautiful woman in front of him, who looked completely devastated. And it was entirely his fault.

"Shelley," Jeffrey began in her defense. He did not care for the manner in which William Weatherly spoke to Yvette. "I can explain everything—"

Yvette placed a hand on Jeffrey's arm to silence him, giving a brief shake of her blond head. "No, let me, Jeffrey," she whispered to him, before facing Lord Shelley.

"William, I am very sorry. And as for Jeffrey and me . . ." Yvette looked guiltily between the two men. "I have been desperate to speak to you about this for days." She turned back to Jeffrey, her expression full of anguish. "If you would please excuse us, Jeffrey? I would like a word with Lord Shelley in private."

Not knowing what Yvette planned to do, Jeffrey was loath to leave the room. After learning of his senseless wager, would the lure of becoming a duchess be too strong for her to resist? Was Yvette going to apologize and beg Lord Shelley's forgiveness in the hope of garnering that sought after proposal after all? Or was she going to tell him that she wished to marry Jeffrey instead?

With his heart in his throat, he nodded reluctantly, giving Yvette one last lingering look before leaving her alone with Lord Shelley.

* * *

Rendered speechless by what he had just seen, William Weatherly stared at the beautiful woman he intended to marry. Dressed in a stunning emerald green gown that flattered her petite figure and her silky blond hair arranged fashionably around her face, she looked as gorgeous and alluring as always. Oh, how he wished to kiss those enticing lips of hers! Yet there was a sadness about her he had not seen before. Judging from her expression, she had most definitely been crying. His initial anger at finding her alone with Eddington now faded to worry. If Eddington had caused her unhappiness, he would kill the man. It had taken all William's self-control not to have taken a swing at Eddington before he left the room.

He was not sure what he had just witnessed between the two of them. A lover's embrace? Surely not! Yvette had declared time and again that Eddington was like an older brother to her. Perhaps she had been upset by something else entirely and Jeffrey was merely comforting her. Either way, William did not like the situation.

Yvette stood quite still, gazing at him, looking unsure what to do.

"Yvette, my dear," he began broaching the subject that had been a thorn in his side for weeks. "Your so called 'friendship' with Lord Eddington . . . well, I must say, it is highly unusual and I don't care for his familiarity with you. If you are going to be my wife, you simply cannot continue to be on such intimate terms with him. I just cannot allow—"

"William," she interrupted him, looking flustered. She took a step toward him, and then hesitated. "That's just it."

"What is?" William was confused by her words.

"About being your wife," Yvette said, her voice very low

and shaky. "I know you have yet to ask me in any formal way, but your intentions have been clear enough."

He smiled, realizing she was worried that the delay meant he had changed his mind. Yes, he was upset with her for being alone with Eddington this evening and he had made that quite clear, but he still wanted her to be his wife. "I have every intention of asking you to marry me, Yvette. I would ask you now."

She gasped, her face pale. "Oh, please do not."

"Excuse me?" Surely he had misheard her!

With her eyes full of what could only be described as torment, she looked on the verge of tears once again and William's heart flipped over in his chest. Whatever could be the matter to upset her so? A niggling feeling of unease crept up his spine.

"Oh, William, I beg you, please do not ask me. I am not worthy of the honor."

Stunned, he stared at her in disbelief. "Yvette, my dearest, what are you saying?"

She said nothing but stared at him. A tear slid down her soft cheek.

"Yvette?" he asked again, his mouth dry. He stepped toward her, until he stood close enough to place his hands on her shoulders. "What do you mean?"

"I am afraid that things . . . my feelings . . . have changed . . . and I . . . I have feelings for someone else, William."

His head pounded and the blood rushed from his face. Damnation! He had been quite certain of her affection for him! What had happened? Had she been playing him for a fool? She couldn't possibly be turning him down when he had not even asked her yet!

"You don't know what you're saying, Yvette. I am going to be a duke!"

She looked up at him, taking one of his hands in hers. She squeezed tightly. "I am very much aware of your title, William, which is why I am not worthy of such an immense honor. So, I beg you, please do not ask me to marry you."

William grew quiet, trying to take it all in. The disappointment was crushing. After all the time he'd spent courting her, finding favor with her family, and deeming her worthy of being his duchess, Yvette Hamilton was not going to accept his offer of marriage. It was unbelievable. How could such a thing happen? To him?!

Yvette was not in love with him.

"Is it Eddington?" he asked finally, knowing in his gut what the answer would be.

She looked him square in the eye and admitted, "Yes. I am in love with him."

"I see." He blinked rapidly and took a deep breath, attempting to maintain his composure. He removed his hands from hers. He had never been more astounded in his life. A woman had never turned him down before. Never.

"I am so sorry, William." Yvette began to explain, "I had wanted to tell you as soon as I realized the truth myself, which was only a few days ago. But you were so ill . . . and I couldn't see you."

"Yes, that would have been useful information. I might have passed up attending the Duke of Rathmore's ball this evening." William would have preferred to suffer this humiliation in the privacy of his own home. It was now quite clear to him why Yvette had sent him a flurry of notes the last three days, asking if he was well enough to see her. If he had known how important it was, he might not have let his vanity keep him from seeing her when he was not looking his best. It also explained Lucien Sinclair's unexpected attempt to see him this morning.

"I did not wish for you to learn of my feelings for Jeffrey here tonight, truly I did not," she said softly.

"On that score I believe you, Yvette, and I thank you for trying to spare me this."

"I have enjoyed our time together, William, and my affection for you was honest, I assure you. However, my feelings for Jeffrey caught me quite off guard. I don't know that I can explain what happened with him."

William lifted his chin, not able to bear hearing about her amorous sentiments for Lord Eddington. Never had he disliked a man more. "I suppose it's best to know the truth now before entering into a marriage together."

"Yes." She nodded in agreement, her eyes sad. "I am so very sorry."

"Well, I guess that is all there is to say." He forced a smile he did not feel. "We can part as friends, I hope?"

"Oh, yes." She gave a halfhearted grin back at him. "Of course, I shall always consider you a dear friend."

"I am happy to hear that." He took a deep breath. "Then I shall take my leave of you now and return to the ballroom."

"William, I . . . There is . . . one more thing you ought to know . . . ," she said with great reluctance, wringing her hands together in front of her.

"Yes?"

"Lord Rathmore is going to announce my engagement to his son this evening."

His stomach roiled at her words. William could take no more. This was rubbing salt in the wound, so to speak. Although to her credit, she did look mortified by the prospect. At least he had the comfort that there had only been rumors of their impending engagement and nothing certain. Aside from her family and his mother, no one else knew for certain of his intentions to marry her. He said, "Then I hope you understand my desire not to remain for the announcement."

"I understand completely."

Again, he forced another smile at her, fighting the urge to take her in his arms and kiss her one last time. Filled with disappointment and regret, he said, "I wish you and your family a most joyous Christmas, Miss Hamilton."

"I wish the same to you and your family, Lord Shelley."

They had reverted back to their formal beginnings. With that, William held his head high and left the room.

33

Pipers Piping

Yvette waited for a full half hour before she was calm enough to return to the ballroom. She had no desire to go, but she made the effort. The noise of the ballroom no longer seemed festive to her. Still quite angry with Jeffrey and feeling terrible for Lord Shelley, she managed a weak smile for the friends who greeted her. Now she only wanted to find one of her sisters and return home. This evening had disintegrated into a nightmarish mess.

"Yvette!"

"Lucien?"

Her tall and handsome brother-in-law caught up to her. With an indulgent smile, he said, "They've been looking for you everywhere. Your presence is requested in the gallery right away."

She shook her head, fighting the urge to cry. "Oh, Lucien, will you please take me home?"

"Why?" His green eyes looked at her with sudden concern. "What's wrong, Yvette?"

"Jeffrey." It was all she could manage to say, but in essence his name said it all.

"What has happened?"

"I don't wish to talk about it now. I just need to go home."

Lucien gave her a sympathetic look and attempted to calm her. "Oh, Yvette, I have been friends with Jeffrey Eddington for most of my life and we have been through a great deal together. But I have never seen him act the way he does with you. He is head over heels in love with you and he would never do anything to hurt you. Not intentionally anyway. If he has hurt you, I am certain he didn't mean it."

"That's what Jeffrey said too," Yvette murmured. "But I just feel so strange about everything now, knowing what he did. . . ."

"Then see him, talk to him. Don't go home and hide, Yvette. Running away doesn't solve anything."

"But Lucien, you don't know what he—"

"But I do know you. And Jeffrey," he interrupted her, "and I know enough to see how much you love each other. Go to him."

Yvette paused, unsure what to do. Perhaps Lucien was right.

"There you are, my girl!" a jovial voice called to her.

Yvette was suddenly face to face with the Duke of Rathmore, whose eyes were twinkling with delight.

"Oh, Lucien, I see you have found her!" Maxwell Eddington said. "Yvette, my dear, we've been looking for you everywhere. It's almost midnight and I've waited long enough! It's time to make our announcements. Jeffrey and Janet are already in the gallery, waiting for us to join them."

"Oh, Your Grace," Yvette stammered. She looked nervously to Lucien for help. "I'm . . . not feeling at all well. I'd rather wait—"

"Nonsense!" Maxwell Eddington cried, dismissing her worries.

Lucien nodded at her, smiling. "Go."

"Excuse us, Lucien." The Duke of Rathmore took Yvette's arm and began guiding her to the main hall. "You look well enough to me. In fact, you look lovelier than I've ever seen you. It's just the excitement that's got you all aflutter. Besides, it won't take but a minute or two. I can't wait to see the expressions on everyone's faces when they hear our exciting news!"

His smile was so infectious that Yvette could not resist him. Helplessly, she followed the duke up the marble steps to the small gallery overlooking the main hall, where many of the guests had assembled. She searched the crowd below for her sisters, but could not locate them. She gave a silent prayer that Lord Shelley and his mother had left already and would not bear witness to this event.

The Duke of Rathmore escorted her to the gallery, where his new wife and his only son were waiting.

Jeffrey had the decency to look sheepish when he saw Yvette. With questioning eyes, he took her hand in his and drew her to his side. "You don't have to do this if you don't wish to marry me," he whispered in her ear. "I can tell my father we've called it off."

"Is that what you want?" Yvette whispered back. "For me to call it off?"

Maxwell Eddington gave a signal to the orchestra and they ceased playing. The large crowd of elegantly attired guests grew hushed in anticipation. In his booming voice, he began, "Ladies and gentlemen, I am sorry to interrupt your revelry, but I wish to thank you for coming to my annual Christmas ball."

The crowd below cheered in agreement.

"You know it isn't what I want," Jeffrey murmured fervently. He squeezed her hand in his. "I want to marry you more than anything in the world. But what I want doesn't matter. All that matters to me is what you want, Yvette."

"I have wonderful news to share with you this evening!" The duke's voice boomed across the wide hall. "News I hope you will be as happy to hear as I am to share it with all of you."

A sea of interested faces looked up at the gallery in expectation.

Yvette stared at Jeffrey Eddington, tears welling in her eyes.

She had loved this man for longer than she could recall, certainly long before she'd realized it. The day she had first met him in the bookshop, while she was atop a ladder and he entered looking so striking and debonair. He had bowed elegantly to her, making her feel like the fairest lady of them all. Jeffrey had always had the ability to make her feel that way. He made her feel special all the time, even back when he'd allowed her to have a first taste of champagne when Juliette and Harrison became engaged. Jeffrey had teased and adored her for years.

All her life she had been longing for someone or something to make her feel special and important and needed, and it had been right in front of her the entire time. She had gradually come to rely on him, to need him, to want him, to love him. She could not imagine her life without him in it.

"Yvette?" Jeffrey asked, his voice a bit more anxious.

"I am sure some of you may find this news quite surprising for many reasons," the Duke of Rathmore continued to talk to the crowd, drawing on his considerable charm and flair for drama to keep them in suspense. "My life has not been without scandal, as you are well aware." With a sly wink and a mischievous grin, he leaned over the balustrade and his guests smiled indulgently at him. "So while this announcement may cause a greater scandal, in some ways it rights a terrible wrong done long ago to two people I love dearly."

The waiting crowd grew hushed, eager to hear the duke's great revelation.

Jeffrey squeezed her hand again, prompting an answer from her. Yvette knew that if she didn't say something, Jeffrey's father would announce their engagement whether she wanted him to or not.

What did she want? For all that she had wished to be a duchess, she now knew deep in her heart that William Weatherly was not the man for her. Letting him go had been the right decision, for she did not truly love him.

She loved the man who held her hand and looked at her with such longing.

"I am happy to announce that I have married again. Janet Rutherford has consented to marry me, so I would like to introduce you to my beautiful new wife," the duke told the crowd, drawing Janet to the balustrade beside him, presenting her. "The Duchess of Rathmore."

As the new duchess gave a little wave and smiled happily at the crowd, a low buzz of voices began to grow below the gallery. Murmurs and mumbles of surprise and censure echoed around the great hall.

"Yvette, I love you," Jeffrey whispered softly.

She stared at him, her heart racing. He had finally said the words to her!

Jeffrey murmured in her ear, "I want to marry you. I can explain that stupid bet. It means nothing, I swear to you. I'm not half good enough for you, but marry me and I will spend the rest of my life making you happy."

Yvette smiled at Jeffrey. "I love you too."

Looking astonishingly relieved, Jeffrey pressed a tender kiss to her cheek.

"But there's more good news! This is a doubly joyous night for me. For I am a very proud father as well. It seems *both* Eddington men are no longer bachelors!" Maxwell Eddington called down to the buzzing and wide-eyed guests.

If they were shocked at the fact that the scandal-ridden duke had married his former mistress and the mother of his illegitimate son, they were stunned into silence by the news that Jeffrey Eddington, the infamous and notorious rake, was about to be married. They waited, hanging on the Duke of Rathmore's every word.

"My son, Jeffrey Eddington, is engaged to marry the very beautiful, Miss Yvette Hamilton!" the Duke of Rathmore declared loudly.

The guests erupted into gasps of surprise and then shouts of congratulations and applause as Jeffrey and Yvette walked to the balustrade hand in hand, both grinning broadly.

Unfortunately Lord Shelley had not been able to escape Rathmore's ball before the announcement. He did not applaud with the others but watched the proceedings with a heavy heart. Seeing Yvette up in the gallery, standing beside Eddington with a smile on her pretty face, he shook his head in disbelief. His long desired plans for the evening had gone terribly awry. It was quite unbelievable to think that he, the future Duke of Lansdowne, had been thrown over for an illegitmate son. Eddington might be the bastard of a duke, but he was still just a bastard! William longed to get the hell out of there, but if he left now, it would look bad and people would talk. He couldn't abide the idea of anyone pitying him or laughing at him behind his back.

Standing beside him, Wilhelmina Weatherly, dressed in dark gray silk, gave her son a questioning look. "Whatever happened, William? I thought that you and she—"

"I've changed my mind, Mother," he answered brusquely, not quite meeting her eyes. He was simply not in the mood to discuss the end of his courtship of Yvette Hamilton with his mother. He didn't even want to think about it himself. It was then William saw Jane Fairmont making her way toward him through the buzzing crowd.

"Good evening, Lord Shelley." She smiled warmly up at him, her sultry green eyes looking a bit worried. She looked to his mother with a deferential nod. "Lady Lansdowne."

"Oh, Miss Fairmont!" William's mother said. "It's so nice to see you again!"

William was pleasantly surprised by how pretty Jane looked this evening. Had she done something different to her chestnut hair? Dressed in a gown of rich red, she was far more beautiful than he remembered her being. He favored her with a smile.

"It is a great pleasure to see you again, Miss Fairmont," he said.

"What do you think of the Duke of Rathmore's news?" she asked them. "Isn't it exciting?"

"I'm not sure," the duchess began with a little frown. "It's quite scandalous of the duke to marry his former mistress. But that man has always done exactly what he wanted."

"I, for one, couldn't be happier for him. For him *and* his son." William stressed that point. It was always better to keep face. Besides, if he acted happy for Yvette Hamilton, no one would think she had thrown him over. He paused, looking toward Jane. "I believe the orchestra has begun playing again. Would you care to dance with me, Miss Fairmont?"

Her sweet smile deepened. "I would love to, my lord."

"Please excuse us, Mother." Feeling better than he had all evening, William Weatherly took Miss Fairmont's arm and led her to the ballroom with his head held high.

"I simply don't believe it," Cecilia Hamilton cried in despair to her husband. "Yvette was so close to marrying a duke! He was about to propose to her, for heaven's sake! And she ends up with that rogue, Eddington!"

Randall Hamilton, his bushy brows furrowed in disgust, shook his head. "My brother's daughters never had a bit of sense or ambition in such matters. They all take after him. And Thomas never aspired to be anything more than a two-bit bookseller."

Cecilia wiped away a disconsolate tear with her lace-trimmed handkerchief. "They are just like their silly mother too! But I thought, out of all of them, that Yvette had more sense than that. Oh, to throw over a duke for a rake! It isn't to be believed! After all the care I've taken with the girl!"

Randall sighed heavily. "There's nothing for it. Yvette has made her choice, Cecilia. And quite publicly too, I may add."

Cecilia sniffed. "Oh, I don't know how I shall face my friends now."

"The same as you always have. Come now, Cecilia, we need to drag Nigel from the gaming table before he loses even more of our money. It is time to take our leave."

"Oh, but, Randall, I don't know how I shall bear the disappointment! We almost had a duke in the family!" she wailed. Cecilia always focused on the negative, losing sight of the fact that one of her nieces had married a marquis and one an earl.

"Well, I suppose having the illegitimate son of a duke is the closest we're going to get!" Randall Hamilton took his dissatisfied wife's arm and marched from the hall.

James Granger Eddington stared up at the gallery in utter astonishment. Had he heard his uncle's words incorrectly? But no! There were his cousin, Jeffrey, and Yvette Hamilton standing together for all to see. Engaged. About to be married. It was impossible. He had had it on the highest authority that Lord Shelley was set to propose to Yvette this evening! Nigel Hamilton had sworn to him that the future Duke of Lansdowne was going to marry his cousin Yvette Hamilton. It would be the last time that James trusted that inveterate gambler.

How on earth had the tables turned so drastically? James shook his head, thinking perhaps he was seeing things. He had consumed quite a lot of liquor this evening, more than he usually did. He rubbed his eyes and looked again. There they were still, the handsomest couple at the ball, waving happily at the crowd.

Not only had he lost the largest wager he'd ever made, but his damnably handsome cousin had won the girl James had been fantasizing about for months. It seemed that Jeffrey always got what he wanted when it came to beautiful women.

Well, his cousin may have inherited good looks and charm, but he wouldn't inherit Rathmore's estate!

"James! I've been looking for you!" Lady Amelia Wells,

his fiancée, hurried over to him. "Can you believe what your uncle has done?"

"Nothing Uncle Maxwell does surprises me anymore."

"Oh, but to marry that horrid woman after all these years! A ballet dancer! It's just giving rise to that ghastly scandal all over again. How shall we face it?" she cried to him, her big brown eyes full of worry.

"Be glad it's old Rutherford he married and not some young thing who can give him a brood of children to be his legal heirs, Amelia." James shrugged, not particularly worried about his uncle's antics. He was more concerned about losing the bet to Jeffrey.

"Yes, I understand that, but still, people are talking about us," she said.

"There's nothing for it. When Uncle Maxwell dies, I become the Duke of Rathmore and everyone will forget about this debacle."

Amelia didn't look at all pleased by his answer.

James sighed heavily. "Act happy about it, Amelia. You're still going to be duchess one day. Grin and bear it and act as if nothing is amiss and we are pleased as punch by Uncle Maxwell's marriage. That will squelch scandal more than if we show we are appalled by him."

James would pay Jeffrey what he owed him, but still, in the end, he'd won the big game over his cousin. Safe in the knowledge that the duke's old mistress/new wife was no longer of an age to bear children and there would be no new heirs on the horizon to take his place, James, not Jeffrey, was destined to be the next Duke of Rathmore!

Plastering a brittle smile on his face, James lifted his glass in congratulations to the happy couple. Both of them.

* * *

The four Hamilton sisters stared up at their youngest sister on the gallery with Jeffrey Eddington, both of them looking quite happy and in love.

Paulette whispered low to Lisette, "Well, I suspect they managed to sort things out between them."

Lisette grinned in delight. "Of course they did! I couldn't imagine Jeffrey doing anything to deliberately hurt her."

"Well, neither could I, but you must admit it was a shocking story."

"What was a shocking story?" Juliette asked, overhearing them.

Lisette shook her head. "Nothing. Yvette may tell you later, but it's nothing to worry about now."

Captain Harrison Fleming looked smugly at his wife. "I told you so."

Juliette stuck her tongue out at him.

Colette beamed with happiness that her little sister had found love with Jeffrey Eddington. She glanced around the crowded hall, taking in the reaction of the others. Then she turned to her husband. "Everyone seems to be accepting the news of the duke's marriage fairly well, don't you think?"

"As well as can be expected," Lucien agreed. He gave Colette a wry glance. "After what my own parents went through together, nothing about marriages can surprise me anymore."

"Oh, Lucien," she said, placing a light kiss on his cheek.

"Congratulations on your sister's engagement!" Lady Katherine Spencer hurried to Colette's side, squealing in delight with the news. "I'm so very happy for Yvette and Lord Eddington. I've always thought they would be perfect together!"

"That is so kind of you to say, Kate," Colette said to

Yvette's dear friend. "We're very pleased with the arrangement."

Kate's voice dropped to a furtive whisper. "I was quite afraid Yvette would end up terribly unhappy if she married Lord Shelley. I am relieved to discover that she has changed her mind on that score."

Colette held up her fan and whispered back, "So are we!"

34

The Night Before Christmas

"You take my breath away, Mrs. Eddington."

Yvette paused in the doorway of the bedroom, hesitant. "Say it again."

Jeffrey smiled in amusement. "I like your hair all loose like that. You look beautiful."

"No." She shook her head. "The other part."

"Mrs. Eddington?"

She nodded happily. "Yes."

The loving look he gave her, made her heart flip over.

He held out his hand to her. "Come to me, Mrs. Eddington."

Yvette practically flew across the room to him, her delicate white silk nightgown fluttering around her as he scooped her up into his arms.

They had married quietly that morning in a small London chapel with only their families there to witness the event. Wearing a simple gown of the palest pink and carrying a bouquet of white roses, Yvette had walked down the aisle with her two pretty little nieces, Sara Fleming and

Mara Reeves, as her flower girls and said the vows that made her Jeffrey Eddington's wife. No, it hadn't been quite the grand society wedding she had once envisioned for herself, but it had been perfect in every way, in spite of its hasty and impromptu preparations. She and Jeffrey had decided on the night of the Christmas ball that they didn't want to wait any longer to be married.

After a wedding celebration at Devon House with her sisters and brothers-in-law, her mother, and the Duke and Duchess of Rathmore, Jeffrey had brought her to his townhouse for the evening. They would have a proper honeymoon after Christmas and were planning a trip to the south of France, Spain, and Italy.

But for tonight, on Christmas Eve, they were finally alone together in Jeffrey's London townhouse as husband and wife. Well, Yvette supposed it was her home now too. And here she was in Jeffrey's bedroom, or rather her husband's bedroom! She had given the room a nod of approval for its surprisingly simple and masculine look, decorated in hues of rich brown and deep blue. The logs glowed with the warmth of the fire to banish the December chill, and candles flickered around the room, casting the room in golden shadows.

Yvette planned to add her own touches at some point, but for now it was perfect.

Jeffrey carried her to the bed, and her heart raced at what she knew was to come. He placed her carefully on the soft, midnight-blue counterpane and lay down beside her. She wrapped her arms around his neck and pulled him close, breathing deeply of his now-familiar and comforting spicy scent.

"No regrets?" she asked.

"None at all. I'm happier than I've been in my entire life."

She smiled. "Me too."

Never had she felt such peace and contentment. Yvette had always been looking for something grand to make her feel important, thinking that would make her happy. Not satisfied with what she had, she longed for admiration and the acquisition of pretty objects to give her a sense of fulfillment.

But now with Jeffrey, those other things no longer mattered. Everything else paled in comparison to being in love with this man.

"Thank you for forgiving me for the ridiculous wager with James. As I said, I only made it as a reason to be near you, to stop you from marrying Lord Shelley because I knew you wouldn't be happy with him. I think I loved you even then, but was too stupid to realize it."

"I'll agree to that." She kissed his cheek playfully.

"I'll have you know that I dissolved the wager with my cousin and refused to accept his payment." He smiled wickedly at her. "Even though I won."

She laughed at him. "Yes, you won. You married me by Christmas."

His expression grew serious. "Yes, I won. By the luck of the heavens, I won the most beautiful, the most wonderful, the most loving woman in the world to be my wife, when I don't deserve her."

"Jeffrey," she whispered, overwhelmed by his sweet words. "Please don't say that you don't deserve me, because it's not true. And I'm very sorry that I doubted you."

"No . . . I was the idiot. And that you still chose to marry me when you could have been a grand duchess leaves me speechless."

"I chose you because I love you."

"I love you."

"And your kisses make me mad with desire for you."

"Do they?"

"Yes. Very much so."

He pressed a soft kiss against her cheek. "Like this?"

"Yes."

He kissed and nuzzled her throat. "And this?'

"Oh, yes," she said, her pulse beginning to race at the feel of his warm mouth on her skin.

He kissed his way back up to her mouth, placing his lips ever so gently against hers. "This?"

Yvette whispered excitedly, "We're married now."

"Yes?" he questioned.

"So we don't have to stop."

"No. We don't." His mouth came down over hers, taking her in a heated and torrid kiss.

She sighed and simply melted into him.

Plundering her mouth with his tongue, Jeffrey moved his body closer to hers and Yvette pressed herself against him. With both of them dressed only in their nightclothes, she could feel the length of his body quite clearly, which both fascinated and excited her.

Liquid heat seemed to fill her veins as she stretched back against the pillows and Jeffrey covered her body with his. The weight of him above her sent a thrill through her and she wrapped her arms tighter around him, sinking her fingers into his thick dark hair. Their kiss grew more ravenous, their tongues intertwined and their breaths intermingled.

Oh, how wonderful it felt to be kissed by him! And how much she wanted him!

The desire between them increased with each passing second until Yvette thought she would expire from the yearning need within her. Jeffrey's breath sent shivers of delight along her spine, as his hands moved over the curves of her body. Through the thin silk of her night-gown, he cupped her breasts and she caught her breath at the sensation.

Jeffrey tore his mouth from her, murmuring her name. Before she had a chance to protest the end of their kiss, he rose up. With a swift movement he slid his nightshirt over his head, tossing it to the floor. Now that he was naked before her, she forgot to breathe at the sight of him. Slowly, she placed her hands against the expanse of his broad chest, skimming her fingers over the smooth planes of his skin. He sighed and let her explore.

Oh, he was glorious! Like the classical statues of Greek gods she'd seen in a museum once. She pressed her lips against the warmth of his chest, leaving light kisses along the width of him. With a tentative hand, she reached down and took hold of him, amazed by the heat and softness of his rigidity. She gave a gentle squeeze and he groaned in pleasure. Overwhelmed, she removed her hand and looked up at him.

With his eyes on her, he reached down and slid her white silk nightgown up the length of her thighs. She reached down with both hands and assisted him, pulling the material higher and lifting her arms over her head, as he removed the garment from her completely. Laid bare, she trembled and sank back into the pillows, her breathing shallow.

"You're perfect," he said, his voice husky with desire as he gazed upon her nakedness. He cupped her face in his hands. "I love you."

"I love you."

He leaned forward and covered her naked body with his own. The contact of bare skin against skin was deliciously intimate and the heat emanating from him seemed to meld their bodies together. Again, she slid her arms around him, her hands running up and down his back, feeling the taut muscles that held him securely above her. He settled himself between her thighs and the powerful force of that intimate placement took her breath away. She arched her back in response, longing to be even closer to him.

Jeffrey brought his lips to hers again, kissing the sighs of delight from her mouth. His lips then moved along her jaw, down her throat and to her chest, kissing her breasts and nipples. Gasping in excitement, Yvette spread her fingers into his hair again, pressing his head into her. The feel of his slick tongue on her breasts was exquisite. An incredible wave of desire, an aching need, swept over her as his mouth moved lower, kissing the flat planes of her abdomen, swirling his tongue into her belly button.

Yvette stilled as his fingers, ever so gently caressed her heated skin, trailing a path down between her thighs. She arched up and her mouth went dry as he touched her most intimately, dipping a finger deep inside of her.

"Jeffrey," she murmured low, a bit panicked.

"Shh, it's all right. Just relax. Let me," he said in a soothing whisper before covering her mouth with his once more.

She closed her eyes, even though she knew he watched her. With expert skill, he pleasured her with his hand, stroking and fondling her, until she forgot to think, forgot where she was, forgot her name. Over and over, his fingers swirled and touched her in ways she had never imagined, never dreamed of, bringing her to the brink of an intense yearning and desire. Her arms went slack, her head fell back on the pillows, and her breathing became rapid as she gave in to the overwhelming waves of utter bliss that crashed over her. When she cried out his name at the height of her pleasure, he held her and kissed her back to her senses.

Yvette clung to him, breathing in great gasps, in awe of what had just happened to her body. "Is that it?" she asked in wonder.

Jeffrey smiled wickedly, his eyes dark with desire. "We haven't even begun. . . ."

"Oh, my," was all she could manage to say, but she smiled in anticipation.

He rose up and moved over her again. Bracing his hands on either side of her, he settled himself firmly between her thighs. She stared at him, holding on tightly, her fingers pressing into his back, as he kissed her again. With a gentle movement, he entered her like a sword in a sheath. She held her breath, pressing her lips together, growing accustomed to the fullness of him inside of her. As Jeffrey began to move within her, slowly she exhaled, releasing the initial pain. Little by little, that yearning need returned and she began to arch against him, meeting his thrusts with eagerness.

The aching pleasure blossomed within her again and they moved together in timeless rhythm, losing themselves in each other's bodies, which were slick with sweat. Soft whispered words, sweet kisses, and gentle caresses suddenly gave way to driving need and mounting desire. His motions became more forceful, more urgent and demanding as he plunged into her. She welcomed him, matching his thrusts with her own. All her focus centered on the two of them and their love for each other.

The waves of sheer bliss enveloped her once again and what felt like a million tiny stars exploded around her. She screamed his name as he drove into her, finding his own heated release. As he called to her, an added thrill coursed through her, increasing her pleasure. Feeling faint and with her body tingling in every way, Yvette lay there motionless.

Jeffrey collapsed on the pillow beside her, spent and panting for breath. He then cradled her in his arms, kissing her face, smoothing away her hair, which had become tangled around them. Together they lay, until their breathing returned to normal.

"Oh, Jeffrey, I don't even have words," she said at long last.

He smiled at her. "You liked it?"

"Oh, God, yes! It was amazing."

"Not *nice?*" he teased.

"Not even close to nice." She knew he referred to her descriptions of William Weatherly's kisses. Those nice little kisses paled in comparison to the wonder of what she had just shared with Jeffrey! "It was spectacular. Wonderful. Earth shattering."

"Earth shattering, you say?" He smiled wolfishly at her. "I'll take that."

Yvette released a long sigh. "I'm so happy we didn't have a long engagement."

He laughed low and deep at her words and pulled her closer to him. "I am too."

"My sisters will be so jealous."

Confused, he asked, "Why?"

"Because I now know the truth about the infamous Jeffrey Eddington!" She giggled helplessly.

"And just what would that be?" He stared at her, incredulous at her pronouncement.

"Well, as you know . . . your reputation with the ladies being what it is . . . we've all wondered about you."

His blue eyes twinkling, he seemed vastly amused by that. "Have you now?"

"Oh, yes! How could we not be?"

"Who would have thought nice girls like you discuss such things?"

She looked up at him helplessly. "Well, we do. Much more often than you think."

"Well, I hate to disappoint you, my dear wife, and your lovely sisters, but my reputation is vastly exaggerated."

"But you said you'd kissed hundreds of women!" Yvette cried in protest.

"Kissed, yes." He shook his head. "Bedded, no."

"What do you mean?"

"I have kept mistresses, but not as many as your vivid imagination would allow for. Contrary to popular belief, I did not indiscriminately bed every woman who crossed my path."

"Oh."

"Oh?" he questioned with a laugh. "You sound disappointed, Yvette."

"No, I'm not at all. Just taking in this different side of you."

"And?"

"And it makes me happy." Yvette paused and looked at him. "You don't have a mistress now, do you?"

"I did, but she ended it months ago when she realized even before I did that I was in love with you."

"Truly?" Yvette asked in amazement.

"Truly." Jeffrey placed a sweet kiss on her mouth, as if to emphasize his words. "And I will never have another mistress, I swear to you. I have only the most beautiful wife in the world to make my life complete."

"Good, because I might have to kill you if you had a mistress," she said with a smile.

"Thank goodness I'm safe then." He kissed her again.

"Just a moment, Jeffrey." She wrinkled her brows in confusion. "Then why does everyone think that you've been with scores of women if it isn't true?"

He paused before saying, "Because it was easier to let everyone believe the worst about me."

"Why?" That made no sense to Yvette. "Why on earth would you want people to think the worst of you?"

With a heavy sigh, he squeezed her tightly to him. "Because of what I was, it was easier for everyone to think me an irresponsible rogue and not take me seriously. It suited my purposes. No one suspected me of doing what I was really doing."

"You're referring to the secret work you do for the government?"

"Yes."

"That you won't tell me about?"

"It's not that I won't tell you, Yvette. It's that I can't tell you about it." He hesitated. "Let's simply say I gather very sensitive information from certain parties in a somewhat clandestine manner and pass it along to other parties in need of such information." He flashed her a smile. "It's really quite amazing the things people will tell me at a party while they are drinking and no one suspects my motives. Anyway, I perform a necessary service and having people believe me a careless playboy whose sole purpose in life is pleasure suits my purposes remarkably well."

Yvette sat up and stared at the man beside her. "Jeffrey, how can I not have known this about you all these years?"

He gave her his most charming smile. "Because I didn't want you to, my lovely. No one knows about my profession, except Lucien and Harrison, and my father, of course."

She leaned down on top of his chest. "And now me."

"And now you." He kissed her.

"I won't tell anyone, I promise."

"I know you won't. But I think it is time for me to retire from that line of work now."

Yvette placed kisses over his bare chest. "Why is that?"

He gazed into her eyes. "Because it can also be very dangerous, and I've done more than enough, and now I would much rather spend my time at home in bed with my beautiful wife."

Yvette shivered with desire at his words. "That is the most wonderful idea I've ever heard."

"No . . . I think this is. . . ." Jeffrey drew her against him, covering her mouth with his and rolling on top of her once more.

35

Christmas Day

"Well, here is the married couple now!" Juliette called out as Yvette and Jeffrey entered the great drawing room of Devon House late the following afternoon. A light snow was falling outside, dusting the ground in white, as evening began to fall, but inside the family had gathered together on Christmas Day. The scent of evergreens and pinecones filled the air as well as the delicious smells of Christmas dinner.

Jeffrey and Yvette were instantly enveloped in congratulatory hugs by everyone as if they had been gone for weeks and not just one night, but Yvette didn't mind in the least. Nothing could have made her happier than to have all the people she loved most in the world under one roof. Her mother, her sisters, her brothers-in-law, and her little nieces and nephews. And especially her husband. Yvette was thrilled that even Jeffrey's parents were joining them as well.

Cries and shouts of "Merry Christmas!" filled the air.

All of the children were playing near the large Christmas tree, excitedly looking at their presents and playing with their new toys. A traditional Christmas feast was planned for supper, with a goose and roast beef and Yorkshire pudding, and the jovial mood in the drawing room was typical of a Hamilton family holiday get together.

Yvette and Jeffrey went to sit by her mother first. Genevieve Hamilton was growing stronger and her health continued to improve a little more each day. Still as outspoken as ever, she smiled joyfully at them. She took Jeffrey's hand in hers.

"I am so very happy that you have married my daughter. You have always been good to me and now you are my son. *Vous avez toujours été bon avec moi et je vous ai toujours bien aimé. Vous êtes maintenant un vrai fils pour moi.* I love you, Jeffrey," her mother said to him.

Genuinely touched by her words, Jeffrey kissed Genevieve's cheek. "I am happy to be your son, Mrs. Hamilton, and I am even happier to be married to your daughter."

"They are all married now. Each one of my girls is happy," Genevieve said with a contented little sigh. "This is a very joyous Christmas. *C'est un Noël très special. Toutes mes filles sont maintenant mariées. Je suis heureuse.*"

"And we are very glad that you are here with us to share our happiness, *Maman,*" Yvette said. Recalling how close they had come to losing her, Yvette gave her mother a fierce little hug.

"Yvette, come over here!"

Leaving her husband with her mother, Yvette went to see what her sisters wanted. The four of them were gathered together near the mantel, looking at her most curiously.

"So?" Paulette whispered, her eyes twinkling with impishness. "How was last night?"

Lisette, Colette, Paulette, and Juliette looked at her expectantly.

Her cheeks warming a little, Yvette smiled knowingly at her older sisters. "It was quite incredible."

"We thought as much." Juliette winked at her. "How could it not be?"

"It was even better than I imagined," Yvette managed to add before covering her heated cheeks with her hands.

"We won't go into details now. We just wanted to make sure you had a wonderful night," Lisette said in a low voice.

"Oh, I did!"

Colette smiled at her. "Well, we think that you and Jeffrey are the most romantic story of all of us."

"You do?" Yvette was incredulous.

Paulette nodded her head. "Yes, we've been talking about you. It's very romantic and unexpected to fall in love with someone you've known for so long, don't you agree?"

"Anyone can be swept off their feet by a stranger, but to suddenly feel that way about someone you've always known is quite extraordinary," Juliette said.

Yvette stared at her sisters, smiling, and nodded her head. "Yes, it is. Very extraordinary."

"What are you lovelies whispering about so intently over here?" Jeffrey asked the five of them as he joined their little circle near the fireplace.

Blushing, Paulette laughed nervously and blurted out, "You."

"Me?" Jeffrey stared at them. He exchanged a glance with his wife as the girls tried to restrain their giggles.

"I told you so," Yvette whispered to him.

"Well, I hope you did me proud," Jeffrey said with a mischievous smile at his wife.

"Yes," Juliette said boldly. "She did."

Then Jeffrey rolled his eyes. "What am I going to do with all of you girls?"

Colette spoke up. "We were just saying again that now you really are our brother and how happy that makes us."

"Ah yes, now the title of brother is official." He beamed at them.

Yvette loved the fact that Jeffrey was very special to her sisters, but he belonged only to her. She gave him a flirtatious look. "But you're not my brother."

"And for that I am most eternally grateful." Jeffrey took Yvette's hand in his and drew her to his side. "And you four beautiful girls are now truly my sisters, which makes me the luckiest man in the world."

"It's all worked out quite wonderfully, hasn't it?" Lisette said, looking at them fondly.

Jeffrey grinned broadly. "It certainly has."

"Everyone, may I interrupt you for a moment, please?" the Duke of Rathmore called out, looking about the drawing room with his masterful presence.

Yvette shared a questioning glance with Jeffrey, who stood beside her. Her husband gave a helpless shrug and raised his brows, obviously not privy to whatever his father was about to say.

With the family directing their attention at him expectantly, Maxwell Eddington stood in the center of the room, his expression full of excitement. "It seems I have yet another announcement to make. I was going to wait until supper, but I simply can't contain myself any longer." He smiled pointedly at Jeffrey. "This one concerns my son. And his wife."

Again, Yvette met Jeffrey's eyes. What on earth was the duke up to now? Was it some sort of extravagant Christmas gift? He'd already told them yesterday that he would be giving them Eddington Grove as a wedding gift.

"The news of my marriage to Janet Rutherford has done more than incite the gossips to talk about me." Maxwell Eddington smiled broadly at his wife. "It has also raised some valid questions about the line of heredity. A few of my powerful friends and my legal experts are investigating the matter now, but there is a distinct possibility that since I married his mother, my son Jeffrey can be declared legitimate. And if that is the case, it only stands to reason, therefore, that as my lawful and only son, he also can become my rightful heir."

The room grew silent. Wide-eyed at the news, everyone stared at the Duke of Rathmore and then at Jeffrey.

"Is such a thing even possible?" Jeffrey managed to ask.

"Yes. It's a bit premature, of course, and I don't know if it will even come to pass, but the possibility exists and I couldn't resist sharing the good news. I thought it made a most wonderful Christmas gift to my son and daughter-in-law." Maxwell Eddington positively beamed with pleasure and pride.

The silence in the room continued. No one uttered a word, aside from the gaggle of children chattering and playing at the other end of the drawing room.

Yvette looked at her husband, who still appeared dumb-struck. Jeffrey's blue eyes were wide with stunned disbelief.

"Father?" he asked.

"Isn't it wonderful news, my boy?" the duke asked, his expression elated.

"We are so thrilled by the possibility of being able to make this happen for you, Jeffrey, darling," his mother added, tears of joy welling in her eyes. "Aren't you happy to hear it?"

"Of course, I am . . . ," Jeffrey said, although he still seemed shaken by his father's declaration.

Everyone else remained silent. What the Duke of Rathmore had proclaimed was highly unusual, but at the same time, it made perfect sense. Since Maxwell had married Jeffrey's mother, then Jeffrey could no longer be considered illegitimate, could he? Still, the laws were quite clear and it would take some doing to have him declared the heir.

Lucien recovered first, rising to his feet. "I think it's the most astounding news, but surprisingly fitting. No one deserves such good fortune more than my oldest and dearest friend. And it only adds to my happiness for Jeffrey and Yvette. I think we should all celebrate!"

"This is a most merry Christmas!" Colette added, with a bright smile at the duke. "Since we have joined our families, nothing could be better, but now you've made it quite perfect, Your Grace!"

As everyone began to give their congratulations, Yvette turned to Jeffrey, wrapping her arms around him, holding him tightly for a moment. She kissed his cheek.

"This is most unexpected," he whispered in her ear. "I don't even know what to think."

Yvette whispered back, "Whatever happens doesn't matter to me. I have you and that's all I need."

Jeffrey suddenly seemed to regain his composure, flashing her his charming grin. "To think that I might be able to make you a duchess after all."

Yvette shook her head, her eyes welling with tears. "You already made me feel like a queen."

He took her by the hand and led her across the room.

"Where are we going?" she asked as she followed him.

He stopped and turned to face her, giving her his most

charming smile. "To stand right here under the mistletoe, so I can kiss you in front of everyone and no one will mind."

She stared up at him, filled with joy that he was her husband.

"Merry Christmas, my beautiful bride."

"Merry Christmas, Jeffrey."

He leaned down and kissed her.

Books by Bestselling Author
Fern Michaels

___The Jury	0-8217-7878-1	$6.99US/$9.99CAN
___Sweet Revenge	0-8217-7879-X	$6.99US/$9.99CAN
___Lethal Justice	0-8217-7880-3	$6.99US/$9.99CAN
___Free Fall	0-8217-7881-1	$6.99US/$9.99CAN
___Fool Me Once	0-8217-8071-9	$7.99US/$10.99CAN
___Vegas Rich	0-8217-8112-X	$7.99US/$10.99CAN
___Hide and Seek	1-4201-0184-6	$6.99US/$9.99CAN
___Hokus Pokus	1-4201-0185-4	$6.99US/$9.99CAN
___Fast Track	1-4201-0186-2	$6.99US/$9.99CAN
___Collateral Damage	1-4201-0187-0	$6.99US/$9.99CAN
___Final Justice	1-4201-0188-9	$6.99US/$9.99CAN
___Up Close and Personal	0-8217-7956-7	$7.99US/$9.99CAN
___Under the Radar	1-4201-0683-X	$6.99US/$9.99CAN
___Razor Sharp	1-4201-0684-8	$7.99US/$10.99CAN
___Yesterday	1-4201-1494-8	$5.99US/$6.99CAN
___Vanishing Act	1-4201-0685-6	$7.99US/$10.99CAN
___Sara's Song	1-4201-1493-X	$5.99US/$6.99CAN
___Deadly Deals	1-4201-0686-4	$7.99US/$10.99CAN
___Game Over	1-4201-0687-2	$7.99US/$10.99CAN
___Sins of Omission	1-4201-1153-1	$7.99US/$10.99CAN
___Sins of the Flesh	1-4201-1154-X	$7.99US/$10.99CAN
___Cross Roads	1-4201-1192-2	$7.99US/$10.99CAN

Available Wherever Books Are Sold!
Check out our website at **www.kensingtonbooks.com**